PRA
LYING I

"As the bodies pile up, so do Urban's trademark twists, and readers will surely be shocked by the novel's final reveal." —*SLJ*

"Great chemistry and entertaining, nonstop turns of plot steer the ship."
—*Booklist*

"Psychologically and emotionally stirring." —*Kirkus Reviews*

"This cleverly plotted mystery and its earned, complex solution . . . boast numerous exhilarating twists and red herrings."
—*Publishers Weekly*

"A twisted tale of betrayal, heartbreak, and revenge, *Lying in the Deep* is shocking from the very first page. As gory as a slasher and as fun as a comedy, this book is a must-read for thriller fans."
—Jessica Goodman, *New York Times* and *USA Today* bestselling author of *The Counselors*

"Diana Urban is the Agatha Christie of today's YA audience. *Lying in the Deep* had me utterly engrossed from the jaw-dropping prologue to the final murderous twist. An absolutely thrilling and romantic read all the way through, and I can't recommend it highly enough."
—Jessica S. Olson, author of *A Forgery of Roses*

"Whatever your age, this twisty and surprising thriller—with gorgeous settings, swoon-worthy romance, toxic friendships, and a surprise around every corner—will keep you turning the pages as fast as you can. This is storytelling at its best!"
—Hank Phillippi Ryan, *USA Today* bestselling author of *Her Perfect Life*

LYING
in the
DEEP

Campus On Board

Passenger: **Jade Miller** Cabin: **417**

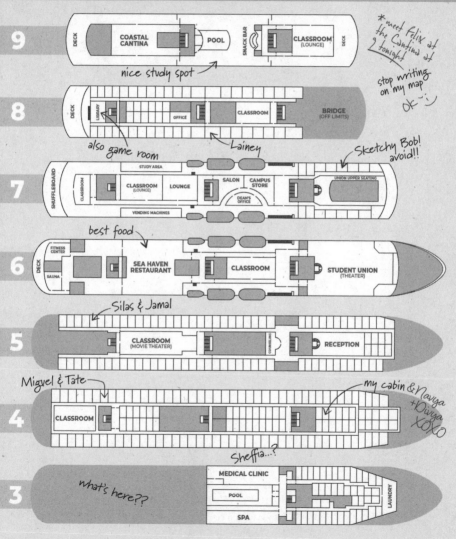

9 — Coastal Cantina · Pool · Snack Bar · Classroom (Lounge) · Deck

nice study spot →

* meet Felix at the Cantina at 9 tonight

stop writing on my map

OK :)

8 — Deck · Library · Office · Classroom · Bridge (Off Limits)

also game room

Lainey

Sketchy Bob! avoid!!

7 — Shuffleboard · Study Area · Classroom (Lounge) · Lounge · Salon · Campus Store · Dean's Office · Vending Machines · Classroom · Union Upper Seating

6 — Deck · Fitness Center · Sauna · Sea Haven Restaurant · Classroom · Student Union (Theater)

best food

5 — Classroom (Movie Theater) · Counseling · Reception

Silas & Jamal

4 — Classroom

Miguel & Tate

my cabin & Navya + Divya XOXO

Sheffia...?

3 — Medical Clinic · Pool · Spa · Laundry

what's here??

Also by
DIANA URBAN

Under the Surface

LYING
in the
DEEP

DIANA URBAN

putnam

G. P. PUTNAM'S SONS

G. P. PUTNAM'S SONS

An imprint of Penguin Random House LLC, New York

First published in the United States of America by Razorbill,
an imprint of Penguin Random House LLC, 2023
First paperback edition published 2024

Visit us online at PenguinRandomHouse.com.

The Library of Congress has cataloged the hardcover edition as follows:
Names: Urban, Diana, author.
Title: Lying in the deep / Diana Urban.
Description: New York : Razorbill, 2023. | Audience: Ages 14 years and up.
| Summary: When her boyfriend leaves her for her best friend, Jade joins a semester long cruise
program unaware that the two are also onboard, and when her ex-boyfriend is murdered and his new
girlfriend goes missing, Jade must dig into her shipmates' lives to find the murderer and clear her name.
Identifiers: LCCN 2022051331 (print) | LCCN 2022051332 (ebook) |
ISBN 9780593527603 (hardcover) | ISBN 9780593527610 (epub)
Subjects: CYAC: Cruise ships—Fiction. | Murder—Fiction. | Missing
persons--Fiction. | LCGFT: Detective and mystery fiction. | Novels.
Classification: LCC PZ7.1.U73 Ly 2023 (print) | LCC PZ7.1.U73 (ebook) | DDC [Fic]—dc23
LC record available at https://lccn.loc.gov/2022051331
LC ebook record available at https://lccn.loc.gov/2022051332

ISBN 9780593527627

1st Printing

Printed in the United States of America

LSCC

Design by Tony Sahara
Text set in Warnock Pro

For Grandma Gloria

```
/\ /\
 0 0
>o<
```

PROLOGUE

NOW

I didn't realize there'd be this much blood.

Yeah, he'd said there was blood all over the room. But I thought of how my mother would always huff and say things like "Oh, Jade, you got ice cream all over yourself." I'd glance down, expecting to be covered in chocolate goo, and there'd be this one lone dribble trailing down my shirt. Everyone always exaggerated these kinds of things.

But nope.

Not this time.

This time, there was literally blood *all over the room.*

A sea breeze rustled the curtains hanging from the wide-open French balcony doors, and even though I'd just been out on the top deck, I shivered, goose bumps coating my arms like a rash. I took another step into the suite to get a closer look, still gripping the cabin doorframe as though it could anchor me to a reality in which my best friend was still alive.

Well, ex–best friend.

That ship had sailed months ago.

Red slashed the ruffled white sheets, most of the blood pooled on the left side of the bed, like that's where it started. Like that's where she'd been stabbed. Smears of it angled off to the right, toward the balcony—had she been dragged?—and there were even some maroon flecks on the ornate opaque room divider at the foot of the bed, separating the bedroom from a small living room area. One of the beige armchairs—the one closest to the balcony—hadn't escaped the splatter.

Smudges streaked the balcony's stark white doorframe, too, the door open, ominous, like a gaping void before the endless sea.

The buzzing in my ears drowned out the voices behind me in the hall—yelling voices, frantic voices—and I thought of the blood staining my own shirt's hem. I tugged my jacket closed, hiding it . . . praying they wouldn't think I did this.

After all, there wasn't a snowball's chance in hell she'd survived.

There was so much blood, too much blood, and the way the balcony rail was coated in it . . .

But then a thought crossed my mind, a thought that made me falter back a step, that made bile rise in my throat and shame burn my cheeks.

Yet I couldn't help but think it.

That spoiled, selfish brat got exactly what she deserved.

1

THREE WEEKS EARLIER

Oh, for crying out loud. I could count the number of times I'd ever left California on one hand, and now here I was in the bustling port in Amsterdam, waiting to embark on Campus on Board, surrounded by chattering classmates, aka potential new friends, about to set sail on the greatest adventure of my life for an entire semester, daydreaming about murder again.

There was no stopping it. Every time there was the tiniest lull in my day, my mind would snap to vengeance. Murderous vengeance. It was getting exhausting, honestly.

It'd been two months since the love of my life, Silas, dumped me for my best friend, Lainey.

Via text message, no less.

He'd been spending the summer interning at her dad's pharmaceutical company in Boston, and yeah, putting an entire country between me and them might strike you as a recipe for disaster. But I never in a million years imagined it'd end that way, let alone at all. Silas and I had fallen in love at first sight, like that cheesy stuff that happens in the movies, but *real*. It happened the first Friday of freshman year, when my new roommate, Lainey, dragged me to a frat party, wild and wicked, determined to break my lifelong sobriety streak. We'd been clutching red Solo cups filled with God-knew-what in the corner of some packed living room that reeked of cheap beer, tittering over the tequila she'd snuck in in a flask, like that somehow made us fancier than everyone else.

For no reason at all, my gaze had flicked over her shoulder, and there he was on the staircase. Arms crossed, sans beverage, leaning against the wall as he scanned the packed room, tall, tan, and lean, with this sharp jaw and thick, sideswept chestnut hair. Not a moment later, his sparkling hazel eyes found mine. Like fate.

I had no clue Silas was Stanford's newest baseball star, no idea he was destined for the majors and the fame and huge contracts that came with it. All I cared about was how his lopsided grin turned my insides to mush, how everything else in the room seemed to disappear, even Lainey, even the bass blasting from a speaker perched on the windowsill next to me.

He was my first everything, and then, after nearly two years together—two years of cheering him on from the bleachers, of clinging together beneath his bedsheets, of planning a future together—all I got was a stupid text.

I'd memorized it. Memorized every word, searching for meaning in the letters, hunting for some logical explanation.

Hey Jade, it's over. We haven't been working for a while. I'm with Lainey now and it's not up for discussion. We're both blocking your number, so don't bother trying.

Brutal, I know.

As for Lainey, my supposed BFF . . . she'd totally iced me out. No text, no DM, nothing.

We'd been roomies since freshman year, though let's be real—

4

as the daughter of one of America's wealthiest pharmaceutical tycoons, she could've easily snagged a fancy off-campus loft. But she wanted a "normal" college experience—and what Lainey wanted, Lainey got—so she wound up in the dorms with me. I was as "normal" as they came: a broke nerd raised by a single mom in rural California who only managed to swing Stanford on scholarship.

We'd instantly glommed together despite the differences stretching between us like a chasm—me, eager to bust from my shell, a loyal confidant, a motivating study partner; she, a magnet for attention and an easy flirt, the way she'd flash her radiant smile and make you feel like the sun was shining at night. She was stunning, because of course she was, with her silky platinum hair, eyes blue as the winter sky, rosy high cheekbones, and rosier full lips. Forget the money—Lainey could steal your heart just by breathing, charm you with a glance, convince you of anything. She could get whatever the hell she wanted, even if she didn't already have it all.

Apparently, that included the love of *my* life.

Hence, murder. Lots and lots of daydreaming about murder.

Poisoning Lainey's tequila might do it, though shoving her off her dad's penthouse balcony would be way more gratifying. I imagined sneaking up there as she stretched on a lounge chair sunbathing, her smooth, creamy skin tanning like my pale, blotchy skin never could. I imagined chucking her phone so she'd scramble to the edge and watch it sail twenty stories down. I imagined pushing her so hard, she'd flip over the rail, legs tumbling over her head. I imagined her shrieking the whole way, and moments later, the satisfying spl—

"Oh my actual God, why am I not getting *any* signal right now?" The tall boy waiting in line behind me brandished his phone every which way, tearing me from my blood-spattered thoughts. "It's not like we're in the middle of nowhere."

"Maybe it's a dead spot?" I suggested unhelpfully, tugging my thick, dark curls into a low, messy bun so they'd stop whipping in my face in the unseasonably cool breeze.

"But this is our last chance to have cell service till the first port." As though he could reason a signal into existence. "Gah, this is gonna be torture. Can you believe we only get fifty megabytes of internet a day? That's nothing. How do they expect us to get any homework done? Scoot up, by the way."

There was a huge gap between me and the person ahead. "Oh, sorry. Jet lag." And homicide.

I slung my backpack onto my shoulder and wheeled up my two heavy suitcases. Embarkation seemed like a bajillion-step process after getting zero sleep in two days. After this check-in line, we had to wait in another line to drop off our luggage, then yet another line to board, then—you guessed it—another line to register inside. I hoped I'd have enough time before lifeboat training to scope out my room, though at this point, things were looking bleak.

"No worries," said the boy. "You didn't fly in *this* morning, did you?"

"Yep, I did." My scholarship covered Campus on Board, but no extras like hotel stays, so I decided to fly in the same day as embarkation. Naturally, my flight from Sacramento to New

York was delayed four hours, so I missed my connection to Amsterdam, rebooked to a later flight, and soared over the Atlantic in a state of sheer panic. Extremely on-brand for me.

"Oh my God, you must be absolutely dead right now. I'm Miguel Diaz, by the way?" He said it like a question, peering at me expectantly, like I might recognize his name.

Nope.

Still, I gave him a warm smile and stuck out my hand. "Jade Miller." I was usually shy with strangers, but it was so much easier when they were super talkative. Like Lainey. It had been impossible not to warm to her immediately.

He gave my hand a little jiggle. "Do you have service?" Talk about a one-track mind.

I shrugged. "I don't have a global data plan."

"Oh, weird."

Not that weird if you were pinching pennies. My cheeks flushed. "Well, I don't want to be tethered to my phone whenever we're at port."

Thinking of all those port stops—eleven countries in four months!—and soaking in all those cultures made excitement fizz through my veins like shaken soda. If anything could piece my shattered heart back together, it was this.

"The semester will be over like that," I said, snapping my fingers. "And I don't want to waste any of it staring at a screen. I want to be present."

That, and I didn't want to be tempted to Instagram-stalk Lainey and Silas at every port.

My heart clenched to think how Lainey and I had planned

this trip together, huddled on our shaggy dorm room rug over brochures she'd requested via snail mail so it'd feel more real than scouring a website, dreaming of clubbing in Greece, sunbathing in Malaysia, tasting authentic sushi in Japan. This was supposed to be *our* adventure. But she couldn't possibly show her face here after what she did. We'd originally planned to room together, but when I logged into my CoB portal, my room assignment was back to pending. Plus, she hadn't bragged about CoB on Instagram in months, which basically confirmed it.

"Okay, so I totally dig this whole *Eat, Pray, Love* vibe you've got going on"—Miguel waggled a finger at me from head to toe—"but if I don't get my videos uploaded, I'm going to lose followers, so."

"What kinds of vid—"

"Skincare tips! I'm almost up to a million subs on YouTube. And that's not including Insta and TikTok—"

As he rattled off his metrics, I scanned the long line ahead of us. Fat chance I'd get to snag the bed I wanted. For whatever reason, I never received my roommate assignment, but I knew I'd have two of them, since I could only afford the small cabins with one single bed and a bunk bed. Something about bunks freaked me out; I worried I'd roll off the top or be crushed on the bottom—

My breath hitched as something familiar, so familiar, caught my eye two lines over—platinum hair coaxed into loose beach waves shimmering in the sunlight. But, no, it couldn't be . . . So many girls styled their hair that way. Though as I kept staring, her cackling laughter dispersed in the air like a virus, turning the fizz in my veins flat. I knew that laugh, the mockery it implied. And as she turned, her sparkling grin coming into full view, I saw I was right.

There, two lines over, was none other than Lainey Silverton.

She had some gall showing up after all. As usual, she was all sleek and sharp edges, her powder-pink blazer probably costing more than my tuition. She had one elbow perched on her Louis Vuitton suitcase's handle, wearing her usual bug-eyed Gucci sunglasses, her large gold hoop earrings swinging as she jabbered excitedly to—I couldn't tell. A group of chattering middle-aged couples behind her blocked whoever it was from view. I leaned to get a better look, standing on my tiptoes, gripping the handle of my suitcase to balance myself, and—*no*. My stomach dropped directly into my uterus.

This couldn't be happening. There was absolutely no way this could be happening.

It was Silas.

He was never supposed to come on this trip. How could he even afford it? Had Lainey bought his way on? Oh God. How could this be happening? How—

"Are you okay?" Miguel asked, finally noticing I wasn't paying attention to a word he was saying. He followed my shocked stare and scowled. "Oh, Christ, it's *that* girl."

I winced. "You know her?"

Miguel nodded. "Lainey, right? Yeah, she's also gunning for the student YouTuber role."

"Wait, what?" I shook my head, confused. "I thought they picked the student assistants ahead of time. Didn't they all board a day early?" I'd applied for a student assistant role since it came with a grant but didn't get picked because I was already on full scholarship.

"Mm-hmm, but the person they picked had to drop out of CoB last minute. They're doing this super-ridiculous audition process, which, whatever—"

"Well, what the hell is she doing in *that* line?" That line was for the "lifelong learners"—grown-ass adults who wanted to study and sightsee with the rest of us college kids—but it was hard to tell them apart from the parents swarming their kids, readying to bid them bon voyage.

In fact, now that I had a clearer view, I spotted Lainey's dad nearby—Boston big-shot Derek Silverton, CEO of Sanatek. I almost didn't recognize him without his usual sports coat. Now he wore a striped navy polo shirt and khaki trousers, though his graying, dark hair was slicked back as always, his mouth set in his usual smug expression as he stared at his phone. I bet they'd spent the day leisurely sight-seeing in Amsterdam. How nice for them.

"So apparently," said Miguel, "she got one of the big suites on an upper deck. I bet she totally bribed someone. There's no other way."

I jabbed my cheek with my tongue and narrowed my eyes. Wow. She really did get whatever the hell she wanted, didn't she? And she was beautiful, charismatic, heir to a freaking fortune.

So why'd she have to take Silas, too?

It wasn't right. It wasn't *fair*. I curled my hands into fists and wanted nothing more than to smash the glass barriers lining the dock and slice her with the shards—

"If she bribes anyone for the YouTuber role," said Miguel, glaring, too, "I'll flip the hell out. You know, getting that could totally put me on the map as a travel influencer. Don't get me wrong, I love the skincare stuff, but free moisturizer isn't exactly on par with a free stay at a five-star hotel in Fiji, you know?"

I scoffed. "Meanwhile, she could afford any five-star hotel she wants."

"Exactly! So, wait, how do *you* know her?"

"She ruined my life."

Miguel's plucked eyebrows shot up, and he gaped at me. "Go on . . . ?"

Ugh, I didn't want to get into my whole depressing life story right now. "Let's just say, we used to be best friends, and now we're not."

"But why—"

"You know what?" I said, eager to change the subject. "If you want to beat her for that role, I bet CoB would love some boarding footage. All the past YouTubers boarded separately, but I bet so many people want to know what this process is like. And *she's* clearly not bothering."

Miguel's eyes lit up. "Oh my God," he muttered, like he couldn't believe he hadn't thought of it himself. He whipped out his phone again and started taking a panoramic shot of the pier as I stared at Silas, my chest filled with such an aching yearning, I thought it might pop.

He wore that lopsided grin of his, pointing out something about the *Sea Voyager*—the gleaming white vessel at the end of the pier that'd be our home for the next four months. He was finally free of his arm sling—the one he'd worn most of the summer as his Instagram feed filled with photos of him and Lainey, photos I'd pored over, sobbed over, wondering what went wrong. Lainey pressed a hand to his shoulder, leaning close, probably to tell him something without her father overhearing. Silas laughed, eyes glittering with amusement, and I swallowed hard as the breakfast sandwich I'd scarfed down on the plane threatened to come back up.

Miguel tapped my shoulder. I turned, and his phone was in my face. "So, tell me your name, where you're from—"

"Gah, not me." I raised a hand, hiding my face. "I look like death right now."

He stopped recording and scanned my face, quirking a brow. "You're not wrong."

I snorted. "Thanks."

"When we're on board, remind me to introduce you to caffeine gel." He turned to the person behind him and made a cooing sound, liking whatever he saw. "Hi, hi! I'm shooting footage for the CoB YouTube channel, mind if I ask you a few questions?"

Whoever it was grunted something that sort of resembled *Yeah*.

My attention slid back to the happy couple. I still wasn't sure what shocked me more—how the breakup came out of left field or the callousness of it, the unwillingness to talk, blocking me as though *I'd* done something wrong. Or maybe it was how both people I loved most in this world had betrayed me so epically.

"You're the best," said Miguel. "So, tell me your name, where you're from, and what your day has looked like so far—"

"I said, yeah, I *do* mind," someone said gruffly. I glanced over at the boy Miguel was harassing, instantly getting brooding vibes from his charcoal-gray army jacket over a black T-shirt and distressed black denim. His long black lashes hid his eyes as his thumbs roved over his phone screen, but when he finally glanced up, raking back his dark tousled hair, I saw his eyes were such a deep shade of brown, they were almost black. They flicked to mine for the briefest moment before focusing on his screen again.

"I promise this'll just take a sec," Miguel persisted.

The sound of Lainey's tinkling laughter floated over— apparently at something Silas had said. She flirtatiously whacked his arm before sneaking a peek at her phone. She never could stop checking her social media notifications, thriving on likes and attention, despite her claims that she hated it.

"I don't have a sec," said the brooding boy.

Lainey was scanning the crowd now, a hand on her hip as she took in the scene—

"Um, you literally have so many seconds right now," Miguel said, motioning to the line. This time, the boy ignored him.

Lainey shaded her eyes despite her huge sunglasses—

"Yeesh," Miguel bristled, back at my side. "This guy thinks he's the shit."

But I was too focused on Lainey to respond, or even care. Her line of sight was about to reach me—

And there it was.

Lainey stilled.

All I could see were those bug-eyed black lenses, but I knew she'd spotted me. She pursed her full lips, her whole body going stiff, and the air seemed to run out of oxygen despite the sea breeze ruffling my curls. There was no joy in seeing me—only dismay. Silas was staring ahead at the *Sea Voyager* again, seeming to say something to Lainey, something she was ignoring.

Finally, he glanced at her. I couldn't hear him from here, but I could read his lips—lips that used to roam all over me. *What's wrong?* After throwing one last bitter look my way, she said, loud and clear, "She came anyway. She's right over there."

Of course I came anyway.

I wasn't the one who stabbed my best friend in the back.

I wasn't the one who stole the love of her life.

I wasn't the one who stomped on her soul with no remorse.

And now that spoiled, selfish cow was going to ruin this trip—a trip I'd been looking forward to for *years*.

Little did I know how much chaos she'd sow.

2

As I waited in the registration line on board to get my ID card, I took in my surroundings, mouth agape—this place was way more glam than I'd expected. The stained-glass, skylight-topped atrium soared three decks above the crowded reception lobby, each level fitted with ornate brass railings and bedecked with oil paintings and bronze sculptures.

But as I made a beeline to my cabin on Deck 4, my surroundings became a blur as the way Silas had spotted me before needled my mind. Surprised recognition had filled those honeyed-hazel eyes, and he'd flinched a bit, seeming to stop breathing as he soaked in the sight of me. I could swear he almost took a step toward me. But then those beautiful eyes turned cold as an iceberg as he clenched his square jaw and balled his hands into fists.

Like *I'd* done something wrong.

Technically, if I hadn't asked Lainey to get that summer internship for Silas at her dad's company, none of this would've happened. But at the time, all I cared about was making sure Silas didn't drop out of Stanford.

After he shattered his throwing elbow in a skiing accident last spring, Stanford revoked his full scholarship since his injury wasn't baseball related. All the physical therapy in the world wouldn't bring him back to full strength. But, like me, he couldn't afford Stanford otherwise—not without some serious financial aid.

"Dammit, Jade, what'm I gonna do?" he'd asked as we huddled on his bed, gaping at the email on his phone, eyes watering—not from pain, but from devastation over losing his future. *Our* future. We'd talked of getting married after graduation, of me starting a remote business so I could travel with him wherever he played ball. I never wanted to be tethered to some desk in a cubicle farm anyway, or take orders from some micromanaging boss with a power trip.

So this plan was perfect.

It was *freedom.*

And now it was gone.

"Don't worry. Everything'll be fine." I'd cupped his cheek, wiping away a tear with my thumb.

He'd leaned into my palm. "I lost *everything* . . ."

"Listen. Everything seems terrible now, and it's going to feel terrible for a while. But you're strong and determined and capable, and you'll get through this."

"How?"

I dropped my hands. That, I didn't know. Anguish clawed at my insides. I wished I could take back that terrible weekend, that I'd insisted he stay with me instead of goofing off with his buddies at a ski lodge at Lake Tahoe. But I wasn't possessive like that, even after seeing what happened with Mom and Dad. Especially then. Trust is freedom.

I *needed* freedom.

"You can take out student loans, can't you?" I'd suggested.

"Not halfway through like this. The interest rates would kill me . . . I'd be buried in debt forever. I'm gonna have to drop out."

Then he'd probably move back home to Tennessee. My chest compressed. "*No*," I'd choked out. "You can't."

"Well, what'm I gonna do with a history degree, anyway?" Silas never wanted to do anything other than play baseball.

"You can switch majors—"

"To *what*? I have no idea what I'd even want to do."

I'd known for ages I wanted to be a solopreneur—to code an app, market the hell out of it, rinse, repeat, until I found a big hit. And all I'd need was a laptop. My career could blossom without ever having to put down roots, without ever feeling *trapped* like I'd felt growing up. So double-majoring in communications and computer science had been an easy choice. I'd never floundered like this.

"How about sales?" I'd suggested. "You're charming, clever, good at convincing people of things. You could probably switch to a comm or econ major for that."

"Huh." He scratched the scruff on his jawline. "Maybe . . ."

My brain whirred, calculating the classes he'd already taken and whether they'd meet the liberal arts requirements for communications majors, whether he'd still be able to graduate on time. But that still didn't solve those hefty tuition bills. It must've been so easy for people like Lainey, whose dad footed her tuition. She'd never had to think twice about it . . .

I gasped. "Oh! I've got it!"

"What?"

"Lainey's dad! He's the CEO of that massive pharmaceutical

company in Boston. I'm sure she could get you a paid internship there over the summer." I grabbed my phone.

"How do you even know they have paid internships?"

"Pfft," I said, googling, "those Big Pharma companies cough up. Yep, see? Here's their career page. They have internships in a few departments, including sales. All paid, look. 'Interns will receive competitive compensation . . .' Oh, and here, 'All interns will be considered for full-time positions based on their performance—'"

"Aw, c'mon, Jade. Intern pay would barely put a dent in my tuition."

"But it'd help. Loans could cover the rest."

"The interest rates—"

"But d'you know how good a full-time job there would pay? Lainey's dad's, like, a gazillionaire. I bet you could pay off your loans in just a few years."

"Huh. Maybe . . ."

Once I asked Lainey, and she got the thumbs-up from her dad, I convinced Silas to take the gig. Biggest mistake of my life, apparently. But it wasn't like I'd done anything malicious—

"Oof!" Someone whaled into my bulging backpack, nearly whacking my skull into an ornate, etched glass wall sconce.

"Watch it," a girl with flowing auburn hair and bright red lipstick snapped as she maneuvered her brown monogrammed Louis Vuitton suitcase—just like Lainey's—around me.

She looked kind of familiar from somewhere but sped down the hall before I could place her. I glanced at the nearest door.

417. My cabin. I'd been standing here like a zombie, lost in my thoughts.

I unlocked the door with my ID card and peeked inside, clutching that sliver of hope I'd somehow beat my roommates here to snag the single bed.

No such luck. My roommates' belongings were already strewn across the cramped cabin, like their luggage had spontaneously combusted upon entry. No sign of said roommates, though, and the single bed was clear except for an elephant-shaped towel animal, my two suitcases propped next to it.

I picked up a sheet of torn notebook paper on the pillow.

> Hi, roomie! This bed is yours. We went to the merch store to pick up some stuff. Can't wait to meet you! XOXO Navya

Welp, now I felt like a selfish sack of shit.

Shaking off my guilt, I dumped my backpack on the bed and took in the space. The interior room had no windows, and the bunks spanned half the wall opposite the door, a small metal ladder angled at one end. Faux granite shelves the color of toasted mauve separated the bunk bed from mine, which converted into a couch along the right-hand wall. A matching closet stood next to the door, which fit a small flat-screen TV in a cubby, and a tiny vanity was nestled next to the minuscule bathroom. I switched on the lights—the sink bore the same granite detailing as the bedroom, and there was hardly any counter space, but some clever storage was built in beneath the sink and above the toilet.

Back in the cabin, the burgundy carpet and quilts, crown moldings, oil paintings above the bed, and all that faux granite gave it outdated yet regal vibes. Cramped, for sure, but nothing I wasn't used to.

Since I had a bit of time before lifeboat training after all, my nesting instinct kicked in. My roommates had left me a few hangers, two closet drawers, and one of the shelves between our beds. One suitcase had all my liquids: shampoo, sunscreen, body wash, oil to tame my thick, curly hair, crap like that. I hauled all of it into the bathroom and crammed it into a shelf.

That suitcase also had all the snacks I'd loaded up on at the Dollar Tree to hold me over on port days. My scholarship only covered tuition and housing, so I'd have to stretch my cashier earnings from the summer over the entire semester for things like excursions, and that meant eating on the cheap. I left them in the suitcase and rolled it under the convertible bed, where it barely fit.

I'd almost finished stacking my underwear in one of the closet drawers when the door burst open, and two girls squeaked, "She's here!" One of them extended a hand to me. "Hi, I'm Navya."

I grinned back, taking her hand. "Jade. It's nice to meet—"

But I was cut off by a bear hug from the other girl. "Hiiiiii. I'm Divyaaaaa. We're gonna have a blaaaaast." She trailed the last syllable of each sentence.

"Navya and Divya," I said as Divya released me and tossed a plastic bag onto the bottom bunk. "Are you two . . . ?"

"Yep, twins." Navya tucked her shoulder-length ebony hair behind her ears. No wonder they didn't mind bunking. "Fraternal."

I actually would've guessed they were a year or so apart—they both had similar, curvy frames and rich golden-brown skin, but Divya was a bit taller, her hair longer and her cheeks rounder than Navya's high, defined ones, with fuller lips and a mole at one corner. Both of them had long, curled eyelashes that put Lainey's heavily mascaraed ones to shame.

"We're both prelaw, too," Navya went on, "but I'm at Harvard and Divya's at BU."

Boston, I thought with a shudder. Where Silas and Lainey had torn my heart to shreds.

Gah, I hated this game my mind was playing, connecting every dot to *them*.

"I knew Harvard would never let in both of us," said Divya, brushing her long hair with fast, frantic strokes, "so I let her have it." She quickly tied it back in a loose ponytail that rippled in ebony waves over one shoulder, then disappeared into the bathroom.

Navya rolled her eyes. "She always says that. But I know she applied to Harvard. It's kind of a miracle she got into BU. Anyway . . ." She reached into her own plastic bag and pulled out a white T-shirt. I recognized it as the CoB itinerary shirt—the design bore a world map surrounded by flags of the eleven countries we'd visit this semester. Students always wore these in their Instagram pics during port stops. "I got you this. A few of the YouTubers mentioned they sell out fast, so."

"Nice, thanks! I thought the merch store didn't open till tomorrow, though."

Navya's smile fell, and she threw a wary look toward the bathroom. "Er . . . Divya knows one of the student assistants who's running it this semester and got him to sneak us in."

"Oh, cool."

"Yeah . . ." Her voice was strained. Maybe she wasn't a rule-breaker like her sister. "Anyway, I took a wild guess and got you a medium; hope that's okay." She sized up my narrow frame.

"Totally, it's perfect." I took it and raised it to my chest. I preferred loose, flowing shirts anyway. Formfitting clothes made me feel like I was suffocating. "Thanks!"

"No worries. It was twenty-eight bucks . . . ya know, just whenever you get a chance."

Heat crept up my neck. I didn't expect her to shell out for a stranger, of course, but I would've done without this shirt otherwise. Now I'd have to make do with a granola bar instead of local cuisine at an extra port stop. Still, I dug through my purse, fished out my wallet, and forked over the cash.

"By the way," said Navya, opening a hidden shelf under the vanity, "this is where we're keeping snacks. Help yourself—ya know, within reason, obviously."

"Ooh, nice." I tugged out my own suitcase, showing her my stash. "Same goes for you two."

"Awesome—"

Divya reappeared from the bathroom clutching two of those mini booze bottles they handed out on planes.

"Oh, come on, Divya," Navya groaned as I shoved the suitcase back under my bed. "Day one? Really?"

"What?" Divya tucked the bottles into her small beige purse. "We're in Europe. Eighteen's the drinking age here. It's ridiculous that CoB limits it . . . like we're high schoolers or something."

"If that were true, they wouldn't let us drink at all," Navya snapped.

Divya opened her mouth like she wanted to argue, but I cut her off. "Anyway, we better move." I opened the closet and stood on my tiptoes to tug out three puffy, bright orange life jackets. "Lifeboat training's in five minutes!"

The rest of the afternoon was a blur of information as we were shunted from one orientation activity to the next.

I tried to pay attention. I knew I should've learned the evacuation safety protocols, the procedures for disembarking at each port, where the medical clinic was located. I should've laughed along with everyone else at the bubbly dean of programming Candace Jackson's jokes during her welcome speech in the Student Union. I should've been impressed by the enormous space fitting all seven hundred passengers that was as extra as it gets despite its basic name—a majestic, glittering chandelier dangled over the stage from an ornately painted ceiling reminiscent of a Michelangelo fresco, red velvet curtains draped the windows lining the balconies, and golden beams separated rows of plush red armchairs with a granite-topped table nestled between each pair. I should've been mind-boggled by how the *Sea Voyager* seemed to defy the laws of physics to fit so much inside. I should've been excited, so excited, to start this journey.

But I kept spotting them.

Lainey and Silas.

Once was while out on deck, watching a lecture on the lifeboats; they held hands in the next group over, and Lainey kept hurling furtive glances my way. Another was when passing Lainey's door on Deck 8 as she struggled to unjam it, laughing with Silas that *of course* she already needed to call maintenance, until she spotted me and scowled.

And somehow, the impossibly spacious ship seemed more stifling than the tiny house I lived in with Mom. The threat of the happy couple's presence lurked around every corner, and jealousy spread through my veins like venom whenever I saw how affectionate they were. She was always caressing his arm or leaning in for a kiss. I was always on the verge of hurling.

I'd thought this trip would put an entire globe between us, but instead, here they were, everywhere I turned.

I finally seemed to have lost track of them as everyone gathered at the ship's stern to wave farewell to the parents who'd lingered or returned to the pier to watch the ship sail off. Navya, Divya, and I raced along the open teak promenade on Deck 9 to snag a spot, squeezing behind a massive, Roman-style bronze bust on the terrace to huddle against the railing. I took a deep breath, soaking in the crisp, salt-laced air and the sight of students crowding the lower decks. "I can't believe this ship has enough cabins for all these people," I said.

"I can," said Navya, clutching her cardigan closed against the sea breeze whipping past. Divya, however, didn't seem to give a damn about the cold—or maybe her frantic waving kept her warm. "Our room's basically a glorified coffin."

I laughed. "It's not *that* bad."

"Are you kidding?" said Navya. "I can't even fit a quarter of my clothes into the closet."

"It's all in the folding. I can show you later. I'm used to small spaces."

She threw me a sympathetic cringe. "Was your dorm at Stanford tiny, too?"

"No, God no." The room I'd shared with Lainey seemed like a palace compared to my bedroom back home, if you could even call it that. "My mom's house is tiny. And I mean, it's a *literal* tiny house."

"Wait, what?" said Divya, catching her breath. Apparently she'd heard us over her hollering. "Like a dollhouse?"

Navya swatted her arm. "Don't be dense." To me, she said, "Like that show on HGTV, right?"

I chortled. "Yeah, pretty much."

After Dad disappeared, Mom wanted to go off the grid, so she sold our ranch in Sacramento and moved us into a tiny house outside the city—one hyper-compartmentalized room plus a bathroom that was basically a closet with plumbing. She took self-sufficiency to an extreme, not even willing to trust things like basic city infrastructure.

"You watch HGTV?" I teased, eager to change the topic.

Navya rolled her eyes. "Our mother's obsessed. It's on twenty-four seven."

"Nobody forces you to watch it," said Divya.

"Well, it's *right* there, all the time." Navya pushed her wind-blown black hair from her eyes.

"Did you have your own room, at least?" Divya asked, swiveling the subject back to me. I guessed the twins didn't have to share growing up.

"Eh, it was more like a shelf above the kitchen." I waved it off like it was no biggie, but really, I'd been desperate to escape. Mom couldn't afford to send me to college, and Dad would never fork over that kind of cash when his priorities were clearly elsewhere. So all throughout high school, I studied like my life depended on it.

And in some ways, it did.

I'd felt so stifled by the lifestyle Mom had stuffed us into, with her rigid rules, her distrust, her paranoia. It felt like the walls themselves would squeeze the air from my lungs at any moment.

In the end, all that studying paid off. I won the Pendant Grant, a full-ride scholarship a wealthy local benefactor gave each year's Sandy Hill valedictorian. It let me go to Stanford, and even covered CoB. Mom was thrilled I'd be going to college so close to home, though she'd tried talking me out of CoB.

But nothing could keep me from this.

"Do you have any siblings?" Divya asked.

"No," I said. "Only child."

"So you just live with your mom?"

"Yup."

"What happened to your dad?"

"Divya!" Navya poked her arm.

"*What?*"

"No, it's fine," I said. I'd wished someone had told *me* what happened to Dad when he vanished. At the time it'd seemed like some monster had plucked him from their bedroom window without leaving a shred of evidence behind. "When I was ten years old, he—"

The ship blared its horn, cutting me off. And as it started drifting from the pier, everyone burst into excited applause.

I reflexively joined in, grinning from ear to ear as giddiness made my fingers and toes tingle. This was it! We were officially setting sail for England, with a whole semester ahead of breathing in the sea air and seeing all these amazing countries and—

A familiar voice whooped somewhere nearby, and a prickle snaked down my spine.

I leaned over, scanning the rows of cheering students, and spotted Lainey farther down the stern. She held her phone out on a selfie stick, filming herself and Silas waving at the pier amid the crowd, and threw him a dazzling smile. My cheeks flushed as my blood boiled. The cheering din faded to a low hum, obscured by my pulse roaring in my ears.

She was happy. No, *elated*. And it tore my heart to shreds.

Even if she'd fallen for Silas . . . even if she'd been determined to steal him . . . didn't it hurt her to lose *me*?

But the biggest question of all—a question that made my stomach curdle to consider—was: How the hell was I going to get through this semester without literally stabbing her in the face?

3

After a quick break in our room to spruce up—I chose a flowy, floral dress with loose off-the-shoulder sleeves I'd plucked from a sales rack at T.J. Maxx—we filed into Sea Haven, one of the two main restaurants on the ship, for dinner. By then I was so famished and exhausted—I hadn't slept in almost two days at this point—I loaded my plate with things that didn't even make sense together: wild rice with penne drenched in rich tomato sauce, cocktail shrimp and chicken fingers, and a glop of something I'd thought was chicken salad but smelled an awful lot like tuna.

Sea Haven had a retro, glamorous ambience. Round mahogany tables dotted the emerald floral-accented carpet, each surrounded by curlicue-engraved high-backed chairs with matching emerald cushions. I followed Navya and Divya around one of the faux marble columns spanning the length of the restaurant to an empty table for six and collapsed next to Navya, eager to scarf this all down. Miguel stood nearby, black hair freshly gelled, filming people carrying loaded plates from the buffet back to their tables. He spotted me and waved before pointing his phone my way.

I angled my veritable smorgasbord toward him and gave an overly enthusiastic thumbs-up, then suddenly noticed who was sitting behind him, facing away from me at the next table over.

Lainey and Silas.

Because of course they were.

A wave of nausea surged up my throat, and it wasn't from seasickness. Silas was facing away from me, but I could see Lainey's silhouette; she'd only need to glance over her shoulder to spot me. Miguel must've fully caught my reaction on camera, but as the two of them huddled together, speaking in hushed tones, all I could think of was what they might be saying, how I wished I were the one with Silas's hand on my upper back, his lips a breath away from mine.

Miguel pointed his camera elsewhere, clearly realizing any footage of me was unusable.

I couldn't torture myself like this. I couldn't let them ruin this. I had to just . . . ignore them somehow. Yep, that was it. I had to just make new friends, pretend they weren't here, and avoid them as much as possible.

I glanced at Navya, and she grinned back, giving my arm a giddy shake. "Isn't this so exciting? I think it's all finally sinking in—"

"Oh my God, Navya," Divya groaned, "can you *not* say the word *sinking* for the next few months?" I laughed.

New friends.

A new adventure.

A new beginning.

I could do this.

A few more people had settled in at Lainey and Silas's table. Okay, yeah, I was already doing a terrible job ignoring them. But the pale redhead in a formfitting sequined number between Lainey and a cute Black boy looked awfully familiar from somewhere, and not just from when she'd slammed into me in the narrow hall outside my cabin earlier. Suddenly, I placed her—Sheffia, Lainey's clingy BFF from high school. I'd never met her before, but I'd seen pictures on Lainey's Instagram.

I remembered showing my phone to Lainey to ask about one of her Instagram pics early freshman year; she'd been posing next to a pretty girl with long, coppery waves and bright red lipstick in front of a pink stucco wall in LA. "Is this the girl who keeps trying to reach out?"

"Ha, are you Insta-stalking me?" Lainey had teased.

I'd flushed slightly. "I like putting faces to names."

She'd snorted. "Yep, that's her. *Sheffia*." She'd wrinkled her nose like there was a turd under it and scrolled through her own phone before tapping with a flourish. "Deleted!" Lainey had been complaining about this girl for weeks. She'd blocked her number but didn't want to blatantly block her on the socials, so had to ignore her insistent DM attempts.

I'd watched the picture disappear from her feed. "Why do you hate her so much?"

"I don't *hate* her . . . She's just . . . I dunno." Lainey's smile collapsed, and stress lines creased her forehead as she gave me a wary look. As Derek Silverton's daughter, she'd been something of an "it girl" back home, even fodder for tabloid TikTokers at times. And though we'd had a blast our first couple of months as roomies, our conversations had remained pretty surface level. Sometimes I wondered if she didn't trust me not to sell her secrets to the press or something.

I'd sunk next to her on her bed, folding my legs beneath me, and poked her arm. "You can tell me stuff. I promise anything you say is safe with me."

She'd given me a wobbly grin. "I know." She nibbled on her lip a moment longer before her posture relaxed. "It's just . . . she's such a *user*. Lots of my high school friends were."

"How do you mean?"

"Well, they all wanted something out of me—party invites, free designer clothes, tickets to something . . . a private jet to LA." She motioned to her phone, referring to the pic she'd deleted. "I'm just so over it, you know?"

Suddenly it made sense how we'd bonded so fast. As electrifying as her wild energy was to me, I was a balm for her. After years of people like Sheffia glomming on to her like a leech, sucking her dry, I didn't give a damn about posh brands or fancy fashions or social climbing, and she *loved* that. So she flicked off those leeches and squished them under her shoe for good measure, and we became best friends.

Yet, clearly, Sheffia had managed to latch onto her again.

"Yo." A lanky boy with sandy curls, black-framed glasses, and a bright orange polo shirt approached the empty seat next to Divya, jarring me from my thoughts. "Okay if I sit here?"

"Sure!" the three of us chirped as Divya lifted her glass of soda seemingly from under the table. Had she just snuck in some booze? Navya frowned; she'd noticed as well.

He flopped down and whipped out his phone. "Have any of you managed to connect to the Wi-Fi?"

I yawned widely. "No." I'd planned to figure out all that later tonight unless jet lag made me collapse first.

"I couldn't," said Navya. "Our stew said it was working, just slow, but I couldn't get it to load."

Divya groaned. "I heard it didn't work at all half the time last semester."

"Ah, well." He plopped his phone on the table. "Anyway, sup? I'm Tate."

The three of us introduced ourselves. "Where d'you go to school?" I asked.

"BU," he said. Oof, again with Boston. "I'm a business major—"

"Oh my God," said Divya through a full mouth. "I go to BU, too!"

"No kidding! Which school?"

"Law. And you're QSB?"

"Yup, and I'm doing a law concentration."

"Oh, nice!"

As they threw around school lingo, I dug in, remembering how ravenous I was. After a few minutes, Miguel came over and sat next to Tate. "There you are! For a minute there I thought I'd have to sit with Sketchy Bob. Hello, you!" he said to me before introducing himself to Navya and Divya.

"Sketchy Bob?" I asked.

Miguel pointed past me, and I looked over my shoulder—a middle-aged man in a gray baseball cap and matching stubble sat alone, tearing a dinner roll in half and staring at the neighboring table packed with chattering girls. "William," said Miguel. "He's a Lifelong Learner or whatever. But he's so *weird*. Everyone's calling him Sketchy Bob already. Anyway"—Miguel lit up, ignoring my skeptical look—"I see you've met my roomie." He entwined his arm with Tate's and gave it an affectionate pat. "He's gonna help me film stuff, isn't that so nice?"

"No prob, it's good practice," said Tate. "I had to shoot a Tik-Tok for a marketing class last semester, and I was like, what the heck am I doing?"

"You'd never made a TikTok before?" asked Navya, aghast. But when Tate's eyes settled on her, her high cheekbones went pink.

"Nah, never bothered," said Tate. "I'm more into gaming."

"Oh, I can teach you so much." Miguel stood and threw Tate's cloth napkin onto his own seat. "I've gotta grab some grub. Save my seat, boo."

"Sure," said Tate, and Miguel went to join the back of the buffet line. "I hope one of you wants a skincare routine makeover or whatever"—he waved a hand in front of his face—"because I'm drawing a line, and that's past the line."

"Oh, I'm in," said Divya as I savored the tomato sauce drenching the penne. I could basically live off Italian food. "Does he do makeup, too?"

"No clue—"

"Is this seat taken?" a gruff voice asked. I glanced up from my meal and saw it was the brooding boy who'd snubbed Miguel in line earlier. He still wore his charcoal jacket even though it was toasty inside, and his dark eyes roved over each of us.

"Yeah." Tate hovered a hand over Miguel's seat. "But that one's not." He pointed at the next seat over, next to me.

The boy nodded and sat, and immediately poked at his food as the rest of us stared.

"Hello," Divya tried. The boy nodded again, chewing slowly, saying nothing.

I had to rub my lips to keep from laughing when Miguel sauntered back over and recognized the boy from earlier, food nearly sliding off his loaded plate as he froze. He looked utterly conflicted—this boy was objectively hot, but Miguel clearly thought he was a prick.

I was inclined to give Brooding Boy the benefit of the doubt. Maybe he was shy and hated being on camera.

Miguel's eyes darted to the surrounding tables, but they were all full anyway, so with an exasperated huff, he took his seat between Tate and—well, whoever this boy was. "Did you see all those ice cream flavors? I'm gonna need you all to stop me. I have literally no self-control."

I, on the other hand, started shoveling in food faster, excited by the prospect of as much free ice cream as I wanted.

"Can you all believe the size of the rooms, by the way?" said Miguel, changing topics faster than a politician. "I mean, I don't know what I expected, but not *that*."

The corners of Brooding Boy's lips quirked at this, and we exchanged a fleeting look before he focused on his food again.

"Wait, is it just the two of you in your room?" asked Divya.

"Yeah," said Tate.

"Then shut up. All *three* of us are crammed into one room." She motioned between her sister and me.

"But your room's probably bigger," said Miguel.

"Mm, I don't think so," said Navya. "They looked pretty similar in the virtual tour. Only the interior singles were smaller." She'd clearly examined every pixel of the CoB website.

"Where's *your* roommate?" I asked Brooding Boy.

He waved vaguely across the room.

So he couldn't even be bothered to get to know his roommate at the welcome dinner, let alone speak words. Maybe he *did* think he was the shit.

Lainey laughed right then, more of a loud crow that reverberated off the walls and made everyone at the surrounding tables go quiet as they glanced over, straining to see what'd been so funny. Though I hadn't had time to fix my hair before dinner, her blond hair was sleek and shiny like she hadn't just been windblown out on deck like the rest of us, and when she tilted her head toward Silas, one of her diamond chandelier earrings glinted as it caught the light from the brass fixtures overhead.

Miguel twisted in his chair to peek her way and quickly turned back. "Oh my God. I literally can't with her." He spoke softly since Lainey was right behind him. To me he said, "Did you know she has over a million Insta followers?"

"Yeah." I pushed around the food on my plate, appetite gone. I used to help her snap pics for it. Each of her posts was a carousel showing at least four bloopers from the first photo. We always had to stop once we were both laughing so hard tears streaked down her cheeks, ruining her makeup.

"And she doesn't even have a niche or anything," Miguel went on. Divya leaned forward to hear, failing to notice she'd fully dunked her charm necklace into her mashed potatoes. "Like, she doesn't tag any brands or do partnerships or anything. It's all just pointless selfies. She's like a magnet for followers without even trying."

"Maybe it's because of how wealthy she is," I grumbled. "Her feed *exudes* it. People love that aspirational crap." I'd never resented it before, though. She'd always let me borrow whatever, and although I couldn't tell a Prada from a Versace, it was fun to pick through her clothes and play dress-up.

And whenever I'd strike a pose for Silas later, he'd always *un*dress me as quickly as possible. I swallowed down the rock that lodged in my throat.

"Ugh, I can't stand people like that," Navya muttered.

"People like what?" Brooding Boy asked at full volume. All our eyes snapped to him, surprised he'd said anything at all.

Navya shifted uncomfortably in her seat. "Well, ya know. People who are rich and successful without even trying. I mean, it's not like she earned that money herself, right? Her parents are probably rich. She's probably been loaded her whole life. Meanwhile, I'll be working my ass off in law school forever, and I'll graduate buried under a mountain of debt."

Tate snorted. "Cheers to that."

"Interesting." Brooding Boy cocked his head, a glint in his eye.

I squinted at him. "What's so interesting?"

He shrugged. "Just how quickly people judge each other for circumstances they were born into and had no control over, no matter which end of the spectrum they're on." I couldn't place his accent—American for sure, but almost with a touch of British.

I leaned forward, perching my elbows on the table. "Well,

36

listen. I *know* that girl, and I can confirm she's exactly as much of an asshole as Navya thinks she is."

Brooding Boy simply stared back, a slight smile playing on his lips as he considered me.

"You're talking about the blond girl, right?" Tate leaned back to see her behind Miguel.

"Yup."

"Yeah, I thought I recognized her before." He lowered his voice even more. "I think her dad's that Big Pharma douchebag, Derek Silverton. You know, the dude who owns Sanatek."

Divya screwed up her face and shook her head, like, *How the hell should I know that?* Rightfully so—how did Tate even know that?

Tate picked up his cell again. "I wanna google it. I wish the Wi-Fi worked—"

"See?" Navya said to Brooding Boy. "Daughter of a pharma bro. I bet she'll never have to work a day in her life."

I nodded, clucking my tongue. Lainey already seemed to have quite the list of haters on board . . . and I couldn't say I hated it.

Lainey glanced over and spotted me. Her lips twisted into a scowl.

Navya gave a little gasp. "Did she hear me say that?" she whispered. Maybe, or maybe she'd recognized the annoyed sound I'd made, just like I could pick out her laugh in a packed comedy club.

Miguel swiveled again to see and immediately broke into a wide grin. "Oh my God, hiiiii, how are you?" He stretched way

37

back to extend a hand to Lainey, nearly falling off his chair. "It's so nice to meet you IRL!"

She fixed a smile onto her lips and shook his hand. "You, too. You know, it's your fault I own, like, every The Ordinary product."

"Oh my *God*, you've seen my reviews?" Unlike earlier, when he seemed to expect me to know who he was, he seemed shocked she did. Shocked and *delighted*, the hypocrite. "We should totally hang. I'll follow you on Insta once I'm back online, what's your handle?" As if he didn't already know.

So he was one of *those* people—the ones who'd trash-talk someone and then be sweet as sucralose to their face. He probably figured he could siphon some of her followers if he snagged a mention.

The mysterious boy caught my gaze, and we exchanged a judgmental glance, his eyes flashing devilishly. Despite everything, I had to bite my lip to keep from smiling.

As Tate and the twins broke off into a separate conversation and Miguel focused on his phone, I wanted to ask the boy his name, but the question clung to the tip of my tongue as Lainey turned back around and Sheffia hissed, "Is that her?"

So Lainey had told her about me. Like she'd told me about Sheffia way back when.

"Yeah," said Lainey, not even bothering to keep her voice down. Had she told Sheffia the truth about how she'd stolen my boyfriend? Or had she painted me as the villain somehow? "I can't believe she came. It's like she's stalking me or something."

Brooding Boy clearly overheard this as well—his eyes filled with pity as they flicked back to me, somehow seeming to understand she was talking about me. Maybe it was the way my cheeks caught fire. My throat constricted, tears welling so fast my nose had to be turning bright red.

Why had the two people I loved most turned on me like this?

Before the dam could burst in front of everyone, I fled, hurtling between tables and chairs like I was navigating some obstacle course and out into the narrow hall. As I hurried to my cabin, Brooding Boy's sympathetic glance flashed through my mind.

But I didn't want his pity. I didn't want anyone's pity.

I wanted answers.

4

When I was ten years old, after Dad bolted without warning, Mom sold everything we owned and stuffed the rest into garbage bags she dumped on the curb. "Fill this with whatever you want to keep," she'd said, handing me a single cardboard box. "The rest has to go."

"But why?" I'd cried for the zillionth time, devastated Dad was gone, terrified to move away from my friends, horrified to part with even more things I loved. And nobody would explain why any of it was happening.

A pained look had crossed Mom's face before she huffed, "They're just *things*, Jade," yet again ignoring my demand for an explanation. "If you can't let go of this trash, how will you ever deal with losing anything important?" As she walked away, helplessness gnawed on my insides like a feasting shark.

That's how I felt now as I turned Silas and Lainey's betrayal over and over in my mind like a stone that wouldn't go smooth. Abandoned yet again, with no explanation. It didn't even make sense—they were never close. If anything, they merely tolerated each other at group outings, him thinking she was some stuck-up snob, her thinking he was a self-absorbed jock. They'd been in a constant tug-of-war over me, then suddenly took the rope and strangled me with it.

I had to get to the bottom of this.

I had to figure out what went wrong.

But first, I needed a ridiculous amount of coffee.

The twins and I swarmed the espresso machine at Coastal Cantina on the top deck at 7:30 a.m. on our first day of class. Our schedules would alternate between A days and B days, and my A days were more hectic: Global Studies at 8:30 a.m., International Marketing at 11:10 a.m., and World Art History at 3:40 p.m. I only had one class on B days—a three-hour-long Business Writing and Communications workshop in the afternoon.

"Did you get *any* sleep last night?" Navya passed me a mug, a look of concern on her narrow face. She must've heard me tossing and turning all night.

"Hardly," I said. Despite not getting a wink of sleep in almost forty-eight hours, my first night on the *Sea Voyager* had been restless as the ship creaked and groaned in the waves, those sounds drowned out by Lainey's words playing on loop in my mind.

It's like she's stalking me.

But after backstabbing me like she did, I'd assumed she wouldn't come on this trip. I'd hoped to put an entire planet between us for a whole semester. Heck, this trip was *my* idea. I was the one who told her about CoB to begin with, way back in the beginning of freshman year. I'd seen an ad for it in high school and knew no matter which college I went to, I wanted to study abroad in this program, even if I had to burn myself out fundraising to afford it. I'd literally been looking forward to this for *years*. And she *knew* that.

None of this made any sense at all.

I had to talk to Silas next time I saw him. We used to be so open with each other . . . not that we'd been very conversational; most of our alone time was more of the physical sort. But maybe he'd at least explain himself.

"Girl, hit me up next time," said Divya, sipping her machine-brewed cappuccino. "I've got some stuff that'll knock you right out." Navya pursed her lips; if our kindly stew, Julia—who'd already tried teaching me how to make towel animals—found her stash, it could mean expulsion. But before she could retort, Tate and Miguel ran into us, and we all scarfed down breakfast burritos before heading to class.

Global Studies was the only class all students were required to take, so it was a big lecture in the regal Union. It was pretty surreal going to class in a room that resembled a European opera house. I spotted Sheffia in the back, looking perky with her shiny curled tresses and red lipstick, despite the early hour. But Lainey and Silas must've had this class on their B-day schedules.

The five of us split up afterward—Navya and Divya had some ethnic studies class, while Tate, Miguel, and I found shady spots on the top deck under a canopy next to the swimming pool to get our first homework assignment out of the way before International Marketing. There'd been a ton of fascinating classes to choose from, but since I was double-majoring, I didn't have room for electives, so I opted for those that'd help fulfill my communications course requirements at Stanford.

"She's kinda hot," Tate suddenly said in a low voice, nodding at someone over my shoulder. I twisted in my seat to look. There was Sheffia again, sitting alone at a nearby table, arms crossed as she sulked at the glistening pool water, her pink tote bag on the chair next to her, like she was saving it for someone who was a no-show. "Either of you know her?"

I nearly rolled my eyes. "Her name's Sheffia." The only other thing I knew was how she'd clung to Lainey like a cobweb Lainey had tried swatting away, and had somehow spun a new web to tangle her in. Tate stared, awaiting more intel, but I gave a small shrug. "That's all I got."

"Well, someone ought to tell her that shade of lipstick is way too dark," said Miguel.

"Huh. I think it's cute," said Tate.

"You *would*."

Tate frowned. "What's that supposed to mean?"

Miguel quirked an eyebrow. "Oh, honey, just look at your idea of fashion."

Tate glanced down at what he was wearing—a navy-blue CoB sweatshirt and jeans—looking perplexed about what else he should be expected to wear.

The three of us had International Marketing next, so we headed down to the classroom on Deck 6 together, and my heart spasmed when I spotted Lainey in the back row. She pretended not to notice me, and her smooth jawline clenched as she stared at her notebook.

While Miguel sashayed right over to suck up, Tate scowled alongside me. I didn't know much about him yet, but as far as I was concerned, he was basically my new best friend.

Though our professor was enthusiastic, I couldn't concentrate at all—I kept wanting to leap from my plush armchair, race to the back row, shake Lainey by the shoulders, and demand to know why she hated my guts, why she'd stolen everything from me.

By the time class was over, I felt like I'd been buried in wet sand; having a nemesis was exhausting. Eager to replenish, I plodded back to the Cantina, picked the most carbolicious dish I could find—linguini Alfredo and a hearty roll of bread—and plopped myself down at a smaller table. I'd never had a huge group of friends before, preferring one-on-one conversations . . . or in Silas's case, make-out sessions. But now I was meeting tons of new people even more quickly than my first week at Stanford.

Soon after I dug in, I noticed someone brush close to my table and glanced up to see Brooding Boy. He wore his gray jacket again, but this time had a red T-shirt underneath instead of black. Somehow that made his eyes look even more like dark pools of ink.

He'd stopped in his tracks when our eyes locked, and a strange sort of spark zipped through me.

"Uh . . . hi?" I said hesitantly. "You wanna sit?"

"Thanks, but I just finished, actually," he said. "Heading to my next class now."

"Ah."

"Yeah." He gave me a little wave and started toward the door.

"I'm Jade," I called after him. My cheeks warmed, and I bet they were turning pink.

He paused again. "Like the green rock?"

"Uh, sure. I guess." When most people commented on my name, they correlated it to my eyes; I'd inherited Dad's light green irises. Sometimes that made it hard to look in the mirror.

He considered me, rubbing his lips together like he was trying to suppress a smile. "Felix." With a nod, he turned and left.

"Huh," I muttered. What an odd person.

Suddenly, a girl dropped a notebook near the opposite entrance, making a loud slapping noise.

And that's when I noticed Silas, sitting alone at a table next to the door.

He bent to grab the notebook for her and nearly sent his laptop flying since his wired earbuds were still plugged in. But he managed to avoid disaster, laughing at his moment of clumsiness. The girl apologized profusely, though she was chuckling, too. When she rushed off to join her friends, he adjusted the laptop and kept reading, munching on a sandwich.

My stomach lurched at the sight of him, his thick brows furrowed in focus, subconsciously flexing his left arm like he was stretching it. I wondered if it still hurt from his injury last spring.

Just a few months ago, I would have hurried over and wrapped my arms around him from behind or launched myself into his lap for a deep kiss. It somehow seemed like both yesterday and a lifetime ago.

I scanned the room for Lainey but didn't see her or her bestie Sheffia anywhere.

Now might be my chance to catch him alone.

Deserting my lunch, I inched toward him, my pulse racing a million miles a minute. He didn't notice me until I clasped the back of the chair opposite him, and his eyebrows shot up.

"Hey," I said as he plucked the buds from his ears.

"Uh . . . hey." His eyes darted every which way.

"Listen, I don't want this to be weird—"

"I don't think—"

"But I just wanted to talk—"

"—this is a good idea—"

"What do you think you're doing?" a voice snarled behind me. I whipped around. Lainey was standing there, clutching a tray of food.

"Lainey, I just want to talk." My voice came out shaky and pleading, and I wished I could suck the words back in and try again. I hated sounding so desperate.

"Why can't you leave us alone?" She spoke so loudly, people at neighboring tables turned to stare.

Mortification burned my cheeks. "Why are you being like this?"

Lainey slammed down her tray, soup sloshing over the bowl's edge. "Just leave us alone. That request should be enough."

I glanced at Silas, silently begging him to be reasonable, but he merely stared down at his sandwich, unwilling or unable to even look at me—I couldn't tell which. "Silas, please," I said, but he refused to look up.

"Don't you dare," Lainey persisted, tugging my wrist, pulling me away from him so hard it hurt.

"Ow—"

"Just go!"

I stifled a cry in the back of my throat and turned on my heel, fleeing like I had at dinner last night, feeling more helpless than I'd ever felt in my life.

I had to find another way to talk to Silas.

But how the hell was I supposed to get him alone if she was always freaking *everywhere*?

5

It's amazing how quickly you can settle into a routine even when your world is burning to the ground.

Sometime before the next A day, Lainey must've requested a schedule change, because the next time I walked into International Marketing, she was notably missing. It's not like kids played hooky on CoB—where the hell would you hide?

Though we had zero classes together now, I ran into Lainey and Silas everywhere, whether at one of the posh restaurants, a nighttime party next to the pool, the lounge chairs on the top deck, or the library slash game room. And whenever Silas's eyes found mine, I caught a fleeting sadness in his gaze before his expression morphed to stone. It made me think there was a part of him, however small, that regretted what happened. That regretted leaving me.

I missed him, missed *us*, so fiercely it felt like someone had torn out my organs and shipped them back to California without me. And even after what Lainey did, and how she was acting, I missed her, too. I missed the Lainey I'd known a few months ago, when I'd come home to our room after comforting Silas, still in tears after seeing him so upset.

"Jade, oh my God, are you okay?" She'd been on Zoom, sitting cross-legged on her berry-pink comforter. "I'm *so* sorry," she said to whoever she'd been talking to. "Something happened to my roommate. I'll call back later."

I'd shut the door as she slammed her laptop shut, my movements slow and jerky. "They took away his scholarship," I croaked.

"Whose scholarship?"

"Silas's!"

"Oh, no." Lainey enveloped me in a hug, her own eyes red and watery. Whenever one of us cried, the other followed soon after. "Why, though?"

"His doctors say that even with physical therapy, his elbow probably won't ever be as strong again . . . and . . . and . . ." I blabbered the rest of it through choked sobs, how he might have to move back to Tennessee, how we might need to give up all our plans, our dreams.

Lainey stroked my hair as I cried, murmuring reassurances in my ear, letting me get tears all over the shoulder of her peasant blouse, which probably cost a bazillion dollars. When I finally calmed, she said, "You know . . . I know it's hard to see it now, but I'm sure things'll work out in the end. He shouldn't have to leave; there's always a way to finagle—"

"Exactly!" I pulled back from her embrace, wiping my cheeks with the back of my hand. "I've thought of a way to keep him at Stanford."

Her eyebrows shot up, clearly impressed I'd already come up with a solution. "How?"

"You can get him an internship at your dad's company!"

She stiffened, still smiling, and her arched brows rose slightly in surprise that she hadn't thought of it first.

I nodded excitedly, grabbing a bunch of tissues from the box on my desk. "If Silas could get a job at Sanatek after graduation, he'd be able to pay off his loans like that." I snapped my fingers. "I know he doesn't have any sales experience . . . or, uh, pharmaceutical experience . . . but internships are the best way to learn that kind of thing. And he's smart, dedicated, reliable . . . Oh, Lainey, can you ask your dad for this? *Please?*"

And she agreed, because of course she did. She was a great friend, willing to do me this massive favor, to get her dad to hire Silas, even with his lack of experience. Her father might've been a hard-ass, powerful CEO, but he doted on his daughter—his only living child after Lainey's little brother died—and said yes to basically anything she asked.

What Lainey wanted, Lainey got.

But then she wanted me gone.

When we docked in London for our first port of call, I was just as excited for the chance to corner Silas as I was to sightsee. I'd hovered near the group transportation sign-up station a couple of days earlier and seen Lainey and Silas sign up for the bus to the Tower of London on the first port day. Then I'd waited until they ambled off to wherever and signed my name right below theirs.

I *deserved* answers. And now I'd have a whole day of chances to talk to Silas.

So it was too bad Navya, Divya, and I all overslept docking.

"I told you to set the alarm," Navya accused Divya as she yanked up her jeans with tiny hops.

"Why is this *my* fault?" Divya shot back. "You could've set it."

"I was already in bed."

"You could've climbed down. Or Jade could've done it."

"Sorry—" I started.

"No, don't be," Navya said to me. "I asked *her* to do it."

"Oh my God, does it even matter?" Divya shouted. "We have fifteen minutes to catch the bus."

I frantically unclipped my curls and sprayed on some oil mist. I'd have to do without makeup today. But that made me think of Lainey, and my heart clenched. She'd always refused to leave our dorm without mascara, convinced her blond lashes were invisible without it, but I'd always thought she looked stunning either way. The most makeup I ever wore was concealer, but thankfully I wasn't having a breakout at the moment, so I quickly slathered on my daily SPF (Miguel would be proud) and raced out the door with Navya and Divya.

"Are you sure you don't want to come see Big Ben with us?" Navya asked me once we reached the disembarkation line. We'd all thrown on the itinerary T-shirts Navya had bought, but since it was a cool, gray, drizzly day, we wore jackets and sweaters over them anyway.

"Nah, I really want to go to the Tower of London." Though I was dying to see Big Ben in real life. "I mean, c'mon—Anne Boleyn was decapitated there. That's way cooler than some clock tower," I said, not wanting to admit the real reason.

"That's so morbid. I love it," said Divya, her round face lighting up. "Navya, let's switch."

But by the time we reached the front of the line, Navya had

convinced Divya to stick with their Westminster tour plans after all.

The CoB security officer checking everyone out gave me a friendly smile. "ID and green sheet?"

Oh, *crap*. It felt like someone had injected me with liquid nitrogen.

We weren't allowed to leave the ship without our ID card and green sheet, which we got at the pre-port presentation last night in the Union—basically a ton of logistical and emergency information crammed onto a single printed sheet.

My ID was still in the back pocket of the jeans I'd worn yesterday, and my green sheet was God knew where—probably on the narrow counter behind my bed.

"I . . . I don't have them," I said. "Can you *please* make an exception?" I clasped my hands. "The buses leave in, like, ten minutes."

"Five," Navya corrected.

"Five minutes."

"I'm sorry," the woman said, shaking her head, her accent vaguely Russian. "I have extra green sheets, but I can't let you leave the vessel without your *Voyager* ID."

I let out an exasperated huff and turned back to Navya and Divya. Felix was waiting behind Divya, wearing his usual dark ensemble, clearly stifling laughter at my predicament. Ignoring him, I said to the twins, "Can you *please* ask my bus driver to wait for me?"

"How will you get into our room?" Navya asked.

"Oh God." I face-palmed. Our IDs doubled as our cabin

keys—the ID part wasn't printed on them and only appeared in the security system when scanned—and without my ID, I had no way to get into our cabin. "Okay, I need one of you to come with me. Or I can borrow one of your IDs and sprint."

"But then one of *us* will miss our bus," said Divya.

"Um, both of us'll miss it," said Navya, "because you're not going without me—"

I swore loudly.

"Okay, okay." Navya handed me her ID, and I booked it, Felix definitely chortling as I dashed past him. When I reached the elevator well, I waited a couple of moments before deciding it'd be faster to hurl myself down the stairs to Deck 4—not literally, obviously. By the time I reached our room, I was out of breath, and when I returned to the disembarkation line, ID and green sheet in hand, I was clutching a stitch in my side, the taste of metal in the back of my mouth. God, I really needed to start using the fitness center; the one time I'd gone in there, Silas and Lainey had been thudding away on side-by-side treadmills, so I'd avoided it ever since.

I handed Navya her ID and brandished my own at the CoB security lady. **Zofia Dobrowski**, her name tag read. "Here ya go, Zofia."

She plucked it from my fingers to scan it. "Thank you. Have a lovely time."

The three of us hustled through the port, following the CoB-branded blue sandwich boards to the bus pickup point . . . and there was only one bus remaining. The space with the board labeled **Westminster Abbey** was empty.

Navya slapped her thigh. "Ah, crap."

"Oh, no," I said. "I'm *so* sorry."

"Divya's the one who forgot to set the alarm," she said.

"Will you shut up about that?" said Divya.

Someone whistled nearby, and we all turned to look. Felix was poking his head out the door of the bus. "Are you coming or not?" The board next to that bus read **Tower of London**. Had he made sure the bus waited for us?

I grinned. "Guess you're seeing decapitation station with me after all."

Navya shuddered. "Gross."

"*So* morbid," said Divya. "I freaking love it."

As we boarded the packed bus, I scanned each row of chattering students—plus Sketchy Bob, who hugged a backpack to his chest and watched intently as we found seats near the back—and realized Lainey and Silas were missing. They must've switched activities last minute.

So much for cornering Silas today, after all that.

But I didn't have much time to sulk—as soon as we stepped off the bus on Tower Hill, the historic castle on the bank of the river Thames enraptured me. The Tower of London was nearly a thousand years old, which blew my mind; I'd never been inside a building that old before. Once a royal palace and later a prison to foreign kings, English queens, and noble prisoners alike, the tall White Tower jutted from the middle of a courtyard surrounded by two concentric rings of stone and Tudor-style structures.

I'd expected to have to join some super-boring guided tour, but the fortress was basically like a gigantic playground for adults—we could freely explore the grounds, the castle, all of it. Once we were past the ticket booth and inside the outer wall, hoods and umbrellas up to ward off the windy drizzle, Felix wandered off on his own, back to his aloof self, his moment of chivalry quickly forgotten. Miguel went to go stare at the crown jewels before filming his final audition video, and Tate and his new premed friend Jamal, Silas's roommate who'd sat next to Sheffia at the welcome dinner, wanted to see the armory exhibit in the White Tower.

I was more interested in the outer fortress, where they'd locked up prisoners centuries ago, and where King Henry VIII's second wife, Anne Boleyn, spent her final nights before her demise in the courtyard.

The grounds were devoid of many tourists thanks to the dreary weather, giving us space to mosey, but Sketchy Bob trailed behind Navya, Divya, and me as we headed for an entrance to the medieval St. Thomas's Tower. "Oh, no." Navya glanced over her shoulder.

"Is he following us?" Divya hissed.

"It's fine," I whispered back. "Maybe he'll go somewhere else . . ."

But nope. Soon after we entered the first room—what used to be a king's living quarters—he followed us inside and gawked without a word of greeting.

It was totally normal for the Lifelong Learners to go on excursions with the students, but the way he never hung out with the other adults, the way he'd openly stare, his eyes watery, gaping voids—it made the hairs on the back of my neck rise.

We rushed through the first few rooms to lose him along the ramparts connecting each tower. Once we finally did, we paused to examine the graffiti prisoners had etched into the stone walls.

Divya pointed out a particularly intricate inscription. "Can you imagine being so bored you'd carve all this? Like, why not try to dig a hole and escape?"

"Mm," said Navya, "that's not how stone works."

Divya shot her sister a dirty look. "People escaped that way in other prisons. You can loosen one stone at a time or whatever. God, Navya, why does everything have to be—"

"A guard would probably notice, anyway," I said, trying to defuse the tension. For twins, they sure fought a lot, and about the most ridiculous things. "I'm sure it was really hard to escape."

"Maybe," Divya said shortly. "Anyway, I'm hungry. I'm gonna check out the café." Before either of us could respond, she stalked out.

After a moment's hesitation, Navya called, "Wait, Divya!" And she was gone.

Wanting to give them space to work out whatever was going on there, I wandered the ramparts alone for a while. An unsettled feeling kept making me dart glances over my shoulder, half expecting Sketchy Bob to lunge from the shadows, as I read the placards in each room. The one inside Lanthorn Tower revealed it was built sometime in the thirteenth century, and though it'd been gutted by a fire in the 1700s, it was still standing.

Was it weird to find inspiration in a stone tower?

Silas and Lainey had utterly gutted me. And I wanted to survive it. I wanted to relish every moment of this semester, to come out the other side standing strong, independent, fierce. I wanted to endure the test of time and heartache and loss, like this building had.

I wandered to the next tower, the air thick with cool dew, whispers of the past seeming to cling to every surface. I traced my fingers along the stone wall. There was no graffiti in this room. Maybe they'd imprisoned queens here—queens who didn't need to dig into stone to know they'd left a mark on this world.

Queens who'd died here.

A shiver coasted down my spine, and I peered out the third-story window overlooking the courtyard. From here you could see the glass monument marking the spot where Anne Boleyn had been decapitated. I'd read once that the king had ordered her brother's similar execution in the courtyard days earlier, so she would have to watch. I clutched my neck. How awful humans could be to each other. I crossed the room to peek out another window—

There he was. Silas. Right there, at the edge of the cobblestone path lining the fortress's outer ring below. My heart leapt into my throat. He'd come on this excursion after all. There must've been a second bus. He scrolled through his phone as he shifted his weight from one foot to another like he was bored, waiting for something. Or someone.

And I didn't see Lainey anywhere.

I leaned close to the cool glass, my fingers pressed against it. He was so close, and in that moment, I wished more than anything we were exploring this place together. One weekend last year he'd surprised me with a last-minute road trip to Disneyland. I'd never been to an amusement park before, and he was determined to fix that. I remembered racing from ride to ride, licking churro sugar off our fingers, cuddling under the fireworks next to the castle. I'd shrieked with delight as we dropped down Splash Mountain's flume, and again that night in our motel room for entirely different reasons before doing it all over again the next day. It was the happiest I'd ever been.

I thought he'd been happy, too.

Maybe this was my chance to find out what went wrong—

My stomach sank as I spotted Lainey, now that my nose was nearly smooshed into the cool glass. She was stooped next to him, her hood covering her blond hair, stretching a finger toward one of the iconic black ravens roaming the grounds as she filmed it. The raven pecked at the gravel, paying her no mind as she crept closer, summoning it with a coo.

Stay away, I thought. *She'll stab you in the back if you get too close.*

A rock lodged in my throat. I hated this. I wished she would disappear—evaporate into mist like the ghosts who lurked in these towers.

Suddenly, Lainey's eyes snapped up to something high above, but not to me. Horror registered on her face and she froze, time seeming to stand still before she launched herself back, crying out as she landed hard on the cobblestones.

A large stone slab crashed to the ground—right where Lainey had been kneeling.

6

Once, when I was little, I got hit by a car.

The driver hadn't seen me as he backed out of his parking spot. I remembered the shock of something unexpectedly knocking me off my feet. I remembered the pain of the sudden impact to my hip, of hitting the pavement a moment later, palms scraping against asphalt. I remembered how the car jerked as the driver slammed the brakes, and how passersby screamed and gasped.

But most of all, I remembered Mom's shrieks as she hurtled toward me.

"Jade! What the hell's the matter with you?"

Even then, sprawled on the ground after getting hit by a car, it was my fault. Whatever went wrong was *always* my fault.

Now I gaped out the window as Lainey slumped on the ground, cradling one of her hands, her palm visibly red and raw. If I rushed out onto the rampart and she saw me there, she'd think I'd chucked that rock at her. That it was my fault.

So instead, I stayed put. I leaned to see the top of the rampart but couldn't from this angle. *Someone* must've chucked it—it's not like stones leapt from battlements of their own accord.

Her shriek had drawn a small crowd; people hurried from both the outer ring of the fortress and the courtyard with the White Tower through the open archways under the rampart.

"Omigod, are you okay?"

"What happened?"

"Oh, no, you're bleeding!"

I could hear their muffled voices through the glass as Silas helped Lainey to her feet, the closed umbrella dangling from her wrist nearly whacking her in the face.

Several black umbrellas obscured my view, but I recognized a few familiar faces: Sheffia, Tate, and Jamal were clustered together. Divya and Navya were on the outskirts of the crowd, clearly biting back laughter—to anyone who hadn't seen what happened, it probably looked like Lainey had screamed bloody murder from tripping over her own two feet. Even Felix had wandered over to see what all the fuss was about.

As Lainey brushed muddy gravel from her jeans, Sheffia darted over and picked up Lainey's fallen phone, peppering her with questions. Tate followed her.

"Is the screen cracked?" Lainey interrupted.

"No, it's good." Sheffia passed over her phone. "What happened?"

Lainey snapped a picture of the stone. "Someone tried to kill me with that rock!"

Sheffia gasped, and Tate said, "Seriously?"

"No, I made it up for funsies," Lainey said sarcastically, then swatted Silas's chest. "You saw."

"Uh . . . I was reading something . . ." said Silas as Tate scanned the rampart, squinting against the drizzle.

Lainey let out a frustrated cry and pointed a shaky finger at the rampart. "I heard a scraping noise right above me and *saw* the rock slide to the edge. Someone pushed it."

A murmur rippled through the crowd, and now everyone was looking up. But clearly, nobody was on the rampart—at least, not that they could see.

"Someone's over there!" Tate shouted breathlessly. Every head turned in my direction.

My heart stopped dead. He was pointing right at me.

I pushed away from the window, but it was too late. I'd been spotted. I couldn't run—then I'd look guilty as sin. *Shiiiiiit.* This wasn't good.

Okay. Breathe. I just had to stay calm and explain what I saw.

Hesitating would only make this worse, so I darted up the short flight of stairs and out to the deserted rampart. The drizzle was picking up. I flipped up my hood and poked my head over the edge of the chest-high stone wall, my pulse racing as everyone gaped up at me. I expected Lainey's expression to twist with fury when she saw me, like the other day when she found me talking to Silas. Instead, she blanched, eyes wide, and took a step back. "You . . . ?"

"No!" I called down. "Of course it wasn't me, I'd never try to hurt you." Not like she'd hurt me.

"Oh, so you just *happened* to be right there."

"I mean, yeah."

"Then who did it?" Tate asked.

I defensively balled my hands into fists but took a steadying breath. Maybe he was genuinely asking. Heck, maybe he wanted to high-five them. "I don't know, I only saw the rock fall. I couldn't see up here from that angle."

Whoever had done it had vanished like a ghost. And if any place could be haunted, this was it. Goose bumps prickled my arms. Barring the supernatural, as far as I could tell the culprit had three potential escape routes.

One, the tower I'd just left . . . so that option was out.

Two, the metal-grated stairs behind me leading to the court-yard.

Three, the tower across the rampart—they could've stooped out of view from anyone below and raced right through it, continuing along the battlements to the next flight of stairs across the courtyard.

The crowd below had formed so fast, I couldn't tell who'd come from where. Whoever did it could be milling among them now—

"This needs to stop." Lainey's voice trembled and her cheeks went pink, the same shade I'd seen her go several times while arguing with her dad on the phone, when he made her so angry she couldn't stop word vomit from spewing from her lips. "*You* need to stop."

Nerves zinged through me like electricity. "I didn't do this," I cried, shaking. "I was in there when it happened." I motioned to where I came from and shot Tate an angry look, but he was busy wiping raindrops off his glasses with the edge of his sleeve. "I swear to God, it wasn't me."

"Lainey, c'mon." Silas set a hand on her shoulder. "There has to be some other explanation." Hope blossomed in my chest. He believed me.

Lainey threw him a look of disgust, but right then, a gust of wind nearly blew Sheffia's umbrella into Lainey's face, and someone else's umbrella turned inside out.

"See?" Silas brushed back his sideswept chestnut hair. "It was probably just the wind."

"*What?*" Lainey and I said at once. It was fully ridiculous to suggest wind would blow over a stone that size.

"The wind," he repeated, like we'd had trouble hearing. "It pushed the stone off the wall."

Felix raised a fist to his lips, and a few people laughed. Tate straight up snorted.

Lainey shook her head. "That's not—that wouldn't—" She gave up on words and let out a low growl before stomping off toward the restrooms.

"Wait—" Silas started.

"I'm *bleeding*," she snarled without slowing. "I have to go wash this."

As Silas and Sheffia chased after her, a Beefeater—one of the Tower's unmistakable guardsmen in a red poufy uniform and a flower-rimmed top hat—approached the dispersing crowd. He managed to corner Felix, who'd awkwardly lingered behind, to ask what happened. I hurried over, down the metal-grated stairs and under an archway. Maybe he could check the security footage. I had to ask.

From here I could see Lainey and Silas had been standing next to scaffolding that blocked the last three archways under the rampart—renovation work, maybe—but there were no construction workers in sight.

"—must have tripped over it," the Beefeater was saying as I

approached, smoothing down his thick gray mustache.

"I dunno," said Felix. "I didn't see what happened, just the aftermath."

"I did," I said. The Beefeater and Felix both turned to me. "She didn't trip over it. I saw the rock fall." Felix threw me a look I couldn't read.

"Ah," said the Beefeater, "the ghosts must be up to their usual mischief, then." Felix and I gaped as he handed Felix his umbrella, bent over with a grunt, and picked up the stone slab. "Mm. Too heavy for a ghost, I think." He raised and lowered it, demonstrating. "Though that'd make an excellent story for the tours."

He wasn't taking this seriously at all. Maybe people didn't sue each other left and right over here like they did in the US. Or maybe he thought we were being a bunch of drama queens.

He caught my bewildered expression and guffawed. "Don't worry yourself. It was likely from the remodeling work." He nodded toward the scaffold. "Someone must have set this too close to the edge."

Some of the pressure in my chest decompressed.

"But she said it came from there." Felix motioned to the top of the rampart. "She said she saw it slide off like someone pushed it."

The Beefeater chuckled. "The thing of it is, there aren't loose stones littering the battlements people can chuck about."

"Someone could've grabbed it from there," I said, pointing to the construction. "Or from inside; some of those fireplaces are pretty crumbly."

"Does your friend have many enemies, then?" The Beefeater's

eyes twinkled like I was some sort of comical cartoon character.

"She's not my friend . . ." I trailed off. A bunch of people *did* dislike her; Miguel was competing against her, Tate kept strangely glaring at her, Navya resented her easy wealth—

"So, *you're* the enemy?" asked the Beefeater. Felix threw me a sidelong glance.

"No!" Panic fluttered in my chest. "Isn't there security footage?" There had to be some proof it wasn't me. "There's CCTV everywhere here, right?"

The Beefeater chuckled. "You're a regular little Poirot, aren't you?" I had no idea what that meant. He blew air between his lips and glanced around. "Not facing this exact spot, I'm afraid."

A bell tolled nearby. He tossed the stone next to the scaffolding with a grunt and clapped damp dirt from his hands before glancing at his watch. "Ah, must be off, otherwise it's off with *my* head." With that, he took his umbrella back from Felix and headed off.

"Crap," I groaned. "Everyone's going to think I did this."

"Yep." Felix smirked. "Have fun with that."

"Gee, thanks."

As he drifted away, I stared helplessly at the cast-off stone. Could this semester be any more of a disaster?

Yes. Yes, it could.

7

Betrayal can make you do ridiculous things. But in my case, hurling a rock at someone's head wasn't one of them. Too bad no one seemed to believe me.

Even my roommates kept whispering together as we traipsed from monument to monument with Tate and Miguel, places I'd dreamed of seeing for years but could barely even process. My mind kept flashing back to Lainey's horrified expression.

I saw the shock in her eyes as we crossed Westminster Bridge, the majestic Houses of Parliament and Big Ben glowing burnt orange in the dying sunlight.

I saw the fear in her quivering chin as we rode the London Eye, the river Thames below slashing through the light-speckled city before coiling into the distance like a snake.

I saw the scowl twisting her features as I bit into my fish-and-chips, turning the flaky fillets into ash—

"Earth to Jade." Divya set a tall glass of Guinness in front of me.

"Sorry, hi. Yes. Thanks."

After topping twenty-five thousand steps today (according to Navya's Fitbit), we'd landed at the Cat and Goose, a packed pub near Trafalgar Square designated as the CoB evening meet-up spot. It couldn't be any more quintessential English, smelling of dark brew and fried haddock, each flat-screen above the bar airing a different soccer—er, football—match. Buses would shuttle everyone back to the *Sea Voyager* at eleven, except for the lucky ones who could afford to stay elsewhere until the ship left for the next port in a few days. But it'd be my hotel each night.

Shockingly, it'd be Lainey's and Silas's, too. I'd assumed they'd stay in some hoity-toity hotel and that they'd only come here to socialize. But then they unsocially claimed a high-top for two in the corner, forcing Sheffia to awkwardly hover until she eventually flitted to an empty stool at the bar. Tate had gravitated over soon after, ditching us, and Navya had been all pouty ever since.

"Why're you all sourpuss?" Divya shouted to be audible over the din of chattering CoB students. At first, I thought she meant Navya, but she was looking at me.

I groaned. "Honestly? I'm worried everyone thinks I'm some rock-hurling psychopath." I sipped my beer, my upper lip sinking into the thick layer of white foam.

"No, they don't," said Navya. "It was obviously just some freak accident."

"Oh." I flushed. "I totally thought you thought I did it."

Navya pulled a face. "Why?"

"The way you were whispering earlier . . ."

Divya laughed. "We were talking about Tate. Navya's kind of obsessed."

Navya swatted her arm. "I am not!" Though her high cheekbones went pink. "Anyway," she said, clearly not wanting to discuss it, though she'd already confided in me yesterday that she had a massive crush on him, "no, we don't think you did that."

I sighed. "Well, Lainey definitely thinks I did."

"Screw her," said Divya. "If she's absurd enough to think you'd do that, she's not worth stressing about. C'mon, let's do tequila shots and get your mind off it."

Tequila. Lainey's go-to drink. I nearly whacked my forehead. I had to stop connecting everything to her.

"Mm, maybe vodka instead?" I suggested.

"Uh, I don't think—" Navya started.

But Divya was already heading back to the bar with a whoop. Navya sighed, and I quirked an eyebrow at her.

"What?" she asked.

"I'm clearly not the only one stressing."

"Oh." She glanced back at Divya, who was leaning against the bar and waving frantically at the overwhelmed bartender. "I mean, I'm sure you've noticed. Divya drinks a *lot*. She's been drinking every night on the ship so far."

"Ah . . ." I'd only noticed the first night. Maybe she'd been sneakier since. "Sorry I went along with the shots idea."

"No, it's okay. It's not *your* fault."

"Is it really that bad?"

She sighed again. "I mean, it's one thing to party. Our parents were super strict growing up, so, like, I get it. And this semester's sort of a last reprieve before we need to start studying for the LSATs. But it's not just the partying . . ." She trailed off, like she felt guilty divulging her twin's vices.

"It's also the flask," I prompted.

"Exactly. The flask, sneaking booze onto the ship . . ." She trailed off again.

"Did she drink a lot at school, too?"

"Not around me. But I don't know—we don't live together; we're both in on-campus housing. And we both took summer classes, so we didn't go back home—" Navya mummed up as Divya returned with three shot glasses and slid one to each of us.

"God, I love that you can drink at eighteen here," she said.

I sniffed mine. "Yeah, I don't get why the drinking age in the US is twenty-one."

"It's fully absurd," Divya agreed. "If you can join the military and die for your country, you should be able to have a freaking beer."

"But *you're* not going to die for your country," said Navya.

"The point is, we *can*. Other people our age are. It's the principle of the thing!" Divya raised her glass. "Anyway, here's to not stressing about absurd laws and absurd people."

I raised mine and said in a horrendous British accent, "Cheers to that, mate."

"Cheers!"

My shot burned as it went down, heat flooding my insides, and Divya chased hers with a swig of Guinness. Navya took a small sip and cringed as she set the glass down.

"Oh, c'mon, that's pathetic," teased Divya.

"I don't like taking shots," said Navya.

Divya swiped her shot and downed it.

"Hey!" said Navya.

"You just said you didn't like it!"

"I meant taking a full shot at once."

As they argued, my gaze wandered to Lainey and Silas across the room. Technically the twins weren't the only ones who believed me. Silas did, too. Or maybe he'd only been trying to calm Lainey down. I couldn't let him think I'd try to hurt her.

When Lainey went to use the bathroom, I took a huge gulp of Guinness. "Be right back." But the twins barely looked up from their fight as I slinked to Silas's table.

He straightened at the sight of me, throwing me a poor excuse for his usual lopsided smile, those dimples I loved so much only making a slight appearance. "Hey."

"Hey." Being this close to him without being able to touch him made me feel like razor blades were shredding my insides. I gripped the back of Lainey's chair to ground myself. "You know I didn't throw that rock, right?"

He glanced toward the restroom. "Sure." But he didn't seem so sure.

My chest tightened. "Silas." I rounded the table and took his hand, his fingers damp from the glass's condensation. "I would *never* do something like that. You have to know that."

He yanked his hand back. "Why do you care what I think?"

I winced. "Of course I care." I still loved him, even after everything.

"You didn't give a crap what I thought when—"

"Hey!" said Lainey, already back from the bathroom. I expected her face to turn beet red. I expected her to ball her hands into fists and start screaming for me to leave. Instead, her blue eyes went wide as saucers and darted across the room, looking for an escape route.

My stomach clenched. Was she *scared* of me?

I stepped closer, and she backed away.

"Lainey, please," I said, "I don't know what happened, but I didn't throw that rock at you. I would never try to hurt you—"

I couldn't hear her over the garbled pub noise, but her mouth clearly formed the word: "Bullshit."

"It's not—"

"You haven't stopped stalking us this entire trip." She raised her voice. "Even now. You're obsessed."

"That's not true." But it sort of was. "I mean . . . I'm not . . . This was the designated meet-up point."

"Then what are you doing *here*?" She motioned to my proximity to Silas.

"I just wanted him to know—"

"No!" she yelled loud enough so others turned to look, then pressed her trembling fingers to her lips. After a moment, she said, "Stop it, just . . . please, *stop* it," and drew a deep breath, like she was desperately trying to regain her composure. But then her eyes watered, and she screwed up her face. "You're going to ruin everything, aren't you?"

I shook from head to toe, afraid to say anything for fear I'd absolutely lose it. How *dare* she? She was the one who ruined *my* life.

"And what about you?" she said to Silas. "What the hell are you doing, talking to her? After everything she did?" He threw his hands up, like he had no control over my presence.

I furrowed my brow, confused and horrified.

What exactly had I done?

8

Sheer mortification made me turn on my heel and stalk back to my table, though I wanted to stay and demand answers. If I did something wrong, something that hurt the two people dearest to me, I wanted to know. In the weeks before Silas dumped me via text, I'd spoken with both of them via FaceTime, and they hadn't seemed mad. Everything was totally fine. And then suddenly, it wasn't. But if I'd unwittingly done something terrible, I wanted to make it right.

My stomach twisted to see that Navya and Divya were gone, and in their place, Felix sat alone with our abandoned glasses, gripping a full glass of his own. Maybe he was holding the table while they went to the bathroom or something; he seemed prone to random acts of chivalry.

Felix watched me sit next to him, taking a long, slow sip of his dark beer. "Hey, Rocky."

"What'd you just call me?"

"Rocky. You know—green rock."

"It's *Jade*." I grabbed my own beer and chugged the rest, then wiped my lips and sank my forehead into my arms.

After a long pause, Felix asked gruffly, "Fun day?"

I grimaced. "Oodles of fun. Having *such* a blast." My words were starting to slur. I couldn't remember how many drinks deep I was.

"Yeah, I get it," he said. "Sucks to explore a new city. Make new friends. Drink legally. What a drag."

I snapped my head up to glare. His face was closer than I'd expected; he'd leaned over so he wouldn't have to shout. Even in the dimly lit pub, I could see how truly dark his eyes were—such a deep mahogany shade, I could only barely make out his pupils. They glinted with judgment.

"Oh, piss off," I said in my offensive British accent.

But he remained still except for a slight twitch at the corner of his lips.

"Haven't you made any new friends you could bother?" I persisted.

"Nah, not really," he said. I raised a quizzical brow, and he offered a small shrug. "I like to be alone."

I almost said, *Me too*, but stopped myself. "Did you spend the whole day by yourself?"

"Yep." He took another sip, then wrinkled his nose like he didn't care for it. "I saw the Rosetta Stone and Buckingham Palace, then hit up the National Gallery and Portrait Gallery. You can cram in a lot by yourself. It's great."

"Then what're you doing *here*?" I motioned around at all the people he so clearly loved avoiding.

He glanced toward the door, feeling around the back of his chair for his coat. "Well, I can leave. Can't take *that* long to get back to the port by Tube—"

I balled up a napkin and chucked it at him. "No, don't be ridiculous."

He eyed the napkin that fell into his lap, then looked up at me from under his dark lashes. "You really woke up this morning and chose violence, didn't you?"

"Oh geez." I covered my face.

"Anyway, your friends took off. Just so you know."

I snapped my gaze to the door, dismayed.

"They were arguing," he went on. "Divya stormed out, and Navya said to tell you she's sorry, but she had to get her sister back to the ship."

I groaned. Divya had probably downed those shots too quickly. I'd been so wrapped up in my own problems I hadn't noticed.

Problems who were staring at me right now.

Lainey and Silas averted their eyes the moment I met theirs, and my expression soured.

Felix followed my gaze, taking another sip. "Wishing you didn't miss?"

It took a moment to register what he meant, and my cheeks warmed. "I didn't *do* it." I kept watching them bicker in hushed tones. Good. Let them fight. The least I could do was puncture this perfect little balloon they'd been floating in. But then Silas caressed her arm. I glowered, mashing my lips together to keep the lower one from trembling. I couldn't help it—I wished whoever threw that stone *didn't* miss.

Felix's eyebrows shot up, and I clapped a hand over my mouth.

I totally said that last part out loud.

"Wow." He chuckled. "What on earth did that girl do to you?"

"I don't actually wish that," I scrambled to backtrack. "I mean, sure, sometimes I think about killing her." My face went even hotter. "Or, you know, not *killing* her, but willing her out of existence or something. *Poof.*" I mimed casting a magic spell across the room.

Felix peeked at Lainey. "Didn't work."

"Obviously." The word slurred, my tongue thick in my mouth.

"So . . . did she murder your dog?"

I screwed up my face. "No."

"Drive drunk and kill your friend? Burn down your house?"

"No, nothing like *that*. God."

"Hmm. Just thinking of reasons you'd want a person dead."

"I don't—"

"It wasn't something petty, was it? Like getting an internship over you? Or stealing your boyfriend, or—" I must've cringed, because he raised his brows again. "Ah, there it is." He glanced over at Silas. "*He* used to be with *you*."

"Yeah, alright?" I huffed. "We used to be together. And it's not something *petty*. It tore my heart into a million pieces."

"So dramatic," he purred.

"Well, yes! It was!" I said. "We were in love, and she was my best friend, and then over the summer, out of *nowhere*, I got this horrible text from him—" And there I went, telling this aloof prick my entire life story. How Silas interned at Lainey's dad's company in Boston while I was all the way in California. How we ended. How they ostracized me. How CoB was my idea, my dream, yet Lainey showed up with him to flaunt their relationship in my face.

But then I thought of the fear in her eyes when she saw me atop the rampart. And of what she said before: *What the hell are you doing, talking to her? After everything she did?*

"And you know what the worst part is . . . ?" I hesitated, my lower lip trembling. I covered my mouth and shook my head.

"Say it," Felix prodded.

I groaned, rubbing my forehead. "Why're you so interested, anyway?"

He wiped the surprised look off his face and perched an elbow on the back of his chair. "Who says I'm interested?"

"*You're* the one who tried to guess what she did to me."

I finally got a real smile out of him. "Fair." He sipped his beer, but it was almost like he did it just to keep his mouth busy. I stared silently so he'd keep talking. It worked. "I dunno. I'm a psych major. I like to figure out what makes people tick."

"If you like figuring people out so much, why do you like being alone?"

He only shrugged, dragging his thumb along the condensation on his glass.

"Oh, c'mon. That's all I'm gonna get out of you? You're a psych major. Whoop-de-do."

He laughed. "Well, what else do you want?"

"I just told you my life story. You've gotta give me something back. Where are you from? What school do you go to? What's your family like?"

The corner of his mouth quirked. "Small talk. I freaking hate small talk."

"Okay, fine. Be difficult."

He folded his arms on the table and leaned close. "I'd argue you're the one being difficult."

Heat rose in my cheeks—both from his words and his sudden shift in demeanor. "How so?"

"Difficult for yourself, I mean. You're so . . ."

"What? I'm so *what*?"

"Angry."

I crossed my arms and sulked, not caring if that proved his point.

"But the thing is," he went on, "I wonder how much of your anger is displaced."

"What do you mean?"

"It's not just what *she* did to you, is it?"

My stomach sank. "You think it was *my* fault?"

"No." He firmly held my gaze. "He's the one who screwed your best friend and then dumped you. So why the hell don't you want to kill *him*?"

Felix's words ripped the air from my lungs.

I *had* been directing most of my ire toward Lainey. It's not that I hadn't been furious with Silas, though. When he sent that horrible text, when I knew he was sleeping with my best friend, I thought the rage boiling my blood would be enough to melt the phone in my grip.

But something about the whole situation felt . . . off. I couldn't put my finger on it. Maybe it was because I knew them both so well. He'd barely been able to keep his hands off me. She'd trusted me with secrets she'd never told another soul.

And then, boom. Everything changed.

Something *happened*. Something I was missing. And I needed to know what it was.

Just then, Silas leaned across their table to cup Lainey's cheek. I remembered how his fingers used to feel on my face, how they'd move to the back of my neck and wind through my curls, holding me close as his lips moved over mine, softly at first, then hungrier, more passionate, until my legs went weak, and a shiver trailed up between them. But now he was *hers*. She'd won some battle I hadn't even known we were fighting until I'd already been slaughtered.

Hatred, hot and thick, bubbled in my veins like lava, and I couldn't stand her, I couldn't stand any of it, I *couldn't*.

Letting out a strangled cry, I scooted my chair back, grabbed my jacket, and stumbled to the door. I couldn't breathe in this crowded, noisy pub—I had to get out of here.

A cool, misty breeze stung my ears as I stepped outside, and I slipped on my jacket, my teeth already chattering. Our bus wouldn't arrive for another hour. Those iconic black cabs were everywhere, but the ride back to port would probably cost at least twenty-five pounds, and that would eat into my budget worth two or three meals. I'd have to figure out another way back. Maybe I could take the Tube, or maybe the port was within walking distance. I wouldn't mind a long walk—

Suddenly, someone nudged my elbow. "Where are you going?"

I gasped and spun. Felix. He'd followed me. "Back to the ship."

He checked his watch. "We've still got a little over an hour—"

"I need to go back *now*." I started down the street, but quickly stumbled over the damp cobblestone sidewalk. I almost bit it, barely managing to catch my footing. Since dissolving into the pavement wasn't a realistic option, I kept going, fully pretending that hadn't happened.

Felix kept pace next to me, and I refused to see whether he was biting back a laugh. "Going to take a cab?" he asked.

"Nope. I'll walk."

"Do you even know where you're going?"

I whipped out my phone. Even though it didn't have service, GPS still worked. "Sure. I've got a map."

"Well, hang on." Felix stepped in front of me.

"What?" I stilled.

He hesitated. "Just . . . come back inside."

I set a hand on my hip and narrowed my eyes. "What, so you can judge me some more for who I'm most angry with?" What even gave him the right?

"No. You still need to hear about my favorite TV shows, and how I went to high school in Oxfordshire, and what I want to be when I grow up." Oxfordshire—that explained the hint of a British accent, at least. He made a face, like saying any more would be a form of slow torture.

I almost laughed. Almost. Nothing was getting me back in that pub. "I thought you hated small talk."

"I do. But it's better than you getting mugged on some sketchy street."

"It's not that sketchy." I brushed past him and kept walking.

"Maybe not right here, but you don't know the route."

"Nobody's going to mug me—"

He swooped in front of me again. "If you think I'm going to let you walk all the way back to the ship alone, you're out of your mind."

I raised my eyebrows at his worried tone.

The breeze brushed strands of tousled black hair across his forehead, and he let out a breath, like he'd been holding it for a moment. "Please, come back inside—"

"I *can't*," I snapped louder than I meant to. "I can't be in there if *they* are." His eyes softened—not like he pitied me, but like he understood, somehow.

"Well, come on, then." He motioned for me to follow him in the other direction. "Let's get a cab."

I swallowed hard. "I . . . I can't afford it."

"No worries, I got it." He led me to the main road to catch a cab, and despite everything that had happened over the past few days, I'd never been so humiliated.

9

"Wanna split and hit the pubs?" Tate asked as our group wandered past a coat of arms in one of the grand halls at Windsor Castle two days later. Windsor was exactly as you'd picture it—imposing gray stone walls and jutting turrets, with lush paintings, ornate tapestries, rich velvet drapes, and intricately carved mahogany furniture spanning each room.

"Hell yes," said Divya. "Let's do it." She wore this flowing midnight-blue maxi dress with puffy lantern sleeves, but it seemed the chance to party trumped cosplaying royalty.

"Ergh?" Navya sputtered, clearly torn between going along with Tate and keeping Divya sober.

"But we just got here," I piped up on her behalf.

"Yeah," said Tate, "but seen one castle, seen 'em all."

"Then why'd you sign up for this?" I asked. I'd been trying to cram in as much as possible after that humiliating cab ride home with Felix, refusing to let Lainey and Silas ruin London for me. I'd even revisited Big Ben yesterday since my anxiety kept me from focusing the first time. I'd always dreamed of visiting, ever since watching BBC shows with Dad when I was little. But the experience was jarring, somehow; it seemed both larger than life and smaller than I'd imagined, its very proximity dashing my grand expectations. And now that I'd seen it in the flesh, the dream was dead and rotting.

Tate shrugged at my question, eyes roving the room. I bet he was looking for Sheffia; I wasn't the only one signing up for excursions based on who else might be there. I'd seen him doing laps in the pool during Sheffia's early-morning swimming routine, and I was pretty sure he'd mentioned his night owl tendencies. But I hadn't seen Sheffia all day—or Lainey and Silas, for that matter.

"I wanna stay." Navya tugged on Tate's sleeve, getting her nerve up. "C'mon, help me look for cats in the paintings. I'm making a TikTok."

Divya rolled her eyes, but Tate teased, "Well, if it's for *TikTok*," grinning. Miguel had gotten him hooked.

At least Navya and I won that round.

Good thing, too, because this was my last chance to do my World Art History assignment: a scavenger hunt for five British works of art containing symbolism. We had to take selfies with them to prove we'd found them IRL rather than looking them up online. You'd think that'd be easy—doesn't all art contain symbolism?—but the portraits of nobles in rich skirts and fine silks had no clear theme beyond their own self-importance, and the landscapes were just that—ancient cityscapes, step-bridges in forests, white-peaked mountains. Unlike in museums, there weren't placards explaining each piece, so I'd have to interpret any symbolism on my own.

Finally, I spotted a portrait of a young Queen Elizabeth I wearing a crimson, gold-tissue gown, clasping a book to her chest. Another tome was splayed open in the backdrop, clearly indicating she was well learned or some shit, because God forbid you'd assume a royal woman was smart without her literally clutching knowledge.

I hustled over for a picture and unlocked my phone, which opened to Instagram. I'd connected to the free Wi-Fi earlier while waiting in line to get in. Now my feed automatically refreshed to a picture of Lainey and Silas grinning in front of the iconic circular tower at Windsor.

Posted twenty minutes ago.

My stomach sank. They were here. Lainey must've hired a car service to cart them around, lulling me into a false sense of security when they weren't on the bus earlier.

"Can you scoot?" A voice next to me made me jump. It was Miguel. "You're in my shot."

"Copycat," I teased, shuffling over.

"Yeah, well. Haven't had a chance to work on this. Editing those audition vids took forever. What a complete waste."

My eyebrows shot up. "Oh, *no*."

"Yup. That rich bitch got the gig. She totally sabotaged me."

"What do you mean?"

He shook his head. "You know what, I don't want to talk about it. It's humiliating . . ." he grumbled before striking a pose, offering his camera a tight-lipped smile. "Ugh, you'd think the lighting inside a freaking palace wouldn't be utter garbage. Here, I'll take yours." He reached for my phone, then barely gave me a chance to grin before snapping the pic and handing it back. "Gorgeous." Without another word, he sauntered to the next room.

I glanced at the shot and grimaced—my snaggletooth was showing. One of my incisors slightly overlapped a front tooth. It wasn't a huge deal; when I'd complained to Lainey about it once, she'd said, "Oh, stop. I've never even noticed before. If anything, it makes you look even more like Keira Knightley, and she's literal perfection." But I'd always been self-conscious about it. I carefully took a few selfies at better angles, picked a favorite, then uploaded it to Instagram with the caption, *Never thought I'd do homework in a castle. One down, four to go!*

There. Now if Lainey saw that, she'd know it was a coincidence I was here.

I'd lost my group, so wandered alone for a bit, sidling around groups of tourists to snap selfies with a bunch of random portraits. I could sift through them tonight and hunt for symbolism then.

As I examined a centuries-old four-poster bed, wondering if the mattresses back then were even slightly comfortable, a hissing noise slithered through the low murmur of tourists. Someone was arguing in the room behind me, so agitated their voice sporadically rose above a whisper.

I knew that voice.

Lainey.

I edged to the doorway leading to a sitting room I hadn't explored yet and peeked inside. There she was. I couldn't see who she was talking to, but it had to be Silas. I slid back out of view, my pulse thrumming. If she spotted me, she'd hurl more horrible accusations at me.

Silas's voice was too soft and low baritone for me to understand, and I could only catch bits and pieces from her: ". . . too late . . . don't feel safe, though . . . we have to . . ."

My hands shook, and I curled my fingers into fists to steady them. *Calm down, Jade.* If I let myself get this angry all the time, it was no wonder she thought I'd chucked that stone at her.

But *someone* did.

Maybe she did have a reason to be afraid . . .

". . . won't leave me alone . . ."

I couldn't bear to hear any more of this.

I hurled myself back across the room and backtracked my route through the castle, nearly steamrolling a Japanese tour guide and tripping over the red velvet ropes surrounding a body of armor before finding my friends in one of the bedrooms.

Tate was filming Navya cupping her hand under a cat in one of the paintings while Miguel showed him how to time the clips to a trending sound. Divya glommed onto my arm. "Oh, thank heavens. Come, darling, let's take a turn about the room." I giggled.

But this reprieve was short-lived. As we wandered into a ballroom, I spotted Lainey and Silas at the other end. I hung back to hide behind my friends as Lainey panned her selfie stick to capture a sweeping view of the crystal chandeliers hanging from the opulent frescoed ceilings, while Silas shuffled along nearby, hands stuffed in his pockets, eyes downcast.

He looked pointedly miserable.

And they weren't speaking.

Hope bubbled in my belly. Maybe he'd been defending me before in those hushed whispers. Maybe they were in a fight now. Maybe—

"You really are a stalker, aren't you?" someone whispered in my ear.

10

My heart jolted so aggressively I clasped my chest before spinning to face whoever it was. Felix. "I'm not stalking anyone."

His lips upturned slightly, his eyes glinting from the chandelier overhead. "Sure, Rocky."

"Why are you even talking to me right now?" I snapped. "I thought you liked to be alone."

Felix nudged the lavish rug's tassels with the tip of his black sneaker. "I do." His eyes flicked back up to mine. "I also like to call out stalkers."

"I'm not a—"

But he smiled wryly and kept moseying, tailing my friends like he'd been hanging out with us the whole time. I let out a low growl and jogged to catch up, managing to pass Lainey unnoticed, but not before earning a disapproving glower from a nearby security guard.

"I literally just noticed them, okay?" I whispered to Felix. "I didn't even think they'd come on this trip—I definitely wasn't *stalking* them."

"Mm-hmm."

I gently whacked his coat sleeve. "I wasn't."

He gripped his arm in mock pain. "Good God, woman. I see you woke up and chose violence again."

"Wow. You're fully ridiculous."

"You're the one being fully ridiculous. I saw you watching them." He brandished his arms at the paintings. "But look where you are! Look at all this other stuff you could be staring at. Why waste eyeball energy on them?"

That got a chuckle out of me. *Eyeball energy.*

But he'd been expending eyeball energy on *me*. Something deep in my belly fluttered. "You're right," I admitted with a shrug. "But . . . I don't know. I need closure."

"What kind of closure? They treated you like shit. They're shit people. There's your closure."

I gaped at him. At the welcome dinner, he'd accused Navya of snap judging people, but that's exactly what he was doing now. "But they're *not* . . ."

"You were out of sight, out of mind, so he screwed the closest available option. Can't get much shittier than that."

But Silas would never do something so basic as cheat on me because he was horny. He *loved* me. My eyes started to water.

Felix's smirk dissolved. "Sorry. I didn't mean to pry."

"All you seem to *do* is pry." I held my voice steady as I blinked feverishly at the chandelier, refusing to break in front of Felix.

He chuckled softly. "I'm just trying to convince you it's not worth torturing yourself over some selfish assholes."

"But Lainey's *not* a selfish asshole. At least . . . she wasn't before. I'm telling you, something's not adding up." I shook my head. "Hey, you said you like figuring out what makes people tick, right? So help me figure out what happened."

He laughed. "Why are you so desperate for a *reason*?"

"Because the alternative is that the two people I loved most betrayed me for absolutely no reason." I could no longer mask the tremor in my voice. "Because the alternative is that I have to *hate* them."

That, and I didn't want to daydream about murder anymore.

A haunted look crossed Felix's face before he stuffed his hands into his pockets. "One thing I've learned is that there isn't always a logical explanation for everything. And that people aren't always logical. They claw to rationalize things that have no answers. It's why religion exists; people try to explain the unexplainable. Why are we here? What's the point of it all? Aha, there must be some omniscient being with a greater purpose! Et cetera, et cetera."

I huffed. "I'm not trying to figure out the meaning of life here."

"Obviously. That was just an example."

"I just . . ." I trailed off, hesitating.

"What? Say it."

I tucked my hair behind my ears. "I think in this case there *is* a logical explanation. If they just wanted to screw, fine, but that doesn't explain why they're so *angry* with me. And at the pub, Lainey said something weird to Silas . . . something like, 'Why are you talking to her after everything she did?'"

Felix cocked his head. "Huh."

"Yeah. I have to know what she's blaming me for. And if I *did* do something wrong, I want to know. To apologize, even."

"After what they did to you?"

I heaved a sigh. "Oh, I don't know. Either way, if I don't find out the truth, it's going to eat me alive."

Felix clucked his tongue. "Well, I wouldn't want to see that. Way too gruesome."

I bit back a grin. I couldn't help it—his sense of humor made me laugh, even if he was being obnoxious. "You'll help me, then?"

He considered me for a long moment. "Fine. But I'd bet you all the gold in this castle that I'm right, and they're simply selfish assholes."

"Too bad it's not yours to wager."

Otherwise I'd end up very rich indeed.

11

"This is a terrible idea," said Felix. "A5."

"Miss. And it's not," I insisted. "I told you they'd be here."

Lainey would never miss something like a Battleship tournament. She was a nerd at heart, and hypercompetitive to boot. I bet it was why she wanted the student YouTuber role even though she didn't need the cash, and why she'd probably star in the talent show and win the Ocean Olympics later this semester. She'd sign up for it all, craving every new experience life had to offer.

It's what first drew me to her—at least, until she had to experience the love of *my* life, too.

I glanced across Sea Haven at Silas, who was playing against his roommate Jamal at a table next to Lainey and Sheffia. "If we wind up playing together in the same bracket," I went on, "he'll be my captive audience."

Felix had been helping me tail the couple between classes over the past few days, as though they might randomly blurt out the truth. Whether Lainey noticed us or not, she frequently snatched Silas's hand, marking her turf. Sheffia joined them for almost every meal, though sometimes when Sheffia spoke, Lainey's eyes went glassy, like she was restraining herself from rolling them. But most notably, every so often—especially when Felix was around—I'd catch Silas watching *me*, and he didn't avert his gaze. Was he trying to suss out what was going on between Felix and me? Was he *jealous*?

Either way, his renewed interest gave me hope, and I felt like a tiger hunting its prey, awaiting a chance to pounce on him alone. But wherever Silas went, there was Lainey. Grabbing a drink at the poolside bar? She was there. Exercising in the fitness center? She was there. Studying on a promenade? She was there. So Felix let me drag him to this Battleship tournament in hopes of finally cornering him.

Felix prodded a white peg into the slot he'd guessed wrong. "Statistically speaking, this won't work. What're the chances you'd wind up playing against him?"

"I don't know. Guess I'll have to win and see." I gave Felix a challenging look. "F8."

His eyes flicked down to his grid, then back up at me. "Eff you."

"That's what I thought," I boasted as he pegged one of his ships, trying to hide how crestfallen I was. He was right; this was a terrible plan. At this point, I'd have better luck getting answers from someone like Sheffia.

I mentioned this possibility to Felix as he contemplated his grid, but he snorted. "Even if she knows the truth," he said, "you think Lainey's *best friend's* going to tell you anything?" My heart cracked—I was supposed to be her best friend.

"Maybe Silas told his roommate," I wondered. Jamal had randomly sat next to me at the Lisbon pre-port assembly earlier tonight. I couldn't think what to say—surely not, "Hey, how are you, has your roommate mentioned why he dumped his girlfriend last summer?" so instead I'd babbled a compliment about his tattoo. He'd rolled up his sleeve to show me the whole phrase on his dark skin—DO NO HARM—and explained he was from a family of surgeons and doing premed at UPenn. The exact kind of small talk Felix so adored.

"Yeah," said Felix, "because Silas seems like *such* a gossip. J7."

"Miss. Wouldn't you tell your roommate about a major recent life event?" But I hadn't confided in Navya and Divya about our breakup, even though I knew they'd be sympathetic. Part of me was afraid to let them too close in case they, like everyone else, decided they hated me.

"You know," said Felix, "this reminds me—I heard Miguel bitching to Tate about Lainey earlier."

That wasn't surprising. "Oh, he doesn't know anything. He's pissed she beat him for the YouTuber role."

"No, it wasn't that. Something about followers?" He frowned like he was trying to remember. "I don't know, he seemed to think she attacked him in some way."

"*Attacked* him?" I repeated, baffled. Huh. Actually, Miguel had mentioned something about sabotage at Windsor. Felix nudged my Battleship board. "It's your turn, by the way."

I huffed and studied my grid, but it was hard to focus with Felix's dark eyes on me, this strange anticipation buzzing between us. I shook it off. "F9."

"Dammit, Rocky."

"Did I sink something?"

"My sub."

I smiled slyly as he placed that peg. But as he calculated his next move, his eyes locked on mine, as though he could see my grid mirrored in my eyes or something. My smile faded, and something knotted in my chest. Or was it because Silas's head turned my way?

"G3?" Felix guessed, jarring me back to the game.

Just then, a chair squealed against wood, and Lainey stood. There was no way she'd lost that fast, but she was plucking at Silas's shirt and hissing in his ear, obviously demanding they leave. Then she threw me a disgruntled look.

"Aw, c'mon," said Jamal. "I wanted to beat you fair and square."

"Dude, you're clearly winning anyway." Silas offered Jamal a fist bump before loping after Lainey.

"Dammit," I muttered, watching him disappear around the corner.

"Like I said," said Felix. "Terrible idea."

"G9," I shot back.

"Annnnd there goes my battleship."

After losing to Felix (on purpose, pride be damned), I headed down to Miguel's cabin on Deck 4, eager to learn about his beef with Lainey. He'd taped a sign-up sheet next to his whiteboard for guests to appear in his new video series, *Skincare at Sea*, blank except for the top row, since Divya had volunteered as tribute.

When the door opened, a ghoul greeted me, and I nearly flung myself back in surprise.

But it was just Miguel in a sheet mask.

"Girl, it's about time you took me up on that caffeine gel," he said.

"Oh, that's not why I'm here—"

But he was already pulling me inside. He'd once complained how small his cabin was, but it was a palace compared to mine. Two beds stretched across opposite walls, each with a desk at one end. A nightstand and coffee table nestled between the beds, each lined with neat rows of vials and bottles, and they had a porthole. It was so dark out I couldn't see much of the ocean.

"Sup, Jade?" Tate was in bed with his laptop and a notebook propped next to him, his short, spirally blond curls more disheveled than usual.

"Hey. Didn't want to play Battleship? Sheffia was there." I waggled my eyebrows. Tate stiffened. "You're an item now, right?" Navya had whined earlier about seeing Tate and Sheffia at the pool again. Apparently after Sheffia hoisted herself out, he'd wrapped her in a towel and kissed her.

"Nah, we're just having fun," said Tate. "Gotta finish this essay, anyway."

"And I'm too stressed for that ridiculousness," said Miguel as he sat me at the desk and started attacking my face with a makeup removal wipe.

I swatted him away. "Gah, what are you doing?"

"I need to apply the gel on clean skin."

"But I'm not wearing makeup."

"Obviously," he said bitingly. "But oil and sebum accumulate over the day."

With a sigh, I let him get to work. "So what's stressing you out? The whole YouTuber thing?" I prodded.

Miguel's face fell. "Oh, gawd. I *told* you," he said to Tate before asking me, "It's making the rounds, isn't it?"

"Uh . . ." I wasn't sure what he meant. I glanced at Tate, who only shrugged.

"Listen." Miguel crumpled the used wipe. "I didn't do it. That bitch totally sabotaged me."

"Lainey?"

"Yup." He grabbed a vial from the coffee table. Each row of products was arranged by height and color. I'd never be able to find anything that way.

"Wait, what do you think she did?"

"She bot-bombed me." He scrolled to his YouTube page and shoved his phone at me. "On Insta and TikTok, too."

"What'm I looking at?"

"The subscriber count, obviously." He frowned. "Maybe you need more sleep, not eye gel."

"Well, hang on, this is the first I'm hearing about this." I squinted at the number: 1.8 million.

Miguel's shoulders relaxed. "Oh." He set down his phone. "Okay, so, basically, I got a million new followers on each platform, in, like, a day." He squirted gel onto his fingertips and started dabbing it all over my face. It smelled faintly of oranges. The label said something about vitamin C. "People are calling me out for buying followers. They totally think I did it to impress CoB, since I'd talked about auditioning for the student YouTuber gig."

"So . . . you think this is why CoB didn't pick you?"

"Oh, that's the least of it. This could *ruin* me." He sank onto his bed, the rings under my eyes forgotten. "If people think I've been buying followers, that's *bad*. People have been trash-talking me for days, and the internet here's been awful—I haven't been able to upload a defense video. I thought it'd die down, but it's not. If enough people report me, my accounts could get suspended."

What a petty thing for people to get so upset over.

"How do you know Lainey did it?" I said.

Tate was the one who replied, "Seriously? Don't you know who her dad is?"

I'd almost forgotten he knew who Derek Silverton was. "What does that have to do with anything?"

"He's a self-serving, scheming bastard. I bet the apple didn't fall far from the tree."

My stomach sank. I had to say, he was probably right.

I met Derek Silverton a grand total of one time.

Well, two, if you count move-in weekend freshman year, but I don't think it counts if the person you're meeting doesn't look up from his phone as he's shaking your hand.

So let's just count the one time.

When I'd flown home with Lainey last spring break, her father, who liked to dote on his daughter, insisted on taking us to some fancy steakhouse.

"So what's your vision?" he'd asked me, a few glasses into a bottle of wine that cost more than my laptop. Since Lainey's mother was at some actress's baby shower in New York, he had no one to split it with; God forbid anyone should snap a photo of his underage daughter drinking. If she meant the world to him, public appearances meant the galaxy.

"My *vision*?" I'd repeated.

He'd offered a patronizing smile. "What do you want to be when you grow up?"

"Oh." My cheeks had flushed. "Well, I want to start my own business someday."

"What kind of business?"

"I'm not sure yet."

He scoffed. "You don't start a business just to start a business. You need a *vision*."

"Dad, shut up," Lainey'd snapped.

"Like Sanatek's vision," he'd said, fully ignoring her, "revolutionizing health care and making treatment accessible to all."

"Bullshit," she'd mouthed.

"Let me give you one piece of advice," he rambled on, clearly tipsy. "Never let your enemies feel like they have the upper hand, even when they do."

Lainey folded her arms. "Enemies? What enemies? Jade doesn't have any enemies."

"Don't be daft. Her competition. Every business has competition. Even if you're first to market, they'll always be nipping at your heels, and you need to be ready to crush them like the cockroaches they are." He speared a hunk of steak and pointed it at Lainey. "You'd've done well to learn that sooner."

"Oh, what, like that time you wanted me to make Wendy Olsen go bald?"

He tried hushing her, but I exclaimed, "Wait, *what*?"

Lainey snorted. "In eighth grade, I tried out for the lead role in the school play—"

"You know how much your mother wanted you to land it," said her dad. "It should've been yours. You're a good actress."

"No, Mom tried to manifest me being good, but I never actually was. Either way, Wendy Olsen had this *stunning* voice; there was no way I'd beat her—"

"See?" Silverton cut her off again. "There's the problem. You'd already talked yourself out of it. Anyone can beat anyone at anything if they're willing to play all their cards."

"Inviting myself over and sneaking Nair into her shampoo wouldn't exactly be playing *fair*," said Lainey. "That's what he told me to do," she said to me. "Can you believe that?" Then she narrowed her eyes at him, riled up. "Though that's nothing compared to what you've—" She stopped herself, but not before fury warped his features. I had a feeling he wouldn't have let the conversation get this far if he'd been sober.

But then he flashed me a devilish smile. "I never said anything about playing fair."

I decided right then I never wanted to meet Derek Silverton again.

Little did I know, Lainey would never invite me back, anyway.

"Miguel," I said, "I don't think Lainey would've bothered bot-bombing you." Though doubt prickled my mind. It's exactly the kind of thing her dad would've encouraged.

"Well, *I* didn't do it," said Miguel. "The timing's uncanny, don't you think? And the cost would be nothing to her." He buried his face in his hands.

"Is there any way to prove you didn't? Like, to show YouTube and Instagram or whatever?"

"You can't tell where the bots came from," Tate chimed in, like he'd already looked into it. "Maybe YouTube or whoever can trace the IPs, but those fake-follow services probably use VPNs."

"I bet YouTube wouldn't even bother looking into it," said Miguel.

"Huh." I wiped my cheek, still vaguely sticky from the vitamin C gel. I thought back to Tate recognizing Lainey at the welcome dinner, remembering how Lainey had given Sheffia an earful about me. "Could you ask Sheffia about it?" I asked Tate.

His posture went rigid. "No."

"But maybe if they gossiped about it—"

"Don't waste your breath," Miguel bristled. "I already asked him, and he won't."

"It's not that I don't want to help." Tate adjusted his glasses. "If I got trolled like that, I'd fling myself into the sun."

"Then dig for me, bitch," said Miguel.

Tate recoiled. "I just don't want to mess things up with her, blaming her best friend like that."

"Aw, you really like her," I teased.

Tate's cheeks went pink. "I mean, she's cool or whatever, I guess."

Would Sheffia have told Tate things Lainey said about me? She must've seen us hanging out a lot. Maybe it came up. I took a deep breath and asked, "Sheffia's never said anything about *me*, has she?"

Tate made a face. "No—" But then he tilted his head. "Actually . . ."

My stomach dropped. "What'd she say?"

"Uh . . ."

Anxiety tore through me. "Oh, c'mon. Please tell me."

Tate shifted uncomfortably. "Well, at the Tower of London, when you came outside, Sheffia said something like 'She totally did it. That girl's vile.'" A panicked look must've crossed my face, because he quickly added, "I told her, no way. I knew you, and you'd *never*."

I gave him a shaky, grateful, smile, but nausea surged up my throat. Sheffia thought I was vile. Not something banal like *annoying* or *clingy*.

Vile.

12

Portugal's heat felt like a balm after our damp England excursions, and although I couldn't keep the chill of anxiety from permeating my bones, I traded my booties for sandals and jeans for airy sundresses. Navya, Divya, Tate, Miguel, Felix, and I stuck together to explore Lisbon after our field study groups took separate excursions yesterday; my art class had bused to the nearby city of Sintra for our Romanticism unit, where we'd hiked to an eclectic, colorful palace atop a hill and toured some ancient Moorish castle ruins nearby.

This morning I'd suggested Tate invite Sheffia along, wanting a chance to talk to her.

To prove I wasn't vile.

To ask why Lainey thought I was.

But he told me Sheffia already had plans with Lainey.

In lieu of getting answers, I tried soaking in the sights as we meandered through the Alfama district. Colorful, centuries-old stucco homes lined the narrow streets winding up the hills, their grated balconies bursting with overgrown potted plants and laundry flapping in the breeze. On one of them, a tabby cat stared down at us with bright green eyes under the midafternoon sun. Endless bakeries tempted us with pastéis de nata, these egg custard pastries that melted in your mouth. Tourists crowded the streets near sunset, their steps squishing the blue-and-white-tiled swirls and checkered patterns beneath their feet.

But all the while, the word *vile* clouded my mind, and I felt like I was seeing the city through a gritty lens.

As we waited for our order at a fish cake shop on the main drag, Felix poked my arm. "You've been quiet today."

"A lot on my mind, I guess," I said without looking up from my phone. I'd just connected to the free Wi-Fi to spy on Sheffia's Instagram when an email alert from Mom popped up. Guilt leached into my gut. I hadn't written to her in a few days.

"You okay?" Felix asked me as Tate fit an entire fish cake into his mouth to the beat of a trending sound on TikTok, and Miguel muttered, "I can't believe this bitch already has ten thousand followers . . ."

"Oh, it's my mom," I said low enough so only Felix could hear. "She's guilt-tripping me for not emailing more often." If it were up to her, I'd be in touch daily, despite CoB warning parents ahead of time that internet connectivity would be limited. Even Gmail loaded so slowly on board, we were supposed to use our Seamail accounts that looked like something out of the 1990s.

"Well, look on the bright side." Felix perched his elbow on the bar behind us. "At least you still have a mom to email."

My eyes snapped up to his, but he averted his gaze. "Is your mom . . ."

"Both of my parents," he said in a quiet voice.

I'd had no idea Felix was an orphan. Then again, I didn't know much about him at all.

"I'm sorry."

"No, it's fine." He picked up his order of fish cakes and passed me one. "Anyway, I'm not much in the mood for moping." He tapped his cake against mine and took a bite.

But I stood a little closer to him as we waited for the rest of the orders.

When he went to get napkins, I refreshed Sheffia's profile. Lo and behold, a new story appeared, time-stamped five minutes ago. If she'd posted this where she stood, she was a ten-minute walk from here. The grand statue-topped archway in the background was unmistakable—it was the iconic entryway to the city. Sheffia posed in front of it, the head of the tallest statue cut off at the top of the screen, like whoever took the picture gave zero shits.

Maybe I could talk to Sheffia today after all.

"C'mon." I tugged on Felix's arm as we headed back into the street. "Let's take some pics in front of the big arch."

"Didn't you already get pics there?"

"But—" I stammered. I couldn't say the real reason in front of everyone.

"We can see it again on the way back to the ship," Navya suggested. Unlike London, Lisbon's port was right next to the beating heart of the historic district.

"But it's the golden hour," I said, scrambling. "Perfect for pictures."

"Yes, girl." Miguel hooked his arm through mine. "Oh my God, I got Tate into TikTok, and now Jade wants to take selfies? I really *am* an influencer." I cringed. I'd said nothing about selfies, but as far as he was concerned, a picture wasn't worth taking otherwise. At least he'd perked up, though—he'd been depressed all day, worrying about the vitriolic comments on a video he'd posted yesterday claiming he didn't buy those fake followers.

With nothing else on our agenda, everyone caved, and I navigated us back down the main drag as we nibbled on our fish croquettes, warding off the restaurant hosts who slapped their menus to attract our attention and attempted to beckon us to their tables. ("We're *literally* eating right now," Divya kept saying.) When we finally reached the archway, my stomach sank. The grand public square beyond was rimmed with busy cafés and bustling with tourists and locals heading every which way, some posing by the statue at its center—some historic figure on horseback wielding a spear. Finding Sheffia would be like searching for a needle in a haystack—

"Tate!" a voice called out.

Speak of the devil.

Sheffia waved as she jogged over from the statue, then launched herself into Tate's arms, wrapping her legs around his waist and accidentally thwacking him in the butt with her large shopping bag. "Oof."

Navya crossed her arms and pouted.

I caught Felix's eye, which glinted in amusement. He knew this was why I'd led us here. His gaze shifted over my shoulder, clearly spotting something. Or someone. I almost spun, but he said, "Don't. They're watching."

I knew he meant Silas and Lainey. "So?"

"They might think you're stalking them." He smirked. "And they'd kind of be right."

I poked his arm, then remembered his whole "choosing

violence" shtick and instead slid my fingers down his arm to clasp his hand. He gave me a perplexed look. "Go along with it."

"Say what now?"

I thought of how Silas kept looking at me whenever Felix was nearby. "Maybe if we make Silas jealous . . . he'll want to talk."

Felix bit back a laugh but didn't try to free his hand from my grasp.

Navya and Divya tittered at the sight of us. I guessed we'd have to fool everyone to pull this off.

Welp, might as well make this look more convincing.

I wrapped my arms around Felix's torso, and he let me; he even held me close, needling his fingers through my curls that went past my shoulder blades. I was surprised by how comfortably my arms fit around him. Silas was always rock solid in my embrace from years of workouts and training. Felix was lean, but softer around the edges, which felt . . . cozy.

I pushed the thought from my mind. This was just for show, that's all. "How's Silas reacting?"

"Like he might try to bite that statue's head off," said Felix.

I started to turn, wanting to see this for myself, but Felix squeezed my arm, keeping me steady. "Don't look. It'll be too obvious."

To an outsider, it probably looked like we were tightening our embrace. I wished I could see through Felix's eyes for only a moment—

"Annnnd they're off." Felix released me, and something deflated in my chest.

I finally turned to scan the crowd milling in front of the statue but didn't see them. "Where'd they go?"

"Back toward the port."

As Sheffia babbled to Tate and the twins about what she'd done today, Miguel poked my arm. "The sun's gonna set soon. What're we thinking for these pics? The statue or the arch?"

Sheffia overheard. "Oh, there are these big blocks in front of the statue you can stand on so it looks like you're holding it up. We were just over there . . ." She scanned the crowd for Lainey and pouted, unable to find her. "Huh." She glanced at her phone and started texting someone. Probably Lainey, to find out where she went.

But everyone knew—Lainey had ditched her.

As Miguel herded us to the statue, Sheffia hung back with Tate, looking sullen. My chest tightened. She probably felt terrible after being deserted like that. I knew I would. Heck, I *was* ditched by the same person, in the worst possible way.

Maybe Sheffia and I had more in common than I'd realized. Compassion tugged at my heartstrings. Checking on her would be the kind thing to do. I started toward her.

But Felix clasped my hand, pulling me back. "Shouldn't we keep up appearances?"

"I want to make sure Sheffia's okay," I whispered. Felix's eyebrows shot up. Yeah, I'd originally wanted to talk to Sheffia to fish for gossip. But she looked so crestfallen now. I remembered how Lainey and Silas took that two-seater in the London pub, how Sheffia seemed like a wad of gum on Lainey's designer shoes she couldn't help but drag around. If I were her, I'd want someone to commiserate with. "She's obviously hurt Lainey ditched her like that."

"Clever ruse," said Felix.

I dropped his hand. "How much of a slimeball do you think I am?"

With that, I sped over to Sheffia and Tate.

Sheffia had been giggling at something Tate said, her smile not quite reaching her eyes, but even her fake smile fell faster than an anvil. "Oh. Hey."

Her obvious disdain made me falter for a moment, but I pressed on. "I don't think we've met yet . . . I'm Jade." I held out my hand.

She shifted her grip on her shopping bag to give my hand a stiff shake. "Sheffia."

Divya summoned Tate for a picture, so he drifted over, leaving Sheffia alone with me as Felix lingered nearby. Her shoulders tensed, and she refused to make eye contact. Good Lord, what had Lainey said about me?

"I just . . . wanted to make sure you're okay," I said.

Sheffia's expression softened for a moment, but then she furrowed her brow and frowned, like she was trying to look confused. "Why wouldn't I be?"

"Uh . . . your friends kinda took off . . ."

"Oh! No, no worries." She waved off my concern. "I was the one who ran off. They must not've seen where I went."

But according to Felix, Lainey and Silas had been watching. They knew where she'd gone.

If Sheffia didn't want to commiserate, I couldn't force it. I scrambled for something to say. "So, you like to swim?" I cringed at how random that sounded.

"How'd you know?" she snapped, like that was classified intel.

"Uh . . . I've seen you and Tate doing laps?"

"Oh." Her posture relaxed again. "Yeah, I busted my knee in a car accident years ago, and swimming's the only cardio I can do that doesn't aggravate it."

"Yikes, I'm sorry. I got into an accident once."

"Really?" She seemed genuinely interested, but it sounded like my incident was nothing compared to hers.

"A small one, though, in a parking lot. I was fine after."

"Oh. I was in the hospital for a couple weeks. Anyway, yeah, it's nice that Tate comes with; I tried getting Lainey to join, but you know her—she hates to swim."

I laughed, remembering how Lainey had coaxed me into coming to wintry Boston for spring break instead of some exotic, tropical locale. She'd do anything to avoid getting in the water. "It's nice that you two reconnected."

"No thanks to you," Sheffia said.

I recoiled from her shift in tone. "What?"

"You're the one who tore us apart in the first place."

This sudden accusation rendered me speechless, and my fingertips went numb.

"We could've all been friends, you know," she went on. "There was room for both of us—you didn't have to shove me out like that. At least Lainey came to her senses. You're just another social-climbing asshole."

My mouth dropped open, and I wanted to shrink into

myself like a pill bug, desperate to avoid conflict and the crushing weight of this accusation. But it wasn't true. I never cared about Lainey's wealth or connections, and she knew that. In fact, that was the exact reason she wanted to drop Sheffia.

Taking in my shocked reaction, Sheffia pursed her lips. "Sorry, that was blunt. I have absolutely no filter sometimes."

I couldn't just dissolve into the asphalt and let her keep believing this lie. "No, I . . . I'd rather know what she's saying about me. But it's not true."

"Sure," she said sarcastically.

"It's really not. It was her decision to drop you; she called you a user." Sheffia tensed. "She said you used her for party invites and private jets and—"

She raised a hand. "I don't want to hear this."

"Why not? Wouldn't you rather know?"

"It's not true."

"It is, though. You must see how she's been treating you. Why are you trying so hard to avoid the truth?"

Sheffia's sharp jaw stiffened, but her watering eyes betrayed her. Still, she stalked away, saying, "The only thing I want to avoid is you."

13

Sometimes the best way to fight a liar is to outmanipulate them. If Lainey blamed me for her and Sheffia's fallout, maybe she hoodwinked Silas with some similar slander.

I was going to find out.

The eighties-themed pool party CoB was hosting the night after setting sail for the Azores would be the perfect chance to make Silas jealous. If merely standing with Felix had caught his eye, dancing together would surely reel him in. Then I'd get some answers.

"Oh, what," said Felix when I suggested these plans between classes, "so first you wanted me to be your narc, and now you want me to be your boyfriend?"

"Not for *real*." My cheeks went hot. "And some narc you've been—shouldn't you have befriended Lainey and Silas and gotten them to dish by now?"

His lips curled into a smile. "So to make up for my shortcomings, I have to agree to a fake relationship?"

"I mean, not a *relationship*, necessarily. We'd just . . . pretend to be together."

"How's that different?"

"I guess it's not . . ." I bit back a conspiratorial grin. "That okay?"

Felix clucked his tongue. "I don't commit until at *least* the third date." He smiled slyly as he headed to class.

Anticipation bubbled in my chest all day, and once the sun finally slipped beneath the sparkling horizon, I dragged Navya and Divya back to our room to gussy up. They curled and teased their usually sleek, shiny tresses, but mine was naturally a gigantic poof ball, so I spent the most time on my makeup—rich purple eyeshadow on my upper lids and subtle turquoise lining my lower lashes, heavy mascara, and bold magenta lipstick I borrowed from Divya. Once I donned a sequined halter dress, I was almost passable for someone who'd stepped through a time machine.

"Yeah, if it electrocuted you on your way over," said Divya, toying with my hair.

"Hey, this is how it naturally dries!" I darted into the bathroom to spritz on some smoothing oil.

"Can you not be such a jerk?" said Navya.

"What?" said Divya. "Everyone in the eighties looked like they'd been electrocuted. I'm just saying, she nailed the look."

By the time we went to the pool deck and found Tate and Miguel, already two drinks and a flask deep, the party was in full swing, eighties music pulsing from the speakers. The decorations were on point—fairy lights dangled from the canopied promenades, and a disco ball revolved over the DJ booth at the far end of the pool, its neon lights reflecting off the water. The dance floor surrounding the pool was packed with students, Lifelong Learners, and crew alike, some of whom had clearly experienced the eighties for themselves, including our peppy dean of programming, Candace Jackson, who'd let out her usual braided top bun into a glorious Afro. The nights were chilly, so nobody was in the pool, though a few brave souls sat at the edge, dangling their legs in up to their knees.

I clasped my denim jacket over my glittering dress as a breeze ruffled my hair, scanning the crowds for Felix, but he was nowhere in sight.

"I can't wait till we're farther south so we can use the pool," Navya commented as we waited in line for drinks, the occasional treat from CoB in international waters.

"You can use it now," said Divya. "You're just a wuss." Tate and Miguel guffawed.

"I am not! It's obviously been too cold to swim." Navya hugged her arms around her waist.

"Sheffia swims every morning," Divya pointed out, which I thought was unnecessarily biting; Navya was clearly still upset Tate was hooking up with Sheffia. "And the drinks'll warm you up enough tonight."

Navya narrowed her eyes. "We're only allowed two each," she said, more to remind her sister of the drink limit than to argue how much warmth they'd provide.

As I passed in my drink ticket, I danced in place to keep warm. "Speaking of, where's Sheffia?" I asked Tate, who'd politely lingered to wait for me as I got my drink. After our tense encounter in Lisbon, I wanted to avoid Sheffia at all costs.

"Hanging out with that bit—uh, Lainey." I followed his gaze across the pool. Sure enough, Lainey stood on a chair filming the party as Sheffia and a posse of glam-looking girls danced for the camera, vying for screen time by gyrating their hips and flinging their arms wildly. Silas sat at a small round table nearby, staring at Lainey. Someone else was watching her, too—Sketchy Bob, leaning against the railing behind Silas. What a creeper.

"What's your deal with her, anyway?" I asked Tate as the bartender handed me a plastic cup of white wine. "How'd you even know who her dad was?"

Tate wiped his lips after taking a sip. "It's his fault my mother's dead."

My stomach dropped. That was the absolute last thing I expected him to say. "I . . . I didn't realize your mother was . . . I'm so sorry—"

"Dance with me!" Divya interrupted, tugging Tate's arm so enthusiastically, wine sloshed over the edge of his cup. "Oops, sorry."

But he laughed good-naturedly, as though he hadn't just dropped that bomb, and followed her onto the dance floor, leaving Navya stewing next to me. Not that he was available anyway.

What the hell did he mean by that? Surely Derek Silverton didn't *murder* anyone; I would've heard about that. At the welcome dinner, Tate had called him a "Big Pharma douchebag." Maybe it had to do with his company, Sanatek. Last spring, I kept walking in on Lainey's Zoom arguments with her dad, and vaguely remembered her yelling about insurance once. She always mummed up when she saw me, so I hadn't wanted to pry.

Suddenly, someone behind me screamed.

I spun on my heel.

"Oh my God," Miguel shrieked, gaping at his phone. "I can't believe it!" He let out a string of expletives.

"What happened?" asked Navya.

"It's gone. It's just totally gone."

"What is?" I asked.

"My YouTube channel." He frantically tapped his screen, fingers visibly shaking. "Oh my God, and my Insta's been suspended. TikTok, too. This can't be happening. This absolutely cannot be happening."

"Maybe you just have a bad connection—" Navya tried. The ship's Wi-Fi rarely worked out here.

"No, it's not the damn connection," Miguel snapped. "I can't with this right now." He stormed off to sort out whatever was happening.

I glared across the pool at Lainey, filming for whatever video she was working on. If she really did troll Miguel like he suspected, she'd completely sabotaged his online persona. She was like a tornado, indiscriminately ravaging anything in her path.

"Oh, no," said Navya. "I feel so bad for him."

"Me, too—" I started, but my heart stilled; I could've sworn that for a moment, Lainey was looking past her phone.

At me.

Had she seen me scowling at her?

Maybe not. Or maybe she was pretending she hadn't.

But then she passed her phone to Sheffia to keep recording and grabbed Silas's hand, yanked him to his feet, and pulled him to the edge of the mass of flailing bodies on that side of the pool. She released his hand and raised her arms, rocking her hips to the beat. I could hear her all the way from here, belting out the song's lyrics. She'd always made being the life of the party look so easy—never afraid to be loud, to take up space. Silas was grinning, and how could he not? Her boundless energy was irresistible.

A rock formed in the pit of my stomach. Where was my fake boyfriend when I needed him? "Have you seen Felix?" I asked Navya.

"I don't think so . . ." She gave me a sly smile. "So are you two, like, an item now?"

I shrugged, flushing. I didn't want to admit the truth, but I didn't want to lie to her, either. "We're just having fun." Technically true, on Felix's part. Our little investigation was strangely amusing to him—especially after he overheard Sheffia and me arguing. He seemed to think he was one step closer to proving that sometimes, people were simply selfish pricks.

I was starting to think he was right.

I scanned the crowds for him—I rarely got the onboard messaging system to load on my archaic phone, and I didn't know where his room was.

Ah, there he was, one elbow draped over the railing as the wind mussed his already-tousled dark hair, a cup in one hand, the other lazily snapping along to the music.

"Go on," Navya encouraged.

"You sure?" I felt bad ditching her.

"Sure. I'll go dance with those clowns." She thumbed at her sister and Tate.

I hurried over to Felix. "Hey."

"Hey, Rocky. You look . . ." He gave me a once-over, taking in my eighties-inspired makeup. "I'd say astonishing, but I wouldn't want you to think I didn't always think so."

Heat flamed my cheeks. I couldn't tell if he was complimenting or mocking me. "Uh . . . thanks?" I shook it off and held out my hand. "Come with me? I want to continue our secret mission." To make Silas jealous.

"Covert Operation Jelly Inception?"

I bit back a laugh. "That's the one."

He considered me for a long moment with a bemused look before taking my hand. "Alright, fine."

"Sweet." I swiped his cup and set both of ours on a nearby table, then tugged him toward the dance floor.

He froze. "Wait, what're we doing?"

"We're gonna dance."

"Oh. I don't dance, like, as a personal policy." He clasped his hands behind his back.

"Why not?"

He rubbed his lips together. "I'm really bad at it."

"Aw, c'mon. You'll do fine." I reached for his hand, but he kept his fingers firmly locked.

"Nope."

"Can you make a small amendment for *pretend* dancing?"

"*Pretend* dancing?" He made a face. "You're either dancing or you're not."

I gave him my best puppy-dog eyes. "Please?"

He sighed, though he still looked amused. He was probably giving me a hard time for the hell of it, as per usual. "I dunno. I'm going to need to send this to council for consideration." But he smiled slightly and unclasped his fingers, allowing me to pull his arms free. I took his hand again and dragged him into the throng of dancing bodies.

"I'm warning you," he said, "this won't look pretty."

"What if it's not even dancing, though? What if it's just . . . swaying?" I turned, thinking I'd have to cajole him into position, but as I slid my hands behind his neck, he set his on my waist, like it was the most natural thing in the world.

I *knew* he was just giving me a hard time.

"Hmm, swaying," he said. "I guess I can alter the policy slightly. But we're really pushing it." His dark eyes glimmered from the fairy lights strung overhead, and something in my stomach fluttered. It must've been from how close we were. I hadn't held someone like this since . . .

I peeked over his shoulder at Silas.

His hands were on Lainey's hips.

But his eyes were on me.

Felix must've thought I'd stepped closer to tighten our fake embrace, and as we swayed to the music, I felt his hands shift at the small of my back as he tightened the gap between us. We were so close now, I caught the scent of his shampoo, a pleasant mix of spice and teakwood.

"See?" I said. "Pretend dancing isn't so hard."

"Pretend *swaying*," he corrected, his breath warm against my ear. I shivered as the breeze rustled my curls.

"Yes, of course, sorry." I laughed, more to show Silas how much fun I was having than because the joke was funny. But when I glanced back at him, Lainey had spun around, pressing back against Silas as she moved to the rhythm, distracting him. His cheek was pressed to her hair as she reached behind herself, cupping the back of his neck.

No. I needed him to look at *me.* I needed him to see he wasn't the only one who'd moved on.

I needed him to *care.*

"You know what would make this even more believable?" I pulled back to look Felix in the eye.

"You don't want me to twirl you, do you?" he said. "There's a ninety percent chance you'll wind up in the pool, so request at your own risk."

I laughed for real this time. "No, not that . . ." I bit my lip and shifted my gaze to his mouth.

His eyebrows lifted slightly.

Oh God. I was blushing furiously now. This was a terrible idea. Mortified, I tried to change tacks. "I mean, maybe a twirl would help—"

"You want me to kiss you."

It wasn't a question.

My breath hitched. If we kissed, it would be merely for performative purposes. But the way he said it, the way my heart galloped like a wild stallion, the way my cheeks were so hot you could boil tea on them . . . nothing about this felt fake.

"Yeah," I finally said. "I mean, only if you're okay with it, obviously."

He chuckled. "Sure, yeah. This is kind of hilarious."

The disco ball pulsed bright cyan in sync with the chorus of the song, making the fairy lights around us sparkle—almost like the DJ was trying to create maximum dramatic effect for us. We both scoffed at the coincidence, and Felix shook his head slightly. "Of course."

Then his gaze shifted back to mine as he moved closer, his eyes like deep pools of ink. "Are you sure?"

My heart was officially trying to eject itself from my chest. "Yes."

And then his lips were on mine.

A silken heat oozed through my veins, down to my fingers running through his tousled hair, down to my toes that were fully convinced the floor had disappeared. This was nothing like how Silas used to kiss me. His kisses were always soft at first, teasing, testing, until they grew deeper, more passionate. Almost like a performance. But this . . . What was *supposed* to be a performance felt nothing like it. We were completely in sync from the start, and these sparks between us set my heart ablaze. Felix's hands slid up to cup my face, the guise of dancing forgotten as we melted completely into each other. This felt more real than anything I'd ever—

I yanked myself back from Felix. He looked as surprised as I felt, and both of us were breathing hard.

I tore my eyes from his to glance at Silas. He'd gone rigid, fury darkening his expression, and he looked ready to lunge straight over the pool to tackle Felix.

It worked.

Lainey had clearly felt Silas's posture go stiff behind her. She leaned to take in his face, then followed his scorching glare to us.

She looked almost amused as she took in our stance, clearly understanding what had just happened. Maybe she was relieved to think I was falling for another boy. Then her claim on Silas would be secure.

Right then, she spun and planted a kiss on Silas's lips.

My stomach didn't even have a chance to clench before Silas pushed her back, his eyes fixed firmly on us. Lainey caught her balance before she could tumble into the pool, but a few people nearby yelped from what almost happened. Lainey said something to Silas—something I couldn't hear—as others looked on, her hands balled into fists. He'd hardly seemed to notice that she'd almost fallen.

"There ya go," said Felix, having peeked at the damage. "Mission accomplished." He dropped his hands from my arms and walked away, passing the poolside bar and disappearing along the promenade before I could make heads or tails of why he left.

Despite the drama on the dance floor, the song transitioned smoothly to the next one—"Fading Like a Flower." Technically a nineties song—I knew that because it was one of Lainey's favorites. Whenever we'd hit up the karaoke bar with a bouncer who never looked closely at our fake IDs, Lainey used to drag me onstage so we could sing it together. And whenever her Spotify playlist shuffled to it, she'd bound across the room and leap onto my bed, and we'd scream along from the top of our lungs until our neighbors banged their fists against the wall.

Across the pool, Silas stormed off. I expected Lainey to chase after him, but instead she glanced back at me, a pained look marring her features. As the song's chorus blared out, much of the crowd echoing the familiar lyrics, we both stood there at opposite ends of the pool, staring at each other. I could swear her eyes were watering. And I couldn't help it—tears prickled the corners of my own eyes. Did part of her miss me as much as I missed her?

No, of course not.

Otherwise she never would've betrayed me the way she did. This was just false hope talking. I ripped my gaze from hers and rushed away.

Yeah, technically Felix was right. Mission accomplished.

Then why did it feel like I hadn't accomplished anything at all?

14

It took two more days to sail to the Azores, and I didn't see Felix nearly the entire time.

If I'd known it was this easy to avoid someone on board, I would've more effectively dodged Lainey and Silas in the beginning. Or maybe I was overthinking it. Maybe he was holed up studying for a test.

Somehow, that seemed unlikely.

I finally spotted him at the Azores pre-port assembly the night before docking, just before Captain Hwang joined Candace onstage to break the news that we'd only have one day there. A tropical storm was projected to move over the mid-Atlantic archipelago in two days, so we'd depart for Gibraltar—the British territory at the southern tip of Spain—early to avoid it entirely. All-aboard would be at 5:00 p.m. tomorrow. Mumbles and groans rippled through the crowd; anyone who'd booked excursions or overnight trips on the islands—to explore the volcanic crater reserves, hike up the Montanha do Pico volcano, or snorkel off the coast of Marina da Horta—would have to cancel.

I'd tried to catch Felix's eye, but he stared at his phone and rushed out right after Candace's presentation. Maybe he had to cancel a reservation he'd made.

Again, unlikely. He wasn't one for overnight trips.

Since I couldn't rationalize it any other way, I couldn't help but think he was intentionally avoiding me. Maybe he thought our fake-dating scheme had gone too far.

I found Felix in Coastal Cantina early the next morning as the ship docked. He was alone, eating a bagel, reading something on his phone. I hurried over with my oatmeal and mug of coffee. "Hey. Can I join—"

"Rocky." He grinned, looking glad to see me. Huh. "Been a while."

I settled into the seat across from him, fully confused. "Yeah. Uh, listen . . . I wanted to apologize."

"For what?" He bit into his bagel.

"Uh . . . for the other night." My cheeks flamed. "For . . . for making you kiss me."

His eyebrows shot up, and he paused midchew. After a moment so long I thought maybe we were in a simulation some alien overlord had paused, he said, "Okay, first of all . . . you didn't *make* me do anything." He shifted in his seat. If anything, *now* I was making him uncomfortable.

"I don't mean . . . Obviously I didn't hold a gun to your head or anything. But just for putting you in that position."

He blew air between his lips, like he was carefully considering what to say. "It wasn't exactly a position I didn't want to be in."

It took a moment for his words to sink in, and then warmth spread to my fingertips.

Until now, I hadn't considered the possibility that Felix was avoiding me because our kiss felt as real to him as it did to me. That he was avoiding me because he thought I wasn't over Silas. That *I* was dangerous territory for *him*.

But that kiss couldn't have been real.

I mean, yeah, technically it was real. There was even that one moment when the tip of his tongue grazed mine, and all my nerve endings caught fire—

No. I couldn't think about that. Not like that. Because if I did, it meant I'd have to ask myself whether I was in love with Silas anymore. And the way I was so desperate for the truth, the way my heart still ached for him despite *everything*, that couldn't be in question. Why else would this yearning be so unconditional?

"Oh" was all I said as my cheeks reached peak redness—at least, I assumed so, because they were scalding. "So, uh, what have you been up to?" I asked, changing the topic posthaste.

"Ugh, I had this huge psych test yesterday." Felix tore off a hunk of his bagel. "Had to study my ass off. I passed out after the pre-port presentation. You?" Oh. He *had* been studying.

"Not much." I sipped my coffee, feeling foolish for worrying. "You know. Classes. Homework."

"Fascinating."

I squished a napkin and tossed it at his face. "Yeah, like *your* lil recap was a real page-turner."

He grinned, catching the napkin midair. "Hey, you didn't see me scribble down the last answers with seconds to spare. That's the stuff of nightmares."

"Yeah, if zombies were present."

"What, you've never had those nightmares where you're late to school, or you show up on the first day without your schedule, so you can't find your classes?"

I suppressed a laugh. If that was the stuff that scared him, he was way nerdier than I thought.

"Wow," he said. "You're actively judging me right now."

"Correct."

His smile widened before he shook his head. "Anyway, what're you up to today?"

"I don't know, actually. My plans got nixed."

Divya had talked Navya into keeping their nearby snorkeling reservations, but since the return bus ride would cut it awfully close to the *Voyager*'s all-aboard, I canceled mine. I hated eating the cost of my ticket—I'd already made a significant dent in my excursion budget in England and Portugal—but going was too risky; if I got left behind, it'd cost a fortune to meet up with the ship in Gibraltar. Plus, I'd have a tropical storm to contend with. No thank you.

"So, I looked up some things to do right in Ponta Delgada," he said, leaning forward. "Wanna explore some lava tubes with me?"

I laughed. "What does that even mean?"

Turned out, it meant exactly what it sounded like— underground tunnels on the outskirts of the city where rivers of lava flowed centuries ago. Felix signed us up for the longer tour, and I had to admit, it was fascinating. The jagged walls were a striking mix of shimmering oranges and yellows, but there was one section that made my throat constrict as tight as the confined space I'd need to shimmy through. I might've been used to small living quarters, but it felt like the dark tunnel could collapse any moment, crushing me under the weight of all that hardened lava.

But when Felix saw the anxiety on my face, he took my hand and went through first, showing me it was safe.

Afterward, we taxied back to the port city to explore and find food.

It felt like a bona fide date.

Was it a date? It wasn't like we were putting on a show for anyone.

As we wound through the streets, I recognized people from CoB dining at outdoor café tables; we weren't the only ones sticking close to port. The tiled mosaic sidewalks intersecting with the main public square were reminiscent of Lisbon, and we posed over a particularly impressive starburst design, the toes of Felix's black sneakers touching my gold sandals as I aimed my camera lens down.

"Wait, you're covering it," I said.

"Well, where should I go?" Felix shuffled his feet.

"At that corner." I nudged him over, then extended my arm, leaned to check the screen and make sure I was centered, and immediately lost my balance and made a noise that sounded something like "Erff."

Felix reached out and caught me. "Graceful."

But I was too busy laughing to be embarrassed, grasping his arms to stay upright. He laughed, too, and . . . his face was so close to mine. It would only take a small movement to—

"Jade?" Silas. I hadn't even noticed him approaching.

Felix and I jerked our heads back and I scrambled from his arms, dusting myself off as though I'd fallen. "Oh, hey." My insides turned to goo as I met Silas's eyes.

"Uh . . . just wanted to make sure you're okay."

I glanced at Felix, who'd clearly broken my fall. "Yeah, I'm fine—"

Felix took my hand. Wait—Silas was finally initiating contact! This could be my only shot at getting answers. But shaking Felix off could foil our ruse, so I just stood there, my eyes darting between them like a fool.

Silas frowned at our clasped hands. "Jade, can we ta—"

"This place is awesome, right?" Felix asked Silas, as though unaware of any tension. "Too bad we have to jet so soon. I heard the mountain views are epic." Felix put his arm around me. "Guess we'll have to come back someday."

Silas gave Felix a steely look before clearing his throat. "So . . ." he said, shifting uncomfortably. "Are you two—"

"Silas?" Lainey's voice called out. Dammit. "Come look at this!" She appeared from one of the smaller archways lining the storefronts on the left side of the square—she must've been admiring something in a window. When her eyes landed on me, her face fell.

"You should go," I said to Silas, though I was dying to hear what he wanted.

Silas threw me one last yearning glance before trudging back to Lainey. I bit back a smile. *Finally.* He wanted to talk. And he *clearly* missed me—

"Oh, Christ," Felix said, releasing me.

"What?"

"The look on your face." He shook his head and started down the street opposite Lainey and Silas.

"What look?" I chased after him.

"That shit-eating grin."

"Well, what? Our plan *worked*—"

"I can't believe you still care about making that creep jealous."

My gut twisted terribly. "Where is this even coming from? He's finally trying to talk to me. I might get some answers. You really should've let us—"

Felix turned to me. "Oh, please. That's not all this is about, is it? You still *want* him."

I winced, then opened my mouth to retort, but before I could muster any words, he stuffed his hands into his pockets and continued down the narrow stretch away from the public square, away from the port. Anger clawed up my throat, and I couldn't tell if it was because he'd nearly sabotaged our mission . . . or because he was right. I'd never felt so pathetic. I wasn't sure what I wanted to do more: yell after him or storm back to the ship.

I spun on my heel—but all of a sudden, the street seemed awfully . . . dark. The clouds had gone low and slate gray, and a gust of wind rustled a nearby palm tree. Getting lost in a city this unfamiliar would be terrifying, especially considering the *Voyager* could set sail without me.

Crap.

I jogged to catch up to him, then slowed my pace to match his. He stared straight ahead, though, avoiding my questioning gaze, right back to his signature brooding mode.

Well, I could brood, too.

We silently wandered to the booths and canopied tables lining the next street and spilling into a nearby park—some sort of street market. Each stall sold different wares: locally crafted jewelry, art prints, soaps, aromatherapy oils, puzzle boxes. We wordlessly paused at each, scanning their offerings. I wished he'd say something, because I had no idea how to fix this.

"Ooh, look at these," I cooed, distracted by a table with rows of miniature . . . what were they, daggers or swords? The vendor, a short, balding man with a scruffy graying beard, noticed my interest and picked up the one I'd been admiring. An intricate medieval design curled down the brass hilt below a thin, blunted blade, and a few subtle gemstones surrounded a Templar knight emblem on the hilt, glinting with each movement.

"Letter opener," the vendor said in a heavy accent, holding it out to me. "Veja?" *See?* I took it.

"Bullshit," Felix muttered. "That thing looks sharp."

I fingered the end. "It's not, actually." The edges were dull, and the tip—well, yeah, that was a bit sharp, but I bet it wasn't dangerous or anything.

I thought of Mom's collection of miniature brass figures of iconic monuments she'd visited with Dad—the Eiffel Tower, Big Ben, the Colosseum, the Leaning Tower of Pisa—before they had me, before she turned into the recluse I knew. We barely had any room for knickknacks in our tiny house, so she kept them in a display case above the coat hooks next to the front door. But this little thing? This was stunning *and* functional. Mom always complained the mail gave her paper cuts—always complained about everything, really—in her rush to sort through it and discard the clutter. Maybe she'd actually use this. Even if she didn't, she could add it to her display.

LYING IN THE DEEP

"Quanto custa?" I asked, one of the Portuguese phrases Candace had taught us at Lisbon's pre-port assembly. *How much does it cost?*

"For you?" said the vendor, scratching his scruffy cheek. "Forty-five euros." I examined the dagger again—a tiny sticker on the hilt I hadn't noticed before was marked fifty euros. But his bargain was still more than I could pay. I took one last look at the intricate brass work—*damn*, that was cool—and set it back between the other miniatures.

"Thanks anyway—" I started to turn.

"Forty?" said the vendor.

I stilled. Guilt soured my stomach each time I thought of Mom, of how I'd let days go by between emails. Maybe getting her a thoughtful gift would make up for it.

I swallowed hard. "Er . . . twenty?" I knew that was low, but it was all the cash I had left from when I'd exchanged some American dollars in Lisbon. The man crossed his arms and shook his head.

"How would you even get it back on the ship?" Felix asked. "It's a weapon."

"It's not. It's a letter opener."

He scoffed. "You'll never get it past security."

"Thirty-five," said the vendor. Felix was unwittingly helping me negotiate.

I pulled my last twenty from my purse. "It's all I have on me."

The vendor frowned, but before he could reply, Felix whipped out his wallet and pulled out his last twenty as well. "Here." He didn't ask for change.

131

As we walked away, clutching my new dagger—letter opener—I mumbled my thanks, embarrassed to let him cover for me yet again.

"Sure. Though I still don't think you'll get it on board."

I stared at it, poking my tongue into my cheek. Before boarding the *Voyager*, security scanned our IDs and searched any bag bigger than a clutch. Stuffing it in my purse wouldn't work.

But I had an idea.

"Hold." I handed Felix the dagger, then flipped my head and gathered my thick, curly hair at my crown, making a messy bun. Then I took back the dagger and carefully slid it through the bun like a hair stick. "Voila! The magic of curls."

Felix circled behind me, bemused.

As we continued browsing the stalls, our earlier tension defused, Felix kept pointing out trinkets and suggesting other creative places we could hide them.

"And that"—he pointed to one figurine—"can go straight up your—"

"Oh my God." I shoved his arm.

"—shirt." He smiled coyly. "What'd you think I was going to say?"

I just shook my head and laughed.

We wandered past the market onto a narrow street beyond, passing some ramshackle homes, an old clock tower, a church. At one point I reached for his hand, almost like some instinct to be close to him, to touch him, then stopped myself as the edge of my pinkie grazed his. But before I could pull back, he entwined our fingers. I stilled, suddenly overwhelmed by this strange heat surging through me. His dark eyes searched mine, and when his gaze dipped to my mouth, my heart beat so hard I thought it might burst.

As he closed the gap between us, conflict raged inside me.

Part of me was terrified to let this happen, to give him the opportunity to crush my soul the way Silas had.

But part of me wanted him to pull me to that nearby archway where the milling pedestrians couldn't see, to press me against the wall, cup my cheeks, and kiss—

The bells in the clock tower overhead rang so suddenly we both jerked back, startled. "Jesus." I clasped my chest as they chimed a melody indicating the top of the hour. Felix gaped up at the clock tower, and my stomach dropped. "We lost track of time, didn't we?"

"Yup," he said. "It's five."

All-aboard was at five.

We were going to get stuck here.

15

"Should we get a taxi?" I yelled as we sprinted back to the street market, already out of breath. The dagger refused to stay put as I ran, so I tugged it free, letting my curls spill down my back. They whipped behind me as we raced headlong into the wind.

The weather was turning fast.

"I don't see any, just go!" said Felix.

"There's one!" I spotted a cab turning one block over. We rushed over and hailed it.

The driver stopped short and rolled down the window, eyeing us suspiciously. Did it look like we were fleeing after stealing something from the market? "Onde você vai?" she asked. I assumed that meant something like *Where you are going?*

"The port!" I said. "Uh . . . porto."

Felix peered into the backseat. "I don't see a credit card reader. You're out of cash, too, right?"

I groaned. I had no clue how to ask if the driver accepted credit cards in Portuguese, so I whipped out mine, meant for dire emergencies only. This definitely counted as dire. "Do you take this?"

The driver shook her head and raised her window before driving off. I let out a frustrated cry.

"Come on!" Felix tugged my hand, and we kept running,

weaving through the tourists and locals in the public square as I hurled apologies over my shoulder at anyone I bumped into.

When we made it onto the final stretch, a long road running parallel to the ocean, I could see the gleaming *Sea Voyager* still docked in port. But it looked so small from here—we had a ways to go. As we sprinted, I kept visualizing it floating from the dock, and sheer panic propelled me forward despite the sharp stitch under my rib cage.

But when we made it to the end of the pier, it was still there.

I paused to quickly regather my curls into a bun, practically wheezing for breath, and slid the dagger back in.

"Come on!" Felix shouted, his brow gleaming with sweat.

We raced to the gate, where Zofia, the security officer who'd made me go back for my ID the first morning in London, stood shaking her head. "You really like to cut things close, don't you?"

"Trust me . . ." Felix gasped for breath as he handed her his ID. "This wasn't fun."

I hoped he only meant this last bit.

I set my purse on the X-ray conveyor belt and breezed through the metal detector, which beeped angrily. Zofia scanned me from head to toe, frowning. My skirt had no pockets. "My necklace, maybe?" I suggested, pinching the charm.

She gave an exasperated sigh. "Just go."

"Thanks." I picked up my purse and followed Felix up the ramp, muffling a laugh into my hand.

"Welp," said Felix, "I now have exactly zero confidence in our security measures."

Despite the captain's best efforts to avoid the bad weather system, troubled waters reached the *Voyager*, causing the ship to sway enough to send many queasy passengers to bed early.

"I'd think lying down would make it worse," said Felix as Jamal rushed past our table in Sea Haven, gripping his stomach and struggling to keep his balance as a rolling wave rocked the room. I'd overheard him spouting tips to ward off seasickness (placing a patch behind your ear, chewing ginger gum), but apparently, even the best-prepared were susceptible to the ocean's wrath. "Better to stay distracted."

"I agree," I said. To my tremendous surprise, I was totally fine, other than a small tension headache. In fact, I was actively inhaling a ginormous bowl of pasta and had been sussing out this lovely-looking key lime pie they were serving for dessert.

At one point when Felix went to the restroom, Tate slid into his seat.

"Oh, hey, Tate—"

"Why didn't you tell me Sheffia's parents work at Sanatek?" Tate leaned forward, his square jaw clenched, eyes narrowed behind his glasses. "You could've at least warned me."

I blinked at him for a moment, struggling to make sense of why this mattered, and how he expected me to know that. "I didn't—"

"Don't tell me you didn't know."

"I *didn't!*"

"But you used to be best friends with Lainey, right? That's what you told Miguel."

"Right, so I automatically have a roster of all her father's employees' offspring."

Tate tugged his fingers through his short, wiry curls. He was so agitated his fingers were shaking. "Sorry, I just . . . Dammit."

"Why does it matter?"

But he just shook his head, seething. I knew nothing about Sheffia's parents—I hadn't even known Lainey and Sheffia might've met through theirs—but this reaction was bizarre. Maybe whatever happened to Tate's mother was related to Sanatek after all. I bit my lip, considering asking, but I didn't want to dredge up anything painful.

"Seriously, some people just need a job," I said instead. "When Silas got injured last spring and lost his baseball scholarship, he would've had to drop out of Stanford if Lainey hadn't gotten him a paid internship there."

"Wait . . . Silas interned at Sanatek?"

"Yup. It was the only way he could afford to stay in school—"

"Hey," said Felix, returning with two small plates loaded with pie.

Tate scooted his chair back. "Sorry, dude."

"No worries."

"And, uh," Tate said to me, rubbing the back of his neck, "sorry for being a dickwad."

I gave him a sympathetic smile. "It's fine." He was obviously grappling with some serious grief. "If you want to talk later, I'm here."

He offered a small smile. "Thanks, Jade. See ya later."

"What was that about?" Felix asked as Tate loped off.

I sighed. "Oh, nothing."

He watched me for a moment, waiting to see if I'd dish, but I nibbled at the edge of my pie. "So . . . wanna head to the library after this?" Felix asked, jarring me from my thoughts. "You probably want a rematch."

Remembering the intensity of his gaze last time we played Battleship is what finally made my stomach wobble. And even though we'd spent all day together, he wanted to keep hanging out with me. "Sure. But I totally let you win last time."

By the time we headed to the library on Deck 8 an hour or so later, the ship's rocking had calmed to a gentle sway—we were distancing ourselves from the storm, but the damage to people's stomachs had already been done.

"Hey!" shouted a group sitting at the large round table in the middle of the library—Navya, Divya, Miguel, and Tate, who anxiously offered a tight-lipped, sheepish smile.

Divya waved us over. "Yaaaaas, the more people the better."

Felix and I exchanged a look—was his disappointed?—before heading over. A girl in an armchair in the corner who'd clearly been trying to read huffed and scrammed. It *was* kind of a weird choice to combine a library and game room. Divya gave my arm a friendly poke as I sat next to her, and Felix sat on my other side.

"Seriously?" I eyed Navya setting up the board. "Monopoly? This could take hours—"

"Drunk Monopoly," Divya corrected, waggling her eyebrows. That's when I noticed the sharp tang of alcohol in the air. Their water bottles sure weren't filled with water. Navya drummed her fingers on hers and gave me a meaningful look, darting a quick glance to Tate and back. She must've known he'd split with Sheffia and practically buzzed with glee, her excitement trumping any concern over Divya's drinking habits.

"Aren't you afraid we'll get busted?" I asked.

"By who?" said Divya. "Most of the professors are sick, too, and the crew don't care. Gimme your bottles." Once we did, she grabbed her backpack from under the table and headed for the door, probably to the nearest restroom to dump our water and mix some concoction for us. "Oh, yep, you're playing, too."

I glanced up. Silas stood in the doorway. Divya grabbed his water bottle and dashed down the hall before he could even understand what was happening. "I— What?"

Felix stiffened next to me.

Oh, crap.

16

"We're about to play a drinking game," Miguel explained. "With Monopoly."

"Apparently, so are you," said Navya.

Silas rubbed the back of his neck. "Uh . . . actually, I'm looking for some Dramamine. Lainey's real sick."

I couldn't help but notice Miguel's smirk—the first smile I'd seen from him since his socials shut down. But I also couldn't help but remember that time I got the flu freshman year and was so sick to my stomach I couldn't even go to the pharmacy, and Lainey went into full-on caretaker mode. She got me meds, Gatorade, and soup, and I was too feverish to know which way was up, but I could've sworn she'd draped cool cloths across my forehead, switching them out every few minutes for fresh ones. The girl had been a saint.

"The clinic's out," Silas went on. "I tried the store, too, but it's closed."

"The clinic's *out*?" said Miguel.

"Yup," said Silas. "They're restocking at the next port, but for now, everyone's SOL."

"Yikes," said Divya. "Good thing we've all got stomachs of steel, huh?" Tate watched Silas with a sullen pout, uncharacteristically quiet.

"I have some Dramamine," said Navya. "I can go get it—"

"Hang on." Tate clasped Navya's wrist. "Apparently the stuff's a precious commodity."

Navya took a sharp breath, gaping at where he touched her, and a hint of pink flushed her cheeks. But then she looked confused. "We're fine, though. Stomachs of steel, right?" But he didn't mean for Navya to hoard it.

It's his fault my mother's dead.

"C'mon, man," said Silas, his brow furrowed in concern. "She's puking her guts out."

"Can you please get it?" I asked Navya.

She nodded and left while Silas and Tate threw daggers at each other with their eyes.

Speaking of which—no wonder I had a tension headache. I took the thin dagger from my hair and shook out my curls. "Ah, that's better."

"What's *that*?" Miguel eyed the dagger.

"A letter opener," I said. Felix snorted, but I ignored him. "I got it at a street market today." I passed it to Miguel, who admired the bejeweled hilt as Silas sank into Divya's seat next to me, dropped his backpack on the floor, and slapped his room key on the table—Lainey's key, more likely—all while holding Tate's withering glare. He rarely picked fights but was never one to lose a battle of wills.

When Divya returned, she passed our bottles back half full. I took a whiff. "What even is this?"

"Rum and Coke, but more rum than Coke."

"Eugh," said Felix.

"Don't like rum?" Divya asked.

"Don't like Coke."

"Who doesn't like Coke?"

"It's the carbonation," said Felix. "I'm sorry, but burping that painfully is entirely unnecessary."

Divya chortled as she slid into the empty seat between Miguel and Felix, not seeming to mind that Silas had swiped hers. He took a sip, cringing slightly. He never used to drink, prioritizing his baseball performance. But I saw him drinking at that London pub, so things had changed. I vaguely wondered how his arm felt, if he'd ever get back full mobility, if he was still devastated he no longer belonged to a team.

"Alright, here's how this is going to work," said Divya as Miguel passed back my letter opener. I set it on the table. "Wait, where's my sister? She didn't chicken out, did she?"

"She went to grab something from our room," I explained as Felix scooted his chair closer to put his arm around me. Silas side-eyed us until Navya reappeared, out of breath, and dropped a small strip of tablets in front of him.

"Thanks. I appreciate it." Silas slipped them into his pocket but stayed put. So much for taking care of Lainey.

Divya scrolled to the rules she'd saved on her phone and read aloud: One sip for landing on a hotel, or someone's property if they had Monopoly, Chance, or Community Chest. Two sips if you went to jail. Rolling a double would earn you a five-second sip. And whenever you passed Go, you got to tell someone else to drink.

"Christ," Felix chuckled as I groaned.

"Yup, we're gonna get shitfaced," Tate muttered, usually enthused by such prospects.

"Exactly the point, boo," said Miguel, our banker, handing me a stack of Monopoly cash.

Silas gripped the table as a wave made the room tilt. Okay, *that* one wobbled my stomach. "You sure this is a good idea right now?" he asked.

"Feel free to take off," said Felix. "You're looking a bit green."

Silas's eyes became slits. We both caught the double meaning, and my stomach wobbled for a different reason. "Nah, I'm good," said Silas.

"Doesn't Lainey need those meds?" asked Felix.

"She managed to fall asleep before I left," said Silas. "Let her rest a bit longer." Then he turned his attention to Divya. "Where'd you get the rum?"

"At port today," she said as we picked pieces. "Filled my water bottle with it, so easy. Zofia never checks."

We rolled to see who'd go first (me), and I instantly rolled snake eyes, landing on Community Chest, which meant—

"Five-second drink and another sip!" said Divya. Felix snorted, and Silas threw me a devilish smirk.

"Oh God," I said, unsure what exactly I was reacting to. All of it, maybe.

With that, we were off to the races.

I tried to relax and have fun—even Miguel loosened up, and Navya threw shade as she accumulated property faster than anyone else—but with Felix and Silas on either side of me, I felt like a deep-sea diver trapped between two circling sharks. Felix kept finding reasons to touch me, like when he fiddled with one of my curls that had gone extra springy from being in a bun, twirling it around his fingers. I could practically feel the rage thrumming through Silas, and for some reason, it scared me more than it satisfied me.

After only a few rounds, I was fully tipsy and a bit dizzy. The swaying ship wasn't helping. At one point, Felix took my hand and whispered in my ear, "You okay?"

"Yeah." I threw him a reassuring smile. He ran his thumb over my knuckles, and a shiver soared up my arm. And those eyes of his, how they so intensely searched mine, I couldn't look away—

"Dude, you gotta roll," Silas practically snarled at Felix.

"I'm in jail." Felix released my hand and perched an elbow on his chair's armrest. "I'll forfeit a roll." After over an hour of game play, the board was now a terrifying cluster of houses and hotels, and jail was the safest spot. People were drinking on every turn.

Silas sneered. "You can't do that."

"Says who?"

"Like . . . the *rules* do."

"I don't have a Get Out of Jail Free card, and I don't wanna pay to leave," said Felix. "The only way out is to roll a double, and what are the odds? So I'll forfeit two turns."

A muscle in Silas's jaw twitched. "But you *have* to roll." Everyone's eyes bounced between them. "You can't just choose not to."

"Yo, who cares?" Tate snapped at Silas. "It's just a game. If he wants to stay in jail, whatever, man."

"But that's the whole point," said Silas. "You gotta roll, and if you get doubles, you have to leave and play the next turn."

"And drink," said Divya.

"*And* drink," Silas repeated.

Oh, brother. I took a swig of my drink, even though it wasn't my turn.

But Felix only shrugged. "Meh." I nearly spit laughing. Holy hell, he was playing with fire.

Silas's face reddened from how Felix made me laugh—worse yet, at his expense. "Dude, what's your problem?"

"Oop," Miguel said under his breath.

I lightly poked Felix's arm. "Maybe you should just roll."

Felix studied me for a moment, then scooped up the dice, shook them dramatically, and rolled with a flourish. A two and a three. "There ya go," he said to Silas, elbow back on his armrest. "Happy?"

I thought Silas's head might pop.

Meanwhile, Tate was still glowering at Silas, cords of tension cutting the room in all directions.

"Jade, your turn," said Navya an octave higher than usual.

"Anyone have a good playlist?" said Divya at the same time, shifting uncomfortably.

As Miguel started playing some music on his phone, I rolled, landing on Baltic Avenue. "How does nobody own it yet?"

Navya scoffed. "I never waste cash on those small fish." She'd bought Boardwalk and Park Place, going for the kill.

I fanned out my property cards. "But if I want to drink as little as possible," I spoke slowly to counteract the slur, "it's better to buy them so you fools can't build hotels on them."

"Well, maybe." Silas shifted closer to see my properties, reminding me of how we used to play poker each Sunday with the same crew who'd gone on that terrible ski trip. I couldn't care less about poker or stand how his friends' house reeked of weed and old pizza; I was just happy to spend time with Silas, that he wanted me there. I loved when he folded early—he'd lean close, analyzing my hand, murmuring advice into my ear, even if his friends hassled him for it. Poker was the only time I ever rooted for him to lose.

"If you can't build," he said now, "you can't get anyone *else* wasted."

"An exchange I'm willing to make," I said.

Silas's mouth quirked. "Fair."

I dragged my eyes from his to count out cash. After Miguel handed me my property card, Felix took my hand again as we waited for Silas to roll.

But he just sat there, pouting at our clasped hands. "So, what, are you two an item now?"

"Isn't it obvious—" Felix started.

"Why do you even care?" I snapped at Silas.

"Why do I—" Silas stuttered. "Are you serious?"

"Hey, did you guys hear about what Sketchy Bob did today?" said Navya, awkwardly trying to change the subject. "He went snorkeling in this tiny, gross Speedo, and then got stung by a bunch of mini jellyfish."

"Oh my God, is he okay?" said Miguel. As they yammered, Silas gaped at me.

"Yo, it's your turn now," Tate said to Silas.

"Shut up," Silas snapped.

Now it was Tate's turn to go red. "Dude, you just made a stink—"

"I said *shut up.*"

"Can we please be civil?" said Navya. Miguel held a fist to his lips, stifling nervous laughter.

"Ya know what? I'm out." Tate scooted back his chair and stood.

"Aw, no, don't go," Divya cast an anxious look at Navya, clearly afraid she'd end the game without Tate here.

But he was already gone.

The next few rounds were tense—we went through the motions, drinking when we had to, but all the fun had been sapped out of it. The next time Felix passed me the dice, Silas huffed.

"Chill. He was just passing me the dice." I raised them to eye level, showing him, struggling to keep my hand steady. I was verging on plastered.

"Sure."

"What's that s'posed to mean?"

"Oh, please. You've been flaunting you're together all night."

My jaw literally dropped. "You *hypocrite.*" And then I started laughing—a drunken, hysterical laugh. After everything he and Lainey had put me through, he had some nerve. "Are you for real right now?"

Silas's opened his mouth to retort, but Divya suddenly stood. "I need more to drink—" But when a wave swayed the room, she fell back to her seat. "Ugh . . ."

"Maybe just water this time." Miguel picked up his water bottle. "C'mon, I'll take you."

Navya started to stand as well. Oh, no. If Silas and Felix were left alone with me, they might explode. I covered Navya's hand on the table, "No, please stay," I whispered loudly. "It's your turn next."

She let out a low whine.

"No cheating." Divya slurred worse than me. "If she has to drink," she said to me, "make her."

"But—" Navya tried, but Divya and Miguel were out the door.

Not a moment later, Silas asked, "Why d'you think I'm a hypocrite?"

"You're the one who came here to shove your relationship with Lainey in my face."

"You're delusional." Silas fully faced me now, the game forgotten. "I didn't even know you'd be here."

My fingers shook with rage. "You *knew* last semester I was coming on this trip."

"Lainey said you weren't," he said. "She thought you dropped out." And I bet that was only the tip of her lies. But he should've talked to me before believing whatever treachery spewed from her lips.

"Well, maybe if you hadn't ghosted me like that, you'd've known what my plans were."

Silas screwed up his face. "I didn't—"

"Guys, maybe now isn't the time—" Felix tried interrupting.

"You stay outta this." Silas clenched his fist on the table, a cord bulging up his forearm. "Listen, I didn't—"

But I cut him off. "Even before this trip—all those pics you posted over the summer, of the two of you hugging, kissing, being so *perfect* together—"

"Oh, don't be so dramatic."

"I'm *not*. What, you didn't think I'd see those?"

He huffed. "Alright, fine. Maybe I did. I was so hurt, you didn't even—"

"*You* were hurt?"

"Of course I was. I still *am*. I still love you. I never stopped loving you."

My stomach dropped so fast it felt like I was on a roller coaster, plummeting after a steep climb. I'd wanted to hear him say those words for months. But now it felt so terribly wrong.

My head swam from the rum, and I couldn't make sense of any of this. "Then why the hell are you with *her*?"

"Why are *you* acting like this wasn't your call?"

"How was any of this *my* call?" I cried.

"If you hadn't dumped me, we'd still be together."

I took a sharp breath. I never dumped him. That didn't happen.

It felt like the walls were closing in, entrapping me, making it hard to breathe. I never dumped him. That was a lie. *His* lie. I shook my head aggressively. "That's not what happened at all. Don't you dare twist things around like that. Don't you *dare* gaslight me like that."

"It's not gaslighting if it's the truth."

Every nerve in my body felt like a lit fuse.

"*You* ended it," he went on. "I loved you, and you're the bitch who wanted nothing to do with me."

Dynamite detonated somewhere deep inside me, and before I even knew what I was doing, before I could comprehend the consequences, I picked up the letter opener, meaning to plunge it into the table's wood grain. All that rage, all that anguish—I needed to put it *somewhere*, because I couldn't contain the blast.

But right when I drove my arm down, a swell rocked the ship, and as drunk as I was, I teetered off-balance . . . and the blade sank into Silas's leg.

17

I was vaguely aware of Felix cursing and Navya leaping from her
seat, but a tinny buzzing noise filled my ears as I gaped at my
own hand gripping the hilt of the tiny dagger penetrating Silas's
leg at an angle above his left knee, below the hem of his shorts.
Shock permeated every cell in my body, freezing me in place.
Silas didn't try to push me away or scoot back or even scream—
it was like he'd seized up in shock, too.

"I—I'm *so* sorry. I didn't mean to . . ." I swallowed down bile.

"Dammit, Jade." Silas gnashed his teeth together, gripping his
thigh above the blade with one hand and clutching the edge of
the table with the other.

"I meant to stab the table. I swear to God, I meant to stab the
table. I never wanted to hurt you." But that didn't matter now.
Blood trickled down Silas's thigh, staining the chair's edge, but
not as much as I would have expected. If I pulled out the blade, it
might be a different story.

"Don't pull it out," said Felix, clearly thinking along the same
lines.

"Why not?" Navya cried.

"It could bleed worse if she does."

But the blade wasn't going anywhere; I could hardly move a
muscle. "Oh God." My brain swam, and everything seemed to
have warped, fuzzy edges. Navya was a blur racing for the door.

Felix stopped her. "Wait—"

"We have to get help!" she cried.

"No!" Silas yelled. I gaped at him. His face contorted in agony as his eyes darted between mine. "I don't want Jade to get in trouble."

My breath hitched. "What? I . . . I literally just *stabbed* you."

He bared his teeth again; pain seemed to be rippling through his leg in waves. "It was an accident . . ."

"Well, what're we supposed to do?" Navya shrieked.

Felix shushed her. "Just . . . just calm down for a sec." He wiped a hand down his face.

"*Calm down?*" cried Navya. "He has a dagger sticking out of his leg! We have to get a medic."

"No, wait," said Silas. "Get my roommate. Jamal."

"Why?" said Felix.

"He's premed. Maybe he'll know what to do."

"Oh, what, so he's taken a couple of biology classes?"

"His dad's a brain surgeon or something," said Silas.

"Right," I said. "He told me his family is full of surgeons."

Silas nodded. "He might know some stuff. Just *do* it."

Worry lines creased Felix's brow as he met my gaze and hesitated, shaking his head, like he couldn't fathom what I'd done, and my heart fractured into a million pieces. He didn't believe me. I'd lost him. I'd lost *everything*, all over again. "What's your room number?" he asked Silas.

"Seven sixteen," Silas grunted. One deck down.

"Stay with them," Felix commanded Navya before taking off.

"Oh my God, oh my God." Navya paced back and forth by the door. She kept glancing at the blade in Silas's leg, then clasping her mouth and diverting her gaze like she was going to be sick.

"Silas . . . I'm so sorry," I said. "I shouldn't have picked up the letter opener at all. I was just so angry."

You're the bitch who wanted nothing to do with me.

Sweat glistened on Silas's forehead. "Let go of it."

"No, we shouldn't—"

"Every time you move, it hurts."

"Oh God. I'm sorry . . ." I held my breath and gently released the hilt.

The dagger remained in place, but Silas hissed through his teeth. "Maybe that's worse." He grabbed the hilt, holding it steady.

By the time Felix returned with Jamal in tow, Silas's face had gone sickeningly pale. Jamal looked groggy and off-balance—still motion sick, maybe—and clutched a bunch of towels and a first aid kit in a small camo pouch. When he spotted the dagger lodged in Silas's leg, his hooded eyes widened, and he clasped his mouth and made a gagging noise before saying, "Holy—"

"Can you do something?" said Felix.

Jamal adamantly shook his head, swallowing hard. "That's not just a cut, man."

"*Do* something," said Silas.

Jamal cringed, sweat already glistening on his forehead. "I can't."

"Are you premed or not?"

"That doesn't mean anything, man. I've never treated anyone before!"

Felix raked back his hair. "Well, what should we do?"

Jamal dropped everything in a heap next to Silas and knelt, examining the impalement, still clasping his mouth. Then he tore his gaze away and shook his head. "We gotta get a medic."

"No," said Silas. "Then we'll have to tell—can't we just pull it out?"

Felix nodded. "It doesn't look like the dagger went in too deep."

"Still," said Jamal, "if you hit an artery, the dagger could be plugging it. I dunno how much it'll bleed if we pull it out. How'd this even happen?"

I swallowed hard, but Silas spoke fast. "I was being ridiculous, dude; I stabbed myself trying to prove the thing wasn't sharp." He chuckled harshly, wiping his brow. "Joke's on me, I guess."

"Seriously?" Jamal caught the wide-eyed look that passed between me, Felix, and Navya. "What really hap—"

"Dammit, that's what really happened!" Silas raged so loud I was afraid someone down the hall might hear.

Jamal winced. "Okay, okay."

"Now can we please get this thing out of my leg?"

"Is there an artery right there?" Navya asked.

"Guh, I dunno," said Jamal, looking worried. "There's a big one that runs right down the center of your leg. This is kinda off to the side, so . . . maybe it missed? Either way, you're probably gonna need stitches."

"This is ridiculous," I said. "Silas, we need to get a medic—"

Silas braced, then hissed through his teeth, like he was trying to bring himself to pull out the dagger but couldn't. Maybe it hurt too much. He reached for my hand and made me grab the hilt. I gasped. "Pull it out," he said.

"No! We *need* to get help."

"No." Silas shook his head stubbornly. "No one else needs to know this happened. I can't do it myself; pull it out."

"Seriously?" said Navya.

"Silas, please," I said. "It's too dangerous."

"Yeah, dude—" Jamal tried.

"Pull it out."

"No!"

"PULL IT OUT!" He screamed so loudly that I reflexively yanked my arm back, taking the letter opener with me.

Silas cried out in pain as blood gushed from the wound, and Jamal sprung to action, clamping a towel over Silas's leg to stanch the flow.

I backed away, shaking hard, still clutching the letter opener, the blade's tip coated in blood. I couldn't believe what I'd done.

And somehow, Silas's words still echoed in my mind on loop. *You're the bitch who wanted nothing to do with me.*

A blatant lie. I'd wanted *everything* to do with him.

I thought of Sheffia, accusing me of sabotaging her friendship with Lainey. But that'd been all Lainey's decision.

And now my suspicions were confirmed—she must've said something similar to Silas.

Lightning streaked through my veins again, setting them aflame, boiling my blood. She stole Silas from me not just by seducing him, but by somehow turning us against each other. She was a liar and manipulator, and I'd almost let her gaslight me into thinking *I'd* done something wrong. But really, she'd say or do anything to get what she wanted.

She'd tricked me from the start. She tricked me into believing she was a good person, became half of my heart, then took both halves away and left me as an empty shell, turning me vengeful and obsessive. Just like how when Dad abandoned Mom and me, Mom turned paranoid and spiteful. Now I saw why. Lainey had turned me into a monster, too.

And now I was going to lose Felix.

I couldn't bear it.

And it was all *her* fault.

As everyone fussed over Silas's leg, I grabbed the room key he'd dropped on the table and slipped into the hall, hurtling toward the stern, toward Lainey's room. Screw knocking—she'd never open the door for me, and I was too angry, too drunk, too *furious* to wait.

My fingers violently shook, but eventually I managed to jam the key into its slot.

The lock beeped, and I threw open the door.

18

Lainey's cabin was dark save for the light spilling in from the hallway, but I could tell it was enormous.

So much for wanting a "normal" college experience; she'd clearly splurged on CoB. It was more a suite than a cabin—some sort of room divider separated a sitting area from the bed, and she even had a balcony. It didn't seem like much of one, with the rail right up against the door, but most cabins had nothing more than a measly porthole, if that. The door was open, its sheer curtains fluttering in the breeze. I hoped the fresh air helped her feel better, because I had some words to say, and she'd better be ready to hear them.

I glared at her shadowy figure curled up in bed—she'd always been a heavy sleeper—and fumbled for the light switch. But before I could flick it on, strong arms wrapped around my waist, tugging me back.

"No!" I cried as Felix yanked me into the hall and shoved me aside to shut the door. I whirled. "Stop! Let me back in. I *need* to talk to her—"

"Not right now, you don't," said Felix. "Look at yourself." He motioned to the letter opener in my grip, the tip of its blade red with Silas's blood. I hadn't even realized I was still clutching it.

Just then, Tate rounded the corner from the nearest stairwell,

Miguel right behind. They were chortling, lugging full water bottles.

Felix muttered a curse as Tate spotted us. "Yo—" But he froze as he took in my stance and expression. I hid the dagger behind my back, but it was too late. Tate saw it. His eyes flicked to mine, like he was trying to puzzle out what just happened.

Miguel hadn't noticed—he was busy gaping down the hall as Silas limped from the game room, one arm draped over Jamal's shoulders and a bloodied towel tied around his upper leg. Navya darted past them, lugging Silas's backpack, to call an elevator.

"What the hell happened?" Miguel asked.

My stomach churned at the sight of the bloodied towel. Holy hell. There must've been so much blood to soak through like that. My mind flashed to the blade sinking into his leg, to that feeling of tearing past skin into muscle. "Oh God." I doubled over in panic, gasping in rasping breaths, like all the air had been sucked from the hall.

"What *happened*?" Miguel asked again.

"Nothing." Felix rested a hand on my back. "Game's over."

"Why—" Miguel started.

"Just go back to your room, or somewhere else, anywhere else."

Silas threw a grimacing glance my way before disappearing into the elevator bay. "I'm so sorry—" I said before clasping my mouth.

"Come on." Felix put his arm around me. "Let's get some fresh air." He guided me up the stairs, ditching a befuddled Tate and Miguel.

"What've I done?" I asked as we reached the open deck. Though the waves had calmed, wind whipped along the promenade—not as blustery as London, but cool enough to make me shiver. I'd left my denim jacket in the library.

"Dammit, this has gone too far," Felix said in a low, husky voice as he led us around the corner to a deserted, poorly lit area with rows of lounge chairs facing starboard, where a wall blocked the brunt of the breeze. He probably regretted ever helping me play detective, ever getting to know me at all.

The teak deck tilted under my feet, or maybe I was just dizzy, but between that, my panic, and the crystal-clear constellations peeking through a break in the fast-moving clouds, it felt like I could be sucked through a vortex and tumble into the vastness of space.

"I'm sorry, I'm so sorry, I never meant to do that, I can't believe I did that . . ." Tears streaked down my face, and I gasped for breath, trembling furiously.

Felix sat me down on one of the lounge chairs and rubbed my back. "I need you to breathe."

"There was so much blood. What if Jamal can't stop the bleeding? What if he *dies*?"

Felix chuckled.

"What about this is funny?"

"Nothing. Truly, nothing. But I really, *really* don't think he's going to die."

"But all that blood—"

"'Tis but a scratch," he said in a full British accent—I recognized the line from *Monty Python*. I let out an exasperated, shaky huff, then hiccupped weirdly, still struggling to catch my breath. It felt like a zillion rocks were crushing my rib cage.

Felix moved to kneel in front of me, gently pried the letter opener from my grip, then set a hand on my knee. "Just breathe, okay? Big deep breath in." He inhaled deeply, motioning for me to imitate him. I did, and again for a big exhale.

After we repeated this a few more times, Felix said, "Keep doing that, okay? Just breathe. I'm gonna clean this off."

He strode off with the dagger, and I watched him disappear into the men's room by the pool. I'd *stabbed* a person.

My God.

I squeezed my eyes shut and clutched the lounge chair beside my legs, trying to focus on breathing in, breathing out as the cool breeze sobered me up a bit, but my mind raced to make sense of what I'd done. It was an accident, a terrible accident—I'd slipped from the swell when I'd really meant to stab the table. But uncontainable rage had driven me to pick up that letter opener in the first place. That never should've happened at all.

"Hey." Felix was back, dangling my denim jacket in front of me; he must've dashed back down to grab it from the library.

I took it and slid it on. "Thanks—" I gasped; Silas's blood stained my shirt right above where it was tucked into my skirt. I hadn't noticed before. A wave of nausea surged up my throat, and I hugged my jacket closed over the bloodstain, rocking back and forth again.

"Hey, it's gonna be okay." Felix sat next to me again, setting the dagger on the floor. So much for giving that to Mom—I should probably chuck it overboard.

"I don't think it will. It's no wonder everyone always leaves me. I'm terrible."

"Why would you think that?"

"Um, I just stabbed another human?"

"It's not like you meant to."

My breath hitched, and I wiped away a tear. "You believe me?"

He squinched his brow. "Come to think of it, no. You are rather prone to violence."

"Oh my God, stop." I shoved his arm.

"See? Exactly what I'm talking about."

I buried my face in my hands, somehow laughing while still crying.

"No, but seriously," he said, "what do you mean, everyone *always* leaves you?" I glanced up at him, and he was studying me so earnestly, like he genuinely wanted to understand.

My chest tightened from all this repressed anguish before it all poured out of me like water through a burst dam. I'd never shared any of it before, not even with Lainey or Silas, afraid my complaints would bore them, annoy them, drive them away. But I told Felix about my parents—how Mom became reclusive, how whenever Dad took me to the park, to soccer practice, to the movies, she'd nag him to stay home. How he eventually got tenure elsewhere and escaped. I took too much effort, too much time away from his work—it was my fault he left.

"Damn. There's so much to unpack there . . ." The breeze ruffled Felix's hair, and he swept it back. "What makes you think it was *your* fault?"

"Because he left me behind with *her*—" My own choked sob cut me off.

"I'm only guessing here, but do you think maybe he blamed her for being neglectful? Do you think maybe he lost a custody battle?"

I shook my head, reflexively rejecting any explanation other than what Mom led me to believe. But the truth was, I was too young at the time to understand what was happening. "He would've reached out. He would've called me, or emailed . . ." But Mom didn't let me get a cell phone until halfway through high school and had access to all my accounts back then. Who knew what she kept from me? I never confronted or questioned her, too afraid to set her off. Instead, I kept my head down, bided my time, plotted my own escape. By the time I was old enough to contact Dad, maybe he assumed I already hated him.

I wouldn't know; I was never brave enough to reach out and ask.

I told Felix what happened after, how Mom moved us to that horrible tiny house, off the grid, paranoid and secluded, blaming me for everything that went wrong. "So when Silas blamed *me* for our breakup, when that's definitely not what happened, all those feelings came rushing back, and I just . . . I just . . ."

"Had to stab a table."

"Yeah. Guh, I've been bottling all this up for so long. But I think I need help. Real help."

"You know," said Felix, "most people never get to the point where they admit that."

I gathered my windblown curls off to one side. "I guess you can say I've hit rock bottom."

"Oh, I'd hope so. If this isn't your rock bottom, I'm petrified to see what is." He kept his tone teasing, and I gently shoved him again, even as another tear streaked down my cheek. "Have you ever seen a therapist before?"

"No. But when I get home, I should."

"You don't have to wait. All the psych professors on board double as counselors. You could see someone tomorrow. I'll introduce you to Professor Shah. She's great."

"Are you kidding? They're probably going to kick me off the ship tomorrow."

"Mm . . . I really doubt they'll make you walk the plank. That only happens in the movies. Or on pirate ships."

I let out a hybrid chuckle sob. "I mean, whenever we get to Gibraltar."

"I don't think anyone will find out. Silas won't tell, and I won't, either—"

"Navya will tell Divya for sure." Panic clawed up my throat again. "And there's no way Divya will keep her mouth shut. Not that she even should—I *stabbed* someone."

Felix needled his fingers through my hair to cup my cheek, those dark, liquid eyes penetrating mine. "It was an accident."

"Still. I never should've picked up that dagger at all."

After a long pause, he said, "It was my fault as much as yours—" He cut himself off and averted his gaze.

"That's not true."

"I egged you on tonight. Both of you."

"I'm the one who asked you to fake-date me. I'm the one who asked you to help make Silas jealous. You were just playing along."

"No, I wasn't." His eyes flicked back up to mine. "Not tonight."
My heart fluttered.

How was this possible? He'd seen me at my absolute worst.
Yet here he was, staring at me like he never wanted to look anywhere else again. It made absolutely no sense.

"I don't understand. Why . . . How . . ." I struggled to form the right words.

"You seriously don't know?" He shook his head slightly.
"You're sensitive, and compassionate, and kind. Like when you wanted to console Sheffia, even when she was a total asshole to you. You're willing to acknowledge when you've made a mistake, to figure out how you messed up, to fix it. Do you know how goddamn rare that is?"

Warmth spread through me like a sip of hot chocolate. Nobody had ever seen me like this before. Silas used to call me "beautiful" all the time, but nobody had ever bothered to mention what might've been beautiful on the inside. And after Lainey and Silas turned on me, I'd started to fear there was nothing but muck.

"And I think I—" he went on, but stopped himself, chuckling softly.

"What?" I prodded. "Say it."

But he stayed silent, holding my gaze, and I realized we were both breathing harder. Before I could wonder if his pulse was racing anywhere near as fast as mine, he was kissing me, like despite everything that had happened, he simply couldn't wait any longer for this to be real.

I answered his searing kisses with my own, melting into him, hardly able to believe this was happening, that someone could want me despite my flaws laid bare. My heart felt like it might burst as I leaned back on the lounge chair, pulling him with me, on top of me, like the sky didn't have enough oxygen and I needed him to breathe. My veins buzzed with electricity as he deepened the kiss even more, and I wanted to lose myself in him, lose myself completely.

As our kisses grew hungrier, fiercer, he managed to arch my back to untuck my shirt and slide his hands over my bare skin, his palms warm and soft. A longing ache thrummed between my thighs. I wanted his hands all over me. I wanted *all* of him.

Just when my fingers started to drift down to unbutton his jeans, this yearning want overriding any inhibitions, a moan escaped his lips. "We can't do this here."

Obviously, he was right. Anyone could walk by at any moment.

"Your room?" I suggested breathlessly.

"Roommate," Felix grunted. My room was out, too. Either way, I knew we shouldn't go further tonight, not after everything that had happened, and especially not without any protection. "And we should wait until we haven't been drinking." That, too.

Felix kissed me softly once more before sliding off me, and I scooted over so we could lie side by side, my arm crossing his chest as he clutched me close. I nuzzled into his shoulder, soaking in his warmth, his scent of spice and musk. At some point his breathing slowed and he drifted off, his lips making a faint puffing noise with each exhale. But I lay awake for a long time, wondering if he was right, if everyone would keep quiet about what had happened.

If he wasn't, tomorrow might be my last day on the ship.

If only that would be the worst thing about tomorrow.

I had absolutely no clue.

19

Nothing jolts your bones like waking up to the sound of screaming.

I jerked upright with a gasp, and the memory of stabbing Silas flooded back like a tidal wave. Had I really heard a scream, or was I having a nightmare about that terrible moment?

I'd spent most of the night shivering and restless, but exhaustion blanketed me in half sleep until I managed to fully pass out a couple of hours ago. Now my head was a lead weight, lips parched, tongue like a mound of sand. I squinted against the sun peeking over the purplish clouds stretched low over the horizon, leaned over, and searched the floor around my chair for my water bottle, but I'd left it in the library. The breeze flipped up the corner of a large white towel someone had draped over me.

Someone screamed again. Two voices. From inside the ship.

Felix grunted from the next lounge chair over, tugging his own towel up to his chin.

"What the hell?" I said.

"You were kicking," Felix mumbled, like he thought I was insulted he was no longer curled up with me.

"Not that—did you *hear* that?"

"Hear what?" He shaded his eyes.

There it was again. Someone calling for help.

Someone who sounded an awful lot like Silas.

I threw aside the towel and scrambled to my feet. Brown speckles filled my vision from standing too quickly, and I gripped the back of the chair to steady myself.

"Rocky, wait up," Felix called after me as I rounded the corner to the doors and hurtled down the stairs, following the sound of Silas's voice.

I found him in the hall on Deck 8, back against the wall, keeling over with a hand gripping his good knee, swearing loudly.

"Silas?"

He straightened, his face drawn and pale, his sideswept hair disheveled, a look of terror in his eyes. "Oh God, Jade."

"What's wrong?" I asked as Felix caught up behind me. A few people down the hall poked their heads out to see what all the fuss was about.

"It's Lainey. I don't . . ." He hobbled back a couple of steps from her door.

"What's going on?" I insisted.

"Sheffia went to get help. I don't—"

"What happened?"

"I . . . I told her I'd meet her for breakfast before class. Ran into Sheffia . . ." He was nonsensical, his eyes wavering between mine, in utter shock. "There's . . . there's blood all over the room . . ." He covered his mouth like he was going to be sick.

Blood drained from my own face. For some reason, my first thought was that his wound had reopened. I glanced at his jeans, which hid whatever bandage might be covering it. "Do you need to go to the clinic?"

"Not *my* blood."

I gaped at Lainey's door.

"Jade, I think someone killed Lainey."

By the time Zofia corralled Felix, Silas, and me down the hall and into the library, I'd replayed the memory of that blood all over Lainey's cabin a thousand times. There was no dead body. No sign of Lainey. Just blood. Lots and lots of blood. It stained the ruffled white bedsheets, red as rubies, mostly pooled on the left side, like that's where it started. Like that's where she was stabbed . . . or shot, maybe? I hadn't noticed any bullet holes, but I hadn't stayed long enough to search.

Captain Hwang inspected her cabin while Candace ventured to the clinic to see if Lainey had gone for help, even though they'd radioed back that she wasn't there, and one of the security officers checked with Lainey's neighbors to see if they'd heard anything or let her in.

Meanwhile, Zofia kept an eye on us.

I shivered and hugged my jacket closed over my shirt, hiding the dried bloodstain. Silas's blood. But it was nothing compared to the blood all over Lainey's cabin. I'd never forget that grisly scene, especially the streaks on the bed leading toward the balcony, like someone had dragged her, smears coating the rail. The story it told was as clear as the waves breaking the ocean's smooth surface.

Lainey wasn't in the clinic, or in her neighbor's room.

Lainey had gone overboard.

"What's going to happen now?" I asked Zofia, pushing

aside those gory images as she opened the window's curtains, exposing the back deck and, beyond, the endless sea. The table was clear of any evidence we'd played Monopoly here in the library last night. After Felix ran back for my jacket, someone must've put it all away, taken the water bottles, wiped up Silas's blood.

"Depends on what the captain decides," she said.

Silas buried his head in his hands. Whoever cleaned hadn't been thorough enough—dried blood flecked his chair's wooden frame, making Lainey's bloodied room flash through my mind again, along with an echo of my first thought upon realizing she must've gone overboard: *That spoiled, selfish brat got exactly what she deserved.*

But then I remembered the time she invited me and Silas to this silent auction for pediatric cancer she was hosting at Stanford on behalf of her dad's company. Even though it was his alma mater, even though Lainey's little brother had passed away from leukemia years before, he couldn't bother attending. She'd strolled from table to table, flashing her sparkling smile to the guests, her floor-length gown glittering as she bent over and jotted a number on every single item's bid sheet. "Ha, how much are you gonna make your dad spend?" Silas had scoffed.

"He's going to murder you!" I'd said.

She'd only snorted. "It's for the babies. That prick can afford it."

And now she was dead.

A sob escaped my lips. Felix reached for me, but I waved him off. Silas hadn't raised his face from his hands, but still—I couldn't deal with any friction between them. All I could think of

LYING IN THE DEEP

was Lainey, poor Lainey, how terrified she must have been, how much pain she must have felt—

"She has to be *somewhere* on board," Silas finally croaked.

Felix cast him a stony look. "Like where?"

"I dunno. The clinic, right?"

"Candace would've radioed back by now." I glanced at Zofia, and she nodded grimly.

Silas's eyes widened. To think of Lainey clutching her wounds, tumbling over the rail, and crashing into the watery depths below—it was unfathomable. This couldn't be real.

The two-way radio on Zofia's belt crackled. "This is the captain speaking. Mr. Mob, over."

"What the hell does that mean—" Silas started, but then the ship's horn blared three long, resounding blasts.

And then, silence.

After a long pause, I felt the tug of movement to one side, the room seeming to tilt slightly.

"We're turning," I said, breathless.

"Yes." Zofia nodded at the window. "*Mr. Mob* is code for man overboard. Protocol is we circle back and try to search for her." Her voice was monotone, devoid of hope.

Captain Hwang strode in, tall and lean in his bright white uniform, with close-cropped black hair flecked with gray, and a wide, friendly face. I'd seen him around the ship plenty; he enjoyed chatting with the students, the apples of his cheeks shining as he laughed at our misadventures in each country. Now his expression was serious, though his eyes softened as they took in our panicked faces. He extended a hand to me, though we'd already met several times. "I'm Captain Hwang."

He clasped hands with each of us as we stated our names, his grip firm and reassuring, then took a seat. Candace came in as well, wearing her usual jewel-toned blazer and colorful headscarf wrapped in front of her braided top bun. She gave my shoulder a reassuring squeeze before taking the seat between the captain and Zofia.

"Where's the girl who reported this?" the captain asked Candace. "Sheffia, was it?"

Candace tightened her mouth. "Still in the clinic. They gave her something to calm her down . . ."

"Ah." Captain Hwang focused on the three of us again. "Well, as I'm sure you understand, time is of the essence," he said in his Korean accent as Candace opened her tablet to take notes. "If there is any hope of finding Lainey, I need to hear exactly what happened—"

"Can't she be *somewhere* on the ship?" Silas spouted.

At the same time, Felix said, "We heard him shout for help."

And I asked, "Did her neighbors hear anything?"

The captain gave us a tight-lipped, patient smile. "My questions first, okay?" He nodded at Silas. "Tell me what happened."

Silas let out a shaky breath. "I went to get Lainey for breakfast and bumped into Sheffia on the way up. We went into her room, but . . . she was gone, and there was all that blood everywhere, I have no idea what happened—"

"Slow down," said the captain. "How did you get into her room?"

"I have a key—" Silas wiped his upper lip. "Actually, I lost it last night. That's right—the door was already opened."

I remembered swiping that key from the table, *this* table, last night. I checked my pockets, but I only had one key—my own. Frenzied guilt sent shock waves down my spine. If I'd dropped it in the hall, maybe that's how someone had gotten into Lainey's room. I was about to pipe up, but Felix shook his head slightly, a silent plea to keep quiet.

"Why'd you have her key?" Candace prodded Silas.

"She's my girlfriend." Silas's eyebrows furrowed. "But I didn't do this—"

"No one is saying you did," said the captain. "When did you last have it?"

I took it, I wanted to say as Silas frowned, straining to remember. *Right after I stabbed* you. But my tongue went thick in my mouth.

Oh God.

The letter opener.

The thought had crossed my mind when I first soaked in the bloody scene; how blood stained my own shirt—Silas's blood—and how I'd burst into Lainey's cabin last night, clutching that damned dagger.

And there were witnesses. Tate and Miguel saw me outside her room, and I was sure Tate had spotted the letter opener in my grip. Even Silas had glanced down the hall.

Now I understood why Felix had thrown me a silent warning.

Once people connected the dots, they wouldn't just think it was my fault a murderer broke into Lainey's room.

They'd think I did this.

They'd think I killed her.

20

"Let's take a step back." Captain Hwang leaned forward and folded his hands on the table, exuding calmness and authority. Too bad it didn't help my nerves, which felt like they were about to eject themselves from my pores. "When did each of you last see Lainey?"

When I burst into her room with a bloodied dagger.

"I didn't," I said instead, fully panicking.

"You'd never met her before?" asked Candace.

"No, I did. I mean, we used to be best friends. Now we're not. I mean, if she's dead, she's not friends with anyone anymore." Captain Hwang and Candace stared like I was sprouting antlers. "Um, what I mean is, I didn't see her last night, specifically. I mean, I did; I saw her in Sea Haven, across the room, but that was, like, I don't know, six?" Wow, I had to shut up immediately.

"We're not exactly witnesses here," said Felix. "We just heard him shouting for help. You were the last one to see her, right?" he asked Silas.

Silas reddened. "But she was totally fine."

"Not *totally* fine," said Felix.

"Right, obviously," said Silas, flustered. He shot me a worried look, and I almost reached for his hand. Almost.

Candace glanced up from her tablet. "What do you mean?"

Silas's temples glistened with sweat. "Lainey got motion sick, so we left dinner early and went back to her room."

"When was that?" asked the captain.

"Uh . . . I guess around six thirty? But then I was with all of you the rest of the night, until—" He cut himself off, flicking another glance at me, and my stomach clenched. *Until I stabbed him.*

Felix crossed his arms. "We didn't start playing Monopoly until at least eight."

"Dude," said Silas, "she was fine before then. I didn't—"

"Not *fine.*"

"Okay, yeah, she was puking her guts out, but she wasn't *stabbed*, dude—"

"Who said she was stabbed?" Felix narrowed his eyes, his indirect accusation slicing the air between us.

Silas's face went red, but the captain raised his hand. "Please, no finger-pointing. Our top priority is to isolate a time frame when she might have gone over so we can narrow our search. We once had a student go overboard—something like fifteen years ago—and we recovered them."

"Only forty-five minutes later, though . . ." Candace said uncertainly.

Still, my heart fluttered with hope. "Aren't there security cameras?" I asked.

The captain deflated a bit. "Most bigger ships have them. Your congress recently passed a security act mandating them on ships of our size as well, but we have five years to comply."

"They're part of next summer's renovation, right?" Candace asked.

He nodded. "No help to us now." He glanced at his watch and

asked Silas, "When did you and Sheffia go to Lainey's room this morning?"

"Uh, like, seven fifteen, I guess?" Silas's voice cracked. "We usually get breakfast before our eight o'clock class—she always wants coffee, first thing."

Her and me both.

We used to hobble like zombies to the Starbucks across the street before we'd even brushed our teeth. She always had some excuse to cover my drink: she had the app ready, or she was collecting points, or she'd been the one to insist we stay out late dancing. She was kind and generous . . . until she wasn't. A rock lodged in my throat. Lainey was so many shades of gray she might as well have been walking around in monochrome.

The captain rubbed his chin. "Eight until seven . . . eleven hours, then."

Worry lines creased Candace's forehead. "That's a big window."

"It's less than that," I said. Felix shot me a look, but I ignored him. If there was even the smallest chance Lainey was out there somewhere, clinging to something, to *life*, and I could help narrow the search area, I couldn't stay silent. "Silas told us she was sick . . . and I checked on her around eleven, I think? She was definitely in bed then."

"Did she say anything to suggest she was in danger?" asked the captain.

"No, we didn't talk. She was asleep."

Candace tilted her head, confused. "So you *did* see her last night."

"Uh . . ."

"How did you get in, if she was asleep?" asked the captain.

I licked my lips, scrambling for an explanation. The doors automatically locked when they shut, so I couldn't say hers was unlocked, and Silas already said he lost his key, so I couldn't say I borrowed it. "The door . . . uh . . . it was already open?" Like how Silas and Sheffia found it.

"Her door jammed a lot the first week," Silas piped up, setting a reassuring hand on my knee—a hand Felix couldn't see. "Someone from maintenance fixed it, but maybe it jammed again." I remembered seeing her struggle to shut it on day one. Even if that's not really how I got in, maybe it's how her assailant had. Maybe they hadn't used the fallen key after all. Still, it was my fault the door hadn't been shut all the way.

"But you saw her in bed?" the captain asked me.

"I mean, it was dark—I didn't want to wake her up, so I didn't turn on the lights—but I definitely saw her, yeah."

"Are you *sure*?" Felix asked me.

I could see her in my mind's eye, her shadowy form curled up in bed. "Positive."

"Did you see anything suspicious?" Candace asked.

"No," I said. "I didn't go inside, just sorta hovered in the doorway."

"So, wait," said Zofia, "you were the last person in her room last night, and you just happened to be back again this morning?"

My heart lurched. "We weren't the only ones there," I said in a rush. "Tate and Miguel—" I stopped myself, but it was too late.

"Others were present?" asked Captain Hwang.

After the three of us exchanged a look, I gave him a

play-by-play of the evening—who'd played Monopoly, how Tate was the first to leave after a couple of hours, followed by Divya and Miguel a half hour later. I left out the part about stabbing Silas, making it seem like the rest of us simply decided to stop playing before I checked on Lainey, ran into Tate and Miguel in the hall, and went our separate ways.

The captain asked Zofia to get everyone I mentioned to see if anyone saw or heard anything suspicious after parting for bed. Unease clenched my gut. Navya had seen me stab Silas. Surely she would've told Divya by now.

This was going to suck.

Another security officer came in—a tall, burly man with dark skin and a handsome face. Asim, according to his name tag. "I spoke with the neighbors," he said. "Nobody heard or saw anything—no screams, nothing."

"All Lifelong Learners, right?" asked Candace.

Asim nodded. "A family of three on one side, and couples on the other and across the hall. Most said they were asleep by eleven."

I shook my head, baffled.

"Heavy sleepers, maybe?" Silas whispered to me.

"*All* of them?" I whispered back. I imagined some shadowy figure covering Lainey's mouth while stabbing her, and fear surged through me, making my stomach lurch and my toes tingle like a bad case of vertigo. Someone on board did this. Someone *murdered* her. Who the hell could it be?

"Well, get out there," Captain Hwang ordered Asim. "I want all hands on deck keeping a lookout."

"Yes, Captain." Asim headed out.

"Should we make an announcement?" asked Candace. "People will have noticed we turned around."

The captain wiped a hand down his face, then said in a low voice, "I want a better idea of what we're dealing with . . ."

It struck me then that the captain was out of his depth. He wasn't a detective. Nor were the security officers.

As he and Candace murmured together, I whispered to Silas. "How's your leg?"

He pursed his lips. "Hurts. But it's fine."

"Did you go to the clinic?"

"No. Jamal tried to get me to go, but . . . he cleaned it the best he could. He had gauze in his first aid kit, so."

I gaped at his jeans as though I could see Jamal's handiwork through denim. "You didn't need stitches?"

"He still thinks I might—he was paranoid as hell I'd bleed out or something. I'm pretty sure he stayed up all night . . ." He trailed off as Zofia returned with Navya, Divya, Miguel, and Tate. That was fast.

Navya rushed over. "Omigod, are you okay? Where were you—"

"I'm fine," I cut her off. Guilt tightened my chest—of course she would've worried when I didn't come home last night. I glanced at Divya, but she only looked confused; maybe Navya hadn't filled her in yet.

The captain stood so Navya could take his seat, and Divya slumped into the last empty chair between Silas and Zofia, clasping her sherpa robe closed. Her black hair was tangled and matted, like she'd just rolled out of bed. "What's going on?"

Tate asked groggily, leaning against a bookshelf. Miguel stood next to him, a bit green.

"Are we in trouble?" Divya asked.

"No," said the captain. "But one of your classmates might be, and I need to know if any of you saw anything—"

"Who?" asked Divya as Navya said, "What happened?"

"It appears one of your classmates has gone overboard. Lainey Silverton."

Navya and Divya gasped, Miguel's mouth dropped open, and Silas winced, shaking his head in denial. Tate's gaze ping-ponged between me and Silas. Icy tendrils spread through my veins, remembering his eyes snap to the bloodied dagger clenched in my fist outside Lainey's room.

No. He couldn't really think I'd done this.

But after the captain asked if anyone had seen or heard anything strange, Tate cleared his throat. *Crap.* I threw him a pleading look, but he ignored it. "I saw Jade outside Lainey's room. We both did." He motioned to Miguel.

I tried to look calm, to swallow the heat creeping up my neck. "They already know I was there," I said. "I was checking on her."

Tate frowned. "Why were you so hysterical, then?" Felix's posture went rigid.

Dammit, Tate. This wasn't a first—he'd been the one to point me out in that window at the Tower of London—

Oh.

The Tower of London.

Someone had targeted Lainey with that stone slab.

I remembered Lainey's urgent whispers to Silas at Windsor—someone made her feel unsafe. At the time, I thought she was being a drama queen. At the time, I thought she meant *me*.

She was right to be afraid.

But I didn't do this. "I swear, I didn't—"

"Jade was obviously upset about Silas getting hurt," said Navya, trying to help me but failing miserably.

Captain Hwang frowned. "Silas got hurt?"

Navya clamped her lips, realizing she'd messed up.

"Just a small cut," Silas said quickly.

"How?" Candace asked, her brow furrowed.

"It was an accident. I, uh . . . I was checking out this souvenir Jade bought. I wanted to see how sharp it was." Silas laughed, an obvious forced chuckle.

"What kind of souvenir?"

"A letter opener," I said, "designed like a mini sword. It was sharper than we thought." I waved it off like it was no big deal.

"I saw you with it," said Tate, "outside her room." My mouth fell open, lost for words, terrified and hurt. "Well, what? I saw what I saw!" True. I wasn't entitled to him covering for me. But so much for thinking he was my friend. "And I saw him drag you out of there." Tate pointed at Felix. So he'd seen that part, too.

"You did go inside Lainey's room?" the captain asked me.

It felt like the room was spinning, the floor turning into a swirling black hole that would suck me in and squish me into oblivion. "I didn't go any farther in than the doorway. I looked in, saw her curled up in bed, and left. That's it."

Tate huffed skeptically.

"Don't be ridiculous," said Felix. "She was in there for, what, ten seconds? There's no way she had time to stab Lainey and single-handedly lift her over the rail. And she was on the top deck with me all night after that—she didn't do this."

Silas narrowed his eyes at him. "What the hell were you doing up there?"

The corner of Felix's lips quirked. "What do you think—"

I clasped Felix's hand and shook my head. Now wasn't the time to rile up Silas.

A muscle twitched in Silas's jaw, but then he slumped and covered his mouth, too shocked and broken to bristle over this now. Even if he still loved me, he must've cared for Lainey. I knew full well it was possible to have feelings for two people at once.

"Anyway—" Captain Hwang started.

But Felix cut him off. "Aren't these things usually the boyfriend?"

My heart jolted, and Silas blanched. "I didn't do it!" he yelled.

Felix crossed his arms. "No?"

"Please—" the captain tried interjecting, but Silas shouted over him, "No, you jackass. I was in my room all night. Ask Jamal. Like I said, he stayed awake all night after he bandaged me up." Though he'd only told me that part.

Candace's expression had morphed from concerned to suspicious. "How bad exactly was this cut?"

Navya threw me a leery glance, perhaps no longer believing I'd stabbed him by accident, considering what went down afterward.

Holy hell.

"I dunno," said Silas. "Does it matter? Point is, I was in my room all night—"

"You could've done it this morning," Felix said simply.

"Felix!" I exclaimed.

"Well, he *could* have."

"But Sheffia was there, too."

"He could've done it right before that."

The cords in Silas's neck bulged, and he opened his mouth to retort, but the captain raised a hand and his voice. "I need focus, *now*." Everyone went silent. "Okay. Now, where did the rest of you go after witnessing this scene outside Lainey's cabin?"

Tate visibly swallowed, and Miguel seemed to be trying to dissolve into the wall behind him.

"I didn't witness anything," Divya piped up first. "I'd passed out by then." She thumbed at Miguel. "He's *my* witness."

Miguel nodded warily. "She was so out of it, I took her back to her room." Candace raised her brows. Navya gave Miguel a panic-stricken look, but he kept rambling, "Then I went to get water in the Cantina and ran into Tate, and then we saw them outside Lainey's." He pointed to us. "Then—"

"I came back here," Navya cut in, "to put away Monopoly." So, she was the one who cleaned everything up—even Silas's blood. "Then I went straight to our room. Divya was already asleep. I read for a bit, then fell asleep, too. And that was that."

"When you came back here, did you see anyone else in the hall?" the captain asked Navya, but she shook her head.

"Hang on, back to you two." Candace motioned between Tate and Miguel. "Where'd you go *after*?"

"Back to our room—" Tate started as Miguel said, "Down to six—"

Tate shot Miguel a death glare. Divya rubbed her lips, worry creasing her brow.

"Oh. Right," Miguel said in a small voice. "Things are a bit . . . hazy . . ."

"Good Lord," Candace huffed. "You were all drunk as skunks, weren't you?"

"Um . . ." said Divya. "No?" Navya grimaced, while Miguel looked fascinated by something on the ceiling.

Obviously, yes.

Captain Hwang exchanged an exasperated look with Candace. "Alright. Clearly, we have a lot of open questions, but right now we need to focus on finding Lainey—"

"Are you serious?" I said. "We have to find out who did this."

"Once we reach Gibraltar," said the captain, "local authorities will board and do a thorough investigation. They'll do interviews, sweep for fingerprints and DNA—they'll find the truth." Dread slithered down my spine. They'd find *my* fingerprints on Lainey's door and the wall from when I fumbled for the light switch.

"Are we separating them until then?" Zofia muttered to the captain. We all exchanged frantic looks—would they lock us all up for that long?

But the captain shook his head. "I want all our resources on search and rescue. Candace, can you call an assembly in the Union? We should let everyone know what's happening."

Candace nodded and bustled off to make the announcement.

"I should also take that souvenir of yours," the captain said to me.

My cheeks heated again.

"I, uh . . ." I stuck my hands in my jacket pockets. Then I remembered. Felix had set it on the floor next to my lounge chair after cleaning it off. "Oh, I left it out on deck."

The captain motioned for Zofia to follow, and she shadowed me to Deck 9 and out to the promenade where Felix and I had slept last night. I stooped next to the chairs, scanning the floor.

A prickling sensation crept over my skin.

"What the hell?" I pointed between the two chairs we'd slept in. "It was right here."

But now it was gone.

21

Panicked murmurs rippled through the packed Student Union, and I gripped my red-cushioned seat's armrests to keep my hands from shaking. Captain Hwang had just said on-stage he believed a student, Lainey Silverton, had gone overboard, and though he hadn't used words like *fell* or *pushed*—nothing to indicate the circumstances—it was like people knew.

"*. . . couldn't have been an accident . . .*"

"*. . . railings are too high . . .*"

"*. . . that super-rich girl, right?*"

"*. . . she'd never have jumped . . .*"

I squeezed my eyes shut, like that'd somehow plug my ears and mute the murmurs. The captain had asked the seven of us to keep mum on the details, only revealing Lainey's identity so people wouldn't panic about who might've gone overboard.

But it was only a matter of time until someone blabbed. Until those whispers were about Silas and me.

Silas was clutching his head in the front row, surrounded by Jamal and a few buddies consoling him like a bereaved spouse in a missing persons case. A shiver rippled through me despite my numerous layers. Eager to lose the bloodied shirt, I'd dashed back to my room before the assembly and changed into my favorite cozy tunic, leggings, and moto jacket in an attempt to quell my persistent trembling. It didn't work.

A hand on my knee jolted me back to reality. Felix. I entwined my fingers with his.

"Your attention, please," said Captain Hwang. "I need everyone to remain calm."

The room quieted except for a lone sob. Sheffia, in the first row of the balcony seating behind me. She clasped her mouth, cheeks shining with tears. I didn't see Tate anywhere. Despite everything, my heart ached for her, having seen that bloodied room, hearing how her friend was officially missing, alone now in a crowded room.

"We're following standard man-overboard procedures," said the captain, "and are backtracking now to attempt a search and rescue. A couple of ships within thirty nautical miles are assisting as well. But the tropical storm we avoided yesterday is heading in our direction, so we can only go so far before posing a risk to the ship."

"*. . . no way in hell . . .*"

"*. . . drowned by now, right?*"

"*. . . needle in a haystack . . .*"

They were right. Of course they were all right.

I could imagine Lainey clutching her wounds as some shadowy figure dragged her from the bed, wrestled her to the balcony, pushed hard enough to flip her over the rail. I could image her falling, plummeting into the murky depths below, then kicking, straining to reach air as her lungs screamed for oxygen. I could imagine her finally breaking the surface as rivulets of blood flowed from the gashes in her chest, sputtering, splashing, flailing as the ship grew smaller in the distance.

Yeah.

There was no way she could've survived that.

Her forlorn gaze during the pool party flashed through my mind, and a sob scraped at my throat. I'd loved that girl—loved her like a sister. And I was furious with her—not just for taking Silas, but for tearing *us* apart. Her and me. We were supposed to explore the world together, to party and laugh and relish the sights together.

And now she was gone. Just like that. And so *violently*.

I couldn't fathom the permanence of it. I'd been abandoned plenty, but that was different . . . Like with Dad, I'd always known he was somewhere out there in the world, going about his business, and I could reach him if I had the guts or inclination. But there was no reaching Lainey now. Our bad blood would seep through the infinite expanse of time, and we'd never stanch it. She'd died thinking I hated her.

"What if we can't find her?" someone called out.

The captain nodded grimly. "The weather in the Azores is too turbulent for us to return. If we're unsuccessful, we'll turn again and continue on to Gibraltar, where local law enforcement will board and investigate."

Investigate. The murmurs picked up again, everyone's suspicions confirmed.

"In the meantime," the captain went on, "classes will proceed as usual, but at least one of the psychology professors will be available at all times here in the Union for grief counseling—Professor Shah, Professor Gonzales, and Professor Bowman." Grief counseling. As though Lainey had already been declared dead. "Please stick to the common indoor areas, and limit your movements to the classrooms, Coastal Cantina, and Sea Haven. The poolside café will be closed until further notice. Do not wander the ship. Lifelong Learners—I strongly advise you do the same."

A chill settled over the Union.

"And," he continued, "if anyone knows something or saw anything suspicious last night, please come forward—you can talk to me or any of the crew, CoB staff, or professors."

Hisses filled the room like a symphony of snakes.

"*. . . is that her?*"

"*. . . she hated Lainey . . .*"

"*. . . used to date her boyfriend . . .*"

"*. . . heard she had a knife . . .*"

To my dismay, people were darting glances at me. I didn't think it'd happen this fast. I tightened my grip on Felix's hand.

"It's okay." He leaned close to my ear. "Don't panic. You didn't do this. You'll be fine."

But panic bloomed in my chest, and my stomach curdled like sour milk. I couldn't be a suspect. This couldn't be happening.

Though being in denial wouldn't help anything.

I had no clue what to do if I were a murder suspect—I never imagined that would happen. All I knew was, I couldn't risk being taken into custody in a foreign country. If Captain Hwang wouldn't launch his own investigation, I had to figure out who killed Lainey myself.

And I had to do it before we made port.

When Captain Hwang dismissed the assembly, I rushed down the center aisle before hordes of students could clog it, pulling Felix with me. I had only one class today—a three-hour-long Business Writing and Communications class in the afternoon—but screw my attendance right now.

As we tore past the campus store and out onto the promenade, Felix asked, "Where are we going, exactly?"

I stopped short. "I don't even know. I need to *think*. I can't believe this is happening. I can't believe she's gone."

"I thought you hated her."

His words sucked the air from my chest. "I didn't want her to *die*." Not like I'd imagined killing her. That wasn't real, but merely a cathartic daydream to grapple with my own pain. I was never going to *do* it. I gripped the rail and inhaled deeply. The sea beyond was so dark from the overhanging clouds it was almost black. What was once a boundless expanse of freedom now held us captive with a killer. "We have to figure out who did this."

"*We?*" Felix rubbed his neck. "I dunno . . . I think you should lie low—"

"People think *I* did this."

"That's exactly *why* you should lie low."

"Oh God. I'm screwed." I paced back and forth, clutching my jacket closed. "Absolutely screwed. No, wait. The key is not panicking—"

A group skirted around us like a school of fish passing a barracuda, darting wary glances my way.

My stomach clenched. "Okay, yes, definitely panicking."

Felix clasped my arms. "You'll be fine. Trust me. Even if some people think the dagger thing is weird, the boyfriend's *always* suspect number one."

"Silas didn't do this, either."

"Do you know that for sure?"

I sighed. "I know you don't like him . . . and I know he's been a bit hotheaded lately. But he'd never *kill* anyone. And anyway, he has an airtight alibi. It couldn't have been him."

Felix raked his hair back and muttered a curse.

A different group from before spoke in hushed tones nearby, but suddenly one of the boys spouted, "There's no way you could've heard that."

"I did, though!" said Briana, an Asian girl with blue-highlighted hair I knew from my art history class. "I know what I heard."

Felix and I exchanged a look, then sidled closer to listen.

"Did you hear it, too?" the boy asked a tall blond girl with glasses.

"No—" she started.

"She was asleep," said Briana. The blond girl must've been her roommate. "But I couldn't sleep. I was reading, and I heard it right behind my head. Our pillows are right under the window."

"But they have two thick layers of glass," the boy insisted.

Briana's cheeks went pink. "I don't need you to mansplain how portholes work. It was loud enough to hear through the glass, and I *heard* a splash, right outside our window."

An icicle lodged in my chest. "When was this?" I piped up.

"Oh, hey, Jade. Hmm . . ." She tucked a blue tress behind her ear. "I didn't look at the clock; I wanna say it was about two?"

"Where exactly is your cabin?" I asked breathlessly. "What side of the ship?"

"Deck 5, on the . . . uh—" She snapped her fingers. "I always mix them up. This side."

"Starboard," said Felix.

"Yep."

Lainey's room was on the starboard side, in the middle.

"Toward the front or back?" I asked.

"Right in the middle."

I darted a frantic glance at Felix, this confirmation staggering.

The blond girl poked Briana's arm and whispered in her ear. Briana's eyes widened as they shifted back to me. She must not've realized I was a suspect.

My pulse thrashed in my ears. "You should tell the captain what you heard. It'll help him narrow the search area."

Briana squeaked, "We will," and their group dashed past Silas in the exact wrong direction of the captain.

Silas.

How long had he been standing there, watching?

"Jade," he said, looking miserable, his eyes bloodshot and watery. "Can we talk? Alone?"

22

I glanced around; a few people moseyed along the promenade, probably figuring the captain's orders were more out of an abundance of caution than a response to a real threat.

"Let's go somewhere private," I said to Silas, still reeling from what Briana had just said.

Felix stiffened. "Are you sure that's a good idea?"

I knew he thought Silas was dangerous, but if anything, I was the dangerous one. I was the one who'd stabbed *him*, even if it was an accident. "It's fine." I set a reassuring hand on his chest, trying to keep my fingers from trembling. "I'll meet you in the Cantina in a few minutes, okay?"

Felix hesitated for a moment, then squeezed my hand and headed off.

Silas and I went in the other direction and found an empty classroom next to the back deck. The moment he shut the door, I spun to face him and crossed my arms. "Well?"

"I just . . . I have to know . . ." He wiped a hand down his face. "I mean, God, Jade, I can't believe I even have to wonder this . . ."

"What?"

"Did you do it?"

My jaw might as well have dropped to the ocean floor. "Are you serious right now?!" I'd thought he wanted to assure me *he* didn't kill Lainey.

"I mean, you did kinda lose it last night . . ."

"Silas! What I did to you was a total accident. You have to know that. I would never *kill* someone."

"Okay, okay." He raised his hands.

I clasped my mouth, struggling not to cry. I couldn't believe he'd think I was capable of something so horrid.

He pinched his brow. "How the hell is this even happening?"

"I don't know." My voice shook. "And, honestly, that's been my mental state for the last few months. How the hell is this happening?" I gave him a meaningful look.

He grimaced for a moment, then surprised me by wrapping his arms around me. "I'm sorry. I'm so sorry." I almost shoved him away on instinct, but his embrace was so familiar, I collapsed into it, tears prickling my eyes. He threaded his fingers through my curls and inhaled deeply, like he always used to—he'd loved the scent of my shampoo, the fresh mix of jasmine and mint. This was everything I'd wanted for months . . . but it brought me no comfort now.

"*How?*" I eked out. "How did this happen?"

I felt him shake his head against mine. "I don't even know. I keep thinking of how everything was before the skiing accident—everything was *great*. And then it all spiraled so fast. But even after all those things you said, turning around and dating your best friend was low. I'm so sorry. I was just so *pissed*."

I winced and leaned back to see his face, frowning. "What d'you mean, 'after all those things I said'? What *things*?"

"You know. What you said when you dumped me."

I pushed myself away from him, unnerved. "Silas, *you* dumped *me*."

He pulled a face. "No, I didn't."

"Yes, you did." I balled my hands to keep them from quivering. "I know Lainey must've said some messed-up stuff about me, but you chose to believe it. You *chose* her over me."

His eyes widened. "She said she never told you about that . . ." He hobbled to a chair, collapsed into it, and mashed his forehead into his palm.

Now I was downright confused. "About what?"

His hazel eyes grew dark, haunted. "I only ever slept with her that one time. It meant nothing. But why didn't you say anything about it then? If you loved me, you would've let me explain."

I let out a nervous laugh. "I'm so freaking lost right now."

His brow furrowed. "Did you know about that or not?"

"What does it matter? You wound up together, so I *assumed* you were sleeping together—"

"*Once.* One time. It wasn't that big a deal—"

"Oh my God, stop. All I know is *you* broke up with *me* in a text, then blocked my number. So don't try to pull any more of this gaslighting crap, and let's figure out what to do now that Lainey's *dead*, okay?"

He shook his head adamantly. "I never broke up with you in a text."

I cursed and whipped out my phone. "I still have it." I scrolled through my messages until I reached his name, his last text from July—

Wait.

This wasn't right.

The most recent texts were from me—my few measly attempts to get a response before realizing he really did block me. But the most recent from him was **Good night xx**. It was after the last time we'd spoken on FaceTime; he was heading to a baseball game and a party, and afterward, he'd texted me this.

But that awful text from two days later, the one I'd memorized—**Hey Jade, it's over. We haven't been working for a while. I'm with Lainey now and it's not up for discussion. We're both blocking your number, so don't bother trying.**—was gone.

I didn't remember deleting it. I hadn't read it since before leaving Sacramento for Amsterdam. After a while, I couldn't look at it anymore. Maybe the last time, I'd decided to get rid of it for good.

Either way, the text was gone now.

"I . . . I guess I deleted it."

"Or maybe you dreamed it."

"No, there's no way—"

"*You* emailed *me*," he said. When I stared blankly, he went on, "You said you didn't want to be with someone who didn't have a future. You said you knew it was my fault—"

"No! That never happened." I had no memory of that either. This was unreal. I'd never even *think* that, let alone write it in an email. I'd asked Lainey for that internship for him so he'd *have* a future. And even if he didn't—even if he hadn't a penny to his name, even if we had to move to his hometown in Tennessee—I still would've wanted to be with him.

"Yes, it did." He cursed. "I wish I hadn't deleted it. I was so . . .

so *hurt*. I wanted to talk to you so bad, but you said you never wanted me to contact you ever again."

I gaped at him. "Then why did you block my number?"

"I didn't."

"What about all these texts I sent you?" I showed him my screen. "Obviously I wanted to talk."

He studied it, stupefied. "I never got those."

Now it felt like we were both losing it. "Check," I insisted. "Check to see if I'm blocked."

He pulled out his phone, tapped over to his settings, and found the Blocked list. Blood drained from his face. "I swear to God I didn't block you."

But there was my name, in his block list.

"Lainey did this," I whispered. "She must've used your phone to text me, then deleted the text and blocked me." I'd already suspected she'd somehow tricked us into breaking up but hadn't realized it'd gone further than emotional manipulation. This was complete sabotage.

"And then, what?" His tone sharpened. "She phished your email or something?"

"Exactly." My eyes burned with the threat of tears. It felt like she'd stabbed me in the chest from her watery grave. This deception—this complete and utter betrayal of our sisterly bond—hurt more than anything. It hurt more than losing Silas, even.

I should've known better all along.

"Holy—" Silas's shock turned to fury, and he gripped his phone so hard his knuckles turned white.

I shook my head. "I can't believe you thought I'd break up with you over email."

"You thought I broke up with you over text."

Touché.

Silas let out a bitter chuckle. "You know," he said, "she got *so* mad on my behalf. Called you a social-climbing whore." I flinched. "And I was so hurt, so angry, I must've been so damn desperate to believe her." He slammed his fist on the desk.

"What Lainey wants, Lainey gets," I said.

Finally, he huffed and shook his head, grief creasing his forehead. "I mean . . . I guess I should be flattered? How can I be this angry at someone who . . . who's . . ." His voice cracked as he trailed off.

"Did you love her?" The words slipped past my lips before I could stop them. I hated myself for it—for still caring what the answer was, for thinking of her in the past tense, for giving up hope that fast, though I knew it was foolish to have hope at all.

I wasn't even sure she deserved my hope.

"No." He answered quickly. Too quickly. My eyebrows shot up. "I mean, I cared about her. A lot. She was fun. Free-spirited, you know? And she had this wild side . . . I dunno. She sure made things interesting."

I couldn't help but smile. "That, she did."

"And she didn't seem to mind that I wasn't perfect. That's something we both dealt with a lot . . . this intense pressure to be perfect all the time."

I could see that. Though unlike Lainey with her dad, Silas inflicted that pressure on himself.

"But we never had super-deep conversations, you know?" Silas went on. "We partied a lot, drank a lot."

"You cared about her enough to join CoB."

"She convinced me to come. Said it'd distract me from the fact that I lost my spot on the team. I thought what she really meant was, it'd distract me from losing *you*. But I figured, what the hell? Cool way to see the world, and I could do my physical therapy exercises wherever. And she was right—I did need an epic distraction. But then once we got here . . . once we saw you . . ."

"What?"

"Every time I saw you, it was like you were stomping on my chest all over again. She got all uptight; she thought you came here to make us both feel guilty. She called you a hypocrite, since you were the one who'd dumped me." He shook his head. "Now I get why she was so uptight. She thought we'd find out the truth."

This explained why she never wanted me to talk to Silas. Why my presence scared her.

"Wait a minute . . ." I paced back and forth, tugging my lower lip.

"What is it?"

"If she sabotaged *us* like this . . . she might've manipulated others, too. And maybe one of them got furious enough to . . . to . . ." To sink a knife into her flesh. To push her overboard.

There was Miguel's bot-bombing incident.

And did Sheffia still believe I'd caused their friend breakup?

Either way, there was a pattern of behavior. "We have to figure out who else held a grudge against her."

"Hang on." Silas stood, grimacing in pain. "You can't tell anyone about this."

"Why not?"

"If people think we knew Lainey tricked us *before* she died . . . they'll think *we* were the ones who got angry enough to kill her."

Yikes. He was right.

If we each hadn't already had enough of a motive . . . we certainly did now.

23

"What, are you *trying* to give me a heart attack?" Felix said as I slid into the seat across from him in Coastal Cantina. "Being alone with Silas maybe isn't the best idea right now."

My own heart skittered, and I wasn't sure if it was because he suspected Silas or because he cared enough about me to trigger a cardiac arrest. Maybe both. I set down the empty glass I'd just chugged water from and wiped my mouth, still parched. "He wouldn't hurt me."

"It's not just that." He glanced around. "The conversation's shifted from you to him. People are saying *he* did it."

My jaw dropped. "How do you know? Who's saying it?"

"I overheard some of the chatter." He vaguely motioned around.

I narrowed my eyes. "What, because he's *the boyfriend*?"

"Not just that. I heard people talking about the way he pushed Lainey at the pool party."

I groaned. That's right. After Silas watched Felix and me kiss for the first time, and Lainey tried to plant one on him, he'd shoved her back so hard she'd almost toppled into the pool. And lots of people saw it.

"But if people see you two *together* . . ."

"Okay, okay, I get it." I glanced at Felix's plate loaded with a cream-cheese-smeared bagel, pastries, and buttered toast. "Ugh, how can you even think about food right now?" But I swiped a slice of toast and nibbled at the crust, eyeing the nearby coffee machine.

"So what'd he have to say to you?"

I filled Felix in on my and Silas's revelation that Lainey had tricked us into breaking up.

"Huh. I dunno . . ." Felix balled little clumps of bagel and dropped them onto his plate, mulling this over. "I think Silas made up that whole email-phishing thing."

I nearly choked on my toast. "No way."

"Did he show you the email?"

A pit formed in my stomach. "He said he deleted it."

"Mm-hmm. Think about it. Now he can make up whatever cockamamie story he wants to blame your breakup on Lainey. She's not here to defend herself."

"Listen . . . Silas is smart, but he's not *that* smart."

Felix chuckled.

"What, you think he had the foresight to block my number so he could show me it was blocked later?"

He nodded. "Yeah, maybe."

"I don't think so. The way he was talking last night—he was *convinced* I'd dumped him. And it's not like he was trying to cover his ass just now; he admitted to cheating on me."

Felix quirked his brow. "Is that what he called it?"

"I think his exact words were, he *slept with her*."

His jaw stiffened. A prickly feeling crept up my neck—that feeling you get when you can sense someone watching you. I glanced around, but nobody seemed to be paying me any mind.

"This is a moot point, anyway," I said. "Silas has an alibi. Jamal was in their room all night."

"But who else would've done it?"

"Well, let's make a list. Lainey has quite a few haters." I pulled up the Notes app on my phone. "There's Miguel . . ." I typed his name. "Thanks to that bot-bombing incident. He's devastated his profiles were suspended. And he seemed very convinced Lainey bought all those fake followers. Whether or not she actually did it, he believed it." And now that I knew the lengths to which she'd gone to manipulate Silas and me, I wouldn't put it past her.

"Hmm." Felix drummed his fingers on the table. "I can't picture Miguel stabbing someone."

"Before yesterday, I couldn't picture *myself* stabbing someone, either." I shuddered, almost feeling the dagger in my grip, the blade sinking into Silas's leg.

"That was an accident."

"Still."

He blew air between his lips. "Alright, who else?"

"There's Tate. He's had a problem with Lainey since night one—well, more her dad, but still. And the way he was being all accusatory earlier *was* kind of weird—"

"Wait, what's that about Lainey's dad?"

"You haven't picked up on that? Tate has this *huge* grudge against him. Actually, you were there when he first brought it up. At the welcome dinner. Remember?"

Felix tilted his head, straining to recall it.

"Derek Silverton?"

He clamped his lips and shook his head.

"The billionaire?"

"Sorry, I don't keep a running list of billionaires in my head at all times."

"Haven't you heard of Sanatek? It's one of the biggest pharma companies in the country—"

"Okay, yeah, that rings a bell. What does Tate have against him?"

"He told me at the pool party, 'It's his fault my mother's dead,' and just yesterday he found out Sheffia's parents work there and totally flipped out. I think he thinks it somehow caused his mother's death."

Felix tightened his grip on his glass of water. "Opioid overdose?"

I frowned, confused.

"His mother. Was it opioids?"

"No, I know what you meant, but . . ." I thought most opioid overdoses these days happened when people got their hands on counterfeit pills or opioid-laced heroin, not the prescribed stuff. But Sanatek *did* sell opioids; I remembered one time last year Lainey panicked when a professor assigned her a piece on the opioid epidemic. "She's making us publish our features on Medium," she'd told me. "But opioids are Sanatek's biggest moneymaker. If I accidentally say something I'm not supposed to know, and Dad finds out . . . he'll *kill* me."

I'd suggested she ask to publish it under a pen name, and

that's what she did. She'd deleted the article after getting her grade back and seemed to have gotten through the incident unscathed, and I'd forgotten about it till now. Either way, it'd be pure speculation to guess opioids killed Tate's mom.

"I don't know," I said. "He didn't get specific." Still, I added Tate's name to my list. "Who else? Sheffia, maybe?" I thought of her crying at the assembly earlier. "Lainey treated her like scum this whole trip. And remember what I told her in Lisbon? How Lainey called her a user and wanted to drop her?"

Felix cocked his head. "I can't imagine her lifting Lainey over the rail . . ."

I shot him a look. "What, so only a dude would be strong enough?"

"Hmph."

"She's strong. Athletic. I bet she could do it. Maybe she faked a panic attack after 'finding Lainey's room all bloody'"—I made air quotes—"to make herself look innocent." I added her name. "And we have no clue where she was last night." I glanced around the crowded room, and my eyes locked on another pair staring straight back.

A shiver coasted down my spine.

Sketchy Bob.

He wasn't even in the Cantina—he was out on the promenade, staring through the window with this vacant expression. I remembered that prickly feeling a few minutes ago, that sense that someone was watching me.

I turned back to Felix. "What if we're totally overthinking

this?" I whispered, though there was no way Sketchy Bob could hear me out there.

"What do you mean?"

"Look out the window to the right."

Felix looked the wrong way.

"*Your* right, my left. I knew to switch it."

He snorted but looked. "That guy? No way."

"Why not? He's a total creeper." I suddenly remembered something and gasped. "He was at the Tower of London!" Navya, Divya, and I'd had to speed-walk along the ramparts and through a few of the towers to lose him. "Maybe he was the one who dropped that rock on Lainey!"

Felix furrowed his brow. "Just because he was *there* doesn't mean—"

"I saw him ogling Lainey at the pool party. Maybe he's obsessed or something." I glanced back, but Sketchy Bob had vanished.

"Tons of dudes ogle girls," said Felix. I made a disgusted sound. "I only mean, just because he's some weird loner who finds hot girls hot doesn't mean he's a murderer."

I folded my arms. "Why are you shooting down *every* possible suspect?"

"Because there's only one person I think did this."

Silas. "That's impossible. He stayed in his room all night, and he told me Jamal was so paranoid he'd bleed out, he stayed awake *all night*. It couldn't have been him."

Felix cursed, tugging his fingers through his hair.

"Please, Felix. I know you hate him. But if people think he

killed Lainey, and they know about our history, they might think I was in on it. The police might arrest *both* of us. We have to figure out who really did this to save *both* our asses."

Felix held my gaze, his dark eyes filled with worry. "Fine. So who should we start with?"

24

The prospect of grilling people made my nerves sizzle and pop. I hated confrontation to begin with, but throwing murder into the mix whipped up a whole new level of social anxiety. Plus, I knew what it was like to be wrongfully accused. I didn't want to make anyone else feel that way.

But I couldn't just sit and await my own condemnation.

I convinced Felix that we should corner Miguel first. If anyone were to blather and incriminate someone—potentially himself—it was him.

I knew he didn't have class now, so we eschewed the captain's orders and scoured the ship from bow to stern, deck by deck. Nobody tried to stop us—all available crew and CoB staff were out on deck, scanning the ocean for Lainey. We crept along the gusty promenades, roved the packed restaurants, peered into classrooms, poked our heads into the library, fitness center, hair salon, and dean's office, and pounded on his cabin door.

But it was like Miguel had slipped into an alternate dimension.

He ignored the messages I managed to send on the sluggish CoB messaging system, and nobody we asked could recall spotting him, either.

"How has nobody seen him?" I asked as we took the elevator back up to Deck 9. "He loves gossip, and murder's the most salacious kind. You'd think he'd be all over this, TikToking about it or something."

Felix shrugged. "He could be in literally anyone's cabin."

"Do you think he's hiding? Or . . ." Dread snaked through me.

"What is it?" Felix asked.

"No, I'm just being paranoid . . ."

"Say it," Felix prodded.

"Well . . . you don't think something could've *happened* to him, do you?"

Before he could answer, the door slid open, and Divya was standing there, waiting for an elevator.

"Oh, hey, you!" she said. "Is Navya in our cabin?"

"I dunno," I said as we stepped out. "I haven't been there since before assembly."

"Ah, 'kay." She brushed past us to get in. Earlier, when the captain asked Tate and Miguel where they'd gone last night, she seemed to know something . . . something that worried her.

"Have you seen Miguel?" I asked.

"Nope. Haven't seen him or Tate since assembly; I have no clue where those clowns went." She waved as the door started to close. I almost let her go per my usual avoidance of uncomfortable conversations. But I *had* to find out what she knew. I lurched forward and caught the door before it closed. She gave me a questioning look as it slid back open.

"Uh . . ." I stammered, "d'you know where they went last night? After they saw us in the hall?"

A wary look crossed Divya face. "No. Like I said earlier, I'd already passed out by then. Ugh, this headache's trying to murder me . . ." She jabbed at the buttons, even though I was holding the door open.

"It's just that earlier," I persisted, "when we were talking to the captain, it seemed like you knew something. Did they tell you?"

Divya pinched her lips. "I swear, I have no idea."

"You're pretty close to Tate, right?" Felix asked.

"We're just friends." She stepped back off the elevator, looking slightly defeated. "Navya gets all pissy about it, but I don't like him that way. I *told* her I'm into this girl in my politics class—"

"No, I don't mean like that," said Felix. "Did Tate ever tell you about his parents at all?"

She shook her head. "It's just him and his dad. His mom died recently; apparently that's why he wants to go to law school. Something about some lawsuit that never took off, yada yada, justice for other families." Divya snapped her fingers, trying to recall. "Guh, to be honest, we were pretty wasted. I don't remember much else."

"Do you remember *how* his mother died?" I prodded.

"Yeah, actually." Divya folded her arms and leaned against the doorframe. "She was taking meds for some heart condition, and the price was suddenly jacked up. I don't remember if it was that her insurance wouldn't cover it or they couldn't afford it, but either way, she wound up having a heart attack."

"When was this?" I asked.

"Last spring, I think?" she said, confused.

Felix and I exchanged a horrified look. I was willing to bet

Sanatek was the company that had jacked up those drug prices.

And revenge was an awfully good motive for murder.

"I think we should tell the captain," I said to Felix after Divya took off.

He shook his head. "He was pretty insistent on focusing on the search."

"But if we think Tate might've killed Lainey—"

"We don't, though," he said. I narrowed my eyes at him. "Well, I at least want to hear what Tate has to say about all this for himself. Don't you?"

I wrung my fingers. "What if he snaps or something?" The more I thought about it, the more it made sense that Tate had done this. Not only did he have a motive, but the way he'd hurled accusations my way twice now was super sus. Maybe Sketchy Bob wasn't the one who dropped that stone at the Tower after all. Maybe it was Tate. The crowd below had formed so fast, I couldn't tell who came from where, and I'd only assumed Tate had shown up with Jamal and Sheffia. He *had* been hovering behind them slightly. And then he'd rushed to point me out in the window. Later he claimed he hadn't meant to accuse me specifically, but either way, he'd diverted attention from himself.

"You don't really think he's dangerous, do you?" Felix asked.

"I don't know—" I gasped, then whispered, "Look, there he is!"

Tate didn't seem to see us as he rushed down the stairs by himself. Felix and I exchanged a look, then wordlessly crept after him to Deck 6. He hurried into the fitness center, of all places, though he wasn't exactly gym-ready in his jeans and button-down.

I peered at him through the window in the door. "Well, let me go talk to him alone."

"What? Why?" said Felix.

"You're not exactly the king of subtlety," I said. "And I think I might know how to get him to fess up."

"I want to hear what he has to say."

"I'll fill you in after . . . I don't want it to look like we're ganging up on him—"

But it was too late—Tate was rushing back out the door. He stopped short at the sight of us.

"Oh, hey, Tate!" I pretended to only just see him. Felix remained silent.

Tate stiffened.

"Were you working out?"

"I, uh . . ." He patted down his sandy curls, eyeing me warily. "I was looking for someone."

"Who?"

"No one."

That wasn't suspicious at all.

"Are you okay?" I fixed my expression into something resembling empathy. Being confrontational would only make him defensive.

Tate adjusted his glasses, puzzled. "I'm fine . . . ?"

"Good. I just wanted to clear up what you saw last night." I stepped forward, and he backed up in equal measure. "I couldn't live with myself if you thought I had something to do with what happened to Lainey. Your friendship means too much to me."

His Adam's apple bobbed. "It does?"

"Of course." I clasped my heart and pretended Felix wasn't standing right there, judging this little performance. "I thought we had each other's backs. I know you had nothing to do with it, either, even after what happened in London. I mean, obviously that was just a prank." I waved it off like it was no big deal.

Tate's eyes bugged. "You saw me?"

Bingo.

Tate must've hunched low as he slid the rock off the rampart, run stooping to the next tower, out of view, and dashed through it to the next rampart and down the nearest flight of stairs before rejoining Sheffia and Jamal in the milling crowd.

"I did." I tried to keep my face impassive, but I couldn't do anything about the look of surprise on Felix's.

Tate was sweating bullets now. "Then why didn't you say anything? People thought *you* did it."

I had to act like I wanted to help him—like I'd *already* helped him. If he trusted me to protect him, maybe he'd confide in me. Maybe he'd admit to a worse crime.

"I didn't want you to get in trouble. It's not like she got hurt or anything; obviously you just wanted to scare her. But if I told, you could've been thrown out of CoB. I mean, God, you've been through enough."

"What do you mean?"

I swallowed hard. "What happened to your mother . . . I figured, why should you pay for throwing that rock when nobody paid for what happened to her?" I sensed Felix tense next to me, like he was holding his breath.

"You know about that?"

I nodded, steeling my nerves. "I'm so sorry. It's so unfair."

A muscle in his cheek twitched. "Yeah, it is. That jerk-off got a couple months of bad press for jacking up those prices, and then totally got away with it. Meanwhile, my mother *died* so he and his spoiled, stuck-up family could get even richer. It's complete bullshit."

There it was.

I couldn't help throwing Felix a glance. His jaw was taut as he tried and failed to hide his reaction.

Tate noticed this time and took a sharp breath. "Hang on . . . How'd you know about all this? Did I tell you . . . ?"

I stepped back, my pulse racing. "Not until now."

He blanched. "Oh, so now you're going to . . . Listen, I did want to scare Lainey at the Tower. I wanted her to call home to Daddy and cry about it, so he'd for *one moment* see what it's like to know his family wasn't safe. Just for one stinking moment, to feel that stab of fear, right in his chest." He slapped his own chest.

I nodded. "You wanted revenge."

"Not like that. That's as far as it went, and you *know* it—"

"So where'd you go last night?" Felix finally piped up. "After you saw us in the hall?" I remembered the death glare Tate shot Miguel when Miguel told the captain they'd gone to Deck 6.

Tate clasped his hands behind his neck and screwed up his face, struggling for words. Then he let out a low growl. "We went down to six, alright?" He motioned down the hall. "To one of the empty classrooms."

"Why?" I asked.

"We wanted to try some pills." I must've made some judgmental look, because he scoffed. "Oh, please. Your boy does it plenty."

I shifted my gaze to Felix, startled.

"Not him. Silas."

"Silas doesn't mess with drugs."

"Uh, yeah he does. Sheffia told me."

I shook my head adamantly. She had to be lying. "But . . . why go to a classroom?"

Tate blew air between his lips. "We didn't want to bring them back to our cabin in case someone searched it or whatever." But if they could get busted in their cabin, they could get busted in a classroom, too. This didn't make any sense.

"What kind of pills?" Felix asked.

"Does it matter?" said Tate. "Point is, that's where I was, and I've got a witness, so don't you dare try to pull any bullshit." He talked tough, but his face was taut with fear. He knew as well as we did that only one person could confirm this story.

Miguel.

And he was the one person we couldn't find.

25

After Tate bolted, claiming he had to get to class, Felix turned to me with a hint of a smirk on his lips. "So, you didn't chuck that rock after all, huh?"

I flicked his sleeve, then watched Tate disappear into the stairwell. "Like hell he didn't mean to hit Lainey. It fell *right* where she was kneeling."

"I think he was telling the truth," said Felix. "He fessed up to dropping that stone way too easily."

"Only because he thought I *saw* him do it."

Felix shook his head. "I don't think so . . ."

"Well, maybe he admitted that to look innocent of the worse crime," I said. "Like a false confession."

"That's when you admit to something you *didn't* do to get away with something else."

"Okay, fine. But that explains that whole ridiculous drug story."

"I think that was true, too," said Felix.

I crossed my arms, leaning against the wall. "But Tate had a *reason* to want to hurt Lainey. He could've been planning this all along. Maybe while researching Sanatek and Silverton, he found Lainey on social media. She did post about her plans for CoB last spring. He could've applied after seeing that."

Felix dragged his fingers through his hair. "But then why

would he tell people about his mother? Obviously that'd make him look suspicious."

"Seems like he only ever mentioned it when he drank. Maybe he didn't mean to let it slip. And then he spotted an opportunity last night—again, while drunk, maybe even high—and . . ." I made a slicing motion across my neck.

Felix side-eyed me. "So, which is it? Was he plotting this all along, or did he do it on a whim?"

"Oh, I don't know." I rubbed my brow. "All I know is, Tate's only supposed alibi is missing."

He chuckled and rubbed my arm. "Even if you're right—which you're not—and Tate *did* kill Lainey, I'm sure Miguel's fine. Tate's not some serial killer."

A chill zipped through me. "Serial killers don't start out as one."

We headed back to Sea Haven, Miguel's favorite restaurant, and split up to ask around if anyone had seen him or anything suspicious last night. An anxious, morose vibe permeated the walls, and despite the packed tables, it was quiet save for the occasional grunt or moan—the closer we got to the storm, the more the ship swayed, unsettling people's stomachs again.

My desperation for clues trumped my usual shyness, but some people lurched from my path as though I'd sink a blade into their flesh right in the middle of a crowded dining hall. Most listened to what I had to say, though, and reported seeing nothing, apologetic they couldn't help more.

"Miguel . . ." said a Black girl in the buffet line, toying with one of the long braids flowing down to her hips.

"He's that influencer who's always trying to rope people into his videos—"

"Oh, yeah!" She snapped her fingers, and her ladybug-charm earrings jangled. "I do know that kid. He wanted to know about my skincare routine or whatever, and I was like, 'Um, what skincare routine?'"

I chuckled. "Have you seen him today?"

She mashed her lips together, thinking. "Nope. Sorry."

"No worries. Did you happen to stay up past midnight? Hear or see anything weird?"

"Nah." She shuffled ahead and picked up a plate. "Had to sleep with my earbuds in to block out my roomie puking all night. I heard some girl say she heard a splash at like two in the morning, though."

"I heard her say that, too."

She nodded, slopping scrambled eggs onto her plate. "But it coulda just been the waves crashing on the boat, right? Wish I heard it myself."

Just then, I noticed Sketchy Bob sitting by himself at a table near the buffet, watching people load their plates. His own bagel sat untouched on the table, and his eyes lingered on a curvy girl bending to reach a spoon from a tray in the back row. Ugh.

But since staring at people was kind of his shtick, maybe he'd seen something.

I loaded a plate of my own with pastries and headed over. As

I slid into the empty chair next to Sketchy Bob, the couple at the neighboring table turned to gape.

Sketchy Bob might sit with you, but nobody ever sat with Sketchy Bob.

Even he looked flabbergasted.

"Hey," I said. "I'm Jade."

Sketchy Bob stared blankly for a moment, eyes roving from my face down to the cinnamon bun I'd started picking apart. "William," he finally said, his voice more resonant than I'd imagined. You'd never know because he never spoke. Before I could ask about Miguel, he said, "Were you friends with the dead girl?"

Not the missing girl. Not the girl who went overboard. The *dead* girl.

I shifted uncomfortably. "Uh . . . yeah."

He tore off a hunk of his bagel. "You never know when someone will be ripped from this world, do you?"

My mouth went dry. "How do you know she's dead?"

"How could she have survived?"

Captain Hwang hadn't disclosed the state of Lainey's cabin at the assembly; all anyone knew was that Lainey was missing, suspected to have gone overboard overnight.

"What do you think happened?" I asked.

"How should I know?" William popped a bit of bagel into his mouth, crumbs falling into his gray scruff.

"Well, I just thought . . . maybe you heard something? Or saw something?" God, this was a disaster.

"Did *you* see something?" Did he only speak in questions?

"I was asleep," I said. "But someone heard a loud splash around two in the morning."

"Yo, Jade," said someone behind me. I twisted to look at the couple who'd gaped before. "Sorry to butt in," said the boy, Ghassan—he was in my business writing class. "Did you just say you heard a splash last night?"

"Not me," I said. "Briana did. You know her, right? The girl with the blue hair? She was in her cabin on Deck 5."

He rubbed his chin. "Interesting . . ."

"What is it?" asked his girlfriend. William slumped in his seat, back in observation mode.

"I went to get water around then," said Ghassan. "And I saw someone booking it down the stairs."

My eyebrows shot up. "Who?"

"One of your roommates, actually. The one with shorter hair." He motioned to his shoulder, indicating the length. Navya.

I stiffened, surprised. "But Navya said she was asleep—"

"Right, that's her name. I don't think she saw me."

"Where were you?"

"I was heading back from the fitness center—the ice machine in there works best."

"Are you *sure* it was her?" I asked.

"Positive. I remember she was going so fast, she grabbed the rail to fling herself around the corner. I thought she might fall or something. So, yeah, it was definitely her."

I rubbed my brow. "The fitness center's on Deck 6 . . ."

"Yep," said Ghassan.

"So Navya was on Deck 7, *at least*," I said. Lainey's cabin was on Deck 8.

Either way, Navya had told everyone she'd gone to sleep around midnight.

And that was a lie.

It took me a while to find Felix, but he'd wound up back out on the promenade, chatting up a group at a table who were shaking their heads or shrugging at whatever he'd asked. When I took him aside and filled him in, he chuckled skeptically. "There's no way Navya killed Lainey. No way in *hell*."

"No, I know that. But why would she lie? Maybe she saw something."

"Oh. Huh."

"Yeah. Let's go find out."

We found Navya in our room, nestled under her comforter in the top bunk, scrolling through her phone with earbuds in. Not only was she blatantly disregarding the captain's orders to stick to public indoor spaces, but willingly hanging out in this cramped space was a *choice*. Or maybe that was just my hang-up—it reminded me too much of home, of Mom's overbearing presence suffocating me in that tiny house. If I ever had a break between classes, I spent it on deck in the open sea air.

I knocked on the door as we entered to get her attention. She perked up and tugged out her earbuds but winced when she saw it was me. "Oh, hey." As she studied me with those wary, wide brown eyes, I knew she hadn't hurt Lainey.

But she was hiding *something.*

"Hey," I said. "Okay if Felix comes in?"

"Sure, I guess." She glanced around. There wasn't exactly much room for guests.

"You don't have class?" I asked as Felix and I sat on my bed.

"Not for another couple of hours." Her tone was distant. Cold. My heart cracked—she was always so warm and friendly. She climbed down and perched at the edge of Divya's mattress so she wouldn't clobber her head on the top bunk, still gripping her phone.

I motioned to it. "Has the news gotten out yet?"

"Not that I've seen." Another frigid, terse response.

"That's surprising," said Felix.

"A few people on board tweeted about it," she elaborated for him, "but nothing's taken off. Though, I dunno—I'm only using a few minutes of Wi-Fi at a time. You'd think they'd open it up to everyone without data limits today, but no."

"The system's not built for that," said Felix. "Everyone would eat up all the bandwidth and it wouldn't work for anyone."

"Ah," said Navya.

It was only a matter of time until the news of Lainey's death blew up on social media, and then it would be chaos. Had Candace already gotten in touch with her parents? Derek Silverton was so wealthy, I wouldn't be surprised if an arsenal of helicopters and search boats descended on the area within minutes to search for his daughter—though whether it'd be more out of desperation or to milk the drama for his public image, I couldn't be sure.

"You didn't happen to see if Miguel tweeted or posted anywhere, did you?" I asked.

"No." Navya frowned. "Why?" Worry filled my chest.

"We haven't been able to find him," said Felix.

"Oh, huh."

"So, listen." I shifted nervously. We couldn't waste time. "We wanted to ask if you saw or heard anything weird around two in the morning."

"No," Navya snapped. "I told you earlier, I was asleep by then." Her harsh tone took me aback.

"Well," said Felix, "the thing is, someone saw—"

"Heard a splash around then," I cut him off as I caught his eye, shaking my head slightly. I didn't want to accuse her of anything. "On the starboard side, near the middle of the ship—under where Lainey's room is."

Navya visibly swallowed. "Oh."

"If it's true . . . it confirms Lainey went overboard after all," said Felix.

Her eyes widened. "It does?"

I nodded. "And that's when it happened."

"Oh," she said again. Then she remained silent, eyes darting between us.

"So, again," said Felix, "if you saw anything at all—"

"I couldn't have, could I? I was asleep." Suddenly she stood and grabbed her messenger bag, shoving in her laptop. "Crap,

I've got to get to class! Totally lost track of the time . . ."

"I thought you didn't have class for another couple of hours," I said.

"I got confused. Thought it was an A day." She slung the bag over her shoulder. "Uh . . . see you later." With that, she was out the door.

"Well, that wasn't shady at all," Felix muttered.

My eyes widened. "There's no *way* she killed Lainey . . ."

"I'm not saying she did," said Felix. "But she's clearly covering for *someone*."

26

"It has to be Tate," I said as we descended the winding staircase toward the reception lobby under the stained-glass atrium. "The only other person Navya would cover for is her sister, but there's no way Divya killed Lainey. Tate did it, I know it. Oh God. What if he killed Miguel—"

"Nobody killed Miguel," Felix assured me. We'd systematically combed each deck all over again, starting with Deck 9. But it was like Miguel had vanished into thin air.

"It's not like him to disappear like this."

"Maybe he's afraid to get in trouble."

I stilled, gripping the brass-railed banister. "So you *do* think he's hiding?"

"Not for killing Lainey." Felix had passed me a couple of steps, so turned to face me. "I bet he's paranoid he'll get busted for doing drugs with Tate. I'm pretty sure it was their first time trying anything like that."

"If Tate was telling the truth."

"I think he was."

I stubbornly shook my head. I knew what Felix thought— what he wanted me to think. That Silas was the only legitimate suspect. But he couldn't have killed Lainey.

"Maybe there's another reason they went to Deck 6. Maybe Tate went to grab a knife from Sea Haven."

At first I'd assumed Lainey's killer had used my missing letter opener, but I doubted they could've muffled her screams while stabbing her as hard as they would've had to with a blade that blunt. Unless every one of her neighbors slept like the dead, they must've used a sharper knife to quickly slit her throat or something—

"Or maybe"—Felix took a step up so we were at eye level, his hand on the banister millimeters from mine—"you're trying to spin a narrative you want to believe. One that hurts less."

My stomach wobbled, and I wasn't sure if it was because he was right, or what I'd been picturing, or the waves crashing into the boat, or because of how close his hand was to mine, the intensity of his stare, the electricity pulsing between us. It would be so easy to close the gap between us, to sink into his comforting embrace that already seemed so familiar.

But suddenly, a tugging sensation pushed me into the banister, stronger than a wave-induced wobble. "We're turning again . . ." I gripped my mouth while clinging to the rail with my other hand. *Lainey.* They were giving up on her. "*No.* It's too soon. They've barely even looked."

"They probably don't want to get too close to the storm," said Felix. "And the chances of her surviving . . ."

"Oh God." I squeezed my eyes shut. I'd never see her again. As much as she'd hurt me, it killed me to know we'd never resolve this. That I'd never fully understand why she turned on me.

Felix cupped the back of my neck and touched his forehead to mine. "I'm so sorry." I wrapped my arms around him and let him hold me back.

But then my eyes snapped open. "That means we're heading to Gibraltar . . ." I glanced up at the enormous gilded clock behind the brass statues atop the staircase. How long would it take to get to Gibraltar? It had taken at least three days to get from Lisbon to the Azores.

Either way, time was ticking.

"Come on," I said, heading down. "We have to find Miguel."

Felix rushed past me again, blocking me at the foot of the stairs. "Where are you going?"

"Miguel and Tate's cabin."

"That's a waste of time; we already looked there—"

"You don't have to come, but *I'm* checking it again." I skirted around him. "It'll take, like, five seconds."

The corridor on Deck 4 was empty. "Look," I whispered, slightly out of breath, next to the door with Miguel's sign-up sheet. It was ajar. "Someone's home now." Felix's eyebrows shot up.

I started toward it, but he grabbed my hand. "Hang on."

"Why?"

Worry creased his forehead. "If Tate's in there, not Miguel—"

"Oh, so *now* you think he's dangerous?"

"No, I—" Felix set his mouth in a thin line. "I mean, better safe than sorry, right?"

I clucked my tongue but let him go ahead of me and knock on their door. "Miguel?"

He inched the door open. "Hello? Anybody home?" After a quick peek inside, he started to swing the door shut. "Nope, nobody's here—"

"But why's the door open?" I pushed it back open and stepped inside.

Just like the last time I was here, Miguel's bottles and vials were crammed on his desk, as well as the coffee table and nightstand between the two beds. I peeked inside the large closet packed with clothes and towels, then motioned to the closed bathroom door next to us. "Maybe he's in there?"

Felix pounded on the door. "Hello? Miguel? You taking a dump?"

"Oh my God." I shoved Felix as my heartbeat returned to normal, and his eyes glinted mischievously.

There was no response from the bathroom, or any telltale sounds of bodily functions or faucets running.

"See?" said Felix. "Nobody's home. Let's go." He was already out in the hall.

"Hang on, Mr. Know-It-All." If nobody was using the facilities, it wouldn't hurt to peek inside. I tried the handle. The door was unlocked, so I swung it open. Right then, I knew that sight would haunt me for the rest of my life.

Whenever I'd walk into a bathroom, I'd see him hanging from the shower rod, his neck at an unnatural angle.

Whenever I'd drive past a graveyard, I'd see his purple face, his eyes bulging from his skull.

Whenever I'd watch a funeral scene, I'd see his mouth frozen in a last desperate gasp for breath.

I shrieked and stumbled backward, slamming into the closet.

Felix lunged over like he thought I was being attacked, jumping to defend me, then saw what made me scream. "Holy—"

We both stared, rooted to the floor in shock. We were too late to save him. Too late to help.

But it wasn't Miguel.

It was Tate.

27

Your mind can go to weird places after seeing a dead body.

In the moments after, I kept thinking about how I'd never be able to wear these clothes again. The cozy burgundy tunic. The leggings I'd worn so much a tiny hole kept fraying above one knee no matter how many times I'd sewn it closed. The vintage moto jacket, a hand-me-down from Mom.

Even as I raced up to the dean's office to get help.

Even as I watched Captain Hwang press a fist to his lips as he took in the scene.

Even as Zofia and Asim took pictures of Tate's corpse from every angle.

I kept thinking about how I'd have to get rid of these damned clothes. Because they were what I was wearing when we found Tate.

"You two shouldn't be here," Candace said to Felix and me as we waited in the hall, one hand clutching her stomach like she was going to be sick. "Do you have class now?" She gently grasped my elbow to lead me away. "Come on—"

"No, wait," I said. Captain Hwang clustered with the security officers in the bathroom doorway, obscuring our view of Tate. A body bag was splayed open on the bed, awaiting its contents. "Tate knew I didn't believe him. He knew I thought he killed her." I thought of him sweating bullets earlier, begging us to believe him. "He must've panicked . . . Maybe he felt guilty and knew he wouldn't get away with it . . ." *Or, he was innocent, and I was wrong.*

But even if Tate did kill Lainey, I didn't want *this.*

"Are you saying you think Tate killed Lainey?" said Candace as Captain Hwang came into the hall, clearly having overheard.

"I . . . I don't know . . ." A sob clawed at my throat.

Candace set a comforting hand on my shoulder. "Shh, it's okay."

"Can you tell us why you'd think that?" the captain asked gently.

I told them everything, hardly pausing to take a breath—about what happened at the Tower of London, the grudge Tate held against Lainey's father, how we'd cornered him into admitting he wanted revenge.

"Did he leave a suicide note or anything?" Felix asked.

"I didn't see one," said the captain. "Could be on his laptop."

"But—" I tried.

"We should get you two to class . . ." Candace interrupted, then hesitated, glancing at the captain. "Or should we cancel classes for the rest of the day?"

"No," he said firmly. "I want everyone to stay occupied. Tonight, after dinner, we'll have another assembly and explain what's happened. And the psych team should plan to schedule sessions with each student over the coming days."

Candace nodded. "We already talked about that."

"Alright—"

"Captain?" Zofia called into the hall. "We're ready to take him down."

As the captain strode back inside, I leaned to catch a glimpse of Asim clutching Tate around his abdomen while Zofia untied the bedsheet. There was a lot of grunting and shuffling once they freed him, and suddenly, they were carrying him into the bedroom. Felix entwined his fingers with mine and tugged me close, keeping me from getting a better look. He was right—I'd already seen enough to fully traumatize myself.

"Seems Miguel doesn't have class right now," said Candace, frowning at her tablet screen. My heart dropped. This would crush Miguel . . . "Do you know where I might find him?"

"No," said Felix.

"We actually came here looking for him," I said.

Zofia's voice floated into the hall. "Asim, check out this bruising."

"Now, let's see your schedules . . ." Candace kept scrolling.

"Pressure from the sheet?" Asim said uncertainly, making my flesh crawl.

"Looks like you two each have class in fifteen minutes," said Candace.

"I don't know," said Zofia. "It kind of looks like . . ." Her next words were too muffled for me to hear.

"You really expect us to sit through class after—" Felix started, but I tugged my hand free from his grasp and rushed past Candace into the room. She tried to hook the back of my jacket but caught nothing but air.

I froze at the foot of the bed, and bile rose in my throat. They'd closed Tate's eyes, but his mouth still hung open in that last desperate gasp for breath. He was right there, but he wasn't, not really. Everything he'd been this morning—this boy who wanted to see the world, who missed his mother, who sought justice for her, who was torn up over a girl, who'd just discovered his knack for filming videos—was *gone*. Everything he was, everything he'd stressed about, every mistake he'd made, all that conflict and bitterness swirling in his mind, had vanished in a flash.

I slid my gaze to where Zofia still pointed—a deep purple spot on his neck, right above his Adam's apple. Not a line from the sheets pressing into his skin, but oval, like a sour grape.

"A thumbprint." The words escaped my lips like a rush of wind.

Zofia's eyes snapped up to me, but everyone else gaped at Tate's neck, the implication of that mark too terrifying to fathom.

Suddenly, the room burst into noise.

"Someone killed him—" I said.

"You don't know—" said Candace.

"That doesn't mean—" said Asim.

Everyone spoke over each other except for Zofia, who still watched me with narrowed eyes, until Captain Hwang called for quiet, raising his hands. "Please, let's not panic—we have no idea that's a thumbprint. It could be from pressure from the sheet."

My blood ran cold as I glanced at the bruise again, and Felix's jaw clenched.

"Candace, get them out of here," said the captain. "Zip him up," he instructed Zofia and Asim, motioning to the body bag. "We'll wait for the police—"

I tugged free from Candace's grip on my arm. "We can't just *wait*."

"This is outside our purview," said the captain. "Protocol dictates we hand over any investigations to the authorities at the next port."

The authorities. The police who'd scour Lainey's suite for prints and DNA, and probably the same in Tate's cabin. And now they'd find my fingerprints on *both* of their doors, in *both* of their rooms. Felix's, too. And, like Zofia was clearly thinking, we'd been present for both discoveries.

We could be in serious trouble.

"Screw protocol!" I said, panicked. "If there's a killer on board, *actively* still killing, nobody's safe!"

"Jade . . ." Felix touched my arm. He'd gone all quiet—maybe from shock—but I couldn't stay quiet, too.

"No." I held firm despite the panic rising in my chest. "We only just turned around. It took us days to get to the Azores. We can't wait days to figure out what's going on." Nor could I stand for people to suspect me for days. We had to figure out who'd really done this. *Now.*

"It won't take days to reach Gibraltar," said the captain. "We weren't rushing to get to the Azores; now, at full speed, we'll get to Gibraltar in eighteen hours."

Even that seemed too long, with a killer on the loose.

But that meant I had less than one day to prove I wasn't the killer.

Ideally nobody else would wind up in a body bag in the meantime.

28

There should be a law that says you don't have to go to class right after seeing a dead body.

But I didn't make a fuss when Candace dragged Felix and me to our classes (after walking us to our cabins to grab our laptops like kindergartners to our cubbies), afraid to give her a reason to consider locking me up. And though Professor Waxler tried painting normalcy over reality's slashed canvas with his usual three-hour business writing workshop, I couldn't focus as Tate's bulging eyes and Lainey's bloodstained sheets looped through my mind like some twisted carousel.

Felix and I had agreed to meet at Coastal Cantina afterward, so the moment class let out, I zoomed up to Deck 9, anxious to figure out what the hell was going on. But I froze when I spotted Sheffia on the promenade. She was hugging her knees to her chest on a lounge chair, her pink designer tote bag at her feet, still as a statue as she stared out at the whitecaps. Her usual glossy auburn waves were tied back in a messy ponytail, a few loose strands whipping over her eyes and nose. She barely winced, let alone moved to tuck them aside.

The hairs on my arms stood on end. She and Lainey might've reconciled to some degree, but Lainey had treated her like crap this whole trip. Even when they'd seemed glued together at the hip, Lainey had obviously wanted to glue Sheffia's mouth shut.

And Tate had tossed her to the curb over something so out of her control.

But she didn't strike me as a murderer. And however one-sided her friendship with Lainey, and however things ended with Tate . . . they were both gone. She looked so miserable, sitting there by herself. Once she found out what happened to Tate, she'd need *someone* to lean on. Nobody should have to endure that much grief and trauma alone.

I took a deep breath and approached. "Hey, Sheffia."

Her jaw clenched, and a muscle along her temple twitched— her only acknowledgment of my presence. It reminded me of the dark look that had crossed her face when she blamed me for sabotaging her friendship with Lainey.

Still, I sat one chair over, facing her. "You okay?"

Her lower lip quivered slightly, and she seemed to be gnashing her teeth together. Tears streaked down her face, dripping splotches onto her baby-pink sweatshirt. She didn't bother wiping them, or even blinking.

This had to be grief. Before their falling-out, she and Lainey'd probably had countless sleepovers, movie nights, and shopping trips; they'd traveled together, shared a limo to prom, graduated together. And now Lainey was gone, and so brutally. As much as my unresolved tension with Lainey would torture me forever, Sheffia would likely experience something similar.

"I'm so sorry—" I reached for Sheffia's hand, but she flinched back, so I let my arm drop. She finally took a deep, trembling breath and shifted her stony gaze farther from me, like she couldn't even bear to look at me.

I'd been so busy pondering her guilt or innocence, I'd forgotten to consider she might suspect me.

"Jade!"

I snapped my head up to see Silas hovering near the Cantina's entrance. My stomach sank. I shouldn't risk talking to him again. But what could I do, ignore him? As I moved to stand, Sheffia snaked her arm out with almost unnatural speed and latched onto my wrist.

I gasped.

"Tate's dead, isn't he?" Sheffia rasped.

My eyes widened. How'd she know?

Sheffia's eyes darted between mine, watery and urgent. I swallowed a sob and nodded. She released my wrist and covered her mouth with shaking fingers. "Silas . . . he's . . ." But the wind seemed to whisk her words away.

"Yeah, he's right here." I waved him over. Perhaps he was her closest friend now.

He hobbled over, and guilt gnawed at my gut. I did that. I made him limp.

"Oh, hey, Sheffia." He must not have seen her from there. As he sat at Sheffia's feet, she shrank back to give him space, clutching her knees even tighter, her cheeks shining.

He set a comforting hand on her knee, though his own fingers were quivering, and his eyes were red and puffy. "Are you okay?"

Sheffia squeezed her eyes shut, like she wanted to block out every punch the universe had thrown today. *Girl, same.* I wished I knew how to console her, how to make this right. But I felt every jab to my own heart.

"Listen." Silas struggled to keep a tremor from his deep voice. "Everything seems terrible now, and it's going to feel terrible for a while. But you're strong, and you'll get through this. Everything will be okay."

My throat constricted as I met his gaze. That was almost exactly what I'd said to him when we found out he'd lost his scholarship, when he knew his career was finished before it had even started.

Sheffia shook her head, struggling for words, and Silas patted her knee. "We'll get through this togeth—"

She hurtled from the chair with a sob and darted to the stairwell doors, stumbling as a wave rocked the boat. Silas moved to follow her, but I reached for his arm.

"Let her go. She obviously wants to be alone right now." She might've even been afraid of us.

He leaned back into the chair with a sigh, rubbing his eyes. "Ugh. Hell if I know everything will be okay, anyway."

After a moment's hesitation, I said, "There's something you should know."

"What?" said Silas.

I blew air between my lips. "It's Tate . . ." His name soured on my tongue, as did what had to come next. "He's dead."

"*What?!*" His eyes bugged. I told him how Felix and I had found Tate hanging in his shower, about the suspicious thumbprint on his neck, how I thought someone killed him and made it look like a suicide.

"But . . . why . . . why would someone—" Before he could finish the question, he stood, stumbled to the rail, and vomited over the edge. I followed him and rubbed his back as dry heaves consumed him, his whole body trembling. A few people farther along the promenade groaned rudely, but I ignored them.

Finally, Silas stepped back and wiped his mouth, then turned and leaned against the rail, shaking his head. "I can't believe this."

"Come on." I led him back to the chair and sat next to him, rubbing his back again in circular motions as he held his head in his hands, just like months ago, after his skiing accident. He'd seemed like a lost puppy then. To be fair, he'd lost so much, all because he hadn't spotted a rock in the snow. Wrong place, wrong time.

Tate had mentioned something I'd forgotten in the horror of what happened next—that he knew Silas had used drugs. I'd brushed it off as a lie, sure Silas would *never*.

But what did I know? Even before Lainey tricked us apart, he'd cheated on me with her. And there I'd been, thinking we were in love, that we'd get married after graduating, that we were so wrapped up in each other there couldn't possibly be room for anyone else.

I was wrong. How much else was I wrong about? I *had* to know if Tate was telling the truth.

"He told me something earlier today," I said nervously. "Something about you."

Silas clutched the edge of the chair. "Who? Tate?" I nodded. "*What?*"

"He said you've done drugs."

Silas blanched. "Oh." He didn't deny it.

My stomach curdled. "Since when? You never even used to drink."

"It's not that big a deal."

I folded my arms and stared.

Finally, he let out a small huff. "It was only a few times—" He reached for me, but I pulled back. Earlier, when we figured out Lainey had faked a breakup email from me, he'd said, *You said you didn't want to be with someone who didn't have a future. You said you knew it was my fault.*

"When did you start?" I pressed.

His mouth became a thin line.

"Were you high when you went skiing? Is that why you crashed?"

"No," he said firmly.

"Is *that* why they took your scholarship?"

"No, I wasn't high then. That was a freak accident. I never would've done that before careening down a goddamn mountain." He pinched his brow. "They did some tests in the hospital before I went into surgery. I guess it's a standard thing to make sure there are no complications during the procedure or whatever, and there was still Adderall in my system from a couple days earlier, and I didn't have a script."

"Jesus—"

"It's not like I was addicted or anything! I only did it a few times, before some big games, to get my energy up."

"Why would you need it *at all*, though? You were so good."

He shook his head. "My average was slipping. I was spending so much time with you, and I wasn't getting much sleep."

The nerve endings in my fingertips flickered. "Don't put that on me. This was *your* mistake." Whenever I slept over, sleep was never on his agenda, and as flattered and willing as I'd been, he'd always been the one to initiate sex. I wouldn't accept fault for this.

He let out a deep sigh. "It was crap timing. And if Coach Banner hadn't gone and dug around in my locker, they might not've—"

I screwed up my face. "You kept it in your *locker*?"

"Jay drove us to Lake Tahoe right after a game! I didn't have a chance to move it. I didn't know what was gonna happen." He said it like it was his teammate's fault for keeping them on a tight schedule, not his own fault for illegally having prescription drugs in the first place.

"Wow. Just, wow." How'd I been so oblivious to all this? "Is this why you really lost your scholarship?"

His shoulders slumped. "Yeah."

"Why didn't you tell me the truth?"

"Why d'you think? I was scared you'd leave me!"

"Why would I leave you over that?"

"Well, look how sensitive you're being about it now."

"That doesn't mean I'd leave you!"

"Sure," he said. I stared, aghast, and he screwed up his face. "Up until that point, I'd done *everything* right. I practiced all the time, worked out hard, did whatever it took to up my game. I studied enough to swing Stanford. I impressed the scouts, got a good girl, kept my grades up. And then I made one mistake. One stinking mistake. And it made me lose *everything*. So I thought . . . I thought . . ."

He thought I'd dump him over one mistake, too. But his words jarred me for another reason: I'd merely been a bullet point on his list of successes. Meanwhile, he'd meant the world to me.

"And then when you emailed me," he went on, "er, when I *thought* you emailed me—you said you knew the truth, and that's why you wanted to break up. And I believed it."

My breath hitched. "So Lainey knew the truth?"

"No— Well, I didn't think so . . ."

But she must've found out. And she knew me well enough to know I wouldn't break up with Silas over it. I would've been angry and upset, sure, but everyone makes mistakes. I'd loved him enough to stay with him, to get him treatment, to help him through it. When it came to Silas, I'd already been in for-better-or-worse mode. But apparently *he* didn't know that.

I couldn't help but wonder what Lainey saw in him after all this, when it clearly bothered her enough to tell Sheffia about it. She never got serious with anyone, always bored after two or three dates, finding some flaw to pick at until it left too big a scar and she ghosted him. Ghosting always was her MO. Except this time, she'd ghosted *me*, and went through such lengths to take him from me.

"My mother's the only other person who knows." He shrugged, like that was no big deal. She'd always been too busy for Silas, but he'd been driven enough to steer his own ship. Somehow that made the fact that he'd sabotaged his own future even worse. "Coach said losing the scholarship was enough punishment, so he kept it from the media. All anyone else knows is I got injured too badly to keep on playing. But if I fought the scholarship reversal, it would've come out. So I didn't—"

Out of nowhere, Silas was doused in soda. He raised his hands and let out a yelp of surprise.

"Oof!" Felix was suddenly in front of us, holding two plastic cups from the Cantina—one mostly full, the other empty, its contents now soaked into Silas's sweater. I'd barely managed to shift aside in time. "Gah, I'm *so* sorry."

Silas stood, sputtering—some of it had sloshed in his face. "What the hell, dude?"

I wiped my neck, not having fully escaped the splash zone.

"There was a wave . . . I lost my footing," said Felix. "Truly, man, I'm so sorry."

Silas pawed at his face. "Gah, some of it got in my eyes . . ."

As he ambled off to clean up, Felix sat on my other side and passed me the full cup. "Well, you can have this one."

I took it, still trying to register what had just happened. "Uh . . . thanks?" As Felix wiped some soda off my cheek with his thumb, I eyed the remaining brown liquid in the other cup, distinctly remembering him saying he didn't like soda. "You spilled that on purpose, didn't you?"

Felix made a *pfft* noise. "No, I didn't. Like I said, there was a wave." But there was an unmistakable glint to his eye.

"Wow," I muttered, shaking my head.

He suppressed a grin for a moment before his expression fell. "In all seriousness, you should be more careful. If people see you two conspiring out in the open like that—"

"We weren't *conspiring*."

He darted a furtive glance at the crowd nearby. "Well, that's what it looked like. And, you should know . . . I heard security debating whether to lock you both in the brig."

29

"Are you serious?" My throat constricted in panic. "They even *have* a brig on this thing?" I pictured Zofia shoving me and Silas into some dingy jail cell.

"I mean, it's probably just some tiny room."

"How can they think I did this?" I trembled so aggressively soda sloshed over the edge of my cup. "They can't . . . they wouldn't . . ."

"C'mon, you must be freezing." Felix pulled me to my feet and led me into the Cantina, keeping a guiding hand on the small of my back. We found an empty two-seater, and I clasped my hands on the table to keep them from quivering.

"What should I do?" I croaked.

He leaned forward. "We can't let Silas get away with this. And we have to prove it was *just* him. I'm your alibi—"

"Will you stop trying to pin this on him?"

"Will you stop being in denial?" His hands sliced the air.

I tugged back my curls. "It's not denial; it's *physically* impossible."

Anxiety pierced his eyes. "You don't know that."

"Yes, I do. Even forgetting that Jamal is a rock-solid alibi, Silas has been hobbling around all day. You really think he could overpower Lainey when he can barely put pressure on his leg?"

"I think he's faking."

"You *saw* me stab him."

"I think he's faking how bad it is."

"That's ridiculous."

"Is it?"

"Yes!"

"Just . . . hear me out, okay?"

I crossed my arms, considering him for a moment. "Fine."

Felix took a deep breath. "Okay. So, essentially, I think Silas realized Lainey bamboozled him last night when you stabbed him, not today. It was obvious you truly didn't think you dumped him; he must've put two and two together right then. And he's clearly still into you. He said so last night. So later, after Jamal dozed off—because he must've dozed off at *some* point—Silas went looking for you. Maybe he went to your cabin first, I don't know, but either way, he found us curled up on Deck 9. And in a fit of jealousy, he grabbed your dagger and went to wake up Lainey and confront her about whatever she did to break you up over the summer. They got into a fight, it got out of hand. Maybe he threw the dagger overboard after her.

"Then, on his way out, Navya spotted him, and maybe he threatened her to stay quiet. Then he went back to his room, waited a few hours, then pretended to find the bloody mess this morning."

With that, he leaned back in his chair and folded his arms, looking rather pleased with himself. But his theory had several gaping holes, and none of it explained what happened to Tate.

"Are you finished?" I asked.

"Yeah."

I stood so fast my chair nearly toppled back. I'd seen Jamal at a table near the entrance. We were going to settle this once and for all.

"Where are you going?" Felix asked.

"To get Jamal. And if he says he stayed up looking after Silas all night, you *need* to drop this."

"Wait. What if Silas killed her *before* we played Monopoly?"

I shook my head. "He would've acted weird."

"He *was* acting weird."

"He acted like a jealous prick, not like he'd just killed someone. And I *saw* her in bed."

"Maybe she was already dead then," said Felix. The base of my skull prickled. But, no, that was impossible. "You said it was dark—"

"You saw her room this morning. You saw all that blood streaked across the wall. She was alive and fighting when someone dragged her to the balcony. And what about that splash at two in the morning?" I shook my head again. "Whatever happened, happened then, and all at once."

Before he could stop me, I marched across the crowded restaurant.

Jamal sat at a packed table near the entrance, zoning out at his untouched sandwich with bloodshot eyes.

"Jamal?" I said.

He glanced up, startled.

"Can I talk to you for a minute?" I motioned for him to follow me.

He eyed me warily, and my stomach churned. "Uh . . . sure."

Jamal followed me back to Felix, who dragged a chair over from a neighboring table.

"How are you?" I asked.

Jamal collapsed into the seat. "Man, I dunno. You hear about Tate?"

Felix and I exchanged a look. Word was spreading like wildfire. Or maybe Jamal heard it from whoever told Sheffia. Either way, he clearly didn't know Felix and I were the ones who'd found Tate.

"Yeah," I said. "It's awful. Truly awful."

Jamal and Tate had been buddies since before they explored the Tower of London's armory together, though I guessed they weren't close enough at the time for Jamal to notice or care that Tate slipped away for a bit to chuck a rock at Lainey.

"I can't believe he'd do this," said Jamal. "I mean, that boy was up in his feels a lot. He was real bent out of shape over his mom. And I know he was upset about Lainey." Felix and I exchanged another glance. "Still . . . he was just telling me yesterday when we were walking around at port how he couldn't wait for Japan, how he was gonna stuff his face with sushi. Those were his words. Who says something like that and then kills themselves?"

Someone who panicked . . . or someone who *didn't*.

"Anyway," said Jamal, "what'd you wanna talk about?"

I cleared my throat, but Felix launched right into it. "Did Silas leave your room at any point last night?"

Jamal's eyebrows shot up. "Why? You think he shoved Lainey overboard?"

"No—" I started.

"Something like that," said Felix.

We glared at each other.

"Well," said Jamal, "I'm a thousand percent sure it wasn't him. I was up all night. Honestly, I don't think I could've fallen asleep if I wanted to. That whole incident last night sorta made me rethink all my life choices."

"How do you mean?" I asked.

Jamal shrugged. "I always thought I'd be a surgeon like my parents, but I'm not sure I'm cut out for it. No pun intended." He chuckled, then cringed. "For real, though, the sight of blood makes me sick. How can I slice into people if I can't even look at blood?" I remembered the retching noise he'd made when he first saw the dagger impaling Silas's leg.

"Maybe it was because you were already motion sick?"

"Nah, I've felt that way before. I think I've been in denial, you know? Anyway, I'm *positive* Silas didn't leave—"

Felix cursed—Jamal and I both winced—then stood and stormed off. My heart twisted as he disappeared out onto the promenade. Should I go after him or give him a minute?

"What's his problem?" Jamal asked.

I sighed. "He's strung out. We all are."

"Yeah . . ." He zoned out again for a moment. "You know, that reminds me . . ."

"What is it?"

"Tate *did* do something strange last night . . . but nah, maybe it was nothing . . ." He trailed off.

"What'd he do?" I prodded.

"Well, he came over last night after dinner, acting all weird."

"Define *weird*."

"I dunno. Sorta agitated." This must've been after he confronted me about Sheffia's parents working at Sanatek, but before Monopoly. "I asked if he was okay. He said yeah, but he wanted to make sure *I* was okay. You know, because I got motion sick."

"That was nice of him."

"Yeah, totally, I thought so, too. And he offered to hang for a bit. So we were chillin', playing cards, but then I had to go be sick again. And when I came out of the bathroom, poof, he was gone. Took off for no reason."

I rubbed my upper lip. "Maybe he assumed you'd want to be alone. And he didn't want to be, after what just happened."

"What just happened?"

"He broke up with Sheffia."

Jamal raised his eyebrows. "Oh. Were they *together* together?"

"Weren't they?"

"I don't think so. He thought she was hot or whatever, but he told me once—when we were drinking in London—he was sucking up to her to get closer to Lainey."

Tendrils of ice spread through my chest.

"I told him that was a dick move," Jamal went on, "but he laughed it off. And I figured, whatever, that's his business." He looked sheepish, taking in my shocked expression. "D'you think I should've told Sheffia?"

I set my palms on the table, trying to get a grip on what he was saying. "Did he say *why* he wanted to get closer to Lainey?"

The corner of his lip quirked. "Why d'you think?" But the hint of a smile quickly slid off his face. "Man. He must've liked her even more than I thought, if he was upset enough to do that . . ."

But he wasn't. Tate never crushed on Lainey—if anything, he *hated* her. There was a more sinister reason for this, I was sure of it.

I thought of how Tate saw Felix pull me from Lainey's room. Of how he'd seen the dagger, and his eyes flicked up to mine, calculating. He'd probably snagged the room key after I dropped it. Just like at the Tower of London when he saw me in the window, he'd spotted an opportunity to condemn someone else for his crime.

And he was probably careful, so careful. It was my fingerprints the police would find on the door, on the wall by Lainey's light switch. It was probably my dagger I'd shown off to everyone that killed her.

But it wasn't me. I never got *my* revenge.

And I sure as hell didn't want to take the fall for someone else's.

30

I found Felix on the promenade gripping the rail with his arms fully extended, his sharp jaw tense, frowning at the ocean. Something inside me stirred; I felt this powerful urge to kiss him, to promise that we'd get to the bottom of this, to make him feel as reassured as he'd tried to make me feel.

He seemed to sense me standing there and turned to fix his worried gaze on me. "Hey."

"Hey."

"Sorry about that. I just . . ."

"No, it's okay. This is . . . a lot."

Felix averted his eyes to the ocean again and half smiled. "Understatement of the century."

I leaned on the rail next to him. "We have to get into Lainey's cabin." When we'd gone up and down the halls earlier, nobody had been standing guard outside her room.

"Why would we do that?"

"To wipe my fingerprints off the wall."

He suppressed a chuckle. "You keep bleach in your cabin?"

I bit my lip. "No."

"I don't think it'd matter, anyway." He faced me again, keeping one elbow perched on the rail. "There were witnesses."

"But one of those witnesses is *dead*, and—well, God knows where Miguel is. Maybe Tate did kill him, too—"

"He didn't kill anyone."

I backed away from him, tired of spinning in circles. "Dammit, Felix," I snapped. "If you're going to shoot down *every* theory I have that doesn't involve Silas, I don't want your help anymore. I'm *running out of time.* If I get arrested, God knows how long I'll rot in some foreign prison before the US can exonerate me. If they ever do." I crossed my arms. "So am I going it alone from now on or not?"

He stood stock-still, his face a mask of surprise.

"Well?"

"I'm sorry," he finally said. "I'm just worried. I don't trust Silas. I don't know him like you do."

The tension in my shoulders dissipated. "I get that. But you have to trust *me* on this, okay?"

He held my gaze for a long moment, eyes filled with remorse, then blinked it away. "Okay. So . . . you really think Tate killed Lainey?"

I nodded. "Jamal just told me Tate only dated Sheffia to get closer to her." Felix's eyebrows shot up. "Yeah. He was even more obsessed than I realized. We should search his room; maybe he kept notes on her or something. And we need to figure out what happened to Miguel."

"What do you think we'd find that the police wouldn't?"

Panic tightened my chest. "I don't know. But I can't sit still and do nothing, I just *can't.*"

Felix drummed his fingers on the rail. "How would we even get into either room? Lainey's room does have that balcony . . ."

A thrill of vertigo tore through me. "Are you suggesting we climb inside?"

"If a neighbor lets us in."

"I thought you said wiping away my prints was useless."

"Maybe we'd find some clue in there."

I let out a nervous chuckle. "Oh. Uh . . . let's leave dangling over the ocean as a last resort, okay?"

"Well, you don't happen to know how to pick a lock, do you?"

"No. Are the locks even pickable? They're just card readers."

"Hmm, right."

I tugged my lower lip. "What about stealing a master key? Like the ones the stews use."

Felix raised his eyebrows. "Seriously?"

"Yeah."

"I think the stews only have access to the rooms they're assigned to."

"Right. But the security officers must have more access in case of an emergency. Same with the maintenance crew. Like, if someone's toilet floods their cabin when nobody's home, they need to get in to fix it."

"Yup, forgot about those spontaneously combusting toilets."

I snorted. "You know what I mean."

"Mm-hmm. The registration desk is another option," Felix suggested. "They can print any of the keys. Ah, but then there'd probably be a record of someone creating a new key card for the dead kids' rooms. Security might even get an alert."

I cringed at *the dead kids*. "You don't think Tate's still in there, do you?" My stomach turned as I imagined searching his room with his corpse still on the bed.

"No," said Felix. "I'm sure he's in the morgue."

"There's a morgue, too?" A brig, a morgue . . . what hadn't they managed to fit on board?

"Yeah. All cruise ships have one."

"How do you even know that?"

His lip quirked. "Common sense? People have heart attacks and stuff all the time, even if they're on vacation. I'm sure there's a small one in the clinic, or nearby on Deck 3."

Something in my brain lit up. "Oh! Deck 3!"

I dragged Felix inside to the stairwell. A monitor next to the stairs displayed a map of Decks 3 through 9—well, the accessible parts. Most of Deck 3 was grayed out except for a clinic, spa, and pool. I tapped on Deck 3 to zoom in, then pointed. "Look."

"Huh. I didn't know there was an indoor pool down there."

"Not that. This grayed-out part. That must be crew quarters, right? And what about Decks 1 and 2? There's gotta be a staff dining room, engine room, kitchen, stuff like that. And there must be an office for the maintenance crew, too." I cracked my knuckles excitedly.

"Er . . . someone's gonna notice two rogue students snooping below deck."

Most of the crew wore all-white uniforms, though the stews wore tan button-downs, security wore baby-blue polos, and the spa, store, and fitness center staffers wore peach polos. "Maybe the crew don't wear their uniforms while off duty."

"Still, I'm sure they all know each other enough to spot out-siders. It's not *that* big a crew."

I huffed. "What about the stew stations? There's one on each deck, right in the middle." I'd seen our stew, Julia, load her cart there before. "Maybe they keep their keys there."

Felix followed me down the stairs. "If so, I'm sure they keep the stations locked."

"Let's cross that bridge when we get there."

But a minute later, I was tugging on the locked stew station door on Deck 8.

"Time to cross that bridge," Felix remarked.

"I'm glad this is amusing for you."

He raised his hands. "Hey, I'm just saying—"

"Let's try the one on Deck 4."

But that one was locked, too. I muttered a curse.

Down the hall, Julia's cart rattled as she moved from one state-room to the next. We watched as she took a key card from a tray on her cart, unlocked the door, and dropped it back onto the tray with an audible clatter of plastic before propping the door open.

Felix threw me a bemused look that morphed to mild panic when he saw I was seriously considering this. "No way, Rocky—"

"Yes, way."

"This won't work."

"Yes, it will."

After Julia swapped out dirty sheets for fresh ones at her cart and disappeared inside again, I scuttled past the bow stairwell, my pulse racing. Felix trailed me, but I motioned for him to stay put and tiptoed over myself. I'd have to dart past the open door to get to the cart. Rustling noises floated into the hall. I held my breath and peeked inside as Julia stretched a fitted sheet over one of the mattresses.

Now was my chance.

I scurried past the door to the cart and frantically searched the tray up front. Gah, where was that key? Our ID cards were the signature CoB blue. Ah, there was a yellow card—

"Jade, child."

I spun. Julia had come into the hall. "Julia!"

She smiled warmly. Behind her, Felix was clearly searching for somewhere to hide, wearing the guiltiest expression I'd ever seen. There was nothing but closed staterooms over here. Rather than sprint to the closest stairwell as I would've done, he dodged into the nearest shallow alcove and pressed his back and palms flat against the door as though the narrow bit of wall could hide him.

If I hadn't been so panicked, I would've burst out laughing.

"What're you doing down here?" asked Julia, tucking back her frizzy gray hair. "You shouldn't be wandering."

"Well, the thing is, I uh . . ." I stuttered, scrambling. "I need to grab something from my cabin, but I've locked myself out. Could you let me in?"

"Oh, honey, if you lost your key, you should go to the registration desk. They'll need to freeze your old card and make you a new one."

I helplessly glanced at her master key, desperation watering my eyes. *So close.*

Julia's brow furrowed. "Oh, child, I'm so sorry."

I leaned into it and screwed up my face like I was about to cry.

"You poor thing." Julia rubbed my arm. Felix took advantage of this distraction and dashed to the stairwell. "And on top of everything else. Come, I have just the thing." She put her arm around me and started down the hall. Hope filled my chest for a moment—Felix could nab the key himself—but Julia said, "One second," and went back for it before leading me to the stew station.

Inside the tiny room half occupied by shelves stacked with linens and towels, Julia sat me down on a foldout chair with a tan steward shirt draped on the back and busied herself making tea. I grabbed a tissue and scanned the cluttered desk for key cards. No dice. A metal file organizer hung above the desk, but I couldn't see inside.

"You're friends with the missing girl, yes?" She filled a mug at the water fountain.

"Yeah."

"Tell me about her." Julia dropped a tea packet into the steaming water. "What's she like?" She set the mug in front of me and perched on the edge of the desk.

"Uh . . ." *She was a backstabbing jerk.* But I forced myself to think back before then. "She's kind. Silly. You know how they say some people's smile can light up a room, and you're like, that's so cliché, nobody's teeth are made of light bulbs?" Julia chuckled. "Well, hers really could . . ."

It was like the world glimmered in her presence, and not just in the glamorous sense. She even made petty annoyances hilarious. I remembered this one time, some dude sauntered between us as we took photos without bothering to apologize, and instead of getting annoyed, she posed like a pouncing cheetah, wearing this snarling, bug-eyed expression. I managed to snag the shot while he was still in-frame. That pic got millions of likes.

I smiled at the memory. "She always made me laugh."

"She always *makes* you laugh," Julia corrected.

No. She'd made us very past tense before she died.

But I remembered how she'd looked at me at the pool party, her sorrowful gaze crumbling the cool façade she'd maintained all semester. It'd been like the music, the pool, and everyone around us disappeared, and all that was left was this painful chasm splitting the world between us. A chasm we'd never cross.

My throat constricted. "I . . . I don't think she's coming back—" I gripped the desk as a particularly big wave rocked the ship.

Julia set a consoling hand on my shoulder. "Even if she's gone, her memory will live on in you for the rest of your life."

Okay, now some real waterworks were about to start.

But I couldn't let myself feel this. Not yet. If I thought too hard about how Lainey was dead, how she died, how much pain she must've felt, how scared she must have been, how I'd never see her again, I'd sink into a pit of grief as deep as the ocean floor, and I'd never claw back to the surface in time to clear my name. I imagined sitting in some dark, dingy cell with nothing but a hard cot and crusty toilet, trapped for years with nothing but this mystery of why Lainey turned on me to occupy my mind—

Julia's cart clattered loudly past us, down the corridor.

She gasped and darted into the hall to chase after it.

I leapt to my feet, thinking fast, and dug inside the file

organizer above the desk. There were only papers inside. I slid open the single desk drawer—a pack of cigarettes, a box of rubber gloves, a bottle of hand sanitizer. Nothing useful. I shut the drawer with a huff. Then the tan stew's shirt draped on the back of the chair caught my eye.

Oh. That could work.

I snagged it and bolted into the hall.

Julia knelt next to the cart, checking the brake mechanism. Maybe she assumed a wave had caused it to roll down the corridor, but my guess was Felix had shoved it. "Thanks for the tea," I called over my shoulder. I darted into the stairwell, wiping away a rogue tear as I zipped past Felix and down to Deck 3.

"Rocky! Where are you—"

"Shh." I checked the shirt's pockets—no key cards, just a Zippo lighter and a rubber glove (used, it seemed). "Dammit." I dropped my backpack and shrugged off my jacket, but I couldn't wear the stew shirt over my tunic; that'd look fully absurd. After shooting a quick glance up and down the stairs—the coast was clear—I tugged it off.

"Uh—" Felix flushed as he respectfully averted his gaze from my black bra, but I couldn't care less about that right now.

Okay, I cared a little bit.

I pulled on the tan button-down, ignoring the heat creeping into my own cheeks. It was about three sizes too large and fit like a tunic, covering my butt completely. None of the stews ever wore black leggings, but this was the best I could do.

"Hold this?" I shoved my jacket and sweater at him.

"What are you doing?"

"I'm going to see if there's a maintenance office on Deck 3."

"Hang on—"

I pressed a finger to my lips and crept into the hall without letting him get in another word. On this deck, passengers only had access to the medical clinic, the small indoor pool, and the spa. Double doors past the clinic read **Crew Only Past This Point**. I swung them open and breezed through.

My pulse raced as I hurried toward the stern, arms out to stabilize whenever the ship's tilt unsteadied my feet, passing only a few crew members whose eyes slid past me, focused on their tasks or lost in thought. The rooms here seemed like regular cabins, with no indication any homed the maintenance crew. I rounded the corner to the starboard side and passed a bustling dining hall next to a kitchen noisy with clanging pans and clattering plates. People still needed to eat, even after there'd been a murder or two.

After passing the pool again, ignoring Felix's whispered protestations at the stairwell, I headed toward the bow and back around the other side.

No sign of a maintenance office.

Back in the stairwell, I eyed the rope blocking access to Deck 2.

"Maybe there isn't even a maintenance office," said Felix.

"Of course there is. Someone's got to fix the exploding toilets." I unclipped the rope on one side and let myself through.

"Wait—"

But there wasn't time to wait.

On that deck, I passed even more nondescript doors, more

crew quarters. But then I spotted a door with a small plaque reading **Operations**.

That must be it.

I pressed my ear against the door. A couple of men were inside, their muffled speech unintelligible. I backed away, biting my lip. How could I get them out and catch the door behind them? Knocking would do no good. *Excuse me, hi, can you please go somewhere else so I can sneak in behind you and steal a master key?*

But what if there were some sort of emergency—something needing urgent repair? That'd get them out. Hmm. A stew who noticed something broken would probably radio it in rather than come down here in person. Would any sort of mishap alert the maintenance crew automatically? If there was a problem with the piping, or the boiler, or *something*, would it trigger an alarm?

An *alarm*.

Oh.

I reached into my stolen shirt's pocket and pulled out the Zippo lighter.

Yeah.

That could work.

31

"This is the worst idea you've had yet," said Felix as he shrugged on the uniform shirt over his black T-shirt.

"No, it's not," I insisted as I pulled my tunic back on. "I'm just going to set off a sprinkler; I won't start an actual fire."

"Why not pull a fire alarm?"

"What, and freak out the whole ship? No way. This'll just seem like a malfunction or something. It'll probably trigger an alert, and the maintenance crew will come fix it, and you'll have time to search their office for a key."

"Not if one of them stays behind." Felix bunched his gray jacket in his fist.

"It sounded like there were only two people in there. They'll probably both go. It's worth a shot."

Felix huffed. "Where are you going to do this?"

"Some empty common room." I slung on my backpack. "A classroom, maybe. I'll wait for you outside Lainey's cabin after."

"Good, yes, hang around the murdered girl's room. That's not suspicious at all."

"Okay, fine. Outside the Cantina again."

"And what if this doesn't work?"

I checked the time on my cell. "I guess meet me there either way in like . . . twenty minutes? And then we'll come up with a new plan."

"Alright. But let the record show, I think *this* plan's terrible."

"But look at you, going along with it," I shot back before sprinting upstairs. He muttered a curse and headed down to Deck 2.

There were several common areas on Deck 6, so I started my search for a deserted room there. Sea Haven was still packed, and a few students clustered together in the Union's red plush armchairs. Much to my chagrin, all the classrooms here had classes ongoing, so I headed up to Deck 7. One weirdo was on a treadmill in the fitness center—how could anyone work out at a time like this?—and the sauna was probably too moist for a sprinkler to cause enough chaos.

But the classroom across from the hall stood dark and empty.

I slipped inside, flicked on the lights, and scanned the ceiling, vaguely wondering if this was where Tate and Miguel got high last night. There were two sprinklers—one above the door, and one above the whiteboard across the room. Anyone who walked past in the hall could see through the pane glass door, so I switched off the lights. The light filtering in from the hall was enough to see what I was doing.

I crossed the room to the whiteboard. The cushioned chair didn't seem sturdy enough to stand on, considering the unsteadiness of the ship, but I wasn't tall enough to reach the sprinkler otherwise. Maybe I could shove the desk back and stand on that. I strained to budge it, but it was bolted to the floor—

The door opened and closed behind me.

I whipped around, heart beating fast. The bright hall lights obscured a tall, shadowy figure. "Whatcha doing in here in the dark?"

I knew that voice.

Sketchy Bob.

The hairs on my arms stood on end.

"You're not *hiding* in here, are you?" he asked when I didn't respond.

My voice stuck in my throat. I wished Felix were here, but now I was alone with this creep who'd totally obfuscated earlier when I'd asked him about last night. And there was a whole chunk of time afterward while Felix and I talked to Navya when he could've killed Tate.

My fingers and toes tingled as adrenaline coursed through me, fight-or-flight mode activated. Flight would be tricky with him blocking the door, so I curled my hands into fists, trying to remember the maneuvers I'd learned in the self-defense course Lainey made me take with her. Some good it did her, in the end.

"What do you want?" I spat like an accusation.

He turned on the lights and held up a book. "To find some peace and quiet. It's too crowded everywhere else." He seemed even more threatening than he had as an ominous shadowy figure now that I could see his eyes boring into mine.

"Why not just go to your room?"

"Captain said to stick to the common areas—"

"Where were you last night?" I asked, fully panicking.

He studied me, his forehead crinkling like it pained him to realize I was afraid of him. "Wait, you don't think . . ."

"Where *were* you last night?" I repeated, strained.

He opened and closed his mouth a few times, like he couldn't drum up the right words. Finally, he said, "I never would have done anything to that girl. She . . . she reminded me so much of my daughter."

My eyebrows shot up. "You have a daughter?"

"*Had* a daughter. I lost her last year."

"Oh . . ." I deflated like a balloon leaking air just before it could pop. "I . . . I'm sorry."

"Thanks. Never text and drive, okay? It only takes a moment . . ." His eyes watered, and he raised a fist to his lips. I could almost hear the screech and splintering of metal and glass in my mind. After a long pause, he said, "She always wanted to do Campus on Board. So I'm doing it instead. To experience what she should have. To see what she should have." A rock lodged in my throat as he showed me his phone's wallpaper. "There's my girl."

I stepped closer. A smiling girl was posing with William next to an oversized M&M character in Times Square. She had shiny blond beach waves that flowed past her shoulders, like Lainey's.

"Our last trip," said William. "She loved to travel . . ."

So that's why he always stared at Lainey. At all the girls. He was picturing his own daughter, imagining she was one of them.

I'd been so wrong about him. We all had been.

"I'm so sorry about your daughter," I choked out, barely above a whisper.

"Thank you." He switched off the screen, wincing as she disappeared probably for the thousandth time. I'd caught a glimpse at the time—Felix would still be waiting for the maintenance crew to dash from their office, but our twenty minutes was almost up.

"I have to go . . ."

William nodded, and without another word, I ran.

Of all the venues you'd consider a peaceful sanctuary, a library would top that list, right?

But for some reason, it was deserted.

Maybe it was the blood that still flecked the wood grain of Silas's chair from last night.

Maybe people could sense that something terrible had happened here.

Like in the classroom on Deck 7, two sprinklers jutted from the ceiling—one over the doorway and one across the room above the wall-to-wall bookshelves.

I left the door open so I could make a quick escape, dragged a chair (sans blood) under the sprinkler above the bookshelves, and climbed up, out of view from the hall. My pulse quickened as I flicked open the Zippo lighter, thumbed the wheel, and raised the flame to the sprinkler, squinting in anticipation of a deluge.

I waited.

And waited.

I wiped my forehead with the back of my other hand.

Then I waited some more.

I could picture Felix below deck, arms crossed, leaning against the wall, shaking his head and judging me for my ridiculous idea.

Dammit. Maybe this tiny flame wasn't enough to melt whatever inside the sprinkler would open the valve. I lowered my arm and gaped at a small sticker on the ceiling with a red strikethrough over symbols of a hanger and sprinkler, trying to imagine who'd be foolish enough to hang a coat or something from a sprinkler.

Maybe if I tugged on it enough, like this—

Frigid, high-pressure mist surged from the sprinkler so intensely, I yelped and jerked back, tumbling from the chair.

The open lighter flew from my grip as I shot out my arms and crashed onto the floor with a loud thud. My backpack cushioned the blow somewhat, but pain bloomed up my left arm and into my shoulder. I rolled onto my right with a cry, wishing I could rewind the last five seconds, wishing I hadn't been so foolish, wishing this pain could shrink back into an infinitesimal point in my arm and vanish.

I hadn't heard a crack, but my arm might as well have been on fire. By the time I managed to sit up, I was shivering from the high-pressure mist. I scooted back until I hit dry floor, taking rasping, pained breaths.

That's when I smelled the smoke.

I twisted to look behind me and gasped in horror.

The lighter had still been on when it landed on a shelf next to the old cardboard Monopoly box. The edge had caught fire, and flames already consumed the box and were spreading to other games on that shelf. The sprinkler mist didn't reach that side of the room. Why wasn't the other sprinkler going off yet?

Oh, no. My high school physics teacher once showed us a video of a fire fully engulfing someone's living room within thirty seconds.

How fast could it spread through the ship? Would anyone die because of what I'd just done?

32

I scanned the room, trying not to panic, and spotted a red fire extinguisher mounted next to the door. I grabbed it, but it was heavy—searing pain shot up my injured arm, and I set it on the floor. The flames licked the velvet curtains draping the inset shelves, as well as the books on the shelf above.

Oh God—not the books! If those went up, half the room would be set ablaze. I hacked on the smoke already filling the room and covered my mouth with my tunic's collar. I had to endure the pain. I had to do this.

With a grunt, I picked up the extinguisher again, released the safety pin, aimed it at the fire, and sprayed. Foam doused the flames with a hiss as smoke and steam emanated from the damaged shelves.

"Oh, thank God." I dropped the extinguisher and practically flung myself across the room to grab the lighter, but it was no longer lit. I snapped the cover shut, catching my breath.

Now what?

I didn't stick around to find out in case Felix had already headed to our meeting point, but when I reached the Cantina, he wasn't there yet. My teeth chattered as I waited, and I scrunched my damp curls, hoping they'd dry fast. I could move my other arm, so it wasn't broken or dislocated—it just hurt like hell.

We had to stop trying to investigate. I was so desperate to

avoid a wrongful accusation, I was making myself look guiltier by causing all this chaos. I had to tell Candace and Captain Hwang everything—

"What happened to you?" Felix asked as he finally approached, clutching the balled-up uniform shirt.

"Never mind. I think we need to stop—"

But then he flicked a yellow key card between two fingers like a cigarette.

I gasped and grabbed it.

"You're welcome." He chuckled. "I can't believe that worked. One of the drawers was literally labeled 'key cards,' and it was unlocked. Terrible security."

"We'd already established that." I bit my lip, hesitating. Which was worse: digging for answers when we had the opportunity, or doing nothing and hoping for the best, when two innocent people could wind up in jail?

Either way, the temptation to finally get answers was too great. My eyes flicked up to Felix's. "Ready?" I asked.

"As I'll ever be."

We started with Lainey's room since it was closer, and it looked the same as earlier except for the fact that someone had closed the French balcony doors. My stomach lurched from the sight of deep red blood pooled where I'd seen Lainey curled up in bed, from the sharp, metallic smell tinging the air, from those streaks across the far wall that told the story of how she'd struggled. How she'd fought back.

How she'd lost.

If we'd roomed together, maybe this never would have happened.

Why, Lainey? Why did you have to turn on me? I could have protected you.

Or maybe I would've been killed, too.

Felix shook his head, taking in the scene. "Welp, she certainly did disappear. *Poof.*" He imitated how I'd said it at that London pub. I threw him a horrified look, and his face collapsed. "Sorry. That was crass."

"I wish I never said that," I whispered. I should've been more careful what I wished for. My gaze settled on the bloodstained bed again as I cradled my injured arm. I couldn't even imagine what kind of agony she'd experienced when her skin was sliced open.

"Nothing stands out to me," said Felix, jarring me from my thoughts. "Aside from all the blood . . ."

Clutching my stomach, I clenched my jaw to keep my teeth from chattering as I scanned the room. I inched over to the desk, afraid to touch anything or even move lest I shed a strand of hair for the police to find. Though I hoped they *would* be that thorough. I hoped they'd find out who did this.

Lainey's makeup bag was unzipped next to a contouring palette, a tube of mascara, eyeliner, and lipstick, and a notebook was open to a to-do list of homework assignments. A laptop charger was plugged into the wall behind the desk, charging nothing, the wire dangling into empty space. "Huh," I said. "Her laptop's missing."

Felix furrowed his brow. "Maybe she put it somewhere else?"

I searched the bed and gripped my mouth as another wave of nausea consumed me from all that blood. I stood back and squeezed my eyes shut, swallowing hard.

"You okay?" Felix asked.

I nodded and opened my eyes. Lainey's phone was plugged in on her nightstand. But I didn't see her laptop anywhere. "Where's her purse? Ah, here."

Her large beige Hermès tote hung from one of the closet doorknobs. It had no zipper closure, so I could see inside without touching it. "Not in there."

Felix moved to the nightstand.

"Careful—" I started, but he used the stolen uniform as a glove to slide the drawer open.

"Nope," he said. "What kind of laptop did she have?"

"A MacBook. Rose gold. And she had all these pink flowery stickers on it."

We searched the room together, Felix opening her closet, drawers, and suitcases with his makeshift glove while I pointed at what to search next. But her laptop was nowhere to be found.

"Tate must've taken it," I said.

Felix pointed to her phone. "But why not take that, too?"

"Maybe he didn't need it. Maybe he wanted to hack her laptop for something he could use against her dad?" I gasped. "Maybe he wanted to find something to take down Silverton."

"You'd think murdering his daughter would be revenge enough . . ." said Felix.

"C'mon," I said. "If we find Lainey's laptop in Tate's room, we'll have our answer."

I stared at the empty space on Tate's bed where his corpse had been—his skin purple, eyes bugged, mouth agape. I shuddered and shook the image away.

"I dunno, Rocky," said Felix, scanning the room. "It doesn't seem like there was a struggle or anything, does it?"

He had a point—if Tate had been strangled, you'd think there would've been signs of a tussle. But nothing seemed out of place. Even Miguel's skincare potions were lined up in neat rows on the low table between the beds and on the nightstand. Maybe this really was a murder-suicide.

Careful not to touch anything, I slinked to the nightstand and glanced out the porthole, splashed with droplets from the waves pounding the ship one deck below. The sounds were muffled, but you could hear them. I imagined Briana, one deck up, hearing the splash behind her head. The splash of Lainey hitting the water.

We had to find Lainey's laptop. It had to be here.

I moved to open the nightstand drawer, noticing the pain in my arm wasn't so severe anymore; it was more of an ever-present throb now.

"Wait—" said Felix. I froze as he pulled something from the uniform shirt pocket and tossed it to me. The used rubber glove.

"Ew?" I pinched it between two fingers.

"Better than nothing. You shouldn't get your fingerprints on anything."

"Right." Using the glove, I tugged open every drawer I could find, including inside the closet.

Felix flicked open Tate's gaming laptop using his makeshift uniform glove. "Password protected."

"Obviously."

"You can code, right? D'you know how to hack a password?"

"I'm not *that* kind of coder; I have no idea."

"If he did leave a suicide note on here, it could explain everything," said Felix.

I sighed, glancing at Miguel's side of the room. "Huh. Miguel's laptop's gone."

"What do you think that means?"

"I have no clue. Let's keep looking for Lainey's."

As Felix searched the bathroom, I stooped to look under Tate's bed. He kept his empty suitcases there—oh, one of them had some weight to it. I tugged it out and opened it to find a stuffed backpack inside. It looked familiar—light gray and boxy, though lots of people had backpacks like that.

But Tate's backpack was black.

I unzipped it and—"Holy hell."

"Did you find it?" Felix darted from the bathroom.

"No, but look at all this cash!" The bag was stuffed with stacks of US twenty-dollar bills.

Felix blanched. "Why would he have this?"

I didn't get the impression Tate was wealthy—he was here on scholarship, like me, and his mom hadn't been able to afford

Sanatek's drug price hike. I checked the backpack's bulging front compartment and gasped, scooping out its contents.

Gold and platinum jewelry glinted from the dusk sun streaming through the porthole, and one of the charm necklaces—a diamond-encrusted heart—pulverized my own heart to sand. "I know this necklace," I said, breathless. "It's Lainey's. This is definitely Lainey's." I remembered her wearing it at one of her father's fundraisers, the pictures later splashed all over the internet.

"Whoa . . ." Felix sank onto the edge of Miguel's bed. "None of this makes any sense . . ."

"Yes it does!" I shook my head. "Tate killed Lainey and stole this on his way out. This confirms it." But why would Lainey even have all this cash? She always used her credit cards. Maybe she wanted to have it to exchange in each country? I shook the thought away and started stuffing everything back into the backpack, careful to touch it only with my gloved hand.

"What're you doing?"

"Putting this back where we found it."

"Shouldn't we take it?" Felix asked.

I frowned. "But it's evidence. This proves Tate killed Lainey." I shoved the bag back into Tate's suitcase.

"But what if the police think you planted it here?" Felix motioned to me, to what I was doing.

My breath hitched, and sweat beaded on my forehead. Was he right? As careful as I'd been, maybe even a single strand of my hair or DNA would indicate I'd tampered with this bag . . . the very evidence that could exonerate me. Or *would it*? If so, once again my impulsive decisions were hurting more than helping.

"Oh God," I said, frenzied. "We never should've come in here."

Felix cursed. "I had no idea we'd find *this*."

"And her laptop . . . Where is her laptop?" I stared into the suitcase again as though I could will it into existence, but there was nothing else. My gaze shifted to the spot next to the suitcase, where a blotch darkened the burgundy carpet, right next to the low table. It could've been anything, could've been there for God knew how long, but something made me stoop and press my fingers to it. I couldn't tell if it was damp through the rubber glove.

"What is it?" Felix asked.

I hesitated a moment, then knelt and sniffed it.

Oranges.

Just a subtle whiff.

I let out a small gasp.

"What?"

"I visited last week . . . Miguel put some serum on my face, and it smelled like oranges. Vitamin C, I think?" I searched the bottles for the right label. "I don't see it." I ripped off the rubber glove and pressed my knuckle to the splotch.

"Don't—" Felix started, too late.

Not only was the spot damp, but something pricked my knuckle. I yanked it back. A tiny green sliver of glass stuck to my skin. I plucked it free, gaping at it. "A bottle broke."

Felix blanched. "It could've happened earlier this morning . . . ?"

"Would spilled gel still be wet hours later?" I stood and searched all the garbage cans, which still contained trash—Julia must've had orders not to clean this room, or Lainey's. But there were no broken bottles, no shards of glass. "There *was* a struggle." My voice shook. "They knocked the bottles over. Maybe they stepped on that one. Then whoever killed Tate took the broken glass with them."

No better trash can for a murderer than the entire ocean.

"And maybe they took her laptop, too."

"How would they even know Tate had it?" Felix asked.

I worried at my lower lip. "Maybe Navya's not the only one who saw Tate leave Lainey's room with it." Dread curdled my stomach. "Maybe Miguel *has* been hiding."

Felix screwed up his face. "You think Miguel killed Tate . . . what, for that bag of cash?"

"I don't know. He told me he wanted to become a travel influencer and stay in five-star hotels . . . Maybe he thought he was owed this, since Lainey took away any chance he had. Maybe he and Tate fought over it or something . . ."

But something niggled at my mind. If Miguel did kill Tate, why would he hide? It's not like he could stay wherever he was forever—eventually he'd have to leave the ship, and there was only one way off. Well, one *safe* way off. And he'd know hiding would only make him look guilty.

"Oh, I don't know what to think . . ." I glanced at the rows of bottles again. This time I noticed what I should have the moment we walked in.

Something that made my fingers and toes go numb.

"The bottles aren't in order," I said.

Felix looked confused.

"Miguel had arranged the bottles in order of size. Big to small. Then by color. I remember thinking that with this many products, I'd never be able to find anything that way; I'd need to go in order of my routine."

He followed my gaze to the bottles. They were in neat rows, but all out of order—a tall vial next to a short one next to a tall one again, and on and on, with no rhyme or reason. "So?"

"Miguel would've known to put the bottles back the way they were before—or at least done so out of habit. Someone killed Tate and cleaned up after themselves—but it wasn't Miguel."

33

Felix tried to stop me as I hurried upstairs to the dean's office. "Rocky, wait. Think of how much trouble we'll be in for breaking into two crime scenes."

"It doesn't matter," I said. "We have to tell Candace everything."

"But she'll have security lock you up," Felix warned. "They'll lock us both up."

I gave him a forlorn look. "I'm sorry, but staying silent is too dangerous. What if this person isn't finished covering their tracks? Maybe they did kill Miguel. And maybe Navya saw them last night. Hell, they probably know we're onto them, too. We can't just wait for the police to board. Someone else could get hurt before then."

Still, Felix followed me to the dean's office, nestled between the hair salon and campus store, and heaved a sigh as I knocked on the door.

No answer.

"Dammit." I was sick of running around the ship like a chicken without a head. I pounded on the door again, more out of frustration than anything.

The door opened a crack, and someone peeked out—

"Miguel?!" I gasped, pushing the door all the way open. "You're alive!" Relief bubbled through my chest like a cool stream over desert sand.

Miguel's eyes widened, aghast, and deep purple half-moons shadowed them, like he hadn't slept a wink. "Why would I *not* be alive?"

"We couldn't find you anywhere," I said, eyeing his disheveled black hair, which was usually sculpted in place with gel. "Considering what's happening, our minds went there."

"Correction: your mind," said Felix.

I threw him a look, then focused on Miguel. "Where've you been? And what're you doing in here?"

"Um . . ." He tugged his earlobe. "One of the stews found me in the hair salon's back office." When I gave him a confused look, he went on, "Well, it was closed, and I needed a quiet place to work. It's not *that* weird. But Candace told me to wait for her here . . . She had to go talk to the captain." He rolled his eyes, like he didn't have time for this.

"Why not work in the library or something?" I asked.

"I was using the staff internet, okay?" He pulled a dongle from his backpack's front compartment. "I hardwired in."

My fingers went numb. "Did you blow this up online?"

He screwed up his face. "No. I was researching how to get my accounts back."

Wow. People were *dying*—including his own roommate—and all he could think about were his social media accounts. He'd tied his entire sense of self to his social media, and once they disappeared, so had he—it was all he cared about, even when the very real world around him was crumbling.

"What are you doing here, anyway?" Miguel asked.

"We, uh . . . we have something important to tell Candace." I rubbed my lips together, sizing him up. My gut feel was that he was telling the truth. Still, I was wary to admit we'd broken into his room. "Did you happen to see if Tate had another laptop this morning?" I asked instead. "A laptop that wasn't his?"

Miguel winced. "No. Why?"

"Well . . . we think he might've taken Lainey's after . . . well, after he killed her."

Miguel went rigid for a moment, then guffawed, clearly trying to cover his reaction. "Are you seriously trying to frame Tate?"

I bunched my brow. "I'm not trying to *frame* anyone. He hates Lainey's dad—"

"That doesn't mean he'd kill her."

"But we know he was trying to get revenge. We ran into him this morning before he died, and he admitted that in London—" I stopped short at the horrified look that crossed Miguel's face, the way his eyes boinged from his skull, the way his blood seemed to drain from it.

Oh, no.

Heat crept up my neck. "You didn't know—"

"What do you mean, he *died*?" said Miguel.

"I . . . I'm so sorry . . ." Candace must've had Miguel wait here not because he was in trouble, necessarily, but to break this terrible news to him.

Miguel cupped his mouth. "How?" The word was muffled behind his fingers.

"We, uh . . ." I darted a desperate glance at Felix, who unhelpfully cringed. "We found him hanging from his shower . . ."

"*What?* There's no way—"

"We don't think he killed himself. I think someone killed him and made it look like a suicide . . . and I think they took Lainey's laptop. Maybe that's the main thing they were after."

"No." Miguel's watery eyes darted frantically between mine. "It couldn't've been."

"What do you mean?" I asked.

Miguel hesitated, then croaked, "Tate didn't take Lainey's laptop. I did."

Felix and I stared openmouthed as Miguel pulled a rose-gold MacBook Pro embellished with pink petal stickers from his backpack. Lainey's laptop.

"Holy—" I breathed.

"Tate *did* give me the idea . . ." He slid it onto the dean's desk. "I know she's the one who bot-bombed me. I *know* it. So I wanted to find the receipts on her laptop. Then I could prove I didn't buy all those fake followers and get my accounts back." So he wasn't just researching how to get his accounts back—he was researching how to hack into her laptop.

I started to reach for the laptop, then stopped myself. "When did you take this?"

Miguel cringed. "Last night. But I swear to God, I didn't kill her. I didn't *touch* her."

"But . . . how . . . ?" I asked, dumbstruck.

"I saw a key on the floor, right outside her room. I figured it was hers. That you dropped it. I grabbed it, and then later, after Tate and I . . . Well, on our way back to our room, I told him I had to get more water, but I really went back to her room . . ." He trailed off, like we could surmise the rest.

"It was you," I breathed.

Felix swore.

"No, it wasn't!" Miguel narrowed his misty eyes at me. "I could say the same about *you*."

"I was in there for, like, two seconds."

"Mm, sure."

"Don't spin this on me. *You're* the one who has this." I jabbed a finger at the laptop.

"But I didn't even see her," said Miguel, practically shouting now.

I shook my head, struggling to piece all this together. "When exactly did you take it?"

"I don't know. Around three, maybe?"

After the splash.

"Didn't you see the blood?" I asked, breathless. "Didn't you *smell* it?"

"I . . . I was kind of holding my breath. Just tiptoed in and out real fast. I didn't turn the lights on or anything, it was right there on the desk . . . and, honestly, maybe it was earlier than three, I really don't remember, I was so wasted. Please, you *have* to believe me. I didn't kill anyone." Tears were flowing down his cheeks now. I couldn't tell whether they were from sadness over Tate or fear for himself. Maybe both.

"So, let me get this straight," said Felix. "All day, you knew Lainey was dead. And you were still trying to hack into her laptop for receipts?"

"Felix . . ." I muttered.

Miguel hiccupped, pawing away his tears. "Not my proudest

moment. But I knew it was my last chance to prove what that bitch did to me."

"For Christ's sake," said Felix. "The girl's *dead*."

"Good riddance," Miguel spat.

The moment he said it, he clamped his lips like he regretted it. But the words were out, hovering in the space between us like some decrepit ghoul.

But that didn't mean he was guilty.

My own thought from this morning swirled in my mind: *That spoiled, selfish brat got exactly what she deserved.*

"I swear, it wasn't me," Miguel practically whispered.

I believed him. And though Tate wasn't the one who'd nabbed the key, he still could've gotten into Lainey's room if the door had jammed. But *when*? "Are you sure Tate went straight back to your room when you went to grab the laptop?" I asked Miguel.

He rubbed his brow. "I . . . I *think* so?"

"You're *sure* he didn't follow you?" Maybe Miguel was wrong about the time, and Tate snuck in right after. "Was he there when you went back to your room?"

"I don't know; I got right into bed. I was drunk and—" He hesitated, obviously withholding something. "Ugh, I don't *remember*. But, you know, Sheffia *was* pissed at both of them yesterday."

"At who?" asked Felix.

"Tate and Lainey, obviously," Miguel huffed. "Tate told me about how he dumped Sheffia yesterday when we were—*mmph*." He bit his lip.

I almost rolled my eyes. "Oh, stop it already. We know you and Tate tried some pills last night."

Miguel snorted. "Okay, well—*then*. I'm trying to remember exactly how it came up, but basically, Tate asked Sheffia all this stuff about how close Lainey was with her dad, whether she'd ever worked for him, stuff like that. Sheffia was like, 'This is random AF, why are you asking?' So he gave this whole spiel about how awful his company is, and she was like, 'Um, my parents work at Sanatek.' He had no idea, so he kinda lost it. He said he couldn't be with someone whose family devoted their lives to profiting off people's pain."

No wonder Tate didn't want to dig into the bot-bombing for Miguel; he already had an agenda with Sheffia. I frowned. "So, wait . . . Did Tate legitimately like Sheffia?" Jamal had said he was only with her to get closer to Lainey.

Miguel pursed his lips. "Not at first, but . . . yeah, he started having real feelings or whatever. But she *really* liked him . . . Apparently she tried backtracking real hard. Said she hated Lainey's dad—hated Lainey, for that matter. And he was like, 'Bullshit, then why do you spend so much time with her?' And she said the only reason was that her parents sent her here to keep an eye on her."

"*To keep an eye on her*," Felix repeated, befuddled.

I rubbed my eyes, my brain like a fully submerged sponge, unable to absorb any new information. "Meaning . . . to keep her safe?" Then I remembered Lainey's frantic whispers to Silas at Windsor, scared she was in danger. "Was she getting death threats or something?"

Maybe that's why she was so paranoid, so quick to accuse me of stalking her. Heck, maybe she thought I'd sent them.

"I dunno, maybe," said Miguel. "Point is, I bet Sheffia blamed Lainey for losing Tate. And then . . . I dunno, maybe she lost her mind and killed Tate, too."

I tugged at my lower lip. "Eh, I don't think Sheffia killed Lainey." The way she was sobbing at the assembly . . . "But she probably suspected Tate—he flipped out about Sanatek, then boom, Lainey went overboard." I gasped. "Oh, right! She was with Silas when they found Lainey's room like that this morning. Maybe she saw her laptop was missing, and . . . oh no."

"What?" said Felix.

"I bet she thought Tate took it, wanting dirt on Sanatek. But whatever he found on that laptop could ruin *her* family, too. Maybe she was trying to stop him. Even if it meant killing him."

34

"There she is." Felix surreptitiously pointed. "But I don't think this is a good idea."

I followed his gaze to the far end of the Cantina. Sheffia was nestled between Silas and Jamal like a diva between her bodyguards. None of them spoke—Jamal typed on his laptop while Silas fiddled with his phone, but Sheffia watched us, lines etching her forehead in a perma-cringe.

Before I could decide whether to approach her, Divya swooped over. "Jade . . ." Her eyes were red and watery, like she'd been crying. So she knew about Tate.

I enveloped her in a hug, her curvy frame trembling. "I can't believe it . . ." she said, then filled us in on the latest—apparently, rumors of both Tate's death and the library fire had spread like a virus. Everyone was now quarantined in the restaurants, even those who'd eschewed the captain's orders earlier, though passengers expressed different symptoms. Some were terrified a maniacal axe murderer was lurking among us, the fire an attempt to kill everyone. Others were annoyed to hunker down, thinking Tate had committed a murder-suicide and the fire was a coincidence—maybe a smoker taking advantage of the deserted space. A third group was dead set on believing Silas and I were guilty, the fire an attempt to destroy evidence.

I frowned. "What evidence?"

"Er," said Divya. "There may or may not be a rumor that you stabbed Silas's leg in there last night."

My insides went numb. I threw Felix a worried look, but he'd gone quiet, back to the brooding boy I'd known weeks ago. "Has Navya told . . ." I said, flustered. "What kind of evidence would that be . . . Do people think we faked it?"

"So it *is* true!" said Divya. Dammit. My stomach lurched, but she seemed more amused than anything. "Ugh, I'm so mad I missed it—"

I angled my head. "Wait, did Navya tell you or not?"

"No. Sorry, I lied about the evidence thing." She gave me a sheepish look. "I sort of figured it out myself. When Navya put on her jeans this morning there was this huge bloodstain on the knee." She must've knelt on some when cleaning up. "When I asked her about it, she said it was Silas's, but wouldn't say anything else. And then I asked Jamal about it, and he told me Silas stabbed his own leg by accident." Divya snorted. "I knew that was bullshit."

Panic rose in my chest. "It *was* an accident, though! Who've you told?"

"Oh, no one. Don't worry, your secret's safe with me. That guy's such a jerk. But Tate . . ." Her voice cracked. "I thought he was one of the good ones. What the hell's going on?"

"I don't know" was all I said. Despite her promise, I didn't trust Divya to keep anything a secret. "Where's Navya?" I wanted to talk to her before Sheffia and see if she'd seen Tate leave Lainey's room. Now that he was dead, she no longer had a reason to cover for him.

"Over there." Divya pointed at the far end of the restaurant. "She's a mess, though, just FYI."

My stomach sank. "I'd imagine. Listen, can you give us a minute to talk to her?"

"You don't need my permission," said Divya. "I was sitting over there." She thumbed a table behind her; I recognized the group of girls from a couple of my classes. "She won't even talk to me. Like she's the only one hurting right now." Bitterness laced her tone. I gave her hand a sympathetic squeeze before heading over to Navya.

"I hope Divya keeps her mouth shut," Felix muttered as we crossed the busy restaurant.

Worry roiled my stomach. "Me, too—"

Navya glanced up and spotted us, and without a moment's hesitation, she stood and hurried out the closest door.

I sped after her, Felix right on my tail. Outside, a gust of wind immediately blew my hair into my face, and by the time I recombobulated myself, Navya was already halfway down the promenade. She darted a glance over her shoulder and, seeing us following, picked up the pace, nearly colliding with a professor who skirted around her just in time. "Watch where you're going!"

Navya gasped. "Oh my God, I'm sorry—"

"Where *are* you going? Everyone's supposed to stay inside."

"I, uh—" Navya stuttered, breathing hard.

"Bathroom," I told the professor, sidling up next to Navya. "The one inside has a massive line."

The professor pursed her lips, clearly torn whether to

accompany us or continue on to the Cantina. "Well, make it fast, then come straight back."

"We will," I said earnestly.

She nodded and headed off, and the three of us continued toward the restrooms near the pool. When we got far enough away, I reached for Navya's wrist. "Hey, wait up—"

The way she yanked her arm away made my heart sink.

"Navya, *please*," I said. "I know you saw something last night."

"Yeah." She spun to face me with a hard stare. "I saw you stab a guy."

My cheeks flushed. Felix clamped his lips and raised his eyebrows, and I could almost hear his voice saying, *She has a point.*

It was true. And she'd cleaned up the mess.

Whether or not it was intentional, it happened, and I owed her an *epic* apology.

I took a deep breath. "Navya, I'm so, so sorry you had to see that last night. That you saw it, and that it happened. It was an accident; I was drunk, and I was so angry because I thought Silas was gaslighting me, and I picked up that letter opener meaning to stab the table and lost my balance. Still, I should've had a better grip on my anger. I should've known better than to pick up the letter opener at all. There's no excuse for that."

Felix's face slackened as I spoke.

"I was actually going to visit one of the psych professors today," I continued. "I know I need help for some stuff I've been struggling with. I've gotten sidetracked with everything that's happened, but once we get through this"—if I didn't get arrested first—"I promise, I'll get help. I'll do better. And if there's any way

I can ever make it up to you, I will. I haven't thanked you yet for cleaning up—"

"I didn't do that for you," Navya cut me off, though her eyes softened. "I was scared Divya would get in trouble for sneaking booze on board, for it leading to *that*."

My throat burned. "Well, all the same. Thank you. And I'm sorry you had to do it. I'm really, truly sorry."

Navya studied me for a moment that seemed to stretch to the end of time. Did she think I'd committed even worse atrocities after last night?

"And I hope you know," I added, "I had nothing to do with what happened to Lainey and Tate."

"Oh, I know *that* . . ."

Maybe she saw who *did*. "How?"

She bit her lip and shrugged. "I don't think murderers own up to their mistakes like that. It seemed sincere. I believe you."

Oh. I was so relieved, my throat constricted and tears stung my eyes.

She gave me a small smile. "And I appreciate the apology. I'm sorry that asshole hurt you enough to rile you up like that."

"Thank you . . ." I choked out.

She took a step closer. "And, you know . . . you could talk to me about stuff. And a therapist, too, obviously. But I dunno . . . Sometimes it feels like you have a wall up or something. But we're friends. You can let your guard down with me. I might not always have the best advice, but I'll listen."

She was right. Even after she'd confided in me about stuff— her crush on Tate, Divya's drinking problem—I'd kept her at arm's length. But I'd been scared to let anyone get close after Lainey and Silas's epic betrayal. I'd even hesitated with Felix. "Really?"

"Yeah," she said. "I mean, seriously; we're traveling the world together in a coffin—" A pained look crossed her face. "I didn't mean—you know what I mean. That tiny room. We were automatically friends from day one."

A tear slipped down my cheek.

"Aw, don't cry," she said. As she hugged me, I spotted Felix over her shoulder, strands of dark hair whipping across his forehead, watching with the strangest expression—was it worry? We had gotten awfully sidetracked.

"So, listen." I pulled back from Navya. "We wanted to ask you about last night again."

Her jaw stiffened. "Why? I told you, I was asleep—"

"We know you weren't," Felix piped up before I could prod her to confess she knew more. "Someone saw you on the stairs, coming down from Deck 7." I threw him a look, but he ignored me.

Navya's breath hitched.

"Were you up on Deck 8?" I asked gently. "Did you see who came out of Lainey's room?"

"No."

"I know you wanted to protect him, but . . . you don't need to anymore. Tate's gone." At the sound of his name, Navya pinched her lips and averted her gaze. "Navya, if you saw him coming from Lainey's room, we need to know—"

But Navya shook her head. "I didn't. I wasn't on Deck 8 then."

Felix tensed. "Then what did you see?"

Navya crossed her arms and sniffed. "Nothing. I was on Deck 7, okay? That's true. Who saw me?"

"You didn't see *anyone*?" Felix asked.

"No, no one."

"Ghassan saw you," I said. She looked confused. "He's in one of your politics classes. He saw you running down the stairs on his way from getting water in the fitness center."

"Oh."

"What were you doing?"

Navya raked her windblown hair back, looking defeated. "I threw out Divya's booze, alright? By the time I got back to our room, she was passed out, and I was so scared she'd get in trouble for sneaking it on board . . . for getting you drunk enough to stab Silas. So I grabbed her stash, and I threw it overboard."

I stared, stunned. That wasn't what I'd expected her to say at all.

Her shoulders slumped. "I'm so sick of her antics. She drinks so much, and I *know* she does it to get on my nerves. She's been such a brat ever since I got into Harvard and she didn't, like I wouldn't have given my left arm for us to go to the same school together."

I stepped closer, wanting to console her—she looked so stressed, so exhausted from worrying about her sister this whole time. But before I could, Navya turned to grip the rail and stare out over the ocean. "Just . . . please don't tell her it was me, okay? Let her think it was confiscated or something. I can't fight with her anymore . . ."

But I couldn't promise that. Not when it masked the truth.

"I . . . I'll see you later" was all I managed to sputter. When she nodded, I spun and tugged Felix's arm. "Come on."

"Where are we going?"

"We have to tell Candace everything," I said once we were far enough away. "Or the captain, or a professor, *someone*."

"And tell them what, exactly? I think we've hit a dead end here."

"It's worse than that," I said. "We've been shoved backward."

"How do you mean?"

I stilled to meet his eye, giving him a worried look. "Well, what made that splash Briana heard at two in the morning? Was it Lainey hitting the water . . . or was it a bag of bottles?"

35

Felix checked his watch as though it displayed a countdown to Gibraltar. "We're running out of time. And, frankly, before we talk to them, I think we need something more concrete than a bunch of missing bottles. Once they find out we broke into those rooms, it's game over."

I groaned, rubbing my eyes. "So what the hell do we do next?" He shook his head, equally stumped.

There's only so long adrenaline can fuel a sleep-deprived brain. As the sun slipped beneath the horizon, my mind had turned to muddled stew, and my still-damp clothes—the ones I'd been wearing when we found Tate—made me feel like ants were crawling all over my skin.

I hugged my abdomen, my body sore from shivering so aggressively. "Ugh, it feels like my leggings have fused with my soul. I need to get out of these damp clothes and shower—maybe then I'll be able to think straight. I'll meet you back up here in a half hour, okay?" I turned and left without waiting for an argument.

But he followed me into the elevator bay.

"Uh . . ."

He pressed the down button. "If you think I'm letting you walk to your room alone right now—"

"I know, I know. I'm out of my mind," I said, remembering

how he'd stopped me from walking back to the ship from that London pub alone. He gave me a subtle smirk, and despite everything, my stomach did a little flip. But then it knotted as I imagined some masked murderer roving the corridors.

When the elevator door slid open, I half expected some bloodied corpse to topple out. But it was empty. I stepped inside and leaned against the wall, squeezing my eyes shut.

Lainey's blood-splattered room.

Tate's purple face.

Images burned into my retinas that'd plague me for the rest of my life.

Felix touched my arm, and I startled. "You okay?" The doors were already opening on Deck 4, so he waited until we were out in the hall to slide his arms around me, his fingers threading through my curls to cradle my head. "Everything's going to be okay."

"You don't know that," I said into his shoulder.

He didn't respond. Maybe he didn't know how to. Instead he held me tight, and I could feel his heart beating against mine. I could even hear it . . . or were those footsteps?

I glanced over my shoulder, but the hall was deserted.

"Your clothes really are still damp," said Felix, releasing me.

"Told you."

When we reached my door, Felix tucked a curl behind my ear. "I'll meet you here in a half hour. *Please* don't wander off in the meantime." He trailed a finger along my jaw and his eyes lingered on my lips, and something deep inside me fluttered again.

"I won't," I whispered.

He started to close the gap between us, but paused and shook his head slightly, changing his mind. I gave him a questioning look. He only offered a small nod before turning to leave. For a moment I watched him head down the hall toward his cabin before going into mine.

The silence inside hit me first. I only ever came here to sleep, and between Divya's light snoring, Navya's white noise machine, and the sounds of murmured voices and doors slamming in the hall, it was never completely quiet. But with the twins gone and the halls deserted, it was eerily so.

As I closed the door, I crunched on something—a folded, serrated-edged notebook page. I picked it up as something creaked loudly in front of me.

I jerked my head up. What *was* that?

Holding my breath, I gently set down my backpack and stooped to peek under my bed and the bunk. Nothing there besides our suitcases. The bathroom door was wide open, the shower curtain pushed aside, clearly empty.

Sometimes you could hear the creaks and groans of the ship jostling through the waves, so maybe that was the noise I'd heard. But I couldn't quash this eerie feeling that someone was lying in wait, watching, ready to pounce.

And the closet was closed.

I let out a long, slow exhale and edged toward it, reached for the door handle with trembling fingers, and—

The cabin door burst open.

I scrambled back with a yelp and collided into my bed, tumbling onto it.

But it was just Divya.

"Jade! Oh my God, did I scare you?" She shut the door. "I'm *so* sorry."

I gripped the paper against my chest and stood, breathing hard. "It's fine." But it must've been clear I'd nearly had a cardiac event.

"Ugh, this is all such a nightmare," she groaned.

"What're you doing here?"

She tugged out her suitcase from under the bunk and unzipped it. "Sorry, I'll be out of your hair in a sec—what the hell?" Her fingers groped at the empty space where she'd kept her booze.

Navya must've been as quiet as a mouse as Divya snoozed on the bottom bunk, her own drunken snores drowning out the sounds of Navya unzipping the suitcase, the crinkle of plastic as she pulled out the bag.

Divya's nostrils flared. "That bitch." So, she knew.

"She's just looking out for you, Divya."

"Sure." Divya shoved the suitcase back under the bed with a huff. "She's always trying to take things from me. Like whenever I talked to Tate . . . she was *always* trying to get in the middle or pull him aside for herself. I didn't even like Tate that way—we were just friends."

"Maybe she wanted to spend more time with *you*."

She chortled bitterly. "Right. Like how she convinced me to go to BU so we could live in the same city when she went to Harvard? *Pfft.* She just wanted me to see up close and personal how my dreams came true for *her*."

"I don't think that's true . . ."

"You have no idea. You didn't spend your life growing up with her, playing second fiddle to her, your own twin wanting to push you down so she could shine brighter." That wasn't how Navya saw it at all—at least, so she claimed. "I've just had *enough*, you know?"

Divya crossed the room to my bed and shoved her hand between it and the wall.

I crinkled my brow. "What're you—"

She yanked out a Ziploc bag and dangled it between two fingers. Inside were smaller bags filled with something grassy, some pills, a crystalline substance. "At least she didn't get everything."

"Holy— You've been hiding drugs behind *my* bed?" This explained where Tate and Miguel had gotten pills.

She winked. "Nobody would ever look there." She took out the bag of what I guessed was weed. "Though, after last night . . . maybe you're not as straight-edged as I thought." She shoved the rest back in her hiding spot and headed for the door. "See you later."

"Wait a minute," I said. "I really think you should talk to Navya. She got rid of your stash to protect you. She thought you'd get in trouble for what I did, since it was *your* alcohol that got me drunk."

Her hand froze on the doorknob, and she stiffened. "Oh, please. All she cares about is covering her own ass."

"If you resent her so much, why'd you even come on CoB?"

"What's it to you?"

"Seriously?" I motioned to my bed, then their bunk. "You're

my roommates. My *friends*. I want you to be happy."

"You think I don't? Don't get me wrong, I love my sister. It's just that I hate her, too. I wish we could be BFFs like when we were ten or whatever. *That's* why I came here. I tried. I really did. But I'm tired of clinging to this false hope that someday we'll magically get along again." She shook her head. "They say blood's thicker than water . . . but what happens when your own blood tries to drown you?"

You flail and fight until you can escape the riptide.

Just like Mom and me. But Navya clearly loved Divya; this seemed like a terrible miscommunication. Then again, I'd never told Mom how much she'd hurt me, either. I wasn't sure she understood how toxic our relationship had become. I'd never tried to fix anything—instead, I fled. I wasn't sure which was the right path, or if one even existed.

"I'm sorry" was all I said.

Divya offered a small smile. "Me, too." Without another word, she split.

Alone again, I looked down at the piece of paper I'd been clutching this entire time. I unfolded it and read the messy scrawl.

Jade—
I know who killed Tate.
Sheffia

I gasped, and my heart basically stopped. I had to find Sheffia. Now.

She'd been in Coastal Cantina only twenty minutes ago,

sitting with Silas and Jamal. She must've seen me run after Navya and assumed we'd come here. And when I didn't answer the door, sliding a note under it probably seemed safer than scrawling a message on the whiteboard for anyone to see.

I hurtled back into the hall, my still-damp clothes forgotten, and glanced both ways. She'd probably headed back upstairs by now. "Dammit, Sheffia." Why couldn't she have written more? Like where she was going next, or who *did* kill Tate?

I searched Sea Haven first—for what had to be the zillionth time today—then dashed to the Cantina, but there was no sign of her. Miguel sat nearby with Jamal, head resting on his arms, while Candace hovered at the neighboring table, making the rounds, checking on students. I guessed she was done lecturing him, or consoling him, or whatever. I started toward her, ready to tell her everything.

But that's when the screaming started.

Outside. Somewhere on the dark promenade.

The tables near the doors went quiet, and heads turned like gazelles catching the faint rustle of a lion crouching in nearby brush.

Somehow I wound up outside, following the sound—foolish, reckless, my desperate desire to know what happened making me overlook any danger I might face. Others followed me toward the roped-off pool. Safety in numbers, at least.

Night had fallen, and the lights over the canopied promenade reflecting off the pool water cast an eerie blue glow over the deck. Divya sobbed on a lounge chair next to the pool as Navya held her and stared wide-eyed into the water.

"Divya! What happened—" I nearly tumbled over the rope when I stepped over it, but caught my footing, and in that moment, I saw what had made her scream.

Someone was facedown in the water. Fully clothed. Long, dark hair billowed out like red seaweed clumped on a bulging rock, a red cloud of blood swirling like a demonic halo.

I didn't need to see her face. That unmistakable hair. That baby-pink sweatshirt, earlier blotched with tears.

They belonged to Sheffia.

And she was dead.

I swallowed down the bile surging up my throat. "Did you see what happened?" I breathlessly asked the twins.

Navya shook her head. "Divya came out here to smoke or something. I came after her . . . I wanted to stop her . . . and then we saw . . ." She trailed off, motioning to the pool.

I scanned the deck and spotted Sheffia's pink tote bag on its side, some of its contents spilled onto the teakwood—a few pens, lipstick, a notebook. Guilt ravaged my insides so intensely I keeled over, clenching her note in my fist. I'd had it the entire time I talked to Divya. What if I'd looked sooner? What if I'd come here sooner?

"Did she drown herself?"

"Because of Tate . . ."

"They were together, right?"

Whispers, always more whispers, circling the truth but never quite landing it.

Something caught my eye at the edge of the pool, and I inched closer to see blood streaked along the edge. I pointed with a shaking finger, wanting to call people over, but the only sound that escaped my lips was a garbled sob. A nearby group saw me and came over to look.

"Did she fall?"

"Was she pushed?"

"Did Jade bash her head in?"

"I saw Jade run into the Cantina—"

"No!" I said to no one, to everyone, unsure who'd said that. "I didn't do this!"

But I still had her note. *I know who killed Tate.*

They must have killed her, too. And maybe I was next.

So before anyone could stop me, I ran.

36

"Felix!" I pounded on his door, each thunk reverberating in my chest—or maybe it was sheer panic making my heart pummel my rib cage. "Felix? Are you there?" Perhaps he was napping, or maybe I'd misremembered his room number; I hadn't paid close enough attention when Candace led us to our cabins earlier. I pounded once more.

He finally inched the door open, eyes bleary. Nap it was. "What're you . . . I told you—"

"I know." I pushed it open and barreled in, momentarily taken aback by the state of his cabin. Suitcases were thrown open in the middle of the room, belongings piled in jumbled heaps, like he was pulling a Marie Kondo and hadn't yet decided what brought him joy.

"Uh." He let the door fall closed and rubbed his neck. "I got my laundry back yesterday—"

"Sheffia's dead."

His face went ashen. *"What?"*

"She drowned in the pool . . . or maybe she died when someone bashed her head in, I don't know. Either way, someone killed her, and people think I did it."

"Whoa, hang on." Felix clutched my arms. "How did you . . . When . . . I *just* dropped you off like twenty minutes ago—"

"She slid this under my door." I showed him Sheffia's note, told him how I'd gone to find her. How I *did* find her. What people were whispering.

"Well, come on." He pulled me toward the door.

I tugged my hand free. "Where?"

"I want to see this for myself."

Clumps of seaweed hair. Clouds of red blood. I shuddered. "No, I can't. I can't go back out there . . ."

"Could it've been an accident?" Felix asked.

"An *accident*?" I repeated. "I severely doubt it."

He started pacing the short distance between his bed and the door. "Maybe she was running next to the pool, slipped, hit her head, and fell in?"

"Running from what? *To* what? That whole area was roped off."

"It's just . . . none of this makes sense."

I furrowed my brow. "It *does*, though. She saw who killed Tate. Whoever it was was covering their tracks."

Felix grabbed the note from me, studying it like it was written in hieroglyphics. *I know who killed Tate.* I wished she'd written more. If she wanted to warn me, why didn't she elaborate? Why didn't she tell Candace, or the captain, or literally anyone on staff?

Maybe that *was* her next move. Maybe she was afraid and in shock at first, and finally decided to tell someone.

Or maybe she was running from someone.

Maybe the killer chased her upstairs, out onto the deck, and caught her near the pool, right where her tote had fallen. So few people were out wandering, it wasn't impossible to go unnoticed.

As Felix examined the note, muttering to himself softly, my eyes wandered. He had an interior room like mine, but smaller—the bed took up the entire wall next to the bathroom across from a small desk and closet.

Wait.

There was only one bed.

Where did Felix's roommate sleep? I could've sworn he'd said he had a roommate at the welcome dinner, and last night, when we were making out, his palms hot against my skin, and we wondered where to go for privacy . . . he'd mentioned a roommate then, too.

Felix noticed my roving gaze and held the note under my nose. "Why's this so hard to read?"

I grabbed it back and smoothed it down on his cluttered desk. He had a point, I guessed—Sheffia had clearly written this in a hurry. The *w*'s in the second and third words overlapped with the adjacent letters, and thanks to her bubbly handwriting, *know* looked like *knau*, and *who* looked like *uno*.

"*I knau uno killed Tate?*" Felix read.

"Don't be daft. Obviously she didn't mean 'I knau uno.'"

"But what if someone misreads that as *Jade, I know* you *killed Tate?*"

My breath hitched. No matter how I stared at *who / uno*, it didn't look like *you*. "People wouldn't misread it like that."

"Are you sure?"

I squinted at him. He was suddenly acting more paranoid than me. "Um . . . how do you go from *it was an accident* to *people will think you killed her?*"

306

It was like he was talking in circles on purpose.

One of Felix's open suitcases caught my eye, almost empty except for a belt, some American cash, two passports, a crumpled shirt.

My skin prickled all over.

He followed my gaze, and his jaw went taut.

"Why do you have two passports?" I asked.

"Because I go to school in England, obviously," he said without missing a beat.

"Is that a reason to have two passports?"

"My dad was British. Dual citizen."

That made more sense.

"Can I see?" I asked.

"Is now really the time—"

I bent and grabbed the passports before he could stop me and thumbed to the right pages. The photos were identical.

But one was for *Felix Amara* and the other read *Tyler F. Hassan.*

All the oxygen seemed to get sucked from the room.

"Who the hell's *Tyler F. Hassan*?" I demanded.

Felix's nostrils flared. "Rocky, chill. That's my full name. My parents had me before they were married, so my mother's maiden name's on my birth certificate, and that went on my US passport. And I prefer my middle name, so that went on my UK passport with my dad's last name."

"I didn't know you could do that."

"Well, you can."

I pressed a palm to my forehead, confused. Maybe my brain

307

was scrambled from everything that had happened today. "Sorry, I'm just—"

"It's fine. I know—long day."

"Understatement of the century." I mimicked his tone from earlier, collapsing on his bed. "Well, anyway, we have to figure this out." I scooted back against the wall, knees to my chest, and pulled out my phone, navigating to my Wi-Fi settings. I hadn't used any of my data plan yet today.

"What're you doing?" Felix asked.

"Pulling up our suspect list from earlier," I lied. "But . . . oh, geez . . . two of them are dead now." I pretended to backspace their names, and instead typed *Tyler Hassan* into Google. "I still think Sketchy Bob's a very real possibility."

"Seriously?"

"Yeah. You know what I found out?" I asked as I waited for the results to load. As always, my connection was slow as hell. "Sketchy Bob had a daughter who died, and she'd wanted to come on CoB."

Felix's eyebrows shot up. "Really?"

"Yup. And he showed me a picture . . . She looked a lot like Lainey."

"When did this even happen?"

"Earlier . . . uh, when I was trying to find a sprinkler to set off. I ran into him—"

The results loaded. One near the top caught my eye.

Coroner: Couple found dead by son overdosed on opioids

Goose bumps rushed over my skin. Opioids. I remembered

that article Lainey had had to write on opioids for class. *But opioids are Sanatek's biggest moneymaker*, she'd said. *If I accidentally say something I'm not supposed to know and Dad finds out . . . he'll* kill *me.* I tried to keep my face impassive, though my pulse hammered even in my fingertips.

"So, what," said Felix as I tapped that first result, linking to some local Florida news site. "You think it's some sick fairness thing? Like . . . if his daughter can't enjoy being here, why should all these other kids?"

"Yeah, exactly. Hang on, writing this down . . ." I pretended to type as I read.

Toxicology reports from the deaths of Rebecca and Faizan Hassan revealed the couple overdosed on Xanicodine in their Palm Beach home in March 2022. Their son, Tyler, found them a week after their deaths.

My stomach turned over. It must've been horrific to discover his parents' bodies a week after they'd died. Once decomposition had begun.

I shuddered at the mere thought as I googled Xanicodine.

No results. But there were results for a close spelling, Xanicodone.

Xanicodone is an opioid manufactured and marketed by the pharmaceutical company Sanatek. Though Sanatek touts Xanicodone as a low-dose, extended-release opioid—available in 1 milligram (mg), 2.5 mg, and 5 mg—it is double the potency of fentanyl and 100 to 200 times stronger than morphine.

Sanatek.

Derek Silverton's company.

The company that sold the drugs that killed Felix's parents.

That couldn't be a coincidence.

Earlier today, he'd acted like he didn't remember Tate bringing up Derek Silverton at the welcome dinner, saying Sanatek "rang a bell." But if this article was really about his parents, any mention of Sanatek would do more than ring a bell—it'd make his blood boil.

I glanced up at Felix, who watched me closely, his jaw clenched. He'd seen me shudder, the shock register on my face, my ruse of updating the suspect list forgotten.

"What did you find?" he asked, his voice silky as honey.

My heart went into a freefall. "Nothing ... I'm just ... trying to think this through." He'd tried pinning Lainey's murder on Silas all morning, even though it was physically impossible.

Felix, on the other hand ...

I'd passed out in his arms around midnight, my sleep unsettled, but when I awoke to the sound of Silas and Sheffia screaming, he was on the next lounge chair over. I couldn't recall when he moved, so weary from booze and my outburst that I'd tried to fall right back to sleep each time I broke consciousness.

And after talking to Tate this morning, Felix and I had split up in Sea Haven to ask people if they'd seen Miguel or anything suspicious last night. Had he really been questioning people that whole time?

And ... oh God. Had Felix seen Sheffia slip this note under my door as he pulled me into that consoling hug? Maybe she'd been waiting for me at my door and seen me with him—the boy she

LYING IN THE DEEP

knew killed Tate—and scrawled this note. Maybe that's why she kept it vague, in case he read it, too. I thought I'd heard footsteps behind me . . .

Maybe I was right.

Maybe that was Sheffia, running to the elevators.

And when I went into my room, Felix chased her.

No.

My chest constricted, and I swallowed my panic as I scanned the room, searching for something to defend myself with. My dagger was resting on a shelf above the bed he used as a nightstand—

My dagger?!

Felix was the one who'd taken it.

He followed my gaping stare. "Wait—"

"No!" I balled my hands into fists—fists that would never be able to overpower him, though the rage coursing through my veins said otherwise. "It was you. This whole time, it was *you.*"

37

Long story short: Never trust anyone.

My life was an endless cycle of betrayal. Everyone I loved was like a spoke on a wheel that crushed me again and again, showing no signs of slowing, smooshing my spirit like a pancake.

"It's not what you think—" Felix tried.

"You killed Lainey," I spat, refusing to let him lie to me anymore. "Did Tate see you? You stole that bag of cash from her room, didn't you? And then you tried to *bribe* him with it—"

"No, stop—"

"And then Sheffia saw you leave his room, didn't she? She must've seen the look on your face, and she knew, she *knew*—"

Felix reached for me, his eyes pleading, but I scrambled out of reach, careening into his desk.

"Jade, you *know* me." Oh, so he was using my name now, huh? "You know I couldn't have killed anyone."

"I don't know anything about you, *Tyler.*" I hurled the passports at him. "But I do know your parents OD'd on drugs Sanatek sold." I brandished my phone at him, the article still on-screen. A muscle in his jaw twitched as pain darkened his face. Part of me felt terrible for throwing this traumatic memory at him. But I quickly squashed that part. "Don't you dare tell me this is a coincidence. Don't you *dare.*"

He wiped a hand down his face. "Jesus."

I breathed hard and fast, shaking my head. He hadn't been helping me solve this mystery at all. We'd been talking in circles all day, chasing false leads, because he *knew* I was the biggest suspect. He was wasting time until we got to Gibraltar, until I got arrested.

No. He didn't just know I was the biggest suspect. He *made me* the biggest suspect.

Panic and rage ripped through me so intensely my whole body shook. "You came on CoB to kill Lainey. But first, you had to figure out who to frame. And once you found out about our falling-out, *why* we had a falling-out, you knew I was the perfect suspect, didn't you? You got close to me. You egged me on, played our little game of detective, made her think I was stalking her. You murdered her with the dagger *I* bought—"

"*Stop.* Please. My parents' death—you're right, it's not a coincidence, but I swear to God, you've got this all wrong." He stepped closer, trying to cup my cheek, to weave his fingers through my hair, but I shoved him away.

"No! No more. You made me fall in love with you, and none of it was even real. You were trying to frame me this entire time." I'd never said those words to him before, and now here they were, tumbling out in agony.

His own expression was pained, his eyes beseeching. An act, all an act. "No!" he cried. "Goddammit, Jade, it was never supposed to be *you*."

My breath caught. I stared, flabbergasted.

"It was supposed to be Silas," he went on. "But you screwed everything up."

I choked back a sob. I was right. He had killed her, and the others. My blood turned cold. This boy I'd fallen for—this boy I thought could be a love more real than Silas ever was—had murdered three people. What happened to his parents was terrible, but it didn't justify *this*.

Felix dragged a hand through his hair. "It was supposed to be so simple. So damn simple. Silas was supposed to go back to Lainey's room last night, see she was gone, see the blood, and report her missing. He'd have no alibi for the time after dinner. He'd have the biggest motive—wanting to get rid of her to get back together with you. Simple as that.

"But then he stayed in the library playing that ridiculous drinking game. Which, fine, it could've worked anyway, just later." He let out an ironic laugh. "But then you went and stabbed him in the leg and made that whole scene outside Lainey's room." He shook his head, like he couldn't believe how badly I'd foiled his plans. "And then you just *had* to say you saw Lainey in her bed."

"I *did*—"

"No, you didn't," he yelled.

I could've *sworn* I'd seen her curled up in the fetal position. But it was dark; had I only seen the shadows of her comforter, the dark pool of blood, and my mind filled in the blanks—perhaps what it *expected* to see?

"I spent all day trying to figure out how to pin it on Silas," said Felix. "*Silas.* Not *you*."

"How can you be so callous about killing her?" I tried to imagine Felix sinking a dagger—*that* dagger—into her body but couldn't fathom it. "She had nothing to do with what happened to your parents. Even she hated what her dad was doing."

"You've hated her this whole time. Why are you suddenly defending her?"

"I didn't hate her . . ." Tears dribbled down my cheeks, and I angrily wiped them away. "Not really. I used her. I didn't mean to, but . . . I was no better than anyone else. Silas lost that scholarship, and it was all his fault, but I didn't even *see* that." I remembered how surprise registered on Lainey's face when I'd asked for that internship for him; at the time I thought it was because she hadn't thought of it first, but maybe it was because I'd asked at all. "I wanted her to fix everything so badly, I didn't even care that she'd have to ask a favor from her horrible father—"

"Don't do that to yourself. What she did to you was *so* much worse."

A fresh wave of anger surged through me. "Yeah, she lashed out, maybe more than she should have. But she didn't deserve to *die*. And she died thinking I hated her . . . God, how could you do this? *How?*"

And it didn't end there—he'd killed two other people to get away with killing her.

Terror needled my spine. Now I knew the truth, and he was blocking the door. There was nowhere else to run. I glanced at the dagger, perched on the inset shelf above Felix's bed.

He followed my gaze. "Jade—"

But I was already hurling myself across the bed.

He mirrored me, reaching for the dagger, but I got there first. I wrapped my fingers around the hilt—the dagger that had killed Lainey—and swiped it at Felix. He lunged out of reach and slammed back into the door.

"Let me out!" I shrieked.

He raised his hands. "Please, you need to listen to me—"

"You murdered three people! I don't want to hear another—"

Felix's bathroom door opened.

I gasped and stumbled back into the desk again as a girl stepped out.

She was shorter than me, her pixie cut such a dark shade of brown it was almost black, and wore a baggy black sweatshirt over loose jeans. Purple rings shadowing her eyes, her face bare of makeup.

But I'd know that face anywhere.

It was the face I'd seen brighten when I first stepped into my dorm freshman year, flush with the hope of new friendship.

It was the face I'd wanted to bash into the ground when I couldn't understand why she'd stolen everything.

It was the face I'd most wanted to see when I thought she was gone forever.

"Lainey?!"

38

For a moment I was convinced there was a glitch in the Matrix, that the last twenty-four hours had been some vivid, alcohol-induced nightmare, that this entire semester was a figment of my imagination to escape from the pain of getting so epically dumped.

I gripped the edge of Felix's desk, feeling the wooden grain under my fingertips to ground myself, steady myself, to confirm this was real.

And it was.

Lainey stood in front of me. In the flesh. *Alive.*

"Did you mean it?" she asked in a small voice.

I blinked, bewildered. "Mean what?"

"Everything you just said. About not hating me . . ." Her watery eyes darted between mine.

And then I lunged at her.

Lainey let out a small *oof* of surprise as I wrapped my arms around her, relief overpowering every other emotion swirling in my brain, afraid that if I let her go, she'd somehow slip back into the sea. She hugged me back, trembling under her black hoodie.

I released her and scanned her up and down. If she wore bandages under the hoodie, I couldn't see them. "How are you okay? All that *blood*—" But when Lainey and Felix exchanged a quick glance, my heart stilled. Felix didn't seem surprised by Lainey's appearance at all. If anything, he threw her an apologetic look.

I stared at her again, at her shorn off, dyed hair, at her bare face, her baggy clothes.

A disguise.

"Holy—" I breathed. "You faked your own death."

Lainey clamped her lips tight and nodded.

"Lainey, don't," Felix piped up.

"Well, I can't have her think *you* killed me," said Lainey.

I backed away from her as icicles speared my chest. The chaos she'd sowed . . . People suspected me . . . Two people were *dead* . . . "Why would you do this? People think I'm a murderer—"

"Like he said," said Lainey, "it was never supposed to be you." She tried to tuck her hair behind her ears, but the strands framing her face didn't reach. "Ugh, where do I even start? Everything got so out of hand . . ."

"Ya think?" said Felix. "I told you she'd figure it out."

She groaned. "You were right. We should've called it off."

"Called *what* off?" I insisted, nearly shouting. Lainey bit her lip and glanced at Felix, but he merely shrugged this time. "If you don't tell me what the hell's going on right now, I'm literally going to explode."

"Please, don't," said Felix. "The last thing I need is your guts all over my room."

"*Felix.*" Lainey gave him a pointed look.

"Oh, so you really do go by Felix, then?" I spat.

"With friends, yeah," he said. "It really is my middle name." His eyes were sad. I tried not to care.

"How do you two even know each other?" I recalled waiting in line in the Amsterdam port. Felix had stood behind Miguel, laser focused on his phone. He'd overheard us venting about Lainey and texted her, hadn't he? She'd scanned the crowd and spotted me right after. "What, is he some goon you hired to help you?"

Lainey cracked a small smile. "He's not some goon. He's my cousin."

My jaw fell open. "Your *cousin*?" He nodded. How had I never met him, or seen a picture of him before?

Then again, I'd never even met Lainey's mother.

Aside from that time she invited me to Boston, Lainey never seemed to want to merge her worlds, enjoying her relative anonymity at Stanford in the dorms, except for the few fund-raisers her dad made her host and the sparkling social media presence he expected her to maintain. Though one time, when she'd mused how nice it'd be to simply delete all her profiles, I vaguely remembered her mentioning a favorite cousin in England who had none.

"Your parents," I said to Felix. "That article said they lived in Florida . . ."

"They moved there a few years ago, but I stayed in England for college." His father was Faizan Hassan. His mother, Rebecca . . . Amara? "You were right about the passports. I *am* a dual citizen, but that US one is forged."

"The Felix one?"

He nodded. "I kept my nickname so I wouldn't get confused; I figured no one would make the connection." So his mother was Rebecca . . . *Silverton*.

Derek Silverton's sister.

I could almost feel puzzle pieces snapping together in my mind. The drugs Derek's company sold killed his sister.

"Alright." I set the dagger on Felix's desk and tugged out his chair, sat, and crossed my arms. "Explain everything."

Lainey took a deep breath. "Well . . . at first, I just wanted to get away from Dad. He always wanted to turn me into some sort of mini-me. Ruthless and conniving. You know. You met him. Remember how he wanted me to Nair that poor girl's hair to get that part in the school play?"

Felix snorted. "Why am I not surprised?"

"I never told you about that?" Lainey asked. "Anyway, he's always wanted me to work at Sanatek—to make me the public face of the company, VP of PR. That's why he makes me host his fundraisers at Stanford and wants me to look perfect online. But I can never work there. Not knowing all the shady shit they do."

"Like suddenly raising drug prices?" I asked, remembering Tate's mom.

"Psh, that's just the tip of the iceberg. Dad makes himself look so virtuous, *providing access to medicine and health care and all that*." She imitated his voice, shaking her head. "But he's hurt so many people in *so* many ways. Like, Sanatek pays kickbacks to doctors to prescribe that opioid of theirs, even though there are laws against that sort of thing. They market it as safe since it's low-dose—a load of crock. Some doctors are smart to it, obviously, but some only care about making money. It's scary. Dad instructed Sanatek's reps to bribe doctors IRL and either pay them in crypto or disguise them as honorariums—you know, fees for speaking at conferences and stuff. No paper trails, no phone recordings, nothing traceable. Sneaky as hell.

"But he always said if I ever spilled company secrets, I wouldn't see a cent of my trust fund. I have to put on a pretty face and smile and *lie. Sanatek's our family's legacy now*," she imitated him again, "and if I screw it up, I'll screw the family. And after my little brother died . . . I'm *it*, you know?"

"What does your mom have to say about all this?"

Lainey made a disgusted noise. "She wrote me off the moment she realized I didn't want to be an actress, that I wanted out of the spotlight. All she cares about is mingling with celebrities. She doesn't care what Dad does to accumulate all that wealth. Even after everything that went down with Felix's parents . . ." She threw him a sympathetic look.

I shifted my gaze to Felix. "What happened?"

He sighed, rubbing the back of his neck. "They both got hooked on Xani a couple years back. My dad was in a lot of pain from his cancer treatment, and my mom got migraines from all the stress, so she got a script, too. I told them it was a bad idea—I even tried to convince them to smoke weed instead—but my mom believed Xani's low-dose claim. She trusted Uncle Derek, thought he could do no wrong . . ."

"The rest of the family always saw him through rose-colored glasses," said Lainey.

"Because of the money," said Felix. "My parents never could've afforded homes in Florida and Kent if he hadn't helped." His shoulders slumped. "But I should've known better."

"It wasn't your fault," said Lainey.

"I knew they were abusing. Whenever I saw them, they were

321

both so out of it, and they'd lost so much weight. I should've *done* something. But you never think the headlines will happen to you. And then . . . it *did* happen. They both took too much at the same time; I guess they were in pain and thought, 'Hey, can't hurt to take an extra dose.' But that's all it took. They stopped answering my calls, and I was supposed to come home for the Easter holiday anyway, so I did, and when I got there . . ." He trailed off. A haunted look crossed his face, and despite everything, my heart ached for him. "That prick didn't even come to their funeral."

"Not only that," said Lainey, "but Dad paid some firm to scrub the internet of any mention of Aunt Becky and how she died. His own *sister*."

Felix nodded. "There were all these articles, then boom, gone."

"When I googled your name before," I said, "I found one. The article misspelled the name of the drug."

He let out a bitter laugh. "Yeah, a couple obscure ones slipped through the cracks. Still, what could I do, sue my own uncle? He'd *crush* me."

"And right as all that was happening," Lainey said to me, "you asked me to get that job for Silas at Sanatek. After everything I'd told you . . . there you were, like all the rest of them, using me for my connections."

"I'm so sorry," I said. "I was desperate to keep Silas at school—I wasn't thinking."

"I know. And friends are supposed to help each other out . . . I totally overreacted. I think it was the way you assumed I could snap my fingers and do it; I'd been burned so many times by people who acted like that. And when you asked, I'd *just* been talking to Felix about his parents . . . about what Dad did, on top of everything else . . . so it triggered me."

I remembered how he'd been on Zoom when I'd come home from comforting Silas. Her eyes were red and watery—I'd assumed it was because I crying; whenever one of us cried, the other wasn't far behind.

But she'd already been crying over something else.

"Oh." She'd been zooming with Felix. I'd bombarded her with my ask right after she'd learned her father had caused her aunt's death and tried covering it up.

"Yeah," she said. "By then, I was scared I'd get implicated in Dad's dirty dealings, too. I wanted out—to *completely* disassociate myself from him. That's when I came up with the idea to disappear. Heck, the disappearing part would be easy; I knew a guy who could make fake passports and a whole new identity. The same guy I bought our fake IDs from. He's the best.

"But I still had to figure out two things. One"—she stuck up her thumb—"how to disappear without Dad looking for me. And two, how to survive. I never had a ton of cash in my bank account; Dad had me on a strict allowance to make sure I never stepped a toe out of line. So . . . I decided to blackmail him."

"What?"

She nodded. "I wanted to hack his laptop—the one he keeps at the office, connected to this private server. He locks it in his safe every night when he leaves. But I knew his type-A personality would want to track every rep, every dollar they brought in, even the dirty money; there had to be proof of bribery on there.

And maybe of all the rest of it—like how he covered up Aunt Becky's death."

"You know how to hack computers?" I asked.

"I didn't need to. I got this USB that'd automatically siphon things like spreadsheets and text files, so all I'd have to do was stick it into the laptop and wait. So one day I came in to 'surprise Dad for lunch'"—she made air quotes—"and when he went to the bathroom, I went for it." She cringed. "But Silas caught me." My eyebrows shot up, and she nodded. "Yeah, the last thing I expected was for him to pop in to say hi. But he did. And I . . . I panicked. I was literally plugging in the USB; I bet I went red as a tomato, guilty as sin. He asked what I was doing, and in that moment . . . I dunno, I just couldn't think fast enough. So I grabbed his hand and dragged him out of there before Dad could come back and see me scrambling for an explanation.

"But instead of accusing me or threatening to tell on me, he offered to help." She rubbed the back of her neck. "I figured he thought he owed me after I got him that internship. So I gave him the USB. Told him what to do. And a few days later . . ." She yanked a necklace from under her sweatshirt with a tiny USB dangling from the chain like a charm. "And I found so much more than I was looking for. *Terrible* things."

"Like what?" I asked.

Lainey swallowed hard. "I found this one email thread where Dad approved testing some new meds on people living in developing countries before the animal trials were complete." She looked horrified. "He always had to beat the competition, be the first to market, whatever it took."

Yikes. This all tracked with my first impression of Derek Silverton but was no less disturbing. "So you blackmailed him after all?"

"Yup. I used an app to fake my voice, and it totally worked. It freaked him out. He sent me five million in Bitcoin, and I transferred it to an offshore account. It's nowhere near my trust fund, but screw it—I can *easily* start a new life off that."

"So, then . . . why couldn't you pretend to have jumped overboard?" I asked. "Why this whole fake-murder scheme?"

"Dad would see right through that. I've always been scared to swim. He'd *know* I'd never have the guts to jump. And then he'd do everything he could to find me. He'd spare no expense. So, no—he had to think I was murdered. I had to be a victim; it had to look like something I'd had no part in plotting. That's why I wanted that YouTuber role—it had to look like I had no idea what was coming, like I fully intended to keep on living."

"Why frame Silas, though? He *helped* you . . . he got you exactly want you wanted."

"Yeah, I got what I wanted." Her voice went monotone, and she tore her gaze from mine. "And that son of a bitch thought he was entitled to something else in return. As though getting him that internship to begin with wasn't the trade."

39

"What do you mean?" I asked Lainey and caught Felix's eye—he was leaning against the closet, hands in his pockets, and the way he grimly pressed his lips together made dread leach into my veins.

"I went to Silas's place to get the USB," said Lainey, her lower lip quivering. "But instead of just handing it over, he said that if I wanted the files so bad, I had to give him something, too. Otherwise he'd tell Dad exactly what I told him to do."

I felt the blood drain from my face. "So, wait . . . *he* blackmailed *you*?"

She nodded. "I figured he wanted money. Either he'd get it from me, or he'd gain Dad's trust by ratting me out and get hired full-time. It'd be a win-win for him." My stomach lurched. I'd been the one to encourage him to try for a full-time job there. But the fact that he was willing to manipulate someone like that, let alone his girlfriend's best friend, appalled me.

"But I wasn't even sure blackmailing Dad would work," Lainey went on. "And if it did, I didn't know how much I'd be able to get from him, or how much I'd be able to offer Silas. Worse, I knew I couldn't trust Silas. Not after that. Even if I managed to disappear, he'd be around, knowing I'd taken those files, and if news of Dad's blackmail spread, he'd put two and two together. I was a fool to ever tell him anything. But I panicked. And I'd felt so alone . . . Oh, I don't know. I wanted to believe he genuinely wanted to help me. But he *tricked* me." A tear streaked down her cheek. "I'm sorry. I'm so, so sorry."

"Why?" I asked. "What happened next?"

"Well, first I just stared at him in shock, you know? Then he started rambling about how he was risking his own neck for me, that he could've lost everything all over again if he'd been caught, that he could've been arrested, and . . . well, I guess I thought that was fair. I just wanted those files *so* badly, and I was so afraid he'd tell Dad everything. So I put on an act. I pretended I was oh so grateful for what he'd done. For helping me. I wanted him to feel loyal to me, so he wouldn't betray me. So . . . I kissed him."

My whole world tilted on its axis. *I only ever slept with her that one time . . . It meant nothing.*

"I hated myself for it." Tears filled Lainey's eyes. "I hated *him* for cheating on you so easily. I'd always thought he was so devoted to you, but when I made the first move, he was so into it, and . . . well, we didn't stop. He never tried pushing me away or anything."

"Of course he didn't," said Felix. "That's probably exactly what he wanted."

"You think he was trying to bribe her for *sex*?" I asked, horrified.

"Honestly," said Lainey, "I never gave him a chance to say. But he never did ask for money after that."

I clasped my throat. "My God." If Silas really thought that first time meant nothing, maybe it *was* just a favor he wanted from her. "So is that why you wanted to frame him? Because he threatened you?"

"I mean, partly. I was just so *angry*. At him, at Dad, at all these *pigs* who use and trick people to get whatever the hell they want, and always get away with it. I was even mad at you for asking me to get Silas that internship. He wouldn't have been there to catch me, otherwise." She squeezed my hand. "I'm sorry. I know *that* wasn't your fault."

"I understand," I said. "You were hurting."

She sniffed again. "But also, it was the only way I could think of to safely disappear. That way, if he tried to tell anyone I stole those files, nobody would believe him. And CoB was the perfect opportunity. I could make it look like he killed me and threw me overboard—it's totally believable that nobody would find my body in the middle of the freaking ocean. Then I could sneak off the ship at the next port of call and disappear. All it took was a phone call to buy Silas's way into CoB. But for any of it to work, I needed you out of the picture. He made me swear up and down I wouldn't tell you we slept together, so if he thought you found out, I'd lose his loyalty, and I couldn't risk that. So I faked a break-up email from you claiming it was because—"

"Yeah, I know," I said. "He told me today. Because I thought he didn't have a future, and that I'd found out it was his fault he lost his scholarship." She'd known exactly how to manipulate both of us. Even though she wanted nothing to do with her father anymore, he'd taught her well.

She nodded. "Then I texted you from his phone, deleted the text, and blocked your number. It was so goddamn easy . . ."

I gaped at my own phone. "Wait, but that text . . ."

"I deleted it," said Felix. "We were afraid you'd show it to him at some point. You really should change your passcode, by the way, you type it so obviously."

"Jesus. Why didn't you tell me the truth?" I asked Lainey, my face screwed up from the effort of holding back tears. "I would've *helped* you."

Her eyebrows knotted. "I mean, by then, I was spiraling. I didn't know who to trust, besides Felix. And, frankly, it was too risky to involve you; the more people who know I'm really alive, the more likely it is that I'll be found. I knew cutting you off would hurt, but I figured once you heard Silas had killed me, you'd think, *Welp, dodged a bullet with that one!*" She chuckled bitterly. "And I knew you were better off without that creep."

"But . . . your whole relationship with him . . ." I said, aghast.

Lainey stiffened. "I'm a good actress when I need to be."

"You pretended to like him."

"I pretended to *love* him." And Silas was as gullible as a rat seeking out cheese. "I knew in the end it would be worth it. In the end, I'd be *free*."

I could relate to that overwhelming desire for freedom, the feeling of being stifled by a life you didn't choose. Still, thinking of how she'd forced herself to sleep with someone who'd black-mailed her—and possibly intended to extort sex from her—made bile burn my throat. "But after what he did . . ."

She averted her gaze. "I avoided sleeping with him as much as I could. I pretended I was seasick a *lot*."

"Still . . ."

"Yeah. Still," she said darkly. "But you being here threw the biggest wrench in things. I thought for sure you'd cancel when you got the notification that I'd switched rooms. I was shocked to see you in port."

I thought back to that moment on the pier, how angry she'd looked. Because my presence could sabotage her plans.

"I never got a notification that you switched," I said. "I logged into my portal one day, and my room assignment was back to pending. I figured you'd dropped out."

"Really?" Lainey balled the tissue in her fist. "Damn. Didn't expect that."

"Didn't expect a lot of things," said Felix.

"So, what"—I shifted my gaze to him—"you came to help sneak her off the ship?"

"Exactly."

"Please don't tell me you were going to sneak her out in a suitcase."

The corner of his lips quirked. "I was going to sneak her out in a suitcase."

I literally face-palmed. "Oh my God."

Lainey smiled shakily. "Once people thought I was dead, they'd kinda notice me walk through security, disguise or no."

"So that's why you tried so hard to keep me and Silas apart. Why you accused me of stalking you."

Lainey sighed. "Of course. I needed you to stay away from us; I couldn't exactly have you and Silas talk and figure out you didn't actually break up."

"Well, he knows now," I said.

Lainey threw Felix a worried look, but he shook his head. "That bit doesn't concern me," he said. "If anything, it solidifies his motive."

The past few weeks whirred through my mind. "What about that whole mess at the Tower of London? Did you really think I threw that stone at you?"

Lainey bunched her lips. "I honestly didn't know what to think—I was so startled. I'm sorry I blamed you. After Felix talked to you that night, he was convinced you didn't do it, and wanted to call this whole thing off. I never told him about how I broke you guys up. All he knew was what Silas did—how he'd threatened to expose me."

I took a sharp breath. I thought I'd overheard Lainey tell Silas at Windsor that she felt unsafe, but . . . "Did you two argue about this at Windsor?"

Felix's eyebrows shot up. "You heard that?"

"Yeah," I said, "I thought she was talking to Silas."

Felix suddenly refused to meet my gaze. "I was all for framing that prick, but . . . you should've told me *everything*," he said to Lainey. He never wanted me to get hurt, yet determinedly covered for her. And when he called Lainey a selfish asshole the other week . . . maybe, in a way, he meant it.

"I know," said Lainey. "I'm sorry. But anyway . . . by then, I felt like I had to go through with it. I knew the only reason Sheffia came was that Dad suspected something."

"You're right," said Felix. "Apparently Sheffia told Tate her parents sent her to keep an eye on you. Sorry I thought you were being paranoid."

331

"Told you," Lainey grumbled.

"Oh!" I said, remembering what Miguel had told us of Tate and Sheffia's breakup—and Felix's exasperated reaction. "I thought you were getting death threats or something, so her parents sent her, like, in a protective way."

She laughed bitterly. "No. Dad let me come on CoB, but he sent a little spy after me." So Lainey and Sheffia had never truly reconciled. Maybe Sheffia had wanted to, but Lainey always knew she had an ulterior motive. "And if he found out my plans, or confirmed I'd blackmailed him . . . he'd *kill* me."

My eyes widened. "You don't mean that literally, do you?"

"I don't know. If it were a matter of saving his own skin . . . maybe."

"But he loves you."

"He loves himself most of all," she said.

Faking her own death had become a matter of survival. Speaking of . . . "But all that blood all over your room . . ."

Lainey half smirked. "Convincing, right? There are these kits you can buy to draw your own blood. I did that for a while and hid the pouches in the back of my mini-fridge."

"Eurgh," I said.

"Yeah, it was pretty gross." She shuddered. "I put the 'do not disturb' sign on my door for a few days so my stew wouldn't come in and find them. And I got my hair cut and dyed in Lisbon; I've been wearing a wig ever since. Nobody noticed, not even Silas. And then last night, I pretended to be sick again. The storm made it super convincing. I asked Silas to get me some Dramamine, and when he left, I splattered my own blood all over the room and tossed all the evidence overboard. And then I came here to wait."

"Just like that," I said.

She nodded. "Just like that." Without her platinum-blond hair, meticulously drawn face, and tight designer clothing, nobody recognized her. At the time, nobody would've even thought to look twice. "There was a whole chunk of time after dinner when we were alone together, when I was pretending to be sick, that he wouldn't have been able to account for. His fingerprints would've been the only other ones all over the room—even my stew hadn't been inside for days."

"You really thought that would work?" I asked Felix, shocked he'd go along with this. Then again, I didn't really know him at all, did I?

"I did."

"What's even in it for you?" His lies still cut me so deep, I couldn't wrap my mind around them.

"I'm giving him half of the blackmail money," said Lainey.

"I'm not taking it," said Felix. "You need it more than I do. No, I mostly just wanted to help the only family I have left that I don't hate."

Lainey scoffed. "Gee, thanks."

"You know what I mean."

I still couldn't believe they were cousins. Cousins who loved each other, who'd risk it all to help each other.

Even if it meant killing two people to protect their secret.

Fear seared my vertebrae, and I sat straight at the edge of Felix's bed. This whole time, I'd been so shocked by Lainey's revelation, by Felix's true identity, I'd almost forgotten what else they'd done.

Tate's bloodshot, bulging eyes.

Sheffia's clumps of red seaweed hair.

And now I knew the truth. Was I next?

40

My fingertips tingled with adrenaline as panic flooded my system. I couldn't trust them—not after all the lies they'd spewed. I had to get out of here. Was Julia still doing her rounds? Even if they held me back, if I could make it out into the hall, surely *someone* would hear me shriek at the top of my lungs.

But nobody had heard Tate scream before Felix squeezed his fingers around his neck.

Nobody had heard Sheffia scream before Felix bashed her head into the pool's edge.

I had to chance it.

Felix noticed my expression morph to fear first, but before he could react, I zoomed to the door. I was fast, but Felix was faster, and he slammed himself against it. I scrambled for the doorknob anyway, but he held the door shut, and I pulled hard, straining against his full body weight. "Let me out!"

"What're you doing?" said Lainey. "Jade, *please*, you can't tell anyone!"

"You killed two people."

"No we didn't!" Lainey cried.

Felix spun me to face him, keeping a gentle grip on my arms, his expression pained. "You have to believe us. We didn't kill *anyone.*"

I shoved him, and he quickly released me. "I'm not saying she did. *You* did."

"I didn't—"

"STOP LYING TO ME!"

Lainey gripped her throat. "You think I lied to you about what Silas did?"

"No, I believe you about that . . ." I didn't know what to think.

"I didn't kill anyone." Felix set his hands on the door on either side of me, not touching me, but creating a barricade. "I swear it."

"How can I believe a word out of your mouth? You tricked me into— Ugh!" I couldn't say it again.

Our whole scheme to make Silas jealous—agreeing to fake-date me, kissing me in front of him, flirting during Monopoly— none of it was to help me. "When I suggested we fake-date, that was just *perfect* for you, wasn't it?" I spat. Riling up Silas fostered the perception he wanted to get rid of Lainey and back together with me. And perception is reality.

Felix didn't respond—just nodded slightly, pleading again with those sad, dark eyes.

"Ugh, you're disgusting," I said. Because it didn't stop there. The way he always held my gaze so intensely. That almost kiss in the Azores. Those actual kisses on Deck 9, when I'd wanted to give myself to him completely.

I'd let myself fall, and then he'd pulled out the rug from under me so I'd shatter into a million pieces.

"Did you ever even like me at all?"

Felix opened his mouth.

"No, wait, don't answer that. Obviously not. God, I'm such a fool." No wonder he was so quick to forgive me for stabbing Silas—it was all an act, the whole time.

"I really do, though—"

"Cut the crap. You *used* me the entire time to frame Silas."

"It's more complicated than that."

"Oh, spare me. Just be straight with me and admit it."

"You think I *wanted* to fall in love with you?" he said. My mouth went dry. "I risked everything to help Lainey escape a toxic situation—we both did. Getting caught could ruin *both* of us. Everything had to go smoothly. And everything could've gone smoothly. But then there you were, with those perfect green eyes and goddamn empathy, so determined to get your answers, to *fix* everything. You knew something wasn't right, and I had to make sure you didn't figure it out. And then, yes, your plan helped solidify Silas's motive, so I went along with it. But by then . . . gah, you're so annoying! You're persistent, and you're impulsive, and I couldn't get you out of my head."

Out of the corner of my eye, I couldn't help but notice Lainey biting back a smile. My body warred with itself, my heart pumping honeyed heat through my veins while my brain screamed I was in danger.

"After the pool party, I knew," he went on, "but how could we ever really be together? At some point I'd have to tell you who I really was, I'd have to tell you *everything*, and I couldn't. For her sake." He motioned to his cousin.

"So that's why you avoided me after the pool party," I practically whispered.

Felix nodded. "But then . . . dammit, I couldn't help myself—" His voice broke, as did my heart. He knew all along we couldn't really be together.

Lainey's face fell. "I'm so sorry I put you both through this."

I couldn't tear my eyes from Felix's. "I still don't understand. Last night, why didn't you just let me turn on the light in Lainey's room? I would've seen she wasn't in bed, and all the blood everywhere. You could've blamed Silas then—he still wouldn't have had an alibi for right after dinner."

Felix gave me a sad smile. "Because I was terrified for *you*. All I could think was how you had that freaking dagger, and you'd just stabbed Silas, and if I let you spend any more time in that room, everyone would think you did it."

"*Oh.*" My stomach fluttered, but not from fear. "And then . . . I screwed up the timeline."

Felix nodded. "When you said you saw Lainey curled up in bed, I thought I was gonna hurl. I've been scrambling all day, trying to pin this back on Silas. I kept the dagger, thinking maybe I could sneak it onto him somehow, but I couldn't figure out how. But then, Tate and Sheffia—dammit, that was out of *nowhere.*"

Hope sprang into my chest. It seemed like he was telling the truth . . . or was that what I wanted to believe? "So you really don't know who killed them?"

"No."

"*Did* anyone kill them?" said Lainey. "What if they really were freak coincidences? Maybe Tate *was* depressed, and everything that happened set him off. And Sheffia . . ." She squeezed her eyes shut for a moment. Of course, she'd heard me break that news to Felix through the bathroom door. "Maybe she hit her head on the edge of the pool, fell in, and drowned."

Felix finally released the door and backed away from me, rubbing his forehead. "Those would be some coincidences."

"That wouldn't explain the note Sheffia slid under my door," I said. "And what about the backpack we found in Tate's room?"

"What backpack?" Lainey asked.

"Oh, right," Felix muttered. "Hell if I know how it got there."

"Wait," said Lainey. "Does she mean the backpack you put in Silas's room?"

He wiped a hand down his face. "Yeah, we found it in Tate's room earlier. It's still there—"

"Hang on," I said. "*You* put it in Silas's room?"

Felix nodded. "A couple days ago. To help frame him; it was supposed to look like he stole it from Lainey."

"How'd you get it in there?"

He hesitated a moment, so Lainey answered, "Same way I got in here last night." She nodded at Felix, who pulled the master key from his pocket—the key we'd used earlier. "I bribed one of the guys at registration for a master key on day one. Said I wanted to prank a few friends during the Ocean Olympics in November. So easy." Easy for a privileged blond girl.

Wait.

As realization flooded through me, Felix rubbed his lips together, suppressing a sheepish grin. "You twerp!" I cried. "That whole thing with the sprinklers—"

"Yeah," said Felix. "That was entirely unnecessary."

Wow. I'd been played like a fiddle.

"Well, not entirely," said Lainey. "You had to come back here to get the key."

I glared at Felix, and he threw up his hands. "Well, I couldn't exactly tell you I already had one."

"Christ," I muttered. So many keys floating around, first with Miguel nabbing Lainey's key, and now this—

I gasped sharply, realizing something with intense clarity.

"What?" said Lainey.

"Oh, no. No, no, no." I covered my mouth, horror sweeping through me. It was like blank splotches on a canvas were filling in all at once, and I didn't know where to look first.

"What *is* it?" said Felix.

"I know how Tate got the backpack." I paced the short distance between the door and Felix's desk, thinking it through aloud. "He was never in Lainey's room. Miguel was the one who took the key I dropped, not Tate. He's the one who broke in later, not Tate. But Tate took the backpack from *Silas's room* earlier last night. He must've thought Silas killed you . . . oh, *no* . . ."

"Whoa, slow down." Felix gripped my arms, stopping me from pacing. "Why do you think Tate got it from Silas's room?"

"Remember when we talked to Jamal earlier?"

"Yeah."

"Well, after you left, he told me Tate came to his room last night, supposedly to check on him after he got seasick. But when Jamal went to the bathroom, Tate took off. Jamal and I figured he was upset about Sheffia or something. But I think that's when he took it. I don't think he came over to check on Jamal at all. I'd just told Tate how Silas interned at Sanatek." I clasped my forehead, theories filling my brain faster than my mouth could keep up. "I bet Tate meant to steal Silas's laptop to find any dirt he still had from his internship. Maybe Lainey wasn't the only one who wanted to blackmail Silverton. Miguel mentioned he got the laptop hacking idea from Tate—that's why Miguel stole Lainey's laptop, to try to find the bot-bombing receipt."

"I never did that," said Lainey.

"No," said Felix. "I did."

My eyebrows shot up. "Why?"

"I knew he'd suspect Lainey and shoot off his mouth about it, and I wanted you to think Lainey was a selfish asshole who wasn't worth your time."

I blinked for a moment, absorbing this. He'd really tried everything to make me let her go. I shook off the whiplash from this sudden change in topic. "Okay, wait, back to Tate. Silas had his backpack last night in the library—I remember that—and probably had it with him all night. So Tate grabbed the *wrong bag*. And remember how Tate kept trying to pick a fight with Silas during Monopoly?"

Felix rubbed his upper lip. "Yeah, that was weird."

"Maybe he thought Silas was a gold-digging thief but couldn't bring it up without admitting he stole the backpack. And then after Lainey's 'death' "—I made air quotes—"he must've thought Silas killed Lainey for her money." I gasped. "I bet that's why we found Tate looking for someone in the fitness center. He was looking for Silas!" Felix's eyes widened.

Nausea rose in my throat at the terrible conclusion I was

drawing. I remembered how Tate had sweated bullets earlier. "He must've been panicking that he'd get caught with the backpack and look suspicious himself, especially after what he did at the Tower of London. He probably thought no one would believe he took it from Silas's room instead of Lainey's room. And even if he got rid of it, his fingerprints were all over it."

"Why not throw it overboard?" Felix asked.

"The whole crew was out on deck looking for Lainey! He probably thought someone would see him."

Felix cursed.

"And remember how he acted sort of scared of me? I bet he thought Silas and I were in cahoots. Maybe he thought I was the dangerous one, since he saw *me* with that dagger. Maybe he thought he could reason with Silas, to pressure him into admitting what we did—what he *thought* I did. I bet he brought Silas back to his cabin to show him the backpack he'd found in *his* room."

"But Silas was innocent . . ." Lainey said.

"He probably panicked, too," I said. "He already felt like he lost everything—his scholarship, his future, me . . . and he'd just found out you manipulated us apart. And then to be at the receiving end of *that* sort of accusation, confronted with actual supposed evidence?" I shook my head. "He must've snapped."

Felix nodded along. "Then made it look like a suicide."

"And left the backpack?" said Lainey.

"Maybe he was afraid to take it," I said. "But then when he left, Sheffia must've seen him." I glanced at her note, at her scrawled handwriting. The last thing she ever wrote.

Lainey cringed. "Poor Sheffia . . ."

I thought of Sheffia sitting in Coastal Cantina between Silas and Jamal, watching me with a look of fear in her eyes. Silas had been following her around ever since. "That's why she ran away earlier when he was comforting her . . . or *pretending* to comfort her. Oh God. She could've told me then . . . Why didn't she tell me then?"

"Holy—" said Felix.

The three of us went silent. Trying to frame Silas for murder might've turned him into an *actual* murderer.

"Maybe we're wrong," I finally said just above a whisper.

Lainey's face went stony. "But maybe we're not."

"We have no proof," I said.

"We have to admit what we did," Felix said to Lainey. "We have to show everyone you're alive."

"Why?" Lainey gasped, eyes wide as saucers.

"So we can tell the captain all this. Otherwise Jade could take the fall right along with Silas. Everyone seems to think they did this together, and I don't see a way out of it without telling people what really happened."

"Then this was all for nothing," said Lainey. "*Worse* than nothing—I never meant for anyone to die." She covered her mouth, tears shining on her cheeks. "I wish I could take it all back."

I eyed the dagger on the desk, thinking of how Silas had wanted to cover for me after I stabbed him. Like the accident was some crime and he was doing me a favor—and who knows how he'd want me to repay him? I thought of Derek Silverton, who was sure to play the victim for his daughter's betrayal, even after his company basically committed mass manslaughter. Why do the manipulative bastards always seem to win in the end?

That's when it came to me.

"This doesn't have to be for nothing," I said. "I think we can get you out. We can blame everything on Silas." He certainly deserved it now.

"How?" said Lainey.

"Frame him for the blackmail, too," I said. "He *is* the one who siphoned that data. He lost everything after his accident—a future of wealth and success. Your dad will think Silas wheedled his way into Sanatek, blackmailed him, seduced you for your money. Then when you found him out, he killed you. You'll be in the clear. And so will I, if everyone thinks Silas's motive was your money all along."

"You could've wanted the money, too," said Felix.

"That's why we need evidence pointing to *him*, and him alone. Lainey, I need that USB."

"For what?" She reflexively touched her necklace, the tiny thumb drive containing the demise of an empire.

"I'll plant those files on Silas's laptop. Once the detectives find it—"

"But that'd expose Sanatek." Lainey's voice rose. "Dad might get arrested . . ."

"Good. You said yourself he was profiting from people's pain. And we'd get justice for Tate . . . for everyone he's hurt." I stuck out my hand. "If you need to run, run. But we can fix things, too."

She stared for a long moment, stock-still except for her chest rising and falling. Then her jaw hardened in resolve, and she unclasped her necklace and dropped it into my palm.

41

The thing about betrayal is sometimes, it's justified. As I sat at Silas's desk and plugged the USB into his laptop, rage boiled in my veins to think how he'd threatened Lainey after pretending to want to help her, to think how easily he'd been willing to cheat on and gaslight me, to remember all those weeks I'd teetered between blaming her for tearing us apart and blaming myself for somehow hurting them both.

Yes, I'd made mistakes—but I was willing to own them.

Yes, Lainey had schemed and manipulated—but she'd been in pain, and she was willing to make up for it.

We were imperfect, messy humans trying to escape from something or another, and wanting to do better.

But Silas's escape route was inexcusable. When shit hit the fan, he was willing to *kill*.

Thanks to the master key, breaking into Silas's cabin had taken nothing but a slip of plastic. I practically held my breath as I entered his password; he'd told me it once after his injury when I offered to pull up a menu on GrubHub, and I hoped he hadn't changed it. But it worked. Fingers trembling, I opened his Documents folder—

A scratching at the door.

A key card in the lock.

Someone was coming in.

Crap. I couldn't shut the laptop or yank the USB—whatever files Lainey had blackmailed her dad about needed to be on this laptop. I dragged the folder onto his hard drive, and frantically tapped the brightness all the way down until the screen turned black so the files could finish their slow march unobserved.

And then there he was, filling the doorway, surprise twisting his features. Lainey had been acting for months, but now I had to put on a show of my own.

"Silas!" I flew into his arms, trying not to wince as he hugged me back. "I'm so sorry about before—"

"What're you doing here?"

I leaned back to look at him. His eyes were ringed purple, his skin waxen, his actions perhaps as much a shock to him as the rest of us. "Waiting for you."

"But how'd you get in?"

"Jamal let me in. Didn't he tell you?" Better to blame a person than a lock malfunction Silas could easily test. He shook his head. "Oh. Well, we have to talk. We're in deep shit."

The walls creaked as the ship swayed, and vertigo wobbled my stomach and tingled my feet. Or maybe it was fear. I gripped the edge of the desk, and Silas groaned as he sank onto his bed, an elbow on his good knee, clutching his head. "I can't believe this is happening."

I glanced at his laptop. With the brightness down, I had no way to know how far along the file transfer was. I sat next to him and took a deep breath. "Everyone thinks we did this."

His head snapped up. "I had nothing to—"

"They think we did it *together*."

"How? My leg . . . I was in my room all night."

It was still all about him. How had I missed this when we were together? Everything was always about him—*his* baseball schedule, *his* poker games, sleeping together when *he* wanted to. I was so flattered, so infatuated, I'd looked past it.

"Most people don't know about that. The ones who do think we faked it," I said, latching onto the lie Divya insinuated earlier to wheedle the truth out of me.

His nostrils flared. "You're kidding. Should I show them the gash?"

"You can still walk, though. They think you're exaggerating." And maybe he was.

Silas blanched like he was about to be sick, then frantically shook his head. "No. There's no way. This can't be happening." Seeds of doubt sowed in my mind. I remembered what Lainey had said before—*I'm a good actress when I need to be.* Was she trying to frame him for the other two murders, too?

No. I believed her. I believed Felix.

At least, I thought I did . . .

Holy hell. I had to siphon the truth from Silas's skull. Otherwise I'd never feel right about the proof I was planting.

I clutched his hand. "We have to prove it wasn't us before we get to Gibraltar."

"We'll be there by morning."

"I know."

"How can we prove it?"

"Let's get our alibis straight. If we can account for *exactly* where we were all day, and who we were with, before anyone's memory gets fuzzy, we'll be fine."

He dropped my hand. "Nah, no way." He was panicking. *Guilty.* "What about when I took a leak at, I dunno, eleven forty-five, by myself? I have no alibi then, but that means nothing."

"There's obviously no way you could've killed someone in the time it took to go to the bathroom. Let's walk through today, hour by hour, and write down exactly where we were—"

Silas's laptop trilled.

The files must've finished transferring.

We both stared at the open laptop. Silas's brow furrowed, and my pulse raced. I should've turned down the volume, too. I could see the wheels turning in his mind, wondering whether he'd left it open. He hadn't.

"Do you have a notebook?" I tried distracting him, but he moved to his desk and pressed some random keys to wake the monitor. The screen didn't brighten. He frowned. "Silas, I need you to focus—"

"Were you using this?"

"No."

He pushed a few keys again. "Dammit, why isn't it turning on?"

"Maybe try restarting?" That way at least the folder I'd copied everything into would no longer be open. But I still had to get that USB back. He hadn't noticed it. Yet.

He jammed the power button until the tiny light above the

keyboard flickered off and pressed it again with a huff. "You were sitting here when I came in," he accused, narrowing his eyes at me.

I made a face. "So?"

"I *know* I closed it. After I woke up, I googled stab wounds, and I remember looking at the clock and seeing it was seven thirteen and thinking, *Dammit, lost track of time.* Then I shut it and left, and I remember thinking, *Eh, I should have grabbed it.*"

I bet he remembered it all so vividly because today was so traumatic. Dad used to recount exactly where he was on each anniversary of September 11 however many years ago. He parked at school at 6:45. Gave a microeconomics lecture at 8:15. Heard the announcement over the loudspeaker at 9:50. Silas would probably remember every moment of today like a high-def movie in his mind for the rest of his life. So would I. So would many of us.

"What'd you do to my laptop?" he persisted—on edge. Suspicious. If my theory was right, he'd been on the defensive all day, scrambling to silence anyone who might accuse him of something that would ruin him. Injuring his throwing arm, losing his scholarship, losing *me*, had already destroyed him. He probably couldn't bear to lose any more . . .

"Nothing! I was just waiting to talk to you, like I said." I edged toward the door, but I couldn't flee. I had to get the USB back first.

Silas caught the motion, and his face hardened. "Are you scared of me?"

"Should I be?" I clamped my lips. That was a mistake. He couldn't know I suspected him. He had to think I was fully on his side, that I wanted to help him.

But it was too late—Silas balled his hands into fists, and a darkness crossed his face, a darkness I'd never seen before. A darkness Lainey must've seen when he threatened her. A darkness Tate must've seen when Silas closed his hands around his throat. A darkness Sheffia must've seen when Silas chased her to the pool deck.

I had to fix this. "Silas, please, listen to me." I rushed to him and cupped his cheek, his stubble rough against my palm. "People think we killed them, all three of them. We have to figure this out together."

Silas's shoulders tensed, but he held me anyway, like he wanted to believe me so badly. "How?"

I swallowed hard, thinking fast. "I don't know yet. But you need to know . . . Tate confronted me this morning," I lied. It'd been the other way around. "He said he had proof you killed Lainey, but he wouldn't tell me what it—"

"He did." A muscle in his jaw twitched. "But he was lying."

"What do you mean?"

Silas pursed his lips.

I clasped my hands behind his neck and angled him down to press my forehead to his. "You're hiding something from me. Please, *tell* me. I can't help you if I don't know the whole story." Silas shook his head, his nose brushing against mine.

Finally, he released me. "Show me your phone."

"What?"

"Your phone."

"Why?" I pulled out my phone and brightened the screen, showing him.

"You're not recording?"

"No." Unease twisted my stomach. He was thinking everything through. "You can trust me." I took his hand and sat on the bed, pulling him down next to me. "Tell me what happened."

Silas wiped a hand down his face. "That asshole tried to *frame* us."

I gasped.

"Yeah. He took me to his room and showed me this backpack loaded with cash, and all this jewelry. Lainey's jewelry. He said he found it in my room. I told him it wasn't mine, and he said, 'It sure isn't. But gimme half, and I won't tell anyone.' You know, like he was trying to get me to admit to killing her. He was totally recording it. But I think he did—"

"How'd you know he was recording you?" I asked, though that would explain his recording paranoia.

"I got his phone, after."

"After what?"

"What the hell do you think?" he snarled.

I took a sharp breath. But I wouldn't say it. I wanted *him* to say it.

Silas clenched his fists. "I didn't want to do it. But I saw his phone peeking out of his pocket, you know, with the camera pointing at me. I didn't know if he was live-streaming or what—I dunno if he could've been with our crappy internet—I just wanted him to stop recording. I tried to get at it, and we started fighting, and I . . . I lost it. It happened so fast. But he was trying to *frame* us. I wanted to protect us."

But Tate wasn't trying to frame anyone. He was trying to prove his own innocence.

"Why didn't you tell anyone he tried to frame you? Blackmail you, really . . ."

"I couldn't admit what I did! I *strangled* him!"

So, Silas had killed the person he thought killed Lainey. An eye for an eye. Didn't make it right—especially since he was wrong.

I took a deep, shaky breath. "So what'd you do with the back-pack?" I wanted him to keep going, keep talking, confess to the rest of it.

"I left it there—well, I put it back in his suitcase. And then I strung him up . . . I thought maybe it'd look like he hanged him-self out of guilt. But then . . ." He trailed off, then let out a low growl.

"What? What happened?"

He sat on the bed, cupping his head. "You're going to hate me even more."

I knelt beside him, clasping his good knee. "No, I won't. You can tell me anything, I won't judge you. We'll figure this out together."

Silas rubbed his eyes, then finally spoke. "Sheffia knocked on the door right when I was pulling the sheet up over the towel rod. She obviously heard . . . She knew someone was there, but she thought it was Tate. She was begging him to open the door, said she was sad about Lainey, that she wanted to talk. She mentioned some fight they had yesterday or something, I dunno. Eventually, she gave up. Or I thought she did . . . When I finished cleaning up the mess, she was sitting there in the hall, waiting."

She must've seen the look on his face when he spotted her. She must've known the wrongness of the sound she'd heard, of Silas hanging a corpse.

Tate's dead, isn't he?

"She knew . . ."

"She never said so—she just went all quiet and stalked off. I wasn't sure what she thought, or where her mind went. But I knew eventually someone would find his body in there. I kept trying to talk to her, but she kept running away, and when she didn't, other people were always around. I know you saw us in the Cantina earlier, with Jamal." I nodded. "Well, eventually I did have to pee, and when I came back, she was gone. I thought maybe she went to tell someone. So then I went to your room . . . I was going to tell you everything. I wanted your help." He tightened his grip on my hand. "But then I found her there, sliding something under your door, and when she ran like that . . . I knew she knew."

"So you chased her."

He nodded. "She got into the elevator before I could stop her, but I took the stairs—I almost caught her there." He clamped his lips and screwed up his face.

I shifted to perch on the edge of the bed. "Then what happened? *Tell* me."

"She tried to run into the Cantina, but I grabbed her, covered her mouth, dragged her to the pool. I begged her not to scream, I just wanted to talk it all out. I swear to God, I just wanted to talk. But she was struggling, and she hit my bad leg, and I let her go. She tried to run, but she slipped, right next to the pool. There was this *awful* crack."

My chest tightened. "So, wait . . . It was an accident?"

Silas shook his head. "She was still alive. Her head was

bleeding, and she was trying to get up, but it was like she couldn't get her balance, and . . . I panicked. I thought she'd tell everyone I killed Tate *and* dragged her off to the pool like that. So I pushed her in . . ."

I clasped my mouth and shut my eyes. She'd drowned after all. What an awful way to die. I hoped she'd fallen unconscious first. I hoped she wasn't in pain.

"I'm sorry," said Silas. "I'm so, so sorry. I don't know how any of this happened. It all got so out of control—"

The way he suddenly stopped talking made my eyes flutter back open. He was staring at the dagger, perched on the shelf above his computer.

The dagger I'd put there.

I could see him piecing everything together. Calculating how it'd gotten there. Remembering I'd been sitting right there. Realizing it was me. I stood, my legs shaking. "Silas—"

"You *bitch*."

My heart fell to the floor. So much for even attempting an explanation. Before I could react, he leapt over and grabbed the dagger.

I spun and scrambled to the door, the USB forgotten. But as I turned the knob, Silas slammed into me. It was like Felix holding the door shut earlier, but worse, so much worse, because Felix had barely touched me, and so clearly hadn't wanted to hurt me.

But Silas pinned me against the door, shoving my cheek against it so hard I thought my skull might burst. And when he pressed the blade to my neck, I let out a terrified shriek.

42

"How dare you?" Silas growled in my ear, his breath hot on my cheek. "After everything I did to protect *us*—"

Someone pounded on the other side of the door. "Open the door!"

"Felix!" I pressed my palms against it, wishing I could reach him, right on the other side. He was so close, yet so terribly far. I tried reaching for the doorknob again, but Silas grabbed my wrist and yanked my arm back, my bad arm, the one I'd fallen on in the library when I set off the sprinkler. I howled in pain as he twisted it beyond its limits.

"Jade!" Felix shouted, clearly panicking himself. I wished I'd held onto the dagger until the files finished transferring—but could I really stab Silas again, even in self-defense? I remembered how the blade felt sinking into his flesh last night, carving into muscle and sinew. I didn't want to feel that again.

The door trembled as Felix threw himself against it. But without the master key, he couldn't get in.

Oh. The key . . .

As surreptitiously as I could, I plucked it from my pocket and let it fall to the floor. Felix's persistent pounding drowned out the sound.

"Go away!" Silas shouted at the door, right next to my ear.

I flinched. "Silas, please." I felt for the key with the tip of my shoe. "Please let me talk to you."

"Shut up. You never wanted to help me at all, did you?"

I let out a sob. "Please—"

"Tell him to go away," Silas ordered.

"Let me turn around—"

"TELL HIM TO GO AWAY!"

"Felix, go away!" I sobbed as I felt my toe hit plastic instead of carpet. Got it. I dragged the key closer to the door and kicked it underneath. But with Silas pressed against me, he felt the movement and looked down.

"What's that—"

I took advantage of his looser grip and swiveled, but he quickly pinned me against the door again, one arm braced against my chest and the other gripping the dagger at my throat. But right then, the lock beeped, and Felix shoved the door open.

The sudden movement made the blade press into my skin, and though it was dull, pain sliced my neck. I cried out, but Silas wouldn't release me as he strained to close the door again, putting all his weight into it, crushing me between them. Felix was smart enough not to stick his fingers through the opening, thank God, because Silas was stronger, and he managed to shut the door and flip the deadbolt home.

Felix pounded on the door again as tears spilled down my cheeks. I touched my fingers to the cut on my neck and gasped when they came away slick with blood.

Silas let out a sob of his own and pressed his forehead to mine. "I'm sorry. I'm so sorry. I never meant for any of this to happen."

Bullshit, I thought. *You just cut my throat, and you black-mailed my best friend.* That's what started this whole mess. But I couldn't say that. How would I explain exactly when she'd told me about that without giving her away?

She wasn't completely innocent. She'd manipulated him and set this terrible trap. But then he hammered the nails into his own coffin. Nothing excused killing two people. Nothing excused this kind of violence.

"Please let me go," I begged. "This can all end here. Turn yourself in."

His forearm dug deeper into my collarbone. "No. There has to be another way."

"Please, you're *hurting* me—"

"There has to be another way!" he repeated.

Muffled voices in the hall. "In there," I heard Felix say. Someone had come to help.

"It's too late, Silas," I said. "You have to confess. What're you gonna do, keep us locked in here forever?"

A drilling sound whirred below me—whoever had come to help was already working to remove the deadbolt panel. Silas cursed and raised the dagger in frustration.

"Silas, if you kill me, they'll know you killed Lainey alone—"

"I—"

I wouldn't let him defend himself. "You *killed* Tate and Sheffia—"

Whoever was unscrewing the deadbolt made quick work of it, and suddenly the door flew open with such force it threw Silas and me back. As Silas stumbled into the bed, I caught my balance and breezed past him to the desk, plucked the USB from his laptop, and pocketed it.

After Asim tackled Silas, Zofia wrestled the dagger from his grip. Captain Hwang entered next, shaking his head at Silas in disgust, while Felix ran over and wrapped me in his arms. "Are you okay?"

I nodded, grateful for the safety of his embrace, though my neck and arm were on fire.

"I love you," he whispered in my ear. "I'm so sorry about everything."

My heart swelled, and I let out a small sob. I'd slipped and said I'd fallen in love with him earlier, but I'd fallen before I knew how much he'd lied to me. I wasn't ready to say it back . . . wasn't ready to believe him completely.

"I didn't do anything!" said Silas, struggling against the staffers.

"Dude, don't bother." Felix released me and held up his phone. "I recorded the whole thing."

Felix had been down the hall, keeping an eye out for Silas. I'd told him that if he showed up, to let him come in, to let me try to get him to confess, and to try to record it.

And I'd never let Silas say he didn't kill Lainey.

Silas shook his head in a panic, now handcuffed and sitting on the bed as Asim gripped his arm, and Zofia slid the dagger into a plastic bag. "Is this the letter opener you lost last night?" she asked me.

"Yeah," I said. "He must've taken it, then killed Lainey with it."

"What? *No!*" said Silas.

When the police ran DNA tests on the blood on the blade, they'd find Lainey's. We'd sliced her hand with it before I left Felix's room, and I'd wiped our fingerprints from the hilt. I'd even left the Zippo lighter I'd used to set the library on fire in Silas's top desk drawer. They might not be able to prove who really caused the fire, but at least they might suspect him.

If he hadn't murdered Tate, I never would have tried to set off the sprinklers.

"It's not mine!" Silas cried, gaping at the dagger, wearing this helpless, pathetic look. "I never even saw it before—I mean, I did last night—but I never took it. I swear, I didn't kill Lainey!"

Sure, he'd probably tell the police I was the one who'd stabbed him in the leg.

And yeah, he'd probably tell them he'd found me in his room, that he thought I'd planted the dagger here.

But he'd confessed to killing Tate and Sheffia. And he'd almost killed me.

So really . . . who'd believe him?

43

T he next afternoon, I squeezed into the elevator with Felix and his two enormous suitcases, practically merging my soul with the back wall to make room. But if I thought this was claustrophobic, it was nothing compared to Lainey's ride up to Deck 6.

"You really want to stick it out another three months?" said Felix. He hadn't explicitly asked me to leave with him, but he kept expressing complete bafflement I'd even *want* to stay.

"Yep."

Since the murderer was about to be escorted off the ship, Captain Hwang deemed CoB safe to continue its journey through the Mediterranean, though anyone who wanted to head home could disembark in Gibraltar once the local authorities gave the go-ahead. They'd boarded before dawn and made quick work of collecting evidence in Lainey's room, Tate's room, and the pool. Detectives were still interviewing witnesses and would be for a while—I was in for another round this evening—and a sanitization crew was at work disinfecting everything.

Most people were sticking around, since CoB wasn't offering refunds, and leaving partway through the semester could jeopardize graduating college on schedule. Still, by the time we made it to the reception lobby under the stained-glass atrium, a small line had formed to leave next to the barrier erected before the gangway door.

"Wait here while I settle things at registration?" Felix asked as he steadied the suitcases at the back of the disembarkation line. He had to make sure "Felix Amara's" checkout looked legit, even if he'd registered with false documents and paid his way into CoB last-minute. Amazing what wealth can accomplish.

"Sure."

He headed over to wait behind Miguel, who was handing in his room key.

I knelt and untied my shoelace so I could tie it back up. "You okay?" I murmured at the black suitcase, larger than the blue one.

A soft hushing noise was the only response. I guessed Lainey was fine . . . just anxious as hell. Campus on Board's murdering spree had finally blown up online, and Felix's phone trilled with news alerts once we were within service range to port. It was no surprised the headlines focused on Sanatek's dead heiress— clickbait for the ages—but Lainey seemed shocked that her father was apparently already on his way to Gibraltar. "I didn't think he'd drop everything to come," she'd said, gaping at the article on Felix's phone. "I bet he thought it'd look terrible if he didn't."

Hopefully she'd be long gone before his arrival.

I stood as Miguel zipped into line behind me. Anger bubbled in my belly. If he'd turned in Lainey's laptop sooner instead of hiding and trying to hack it, we wouldn't have wasted time searching Tate's room. We might've pieced things together sooner. And Sheffia might still be alive.

But I couldn't say any of that.

"Well, isn't this déjà vu?" I said instead, and he snorted. "You're taking off?"

"Yeah," he said. "Screw exactly all of this. I have to go to their police station or whatever for more questioning, though." His various creams and gels hadn't managed to soothe his red, puffy eyes, if he'd bothered. He rolled his shoulders and took off his backpack, dropping it with a loud "oof." It nearly toppled into the suitcase containing Lainey, but I caught it in time. "Oops, sorry."

"It's fine," I said, balancing it closer to his feet. "Where'd you sleep last night?"

"I didn't. Just stayed in the Cantina. Jamal, too. They kept Silas locked in the brig all night, but Jamal was too freaked to stay in their room with all his stuff." Miguel set his suitcase on its side and unzipped it. "Ugh, I still have to book a flight home, and they gave me, like, two seconds to pack."

"Jamal's staying, though, right?"

"Yeah. But his roommate wasn't *murdered*. Ugh, this entire trip was a complete disaster. And poor Tate—" He raised a finger. "No, I can't talk about Tate, otherwise I'll start crying again, and these bags under my eyes *cannot* anymore."

"Aw, Miguel . . ." The anger in my gut simmered down. "I'm really sorry." I pulled him into a hug.

"No, stop. See? You're making me cry." It was true—by the time I backed away, his bloodshot eyes had already watered. "Ugh, why would Silas *do* this?"

"He was after Lainey's money," I said without hesitating. Let the rumors fly. "Tate and Sheffia were just unlucky enough to figure it out."

"Oh, damn," said Miguel. "Why kill her though? She was clearly shelling out for him."

I glanced around like I didn't want anyone to overhear and whispered, "I heard he had something on her father—something that could destroy his company, Sanatek."

Miguel's eyebrows shot up. "Like what?"

I filled him in on a few of the juiciest bits Lainey had mentioned until Felix returned.

"All set," said Felix.

While Miguel busied himself typing up a storm on his phone, probably tweeting everything I'd just said, I whispered to Felix, "Can you send your receipts to YouTube or whatever? Prove he didn't buy those followers?"

Felix shook his head. "It's too risky."

"I feel bad . . . He should at least get his profiles back."

The corner of his mouth twitched. "I'll see what I can do."

It was almost time—crew members were hustling over, readying to move the barrier and open the gangway door. Felix's eyes shifted to the suitcase bearing his cousin, brow furrowed, some battle clearly raging inside him.

Then he met my gaze. "Come with me."

Something sparked in my chest and sent jolts of electricity down my spine. What I'd felt for him had been real, and he'd spent all of last night trying to convince me the same had been true for him. But I hadn't let him touch me, not since our relieved embrace after the security officers busted open Silas's door.

"I can't . . ." I eyed Miguel warily, but he was still occupied with his phone. "We can't risk it."

All that mattered was Lainey escaping safely. But leaving with Felix could attract attention. People mostly seemed convinced I wasn't in league with Silas, especially since he'd trapped me in his room and sliced my throat, and I had a bandage covering half my neck to prove it.

"I want to see you again," said Felix.

I'd said those same words to Lainey a few minutes ago. My heart clenched to think how she'd shaken her head. "You can't. To disappear, I need to *truly* disappear. I can't risk Dad finding me. I'll probably never see Felix again, either."

"But how will I know you're safe?" I'd asked.

"You won't," Felix had chimed in as he finished packing his other suitcase. "We can't text, call, email—nothing. We can't say anything to each other about it, either." He'd motioned between the two of us. "All of that's traceable. We basically have to pretend she's going into witness protection." They'd been careful all semester, too, never sending traceable messages to each other, only ever talking in person a few times, including that day at Windsor.

"You'll just have to trust me," said Lainey, "that I can take care of myself. And you can never tell *anyone*."

"I promise, I won't tell a soul," I'd assured her. "I'm so sorry about everything that happened. What he did, what *I* did—"

"Listen to me," Lainey had said, gripping my shoulders. "You did *nothing* wrong. I overreacted. As your friend, I should've been happy to help you get a job for your boyfriend. I was foolish and insecure, and what I did to you the past few weeks was horrible."

"But you'd *told* me how people used you. You'd *told* me you hated your dad—"

"But I didn't tell you all of it. I kept his secrets for so long . . . You only ever knew a fraction of it. So how could you have known? You didn't deserve to be put through hell."

"Still. I should've been a better friend," I said.

She teared up. "Well, I should've been, too."

"Dammit, Lainey. I've missed you so much." And then we were hugging, a rib-cracking hug, unable to ebb the flow of tears. I finally got my answers, and better yet, I got *her* back. But now I was going to lose her all over again. "Who the hell am I supposed to room with next year?"

"Probably some boring loser who blasts music at three a.m. and has sex on your bed."

I smiled now, remembering that, and Felix raised his eyebrows. "Yes? You'll come with me?" he said.

"No, I . . . I was thinking of something Lainey said . . ." I trailed off, biting my lip.

"Well, unlike her, I don't need to disappear forever," Felix whispered, stepping so close his jacket grazed my sweater. He brushed my curls aside and trailed a finger down my cheek. "After the semester ends. We need to see how everything plays out, but once it's safe . . . I'll find you."

"So *dramatic*," I purred, like he'd once teased me. "I won't be all that hard to find."

A smile tugged at his lips. "Stanford."

I hesitated. Would I ever truly be able to trust Felix? He'd claimed I'd gotten to know the real him, that he really was a psych major (he'd taken the semester off), that he really did hate small talk (he'd always been an introvert), that he hadn't been acting much except for, you know, lying about his entire identity.

But the wheels were already in motion before meeting me, and he'd tried to minimize the damage—to protect me, in a way—trying to convince me Lainey and Silas were selfish ass-holes so I'd feel indifferent to the girl who'd die and the boy who'd take the blame. Better than unresolved agony.

I ended up protecting myself, though. Knowing the truth was better than being fed a lie, even if it was a tougher pill to swallow. At least now I'd never have to wonder.

At least now the biggest villains would pay.

The line was moving now, and Miguel huffed as he skirted around us. But Felix didn't take his eyes off me, such hope in his gaze. Despite his lies, he'd offered me acceptance and under-standing. He'd shown me it was possible to love again, and even more fiercely than I'd ever loved Silas. He'd made me want to be a better person. If I didn't agree to see him again, I might never.

I nodded. "Come to Stanford. But we'll need to start at the beginning. That includes small talk."

His dark eyes lit up. "It'll be worth it," he said, then kissed me, deeply, right there in front of everyone, a kiss sealing a promise, a kiss full of hope and forgiveness.

There were so many things about this semester I never expected. Despite all my daydreams about murder, I never imag-ined so much loss. Despite all my desperation for answers, I never imagined I'd find them.

But sometimes the very best things are the ones you expect least of all.

After Felix disappeared down the gangway, I raced to Deck 9 to watch him go through security and leaned against the rail a few feet down from William, who spotted me and tipped his head, offering a warm smile. I returned it, then focused on Zofia at her post on the pier, scanning everyone's ID one last time.

A cluster of intimidating Gibraltarian soldiers stood guard just past her. They hadn't moved since I'd last come up here a few hours ago to scope things out. Two held machine guns at their waists, while a third gripped a dog's leash—a drug detection dog, its pink tongue bobbing with each pant as it obediently sat, a charlatan of cuteness. With one sniff, it could ruin all our plans. My heart raced, and I could only imagine how fast Lainey's was pounding as she was jostled over each seam in the gangway floor.

Later, I'd need to pass that dog, too. Although some things would be better said in person, I wanted to find Wi-Fi and call Mom, and start being honest about how she'd hurt me. If she lacked self-awareness, bottling up my pain would never get her to change. And maybe she needed help as much as I did. Then I wanted to call my father. Maybe Mom was right about him all along. Or maybe she'd been the one who'd cut him off and hidden the truth from me. But either way, at least I wouldn't have to wonder anymore.

"Hey," said two voices behind me. Navya and Divya. I hadn't

seen my roommates since yesterday since I'd spent the night in Felix's room with him and Lainey.

"Are you okay?" asked Navya as they both hugged me.

"As okay as I can be. Are *you*?"

"We'll make it," said Divya. "We're badass bitches." Her eyes glimmered, but a shadow darkened them, too. They'd both forever remember Sheffia floating lifeless in that pool, her blood clouding the water. Though maybe in some weird, morbid way, the experience had offered them perspective. Maybe they could be honest with each other, too. Maybe they could finally mend the gash between them. I hoped I'd be able to help.

Once I released them, they stood on either side of me, watching the first few students tow their luggage toward the soldiers, who stopped people seemingly at random so the dog could sniff their bags. Were drug-sniffing dogs trained to sniff out humans where they shouldn't be?

Felix appeared behind Miguel, chin up, shoulders back, striding from the gangway as he wheeled his two suitcases.

"What!" said Divya. "Your boy toy's leaving?"

I chuckled. "It's fine. After everything that happened . . . I can use some space." Worry strained my voice. If Felix wound up in jail for this, we'd sure have a lot of space.

Two armed officers emerged from the gangway leading a handcuffed Silas between them. I winced at the sight. Navya entwined her arm with mine, and I gave her a grateful, shaky smile. But I was even more concerned about the dog sniffing Miguel now, stretching its neck to get a whiff of his backpack. It would smell Lainey, I knew it. My stomach tied in such awful knots I thought I'd never eat again.

Just then, out of the corner of my eye, I noticed someone storming up the pier, toward the gangway.

And I swear to God, my heart stopped beating.

It was Derek Silverton himself, disheveled and unshaven, his long beige trench coat hanging open and whipping back in the wind. It looked like he'd literally sprinted here from Boston, but of course I knew he'd probably taken a private jet and had been waiting for the authorities to open access to the ship.

I could tell Felix had spotted him as well; he quickly averted his gaze, turning his head so Derek wouldn't recognize him, his own nephew—though, according to Felix, he hadn't seen his uncle in years.

But Derek's gaze was fixed like laser beams on Silas.

I expected him to start screaming at Silas.

I expected him to hurl accusations, to call him something foul.

I expected him to demand justice.

But all he did was growl, "You destroyed everything," before raising a black pistol and shooting Silas squarely in the chest.

I was sure Navya and Divya both shrieked, that William gasped, that people were screaming on the pier and on each of the promenades overlooking it. But all I could hear was the buzzing in my ears as Silas fell to his knees, even as the officers gripped both of his arms.

Even from here, I could see Felix's mouth slacken from shock as the soldiers with the dog tackled Silverton.

Now's your chance, I thought. *Go!*

Instead, Felix looked up, his expression bewildered, and I knew he was searching for me. I knew he thought this would devastate me. He wanted to make sure I was okay. But I couldn't lose him, couldn't stand to see Lainey get caught. They had to get away.

Finally, he found me. Knowing people would be recording this on their phones now, all I did was mouth "Go!" I hoped anyone else would interpret it as "No!"

And that's all he needed to see.

He breezed past the distracted guards, down the pier. As he got farther and farther away, I could almost feel the distance between us pulling taut like bands meant to snap back together. And as he disappeared into the crowded port, I knew my love for him was real, and that I'd see him again.

I shifted my gaze back to Miguel—he was still standing there, frozen, mouth agape. If his tweets had already blown up to the point where Sanatek trended, Derek must've seen. He must've spotted the truth in them and known that whatever Silas supposedly had on him would take him down. He must've thought Silas was his blackmailer, and that he'd destroyed his legacy by killing his last living heir. And he'd lost it. Maybe this was even a desperate attempt to keep Silas from exposing the full extent of his depravity . . . but it was too late for that, now.

Meanwhile, other officers and medical crew from CoB tried to revive Silas.

But I knew he was gone.

I'd lost Silas ages ago, but this sudden finality took my breath away. He'd deserved to be brought to justice. But it wasn't supposed to end like this.

The only silver lining was that Derek had unwittingly secured Lainey's escape. Now there would be no one to challenge the circumstances of her disappearance. No one to contest the presence of those documents on Silas's laptop.

We might've been about to ruin him, but his own vengeance had dug himself the deepest grave.

Betrayal can make you do ridiculous things.

ACKNOWLEDGMENTS

This was by far the most fun I've ever had writing a book, and that was largely thanks to my incredible publishing team and support system.

To my genius editor, Rūta Rimas, thank you for helping me level up this book and my craft, for all the brainstorming Zoom chats, and for your truly epic ability to know exactly what to cut to make the rest sparkle . . . but also, thank you for making me feel so welcome at Razorbill. With you and Penguin Random House, I feel like I've found a home in this wild industry. Thanks also to Gretchen Durning for your fantastic insights and enthusiasm; Kristin Boyle for designing such a striking cover; copyeditor Laurel Robinson and production editor Misha Kydd for polishing this book and making it shine; Jayne Ziemba for shepherding this book to publication; Simone Roberts-Payne for your wonderful support; publicist Tessa Meischeid and marketing pros Felicity Vallence, James Akinaka, Shannon Spann, for all your hard work getting more eyeballs on this book; and the rest of the fabulous Penguin Teen team. Working with all of you is such a delight, and I'm so grateful and humbled for all your efforts championing this book.

I've always wanted to write a murder mystery on a cruise ship, and I truly cannot thank Temple Hill Entertainment enough for making this dream a reality. Thank you so incredibly much, Alli Dyer, Marty Bowen, Julie Waters, and the rest of the Temple Hill team. I especially want to thank Alli for your exceptional notes and guidance along the way, and for steering this ship to excellence.

To my literary agent, Jim McCarthy, thank you for always being in my corner and being such a stellar human to work with. Three books in, I'm still convinced you have magical time-traveling powers that let you start drafting replies to my emails before I even send them. I'm so grateful to you! Thanks also to the rest of the wonderful team at Dystel, Goderich & Bourret.

This book was inspired by the novel *Death on the Nile* and the study abroad program Semester at Sea, so my immeasurable thanks to the late great Agatha Christie as well as the Institute for Shipboard Education.

Thank you so much to the authors who took the time to read and blurb this book: Jessica Goodman, Jessica S. Olson, Hank Phillippi Ryan. Your generosity and kind words mean the world to me!

To the fellow authors I chat with day in, day out—Mike Chen, Wendy Heard, Hannah Reynolds, Jessica S. Olson, Sophie Gonzales, Alechia Dow, Erin Bowman, J. Elle—thank you for being my life raft. It's surreal to know you, let alone call you my best friends, and I would be lost at sea without you. Janella, Mara, Jess, Jennifer, Tom, Shana, Tess, Meg, Akshaya, Laura, Amparo, Aimée, Sarah, Dan, and the entire Clubhouse crew—and oh gosh, so many more, you know who you are—I cherish our conversations and I'm so grateful for you all.

To my parents, Mark and Lorri, to Grandma Gloria, and to the rest of my family, thank you for your love, support, and understanding that I've basically turned into a living, breathing keyboard. And thank you for always encouraging me to take big leaps and believe in myself.

It's now a tradition to thank my cat in my acknowledgments, so here goes . . . Thank you, Kitty, for being my constant writing companion. Sorry about those times I had to plop you on the floor because you insisted on standing in front of my monitor while Jade and Felix were trying to have their adventure.

To my husband, Bryan, thank you for your endless love and support, for tirelessly rooting for me every step of the way, and for believing in me always. Thanks also for encouraging us to go on those cruises; having those memories were clutch while sitting at home and writing this book during the pandemic. And I'm so excited for all the new memories we'll create together. I love you so much!

And, finally, thank you. Yes, *you*! Thank you for picking up this book, for choosing it, for spending time with my characters. Thanks also to my street team, and to all the booksellers, librarians, teachers, and bloggers who've helped get my books into more readers' hands, and to everyone who's posted a kind review, or made a TikTok, or posted on Instagram. I know I'm three books in now, but it's still incredibly surreal to me that you're here, right now, *at this very moment*, reading my words. Having your support means the world to me. So, seriously. Thank you.

TURN THE PAGE FOR A SNEAK PEEK AT AN EPIC
SURVIVAL THRILLER ABOUT FOUR TEENS WHO GET
LOST IN THE PARIS CATACOMBS FOR DAYS.

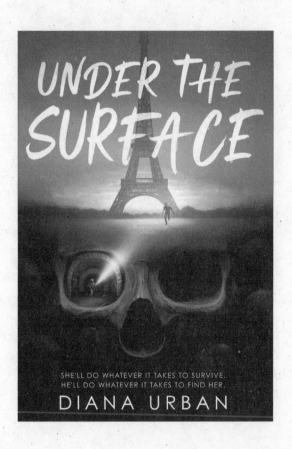

DON'T MISS THIS GRIPPING AND PROPULSIVE
STORY OF LOVE, DANGER, BETRAYAL, AND HOPE . . .
EVEN WHEN ALL SEEMS LOST.

PROLOGUE

Ruby

I never thought I'd die alone in the dark under the City of Light.

That's what they call Paris. The City of Light. Makes sense when you think of the Eiffel Tower glinting in the sun or sparkling at night over the Seine. Or the vibrant paintings bedecking the palatial Louvre Museum. Or the glittering fashionistas strolling the Champs-Élysées. Or the dazzling boulevards with whitewashed buildings gleaming like pearls against the blue sky.

God, I'd kill for some of that light right now.

As I hurtle through the dark, cramped corridor deep underground, my phone's flashlight makes elongated shadows bounce and bob across the craggy walls like a chaotic, ghostly dance, and I have to stoop to keep my skull from slamming into the low, jagged ceiling.

There's no sign of the others.

Terror claws up my chest, and I try not to think of the crunching noises under my boots, try not to think how it's only a matter of time until my phone runs out of power, until my mouth parches, my stomach shrivels, and my legs give out beneath me. Then there'll be nothing to do but curl into a ball and wait for the darkness to become infinite.

Unless *they* get to me first.

No. That can't happen. I won't let it.

I turn a corner and slam my back against the wall, then toggle off my flashlight, plunging the corridor into pitch blackness. But hiding in the dark means my friends won't find me, either. I breathe hard, feeling like I could choke on the dank, humid air, and a sob scrapes my throat. I'm screwed. Undeniably, irrevocably screwed. But I can't spiral. Panicking got me into this mess to begin with.

Keeping my spirits up among six million corpses isn't exactly an easy feat. That's how many are entombed down here in the catacombs, their skeletal remains intricately arranged throughout this ancient labyrinth that stretches under the bustling streets of Paris like layers of rotted casserole squished under a decadent crust. My chest constricts, and it's like I can feel the crushing weight of all six million dead.

And that number's high enough, thank you very much.

A low, rasping growl echoes through the passageway. My heart jolts, and I clamp a shaking hand over my mouth to mask my heavy breathing.

But it's too late.

They found me.

Maybe there are worse things than dying alone.

1
Ruby

2 DAYS EARLIER

"Now's our chance," I whisper to my best friends, Sean and Val, under the shadow of the Eiffel Tower. "Let's go."

It's only our first day in Paris—the culmination of studying my ass off in French class and fundraising to death to go on the best trip in the history of ever—and I'm already trying to sneak away from our class.

"Go where?" Sean frowns and glances at our teacher, Mr. LeBrecque, who for some bizarre reason scheduled us to take in the sweeping views atop the Eiffel Tower while delirious with jet lag. He's gesturing wildly at the engraved names of French scientists and engineers under the first balcony while half the class is verging on a collective collapse and the other's bursting with adrenaline-fueled giddiness.

"To find that bunker." I look to Val for backup, but she's stuck in a stupor.

"I don't think we have time," says Sean.

"But it's literally *right there*."

The secret military bunker I read about—a secret no other travel You-Tuber has covered, as far as I know—is supposedly hidden beneath the south pillar. Which I can see from right here, at this very moment.

Not on my laptop screen. Not on my phone.

With my actual human eyeballs.

I asked Mr. LeBrecque earlier if we could scope out the bunker as a class, but he huffed, "I already squeezed the catacombs into our itinerary for you. This whole trip can't be the Ruby show." A jab at my channel, *Ruby's Hidden Gems*. As much as I respect the snark, it shattered any illusion that my teachers knew nothing of my online endeavors.

And if my teachers know, Dad probably knows, too.

Dad's not exactly sold on my jet-setting aspirations. But it's kind of hard to make it as a travel YouTuber when you can't, you know . . . travel. If it were up to him, he'd swaddle me for eternity—at least, whenever I'm not nursing his hangovers or waiting tables at his restaurant. He wants me to keep working there while I go to community college, and when I told him Val asked me to backpack across Europe with her after graduation, such a tormented expression crossed his round, bearded face that he looked gaunt. This week's as much a trial run for him as it is for me and, for once, I'm not the one most likely to fail.

I can't worry about that now. Not here at the Eiffel freaking Tower. I've daydreamed about this moment for too long to worry about anything except how quickly it will become a memory. I need to savor every minute. Film every nook. Explore every cranny. Even if it means sneaking away from our class for, like, 0.2 seconds.

I tug Sean's jacket sleeve. "Come on."

But Val's still zoning out.

"Val."

"Mm?"

"The bunker?"

"Oh, right, sorry." Val blinks furiously and adjusts her purple horn-rimmed glasses under her black bangs, a sharp contrast to her alabaster skin and vibrant hazel eyes. "Extreme hottie at nine o'clock." I look, but nobody stands out in the swarms of tourists.

Mr. LeBrecque's facing us again. I groan. So much for that.

It's not like Val to waste chances. She's an adrenaline junkie who craves—no, *demands*--attention at all times. Last year when she moved to Starborough, our sleepy suburb north of Boston, she burst into my life like the Tasmanian Devil, dragging me kicking and screaming from my comfort zone. Some of our exploits would give Dad an aneurysm, like breaking into the crypts under Old North Church, white water rafting in the Berkshires, and bribing this cute park ranger to let us camp overnight on Georges Island. But the more daring we got, the more my subscriber count jumped, so after a while I didn't need much convincing.

And look at me now, instigating the sneakage.

"LeBrecque told us to stick together, anyway." Sean motions to the twelve other seniors on this trip. We've distanced ourselves behind them in a futile attempt to keep them from videobombing my slow pans and zooms, oblivious as worms on wet pavement.

"But getting footage of that bunker would make my video pop," I argue. "Everyone and their grandma has posted about the Eiffel Tower."

"Not my grandma," he says, deadpan.

I snort. "You know what I mean."

"Well, we shouldn't."

Val rolls her eyes. "Way to have zero chill."

Sean crosses his arms. Stick a rulebook in front of him, and he'll have it memorized in an hour. He's JROTC and plans to join the military after graduation like his dad, and his towering athletic stature, broad shoulders, faded buzz cut, chiseled cheekbones, and perpetually furrowed brows sure make it easy to picture him in uniform.

And picture it I do. Often.

But getting that uniform will take him away from me.

"Now," Val whispers. "Now, now, now." Mr. LeBrecque's gesticulating at the tower again, and I nod, my fingertips buzzing with adrenaline as Val clasps them.

Sean shoots his hand into the air. "Sir?"

"What are you doing?" I squeak, swatting his cargo jacket's sleeve.

"Mr. LeBrecque, sir," he says, ignoring me as our teacher turns around. "Sorry to interrupt, but is it okay if the three of us head over there for a minute?" He motions vaguely toward the south pillar. "Ruby wants to grab some footage."

Mr. LeBrecque sighs, exasperated, and checks his watch. "Our tickets are for fifteen minutes from now. Be back here in ten."

"Thanks," Val calls back, already making a beeline for the south pillar.

Sean throws me a lopsided grin and steers me after her by the small of my back.

"Oh, shut up," I mutter.

His smile widens. "Didn't say a word."

He doesn't move his hand. I don't want him to. But I speed out of reach anyway.

The electricity between us has been amplifying for months, and now, in Paris, my blood seems to pulse with each fleeting glance, each time a smile curves his lips, like I'm perpetually tripping over a live wire. But I'm terrified to let him touch me, to let those sparks ignite. I can't risk letting him incinerate my soul.

Because that's how it'd end.

That's how everything ends.

So I have to keep myself grounded.

As the three of us search for the bunker's entrance, Sean keeps scouting our class's position.

"Will you stop?" I motion to the iconic wrought-iron lattice pillars surrounding us. "You don't get to see this every day."

His steel-gray eyes flick to mine. "Oh don't worry. I'm enjoying the view plenty." Our gaze holds a beat too long, and my cheeks warm despite the chill in the air.

Sometimes he almost makes it seem worth getting scorched.

It's wild to think Sean used to intimidate me. He's basically had biceps since birth, and if resting asshole face were a thing, he has it. I could never tell whether he was shy or thought he was the shit until senior year, day one, when Mr. LeBrecque partnered us to make a video in French touring Starborough. We trudged to the grocery store after school to get it over with, timid as deer, but when I hit record, Sean brandished his arms and screamed, "Le boutique est grand et à des bananas," and I snort-laughed so hard it hurt. We tried to out-outburst each other in French all afternoon and barely had any usable footage to splice into a cohesive narrative, but he managed anyway—an impressive feat, considering. He's been helping me edit my videos ever since.

"Hey look," Val calls out, pointing behind Sean. "I think that's it."

We hurry over. A cage of rusted green bars blocks a cement staircase descending underground.

"This is it," I say. "I've seen a picture of the door that's down there." It's not visible from our vantage point, but I stick my lens between the bars, against the glass barrier, and film what little I can.

Val slinks under the green railing before the metal door and gives the handle a frustrated shake.

Sean chuckles. "What'd you expect? If any rando could get in, it wouldn't exactly be a secret bunker."

I back up a few feet. "Lemme grab some B-roll, at least."

Val grimaces. "You sound like my mom. *Honey? Grab me some B-roll.*" She snaps and points, imitating her singsong voice. Her parents have their own HGTV show and cart Val around the country to film in different regions year after year. "*Honey? B-roll.*" Snap and point.

"Sorry. I'll try to be less triggering," I say. She laughs, and I kneel to get some of the lattice in the frame and pan across the gate. "Sean, either get out of the shot or look at the stairs." He's watching our class like a hawk.

Distracted, he trips over the edge of the gate's frame and barely catches himself on the rail, then tugs down his jacket's hem. "No one saw that."

"Oh, they *will*." I tap my camera.

He groans. "Please delete that."

"Mm, I dunno. How much will you pay me?"

He laughs softly, his eyes glinting like the beams overhead until they float down to my lips and linger there.

My blood goes warm and tingly like I just downed a steaming café au lait. I slowly rise to my feet and lower my camera as he steps closer, studying my face like he wants to memorize every detail. Electricity sparks through me, and my breath shudders like the sky ran out of air.

"Can I . . ." he starts.

My nerve endings catch fire. This is it.

Our first kiss.

Under the Eiffel Tower.

It's so cliché, I press my fingers to my lips to keep from giggling. Sean sweeps a hand over his buzz cut and averts his gaze, then shoves his hands into his pockets.

Just like that, the moment's gone.

It's for the best. Besides, I don't want to make Val feel awkward—

Wait.

Val's gone, too.

I scan the crowd of tourists swelling under the nearby pillar but don't see her anywhere. Sean sees my expression shift and whips his head toward our class. "It's fine. They're still there."

"Not that—where's Val?"

"Oh." His eyes bounce around, then land back on me. "I don't know."

"Maybe she's trying to find another way into the bunker." Or she spotted something shiny and wandered off, as usual.

"Is there another way in?"

"No idea."

He checks his watch. "Our ten minutes is almost up."

"I know."

"I'll tell LeBrecque—"

I catch his sleeve. "Hang on. She must be close." I spin and race to the right, but there's only an old-timey ticket booth under the pillar, and no other doors or stairs.

"Ruby, wait—" Sean tries.

I veer left, expecting to find a gift shop or something around the corner, but there's nothing but a tall plastic barrier. "Dammit." Frantic, I rush into the crowd, weaving through swarms of tourists. "Val!"

I don't see her anywhere.

By the time I spin around to backtrack, I realize I've lost Sean, too. Crap.